ROMANCE
BY THE BOOK

Visit us at www.boldstrokesbooks.com

By the Author

Revenge of the Parson's Daughter
Or The Lass that Loved a Pirate

Romance by the Book

ROMANCE
BY THE BOOK

by

Jo Victor

2015

ISBN 13: 978-1-62639-353-0

This Trade Paperback Original Is Published By
Bold Strokes Books, Inc.
P.O. Box 249
Valley Falls, NY 12185

First Edition: June 2015

Credits
Editor: Ruth Sternglantz
Production Design: Susan Ramundo
Cover Design By Gabrielle Pendergrast

Acknowledgments

I can't exactly remember how I first got the idea for this story, but I know that reading Joanna Russ's *How to Suppress Women's Writing* was a big part of it. I do remember having an image come to mind of a woman standing in an old house somewhere in England, looking at the painting of a woman dressed as a Regency dandy, and somehow interacting with the woman's ghost. The last piece fell into place when I came across a magazine article about Anne Lister and discovered that someone like the character I was imagining had actually existed in Regency England, and what's more, had left behind diaries—in her own secret code—detailing her love affairs with women.

Anyway, that's where Artemisia came from. I'm not exactly sure about everybody else in the story (although Grace, as you might expect, just showed up one day and proceeded to take over).

It has taken me longer than I ever expected to get this story told, and I've had a lot of help along the way, so I have plenty of people to thank. I am in awe of the work of Helena Whitbread, the scholar responsible for decoding, editing, and publishing Anne Lister's writing; *I Know My Own Heart,* in particular, has been a major source of inspiration and information. Samantha very generously and patiently answered my long list of questions about British food. And although it's been quite a while since high school, my friend Christine—a genuine Yorkshire native—was gracious enough to read the entire manuscript to fact check the British speech and social customs. From one Wise Monkey to another, many thanks. Any errors that remain are of course my fault.

I am grateful to everyone at Bold Strokes Books who helped make this book happen, including Gabrielle Pendergrast who created the fabulous cover. The presenters and participants at the Bold Strokes retreat provided lots of ideas and plenty of encouragement. My editor, Ruth Sternglantz, saved me from myself any number of times in addition to being generally amazing and wonderful. And it should go without saying (but I'll go ahead and say it anyway) that I will be forever grateful to Radclyffe for not only being a huge inspiration and creating a place like Bold Strokes in the first place, but for inviting me to join the jamboree.

My second book. I can still barely believe it. It's a huge, huge thrill.

Speaking of which, all my love, devotion, and gratitude belong to my partner. Twenty-two years and counting, sweet babe. Let's keep dancing.

Dedication

For S., obviously.

Chapter One

Wading through the crowds at Heathrow, hauling her heavy suitcases and overfull backpack, Alex congratulated herself that she'd heeded her mother's advice and shipped her precious books and papers directly from Boston to Leeds. Now all she had to do was pray they arrived safely, and then figure out a way to get the heavy crates to her ultimate destination. But first things first, she had to get herself out of this crazy airport and on to her first stop.

As she maneuvered past a group of flight attendants sporting British Airways uniforms, she shuddered, recalling her previous visit to England and her first experience of culture shock, British style. That particular trauma had occurred only minutes after takeoff from Logan. Considering all the firsts that ascent had represented—first trip alone, first trip to Europe, first flight—it hadn't come as much of a surprise when her stomach began to feel a little funny. In her innocence, she had ordered a ginger ale from the extremely cute stewardess, only to collapse in a choking fit as the searing, spicy liquid hit the back of her throat like a mouthful of drain cleaner. Who could possibly have guessed that—unlike its bland American counterpart—British ginger ale would actually contain a significant amount of real, live, sinus-clearing ginger?

That had been her first lesson in the perils of taking the apparent similarities between Britain and America for granted.

Continuing to weave her way through the crowds, Alex had to smile at her younger self. She had been barely nineteen, after all, embarked on a grand adventure thanks to a junior-year abroad program, wide-eyed and eager for whatever she would find in England, land of her literary dreams. And she had found plenty, including a firm friendship, still going strong after nearly ten years, with her flatmate Fiona Montrose.

What's more, Fiona's grandfather Ian turned out to be both London based and hospitable, welcoming them to his home during various holidays. Fiona was in Australia now, married and expecting her first child, but Alex was looking forward to seeing Ian again.

Finally reaching the subway—oops, Underground—Alex set aside her nostalgic musings to focus on the practicalities of ticketing and boarding. As the train sped along, she thought about everything she had to look forward to over the next year: Her first sight of Yorkshire, whose wild and desolate beauty had inspired so many literary greats. A chance to get some real work done on her dissertation, with no teaching responsibilities or part-time job to distract her. Best of all, she would actually be living in Artemisia's house! Sleeping under her roof, eating in the same dining room, perhaps even sitting in the very chair she used to sit in.

Even now she could hardly believe that she, Alexandra Petrocelli, had been able to capture the Brockenbridge Scholar-in-Residence Fellowship. Not that Artemisia scholarship was as overcrowded as some specialties, but there was still plenty of competition, especially for an award as prestigious as the Brockenbridge. She was still a little dazed, particularly after having discovered that she was only the third American ever to win the award.

Perhaps that was why some of her professors had discouraged her from applying. At least Barbara had stuck by her. Thinking of Barbara made her sigh, so she decided to focus on something else instead. Like Quality Street chocolate assortments, and the delights of Indian take-away; she hadn't been able to find anyone Stateside who could make chicken tikka masala the way she liked it, despite diligent searching. And Ian's housekeeper Mrs. Glendale's roast beef and Yorkshire pudding, her lamb with peas and mint, and best of all, her attention to the manifold delights of a proper tea, right down to clotted cream for the fresh-baked scones. These thoughts happily filled Alex's mind for what was left of the journey.

Once she'd hauled herself and her bags off the train and out of the station into the noise and bustle of downtown London, it took surprisingly little time to hail a cab, and in next to no time, Alex found herself at Ian's front door. The warm welcome she received from Ian and Mrs. Glendale felt like a homecoming, and in a way it was. She was back in England, the home of her heart.

❖

Mrs. Glendale showed Alex to the guest room and left her with the admonition that tea was almost ready. She had barely started to unpack when she heard Ian calling her to come down.

The next three-quarters of an hour or so were a happy jumble of mutual reminiscence and sybaritic wallowing in a tea that exceeded even her fervent expectations, complete with anchovy toast, crumpets laden with butter and homemade marmalade, the longed-for scones with—yes—clotted cream, and best of all, a magnificent Queen of Sheba cake that Mrs. Glendale had baked in honor of her visit.

When the glorious meal had been reduced to a few wretched fragments and the first flood of conversation had died down, a comfortable silence descended, broken only by the hiss and crackle of the fire in the grate and the ticking of the mantelpiece clock.

Alex sighed, partly from contentment, but also with a little regret for days gone by. She wasn't nineteen anymore, which was mostly a good thing, probably, but she couldn't help thinking of the last time she had been sitting in this parlor, when the three of them—she and Fiona and Ian—had been together, laughing through one of their mock-serious arguments over something dear to all their hearts: Emily versus Charlotte Brontë, perhaps, or which of Gilbert and Sullivan's operettas was the silliest. Now Fiona was far away, happily settled and moving on with her life, while Alex was still trying to figure hers out, still on the move, still trying to find a place to belong and, she hoped, someone to belong to.

Ian at least seemed unchanged, a little grayer perhaps, a little thinner, but just as sharp, still full of vigorous good humor from his riot of curly hair to the toes of his old-fashioned boots. His beard and the inevitable tweed jacket gave him rather a professorial air, although as far as she knew, prior to his retirement, he had spent his whole life as a banker. His shrewd gray eyes were fixed on her with an expression she found hard to decipher.

"So, Alexandra. The Brockenbridge."

"I still can hardly believe it."

"Not I. It didn't surprise me one bit to see your name on the candidates' list—you always did have a head on your shoulders."

"Candidates' list? When did you see that?"

"Why, when it was put before the trustees for discussion and vote, naturally. When else would I have seen it?"

"I don't understand. Why would they show it to you?"

"Because I'm a trustee, of course! Maybe I should take back what I just said about your intellect."

"I had no idea you were involved with the Artemisia Foundation...But wait—if you were on the selection committee, is that why—" Alex broke off too late, miserably aware that she had either just grossly insulted Ian's integrity or offered him the chance to confirm her worst fear, that she didn't truly merit the award. She still sometimes worried that it was all a mistake that was going to be corrected as soon as someone realized they had overlooked the real winner.

When the decision was first announced and some of her older, more established—and, with few exceptions, male—colleagues had whispered, not *quite* out of her hearing, their surprise that the award hadn't gone to a serious scholar, part of her had silently agreed. Of course, she had also overheard Barbara's spirited defense of her achievement, which was gratifying, if bittersweet.

Ian gave a bark of laughter. "What, do you think I put one over on the committee for you? Hardly! Why, every one of us knew at least one of the candidates, and most of us knew several. Not that that was an advantage in some cases, believe me. But that would be telling tales out of school." He paused, then continued in a more serious voice. "In any case, it was your own work that won it for you, Alexandra, not my support, though of course you had that. A first-class proposal, and a fresh look at Artemisia's work into the bargain. Not the sort of thing we see every day, more's the pity."

"Oh." Alex's head was spinning.

"Cheer up, Alexandra. By fair means or foul, the fellowship is yours now to do with as you will. I for one look for great things from you over the next year."

"Thank you, Ian. Coming from you that means a lot. I hope you realize I've always looked up to you, and to know I have your confidence makes me feel better." She laughed ruefully. "I confess I've spent half the time floating in a daze of bewilderment and the other half wondering what the hell I'm going to do with myself for all that time, especially after the first few months. I'm not really looking forward to a winter alone on the moors."

Ian laughed in earnest. "Alone on the moors? My dear, Dawson House isn't Wuthering Heights! Even in Artemisia's time it was only a short walk from the village, and by now they've built right up to the edge of the property, including the most appalling little collection of souvenir shops, ye olde tea rooms, and a so-called museum to compete with the official one at Highgate Hall. You should consider yourself lucky if the tourists obey the Private Property signs."

"You can hardly blame me, Ian. I've never been to Bramfell. I've never been anywhere in the North, really."

"Then you've a treat in store. Bramfell's still a lovely little village, despite what they've done to it for the tourist trade. Not much different than when I was a lad, when we'd spend part of every summer in Bramfell with Great-Aunt Oona. And the moor is right there, practically at your back gate, whenever you fancy a ramble. Crags and rocky hills and the vast expanse of cloud-patterned skies, with the whistling wind for company mile after mile after mile. Nothing like it, for my money, anywhere else on earth. Be sure you don't miss it, shut up with your books and papers."

"I certainly won't. As soon as I arrive I'm planning to hike up to Bram Tor and recite Artemisia and Emily Brontë to the hares and hawks. *No coward soul is mine* and all that. I've been looking forward to it since the day they announced the award."

Ian smiled. "That's how my own interest in Artemisia got started. Oona used to tell me stories about her as we tramped over the moor."

"But Artemisia died in 1843! Just how old was Great-Aunt Oona?"

"As you can probably guess, I thought she was ancient, but I doubt she was even seventy when I first started visiting her. She'd never actually met Artemisia, of course, but she knew people who had. Why, her mother had actually been present when Artemisia died, though she was only about ten years old at the time."

"What? I don't remember seeing any little girls in *Artemisia's Farewell*"—she mentally reviewed the painting whose image was tattooed on her brain—"but then I've only ever seen prints of it. I'll take a careful look at the original when I visit Highgate Hall. Maybe she's lurking in one of the dark corners."

Ian snorted. "From what I remember Oona saying, the painting is full of errors—who was in the room, the way things looked, what happened. Apparently the only thing the artist, Smithson, really got right was that Artemisia was present at her own death scene."

"Sacrilege! You'd best be careful, Ian, that no Artemisia Society members are lurking behind the drapes."

He looked over his shoulder in mock alarm, then leaned forward to stage whisper, "You don't mean that some of Artemisia's true and loyal admirers might object to a bit of plain speaking, do you?"

Alex laughed. "Object? For voicing such heresy, they'd probably tear you limb from limb. You know as well as I do that the story of *Artemisia's Farewell* is the real basis for most of the theories about the nature of Artemisia's relationship with Lady Melissa. Forget the rumors, forget the evidence—it was all pure and high-minded admiration with none of that messy, all-too-human adultery to sully their idol."

"Adultery? Don't tell me that's the way you see Artemisia's relationship with Lady Melissa. And you're worried that *I* could get in trouble for speaking my mind. We may have to post a guard at Dawson House during your tenure."

"I wouldn't put it quite so baldly, but I'm convinced their relationship had a significant erotic component."

"Conviction is one thing, but you mentioned evidence." He fixed Alex with a gimlet eye.

She smiled, not the least bit intimidated. "I meant textual evidence, of course. After all, if you consider the implications of, for example, *Dare I with impious hand profane*—but of course I principally have in mind the early revisions, especially in the third draft, the one that was discovered on the back of the Highgate Christmas pudding recipe in 1942—"

"Stop, stop!" Ian held up his hands in mock horror as if to ward off a blow. "I surrender. I should know better than to start a debate with an Artemisia scholar. We'd be at it for hours, and I'm getting too old to stay up so late."

Alex subsided, chuckling, mostly because he was absolutely right. "But in all seriousness, Ian, just what do you believe about Artemisia's work and her relationship with Lady Melissa?" A terrible thought occurred to her. "Good God, you're not part of the Fringe Faction, are you?" All her humor vanished.

"What, those ignoramuses who think that just because she wore men's clothes she was actually a man? Hardly!"

Alex let herself breathe again. "Well, even in this day and age there are still people who are convinced only men can be great writers, and—"

Ian held up his hand before she could really work up a head of steam. Just as well, since she had been known to spend entire conversations on the topic.

"Really, Alexandra, I should hope you know me better than that. As for Artemisia, I believe she was a damn good poet, and an interesting, independent woman, and that's more than enough for me. It's my strict policy to keep clear of all the academic argy-bargy, for fear it might be catching. Clearly, you are more than ready for the responsibilities of the Brockenbridge."

"I certainly hope so. I don't mind admitting I'm a bit apprehensive. I feel like I've been doing nothing but eat, sleep, and breathe Artemisia for the last five years or more. I'm not sure there's anything left to say about her that hasn't already been said, by me or someone else, over and over. I just hope I can fulfill the terms of the grant and present the Foundation with a dissertation that represents a"—she flicked her fingers in air quotes—"worthy new work of scholarship at the end of my stay. I'd hate to have people say that they made a mistake taking a chance on another American as Scholar in Residence, or that the most recent scholar was also the worst."

"Nonsense! Clearly you have the expertise, and the passion. Dawson House will provide the inspiration. You just need to give yourself a chance to settle in and get your bearings. And as for being the worst of the scholars, surely you can at least do better than Heaving Bosoms."

Alex laughed heartily, and Ian joined her. Heaving Bosoms was the nickname bestowed by a reviewer on *Heaven's Blessings*, the actual title having been taken from one of Artemisia's more controversial sentiments, *Desire not Heaven's blessings if they banish earthly joys.* The book had been the astonishing offering of the 1931 Brockenbridge Scholar—the first American to win the award—at the conclusion of his fellowship period.

He claimed that Artemisia had dictated the entire manuscript to him directly from the other side. Furthermore, he had asserted that *Heaven's Blessings* provided proof positive of the existence of a carnal connection between Artemisia and Lady Melissa Dawson, her muse and patron. Thus, he said, he had met the requirements of the Prandall Prize.

His purported proof consisted of numerous sexually explicit scenes between the two women, for which the book was roundly condemned by moralists. Literary reviewers were no kinder, describing it as a hodgepodge of banal dialogue, clumsy prose, and laughable anachronisms. Needless to say, the Prandall Prize remained unawarded, although the book was, predictably, a best seller.

For all its faults, she regarded the book with affection, because the well-worn second-hand copy of *Heaven's Blessings* she had stumbled across in an English bookshop had been her first encounter with Artemisia the person. Of course, it wasn't until she took Barbara's Romantic Poets class the second semester of her senior year that she had first truly come to appreciate Artemisia's poetry. And now, thanks to Artemisia, here she was, about to embark on a genuine academic adventure that could earn significant recognition from her peers. What's more, the Brockenbridge award was not only an almost certain passport to a full-time university position, but if she played her cards right, it would amplify her chances of eventually getting tenure—provided she first managed to produce something worthwhile with her fellowship.

"You're absolutely right, Ian. I don't think it's tempting fate overmuch to predict that whatever I come up with will outdo *Heaven's*

Blessings. At the very least, I can promise to avoid using supernatural manifestations as a source for my research. No crystal ball, no Ouija board, just plain, old-fashioned books and manuscripts."

"Well, speaking of manuscripts, I'm sure I've got the odd letter from Oona tucked away here and there, and though I don't recall her ever mentioning anything to the purpose, perhaps some contain tales of Artemisia. And of course, I've the stories she told me over the years. High time I wrote those down. Once I've got everything in some kind of sensible order, I'll post it all off to you."

"That would be wonderful, Ian, but please—I'd rather have you send me bits and pieces as they come to you. Even the smallest thing might be just the hint I need to spark my research, and I'm anxious to get to work right away. You can always send me updates and revisions later."

"Of course, my dear, if you really would prefer that. I'm so proud of you, and I want to assist you in any way that I can. Which reminds me…" He got to his feet, moving a bit more stiffly than Alex recalled from past years, and left the room.

A few moments later, he returned, holding out a photograph. "I think this will be of interest to you."

Alex looked at it with curiosity. The scene in the black-and-white photo was completely unfamiliar to her. It was an outdoor group of happy-looking children of various ages, all gathered around the seated figure of an old woman who was smiling serenely, gazing directly at the camera in a way that made Alex feel as if she were looking directly at her. From the clothing, Alex could tell that the photo dated from the mid- to late-Victorian period, but beyond that she was at a loss.

Ian pointed to one of the older boys. "That's Oona."

Stunned, Alex looked closer. The sturdy figure dressed in scruffy trousers and a disreputable shirt did have rather delicate features and sported a suspiciously bulging cap that could easily be concealing a quantity of long hair.

"She's got quite a mischievous smile, Ian. It reminds me of yours."

"That's what Mam would always say." Almost imperceptibly, he sighed.

After a moment, Alex asked, "Who's the woman?"

"Oh, that's Janet, of course."

"Janet? Why of course?"

"Oh, the whole village knew Janet. Before my time, you understand, but everyone used to talk about her so much I feel like I knew her myself. She was a great favorite with all the children in the old days. Apparently she had the magical ability to conjure up gingerbread or jam tarts for small visitors, along with a kind word or a lively story, at a moment's notice."

He smiled as if the happy memories were his own, not just reported to him. "And she was always there to soothe a broken heart or offer a word of advice when it was most needed. Seems she was a bit of a matchmaker, too, and more often than not successful. She'd been gone fifty years when I first came to Bramfell, and you'd think she was still around. Of course..."

He stopped, perhaps realizing Alex was too focused on the photo to really listen. Janet's trim figure was dressed simply and neatly in a dark dress of some sturdy material with a hint of lace at the collar and cuffs. Her snowy hair was covered with a sensible white cap sporting a restrained black ribbon. Except for smile lines around her eyes, her face was unwrinkled. She could have been anywhere from sixty to ninety.

Janet wore no jewelry, but there was a bunch of keys at her waist, and on a long cord or chain around her neck was another key, larger and more ornate than the others. In her hands she held a large book with a marbled paper cover that had a tiny rose stamped in one corner, from the looks of it some sort of notebook. It was probably a household account book, since the keys she wore, along with her respectable clothing, proclaimed her status as a housekeeper, the acme of a career in domestic service for a woman. She looked confident and content, sitting in the bright sunshine on a neatly trimmed lawn, surrounded by children who crowded around her with obvious affection.

"When was this photo taken? Do you know?"

"I think it was 1877—it's written on the back."

Alex turned the photograph over. The date was written in faded blue ink. "Yes, 1877."

"It was sometime in July. I'm not sure which day, but I do know it was her birthday—Janet's, I mean. I can't remember now if it was her eighty-seventh or eighty-eighth. The portrait was going to be a gift from the children. They'd all saved their pennies to hire the photographer. Oona was the one who organized it, so the photographer gave it to her. I think he felt sorry for her."

"Sorry for her?"

"Oh, didn't I say? This photo was taken the day Janet died."

"What? The day she died? But she looks so, so—"

"Healthy? Happy? Yes, all that and more. Apparently she hardly ever had a day's illness, and as you can see, she seems perfectly fine. There was no reason to suspect anything was wrong." He paused, looking up and away as if into the distance, or the past. "Oona was the one who found her."

"Oh, no."

"She used to do odd jobs and run errands for Janet, earn a bit of pocket money. She went over next morning at her usual time, and there Janet was, lying on the floor in the upstairs hall, just at the top of the stairs." He shivered. "I think she must have had a stroke, or a heart attack."

"How awful."

"Perhaps it was for the best, hard as it was for the ones who loved and lost her. I don't think she suffered, and clearly she was in good spirits, I dare say right to the end."

"Yes, I suppose that's the best any of us can hope for. Still, it must have been very difficult for your great-aunt."

"Indeed. She and her parents didn't always get on very well, so I think she must have looked to Janet for some of what she missed by way of affection and guidance. I know they were close, and she was always happy to tell me stories about Janet—other than that one. She was housekeeper at Dawson House. Started as a maid, then worked her way up."

"Your great-aunt knew someone who actually worked at Dawson House? I can hardly believe it. How long did Janet work there?"

"Let's see now, I think it was—you know, I'm really not sure, but it must have been a good sixty or seventy years. Oona told me once she started there when she was only in her teens."

"But that means—"

"Oh yes, Alexandra. Janet worked for Artemisia."

For a moment Alex was too stunned to speak. She looked down at the photo again. She was holding in her hands the image of someone who had known Artemisia, spent time with her, served tea to her, actually talked to her—about the daily menu and the silverware count, no doubt, but still, had talked to her. She gazed reverently at Janet's face. This woman had actually known Artemisia.

Her gaze transferred to Oona—who had known Janet, whom Ian had known. And she herself knew Ian. An unbroken chain reaching back into the past, a chain of knowledge and, at least for Ian and Oona and Janet, a chain of strong affection, which she felt privileged to share in.

She looked up at Ian, feeling the wonder, knowing it must be shining in her eyes.

"Oh, Ian! Thank you so much for showing me this, and for telling me about it. Is there any chance that I could..." She didn't dare ask for something so precious, even as a loan, but Ian seemed to realize what she couldn't put into words.

"Keep it? Of course I want you to keep it. Don't worry, it's just a copy. I donated the original to the Foundation years ago, so the museum could preserve it properly. There are plenty of copies, including one on display in the kitchen at Dawson House."

"Thank you. This is so special—you have no idea. You can't imagine what a wonderful gift this is." Ian smiled but said nothing, clearly touched by her reaction. "But I warn you, now I'm more determined than ever to get my hands on your recollections of Oona and her stories. You'd better start on it immediately. If I have to wait too long for the details, I may explode."

Alex made her apologies and called it a night in anticipation of her early train to Yorkshire the following morning.

CHAPTER TWO

A lex woke with a start, just catching the tail end of the announcement that they were pulling into Dunheath, the closest train station to Bramfell. She was slightly embarrassed at having fallen asleep on the train journey north, but the soothing rhythm of the train and the exertions of travel had their inevitable effect.

She disembarked, dragging her luggage into a chill, steady drizzle that managed to insinuate itself down the back of her neck in record time.

"Oh, to be in England, now that April's there!" Alex declaimed sarcastically, wondering how anyone who had actually experienced English weather could ever have penned such nonsense. Was it Browning or Tennyson? She couldn't remember. In any case, whoever it was had possessed a very poor grasp of matters meteorological. Besides, it was July, damn it—shouldn't summer be in full swing? With a sigh, she looked around.

Her next task, the guidebook had assured her, was to make her way from Dunheath to a place called Martinwick, and from there to Bramfell. The book had been somewhat vague about how this feat was to be accomplished, referring to local public transportation but giving no specifics. Now all she had to do was find a Martinwick-bound bus.

The tiny platform was completely deserted, and the wall before her was devoid of any signage beyond a faded marker displaying the station name. Nothing else was visible but a ramshackle building that she sincerely hoped was actually the station office.

And so it proved. The sole inhabitant was an elderly functionary who looked like he might well have taken up his post in Queen Victoria's day and remained on duty ever since.

So far, so good.

But when she asked about the schedule for the bus to Martinwick, he looked at her dubiously. When she repeated her request, carefully sounding out each syllable, *Mar-tin-wick*, he actually scowled.

"Thou'll not find a bus to Mar'ick."

"I beg your pardon?"

"There's no bus on. Mar'ick's got no bus." He was employing the universal response to conversational difficulties with fools and foreigners of repeating the same words over and over, louder each time, hoping that volume would bridge the comprehension gap.

It worked. His statement was suddenly, dismayingly clear.

"There's no bus? But then how do I get to…*Mar'ick*?"

Astonishingly, he favored her with something resembling a smile, accompanied by a strange head gesture, a sort of upward chin tilt aimed in the general direction of the air over her left shoulder. "Thou'll be wanting that Cam, then."

"That what?"

"That'll be me, then, won't it?"

Turning around, Alex saw that the owner of the new voice was standing in the doorway, leaning against the frame, and to judge by her amused expression, had apparently been there for some time.

"Ey up, Cam."

"Ey up, Seth. All well?"

"Aye. Miss here be for Mar'ick, then."

"So I gather."

During this exchange, Alex had been intently studying the newcomer. Medium height, solid build, hair a warm shade of golden brown and almost long enough to brush her shoulders. Not bad. Even better was the way she was standing there, hands in her pockets, with just the hint of a twinkle in her hazel eyes and a bit of a smile for Alex even while she was talking with the railway clerk.

Alex felt herself smiling back. Apparently the wilds of Yorkshire had more to offer than she had expected.

Alex said, "Actually, I'm headed for another town, a place called Bramfell. It's just that the guidebook suggested the best way to get there was by going through Mar'ick."

Cam laughed in an indulgent way that made Alex bristle. "Town! Bramfell's just a village, lass."

Lass? Just who did she think—

"So's Mar'ick, for that matter," Cam said. "If it's a town you're after, the only one hereabouts is Leeds."

With a touch of asperity, Alex said, "I need to get to Bramfell, not Leeds, thank you. This gentleman seems to think you can help me."

"That I can." Cam picked up Alex's two suitcases as if they weighed nothing at all and headed out the door. "See thee, Seth," she called over her shoulder as the door started to close behind her, leaving Alex no choice but to grab her backpack and follow her outside.

"Now wait just a minute. You can't just take my things and—"

Cam didn't bother to reply, merely holding out a hand for the backpack, obviously intending to place it beside the suitcases she had already stowed in the back of her vehicle, a strange sort of truck/van hybrid that had clearly seen better days. Not that it didn't appear to be well-maintained, and so clean it practically sparkled, even in the drizzle, with *Carter's Contracting* stenciled on the side in jaunty red letters backed by a thick white stripe that stood out boldly against the van's dark paint. But no amount of surface shine could disguise the dings and dents it had acquired in what must have been many years of service. Alex was unable to identify the make or model, but something about the overall look of the thing made her think of Eastern Europe—before the Berlin Wall came down. Doubtless its level of comfort and safety were on a par with its appearance.

Shuddering, Alex wasted a moment speculating about the chain of circumstances that had brought the thing to Yorkshire before looking hopefully around for some sign of a bus, taxi, or just about anything else with wheels that she could borrow, rent or steal. Unfortunately, her surroundings did not reveal any alternative form of transportation lurking helpfully nearby. Apparently, it was this van or nothing.

"May I ask just who the h—who you are, and why you've made off with my luggage?"

Cam flicked a casual thumb at the side of the van. "Cam Carter." A pause. "As you can see." Another pause, and a hint of a grin. Clearly she was enjoying this. Alex declined to play along, simply waiting her out.

It took longer than it should have for Cam to give in. When she finally did, her voice gave no hint of annoyance. If anything, she seemed amused to have been bested. "Foundation folk asked me to meet your train, seeing as I was going to be out this way."

Alex was surprised, and not just by the Foundation's choice of emissary. She'd provided them with her itinerary as a matter of courtesy, not because she expected chauffeur service. Which under the circumstances she would have happily dispensed with.

"But how could you be sure who I—" Realizing too late the opening she'd provided, she waited for the riposte, which was not long in coming.

"Can't say as I noticed anyone but you getting off that train."

Touché. Alex smiled ruefully and nodded in acknowledgment of the hit. But Cam wasn't quite finished.

"And an American, headed for Bramfell to boot. Hardly likely to be legions of you wandering about."

Well, at least she hadn't called her *Yank*.

Wordlessly, Alex handed over her backpack. Cam put it inside and went around to the left side of the van and opened the door, raising one sardonic eyebrow. Alex stalked over and got in. She reached for the shoulder belt but couldn't find the end of it. Probably it didn't get much use—she doubted many people would be willing to risk life and limb being ferried around in this thing—and she couldn't be bothered with the contortions that would be required to excavate and untangle the belt. It probably wouldn't make any difference anyway. Even a fender-bender would doubtless crush this thing like a cartoon tin can.

Cam closed the door with brisk efficiency before taking her place at the wheel and buckling up.

After a moment, she looked over at Alex. "Seat belt, please."

"I'm fine, thank you."

Cam didn't respond. She just sat there. Waiting. The eyebrow was again in evidence.

Clearly, the wretched woman wasn't going to start the vehicle until she complied.

"Oh, all right!" Alex fumbled around unsuccessfully in the gap between the seat and the door for a few minutes before getting out of the van to dig out the belt, which had somehow managed to lodge itself behind the seat. Climbing in again and closing the door very firmly—for safety, naturally—she clicked the belt sharply into place. She sincerely hoped the trip was going to be a short one.

Cam favored Alex with a smile that someone else would no doubt have found charming. "Where to, then?"

"Bramfell. Please."

"Aye, lass, but where in Bramfell? Dawson House or Highgate Hall?"

"Dawson House. And my name isn't *lass*."

Another smile. "What is it, then?"

"It's Alex." With difficulty she suppressed the urge to add, *but it's Ms. Petrocelli to you.*

"All right then, Alex, Dawson House it is."

In operation, the van did not quite measure up, or rather down, to its appearance. And regardless of the state of the vehicle, Cam's driving, at least, seemed to be top notch. Satisfied that she appeared to be in no immediate danger, Alex focused her attention on the scenery, at first deliberately to discourage conversation, but after a while she forgot all about Cam, so enthralled was she by the countryside. The area was truly beautiful in an austere way, with rolling hills sectioned by dry stone walls into fields for sheep or cattle, tiny hamlets that were little more than a scattering of cottages, and larger villages with shops lined up beside the road. In the distance she caught glimpses of open moorland covered in rough vegetation and dotted with craggy stone outcroppings. Once she thought she saw a hawk circling.

With a start, she realized that quite some time had passed. Cam hadn't said a single word, yet the silence didn't feel uncomfortable. In fact, it felt completely natural. That was another first. She was grateful not to be peppered with questions, but she wondered at the woman's lack of curiosity. On her previous trip to England, most people had seemed fascinated by her being an American, wanting to know what she was doing in England and what she thought of it all.

Perhaps Cam was angry with her. After all, the woman was doing her a favor, however uncouthly executed, and she hadn't been exactly polite in return. She snuck a sideways glance at her companion. It was hard to tell from the expression on her face.

"How much farther is it to Bramfell?"

"Just ahead." She certainly didn't sound angry. Maybe she had other things on her mind, concerns of her own.

"And here we are." Cam gestured with one hand, indicating the first of a collection of stone houses coming up on both sides of the road.

Alex tried to look everywhere at once, devouring the long-anticipated sight of the place where Artemisia had lived, and loved, and died. It didn't look any different from the other villages they had passed through, except for the names of the shops and pubs, many of which were branded by reference to Artemisia or Lady Melissa, although it was highly unlikely any of these establishments had been around long enough to have enjoyed the custom of either poet or patron. None of them bore the name Anna Thompkins, but that was no surprise. Alex had once tried the name out on a group of her undergraduates, and not a single one of them, English majors all, had recognized Artemisia's real name. Of course, Alex hadn't done any better herself when Barbara had tried the same trick with their class—had it really only been seven years ago? It felt like forever.

A menswear store was named for Mr. Dawson; most people forgot completely about Lady Melissa's wealthy but non-aristocratic husband, perhaps taking their cue from the lady herself. By all accounts he had been most indulgent, allowing her to lavish time, attention, and money on her young protégée without any apparent qualms. Either he was most unsuspicious—or very open-minded—or there had been nothing for him to be suspicious about. Despite all the whispering about the relationship between the two women, most scholars stuck religiously to the assertion that Artemisia and Lady Melissa had enjoyed an emotionally intense, but physically chaste, connection. Alex was determined to prove them wrong, although she had no idea precisely how.

Just ahead, the road forked, with signs pointing to Highgate Hall on the right and Dawson House on the left. Soon they had pulled up in front of a set of modest wrought-iron gates entwined with some sort of creeper and adorned, as Ian had promised, with Private Property and No Trespassing signs. A discreet plaque on one of the posts gave the name Dawson House and, in smaller letters, The Artemisia Foundation.

Cam got out and opened the gates. Alex was a little surprised they weren't kept locked but decided it was probably just as well since she wasn't sure what she would have done if they had been. She reached inside her shirt for the precious door key she had worn on a cord around her neck day and night since it had arrived in the mail along with her letter of congratulations. Cam got back in and they drove up the curving gravel path to the house. The angle wasn't quite right for a good view, and it was hard for Alex to get any sense of the place beyond dark stone walls and enveloping shrubbery.

They pulled to a stop under a tiny porte cochere. Alex got out without waiting for Cam to help her and stepped up to the large, solid-looking door. She stood there, slowly breathing in the scents of wet earth, wet vegetation, and wet stone, imagining Artemisia standing in the very same spot, over a hundred years before. She tried to come up with an appropriate quotation, something suitable for this magical—

"Do you not have a key, then?"

Not trusting herself to answer with anything approaching politeness, Alex stiffly unlocked the door. It opened with a satisfyingly old-fashioned creak, and she stepped across the threshold with Cam close behind. Fortunately the Foundation had long since had the place modernized, and once she had located the light switch Alex could see that they were in a small, sparsely furnished foyer with a stone floor and white plaster walls. Several closed doors on either side no doubt gave access to other parts of the house, and ahead on the right a simple wooden staircase led to the upper level.

Cam shouldered past her and headed for the stairs, carrying both bags, Alex's backpack slung over one shoulder.

"Wait a minute…"

But it was no use. Cam either didn't hear her or didn't care. Alex tramped up behind her. Cam stopped just past the top step, so abruptly that Alex almost bumped into her. In the dim light from below she could make out some sort of built-in shelving unit just in front of them displaying a few odds and ends, but the rest of the upper floor was completely dark.

Cam set down one of the bags long enough to turn a light on, revealing a narrow hall beyond lined with another series of closed doors. With a start, Alex realized that they were probably standing on the very spot where Janet had died. She shuddered.

Glancing back at her as she picked up the bag, Cam said, "It is a bit chilly. Nice cup of tea'll fix you right up."

Of course—the universal British remedy for any problem, be it physical, emotional, moral, or spiritual, with the possible exception of a severed limb. Yeah, she'd be sure to get right on that. All she ventured out loud, however, was a vague "Mmm."

Stepping farther along the hall, Cam asked, "Which room?"

"You needn't trouble yourself. Just leave it all right there."

"No trouble at all." She made no move to set down the bags. Defeated, yet again, Alex pointed at random. Cam opened the door she had indicated, then looked back at her. "Are you sure?"

"Yes, I'm sure."

"Suit yourself, then." She put the bags down just inside the doorway. "Might find it a bit crowded."

Looking past Cam's shoulder, Alex could see that the room she had chosen was the bathroom.

"Thank you so very much." Alex stalked downstairs, this time leaving Cam to follow her. She opened the front door, which had apparently closed on its own, and stood waiting as Cam approached.

If Cam noticed her lack of warmth, it didn't seem to bother her. If anything, it amused her, given the way she was smiling. "What's your mobile number?"

Seriously? This woman was unbelievable. "My phone died right before I left the States and I haven't had a chance to replace it." Not only did that sound like the brush off it was meant to be, it had the advantage of being absolutely true. She favored Cam with a sweetly virtuous expression.

Apparently undaunted, Cam handed over a business card. "Well, no doubt there's a telephone somewhere about. Ring me if you need a lift or want some help getting settled in."

"I'll be sure to do that." When hell freezes over.

The way Cam grinned at her, Alex was sure she'd read her mind. "Till then, Alex." She tipped an imaginary cap as she stepped outside.

Alex shoved the door closed behind her and locked it firmly. She heard Cam drive away, listening to be sure she paused to close the gates. The sound of the engine faded into the distance. Good riddance.

CHAPTER THREE

A lex took a moment to just breathe. She was actually here. She could hardly believe it. Looking around the entrance hall, she tried to decide what to do first. It was like Christmas morning, only better. She decided to start by investigating the rooms around her.

Opening doors and turning on lights, she discovered a little sitting room—rather stiff and chilly looking, a tiny powder room squeezed into what had doubtless been the under-the-stairs storage cupboard, something that might once have been a dining room but now seemed to be a sort of archive area, complete with filing cabinets, shelves full of cardboard boxes, and one or two glass-topped cases— all of which would no doubt repay careful investigation, and best of all, a generously proportioned study lined with bookcases.

The shelves were only about half-full, so there should be plenty of room for her books when they finally arrived. A sleek new computer and what looked like a combination copier/printer waited on a stand beside a large desk that was well stocked with supplies. Even better, nestled into one corner was what could only be a wireless router.

The room also featured two large windows and—yes!—a telephone. Alex looked at the business card still in her hand and, as she stepped back into the hall, flipped it toward the trash can by the desk, not bothering to check whether her aim was true.

The last door she tried led to the kitchen, or more accurately, the kitchen complex, which besides the kitchen itself included a laundry room, a well-filled, scrupulously ordered pantry, a scullery—complete with hand pump and stone sink, doubtless original, and even a sort of bed-sitting room, probably for a caretaker or housekeeper. All told, it took up a good half of the lower floor. Clearly, this was the heart of the house.

The kitchen did have a more-or-less modern stove, refrigerator, and white enamel sink. However, the fireplace itself looked like it hadn't changed at all since the house was built. It was still adorned with various iron hooks, from one of which hung a cauldron fit to stew up a substantial meal, as well as a roasting spit that looked like it could handle anything up to half a sheep. Ovens were set into the stone surround on either side, and the mantel above held a collection of ceramic serving pieces and a small, plain clock. A gleaming copper kettle, large enough to provide a sink's worth of hot water, sat on the hearth, and a fire had been laid, ready to light.

On the wall nearby, just as Ian had said it would be, was an enlargement of the photo he had given her of Janet and the children. Alex imagined that if Janet were somehow able to return to Dawson House, she would feel right at home here.

Beside the fireplace was a high-backed wooden bench, positioned to block any drafts from the back door—all plain lines and no nonsense, but sporting a grudging concession to modern frailty in the form of a few skimpy cushions. On the floor beside it was a work basket with sewing supplies.

The room was not over-large, and no inch of space was wasted, but the effect was snug and cozy rather than crowded. In the center of the room a large, heavy wooden table, scarred but well-scrubbed, offered a generous work surface as well as enough eating space for at least half a dozen people. One place was laid, complete with a linen napkin, a stoneware plate, and a teacup—not a mug, but an actual cup and saucer.

Alex realized that she was hungry and headed upstairs to retrieve the remains of Mrs. Glendale's provisions, stowed safely in her backpack—if she could only get to it. Naturally, when that Cam woman had so helpfully put all her things in the bathroom, she had put the backpack down farthest from the doorway, so Alex had to haul both suitcases out of the way first. How was it possible that they had managed to get even heavier than the last time she had lifted them? Grumbling, Alex reclaimed the food and went back down to the kitchen.

A cheerful red kettle sat on the back of the stove, and tea things were handy on the counter nearby. Alex couldn't resist. She filled the teakettle and put it on to boil, then set about the rest of her preparations. One thing Fiona had insisted on was teaching Alex how to make a proper cup of tea, and she had delighted in the ritual ever since, making sure to rinse the teapot with a little hot water to warm it just before adding the tea leaves. Muttering "Bring pot to kettle, not kettle to pot," she poured in the briskly boiling water, covering the pot with a cozy before setting it aside to steep. In the refrigerator she even found fresh milk—clearly someone was expecting her, and she was grateful.

As she sat enjoying her tea she realized she did feel better, damn it. Shaking her head as if to clear away the last vestiges of Cam's presence, she turned her thoughts to plans for the rest of the day. No sense in wasting any time. A glance at the clock showed it was far too late for hiking on the moors. Probably the most sensible thing to do after she finished eating would be to unpack, then perhaps investigate the study.

Leaving the last of Mrs. Glendale's pastries on the table for breakfast the next morning, she carried her dirty dishes to the sink. They sat there like an affront to the spotless kitchen, but she couldn't bear to deal with them. No harm in leaving them for after breakfast.

Upstairs, she opened doors on an airing cupboard stocked with enough linens for a small army, a closet full of cleaning things, and several interchangeable-looking bedrooms. The Foundation had assured her that she was free to use anything and everything in the house. Alex assumed that either the furniture was all reproduction or it had been deemed to have no historical merit. Much as she would like to imagine that tangible traces of Artemisia's occupancy remained in Dawson House, realistically she knew it to be highly unlikely that anything here had actually once been hers. Presumably anything of real value had long since been removed to the museum at Highgate Hall.

She chose the bedroom closest to the bath, on the side of the house with a view of the moor—or rather, she hoped there would be a view, but when she pulled back the curtains it was already too dark to tell. Suddenly the bed looked very inviting. Maybe if she just lay down for a little while…She sat, pulled off her shoes and socks, and stretched out, not even pulling back the coverlet.

❖

When she woke, the sun was streaming in and some obnoxious bird was delivering its morning broadcast at full volume, from the sound of it right outside the window. Alex groaned and sat up. She felt hungover and all stiff from sleeping in her clothes. She dragged herself into the bathroom and splashed a little water on her face.

What she saw in the mirror wasn't encouraging. She looked positively gaunt, her bloodshot eyes staring out of her too-pale face like red, white, and blue marbles. How patriotic. And her hair! When it got this long it never looked good first thing in the morning, but today was especially bad. She wished she'd taken time to have it cut before she left. She'd just have to hope she could find someone in the village who knew what to do with hair as curly as hers. Another thing to add to her list.

She shuddered to think that she had looked even half this bad the previous day. Why on earth Cam had wanted her number was beyond imagining. Maybe she was one of those flirty types that hit on every woman they met, by reflex. Just as well she hadn't encouraged her. Not that she had so many offers she could afford to be choosy, but still, there were limits.

Eventually she staggered downstairs and into the kitchen, coming to a startled stop at the sight of a tiny white-haired woman standing at the stove, back toward her.

"Uh, good morning."

The woman turned around. "So. You're up, then." She gave Alex an unsmiling once-over that made her wish she had done a bit more with herself than run a brush through her hair. The woman glanced pointedly at her bare feet, and she could feel herself blush.

Still, she plastered a smile on her face and stepped forward, offering her hand. "I'm Alex Petrocelli."

After an uncomfortably long pause, the woman reached out and gave her a surprisingly firm shake. "Elspeth Tate. Mrs."

"How do you do, Mrs. Tate."

"Sit you down. Porridge is nearly ready." She turned her back and began filling the teakettle.

"Thank you, but you really didn't need to make me breakfast. Actually, I prefer to do that sort of thing for myself."

Mrs. Tate put the kettle down with a clank and turned back around, crossing her arms over her chest. "Oh, you do, do you?"

Uh-oh. "It's very kind of you, truly, but you don't need to go to any trouble on my account. I'm used to taking care of myself."

"I see. One of those leave-me-be sorts, are you?"

"Not really. It's just—"

"And next I suppose you'll be telling me there's no call for me to be troubling myself about the place at all now that you're here. After twenty-five years of doing for the Foundation and the Scholars! You'll be taking care of that, too, I've no doubt."

"No, that's not what I—"

Mrs. Tate hadn't paused. "The way you did yesterday, I suppose. Every light in the place left to burn all night, the back door wide open, and food left lying about for that fool cat to help itself to."

As if on cue, the cat in question, a fine big marmalade tabby, made its appearance and began rubbing against Alex's leg.

"I'm sorry about the lights. I was so tired I just forgot about them. I won't do that again, I promise." She glanced at the table but there was no sign of the scone. Either the cat had eaten every crumb or Mrs. Tate had cleared away the evidence. "And the scone—I didn't realize leaving it on the table would be a...Wait a minute, did you say the back door was open? Wide open? But it was closed last night, I'm sure it was. I never even went near it."

"Well, not wide open, truth to tell. More ajar. But open, nonetheless. Never went near it, you say?" She glanced at the door, then back at Alex. In a slightly mollified tone, she said, "Well, it's possible I didn't shut it quite tight behind me yesterday—it's a bit tricky, doesn't always catch the way you think it has. The least little thing can open it again."

"And I'd say we've got that least little thing right here." Alex bent down and picked up the cat, who seemed quite happy to be cradled. "What's his name?"

"Her name. She's Grace."

"Hello, Grace. Scapegrace, by the sound of things." That surprised a sharp laugh out of Mrs. Tate. Shaking her head, she returned to her work.

Alex sat, still holding the culprit, who graciously allowed herself to be petted. "You are a naughty girl, aren't you? Yes, you are. You know you are. Did you eat my scone? Such a bad, bad kitty. And such a pretty kitty. Yes, you are."

By the time Grace had had enough attention and demanded escape, Mrs. Tate had a cup of tea ready for her. Alex took it gratefully. A few blissful sips later it was joined by a hearty bowl of porridge with plenty of butter, cream, and honey, along with a perfectly boiled egg and several pieces of toast—served with blackberry jam so bursting with flavor it had to be homemade. Mrs. Tate waved away Alex's thanks and began washing dishes, leaving Alex to focus on her food. It was all delicious.

After a second cup of tea she felt almost human and asked Mrs. Tate to join her, a bit surprised but pleased when she did so.

As she poured her own cup, Mrs. Tate said, "I always like to see a Scholar with a hearty appetite. Makes me feel I've properly earned my wages." She actually smiled. "Once in a while I've had older gentlemen who could really tuck in, but usually it's the younger ones, like you. Although that last one was such a prune-faced stick, no more appetite than a bird, for all he hadn't seen thirty yet. Old before his time and no mistake. That one's trouble, I said to myself the very first morning, and trouble he was."

"Oh?" The very first morning. Yikes. Alex could only be grateful for her own narrow escape from a similar disaster—at least, she hoped she'd escaped.

"Nothing was ever good enough for him, always complaining. If it wasn't the food, it was drafts, or cold, or damp, or noises in the night. As if anyone staying in Dawson House wouldn't have sense enough to expect a few strange noises or a bit of a chill."

"Of course. It's such an old building."

Mrs. Tate gave her an odd look. "It's not that old, as places round here go." She laughed, but it sounded a little forced. "You Americans seem to think anything still standing after a hundred years is ancient. But I expect you're right."

Alex decided it was best to change the subject, so she asked Mrs. Tate to explain her schedule and any other things she thought Alex should know about.

There turned out to be quite a few things. Eventually Alex excused herself to get pen and paper from the study to take notes. In addition to the details of Mrs. Tate's schedule—including serving Alex "a proper hot dinner" at noon, sharp—Alex was treated to an extensive lecture on household management, Dawson House style. This seemed to principally consist of leaving everything to Mrs. Tate. At first Alex was inclined to argue, especially when it came to things like doing her own laundry, but the housekeeper's expression grew so sour when Alex diffidently suggested a microwave, that Alex immediately dropped the idea.

Having learned her lesson, Alex's remaining contributions to the conversation consisted of "Yes, Mrs. Tate," "No, Mrs. Tate," and "I wouldn't dream of such a thing, Mrs. Tate," until finally the housekeeper was smiling at her again. She even relented so far as to allow that Alex would probably be able to manage on her own on weekends without too much difficulty, so long as she faithfully followed Mrs. Tate's precepts, for which gracious expression of confidence Alex dutifully thanked her.

One thing that was clearly impressed upon Alex—she underlined it twice—was that if anything broke down, no matter how small, on no account was she to attempt repairs herself. The Foundation would have someone in to take care of all that, no doubt a member of Mrs. Tate's extended family, which by the sound of things had been making itself useful to the Foundation for generations.

Alex glanced at the photo on the wall. She wondered whether Janet had been like Mrs. Tate, a benevolent dictator holding absolute sway over her domain, leaving poor Artemisia afraid to pick up her own stockings lest she offend. She certainly looked like someone who would have brooked no nonsense—all for your own good, of course.

Eventually Mrs. Tate shooed her out of the kitchen, saying she had work to do, so Alex went upstairs to unpack, which didn't take all that long, considering how heavy her bags had been. Her room did indeed have an excellent view of the moor, and it looked so glorious in what she was sure was the rare sunshine she decided she could fit in a quick hike before Mrs. Tate put dinner on the table. Tying on her shoes and grabbing a jacket, she headed downstairs and out the front door, planning to loop around to the back of the house.

Ian had been absolutely right—there was a path just beyond the back gate that led straight up to the moor. It was an easy climb and she took her time, pausing often to look back for increasingly spectacular views of the village and surrounding countryside. Far too soon, it was time to head back, but she promised herself that the next time she'd make it all the way to Bram Tor, just as she'd planned.

She had to run a little bit at the end, but still managed to present herself at the kitchen table before the clock finished striking noon, and just as well, too, given the glower Mrs. Tate gave her. However, by the end of the meal all was forgiven. Apparently Alex's appreciation for her cooking—not in the least feigned, for it was remarkably good—made up for a lot of other faults in Mrs. Tate's eyes.

Alex found it strange that Mrs. Tate refused to eat with her. For Alex, it was bad enough being waited on by someone old enough to be her grandmother, but to have that someone standing by without taking part in the meal she herself had prepared was downright peculiar. Mrs. Tate certainly wasn't trying to make her feel uncomfortable— it wasn't as if she were staring at Alex and watching her chew, or interrupting her every five minutes like an over-eager waiter on a low-tip night to ask if she needed anything—but still, it was awkward.

She tried to imagine what it would be like to live in a world where this kind of thing was normal. That was the world Artemisia and Lady Melissa had been born into—a world divided in two, where one group of people devoted their lives to taking care of the other, and everyone thought of it all as natural, inevitable, even God's will—and God help anyone who didn't know their place and keep to it.

She wondered which would be worse—to belong to the group assigned to lifelong drudgery, or to be on the other side, thinking you deserved everything the universe by sheer good luck had tossed in your lap, never realizing your whole life was based on lies.

Looking over at the photo on the wall, she wondered what Janet would have said about it. After all, she had spent, what, sixty years in service, one way and another, if Ian's memory was accurate. And she certainly didn't look downtrodden. Quite the opposite, in fact. What really mattered, Alex supposed, was not how the world saw you, but how you saw yourself, and whether you and the people around you treated one another with respect.

Alex shook her head. Too much thinking for one afternoon.

After Mrs. Tate left for the day, Alex considered going for another walk but decided to try a different kind of exploration instead, heading for the archive room. The files alone proved so fascinating—document after document about the Foundation, the Scholars, and all their research, plus of course plenty of information about Lady Melissa and Artemisia, not to mention contemporaries of theirs like Keats, Wollstonecraft, and Wordsworth—that hours went by before she realized it. It was only her growling stomach that made her finally stop.

Her supper was waiting for her in the refrigerator as promised, and after all that time spent working, she was truly grateful not to have to do more than heat it up. Maybe Mrs. Tate was on to something.

Chapter Four

The next day Alex woke up feeling much better. Mrs. Tate fed her another excellent breakfast, and afterward, since the weather still held, she went for another walk. This time she finally made it all the way to Bram Tor. She spotted neither hawks nor hares during her recitations—perhaps they didn't share her taste in poetry—but the views were glorious and the air was crisp and clean.

When she ran out of poems, she ventured a more-or-less-on-key version of the one Yorkshire ballad she knew. She sang all the way home as well. She didn't have much of a voice, and she expected she was mangling the dialect, but she figured enthusiasm made up for a lot—especially when no one else was listening.

After lunch, Alex figured it was time to pay her respects to whoever was in charge over at the museum. Spending time with some stuffy management type was not her idea of fun, but duty was duty. Besides, she wanted to get off to a good start with the local Foundation officials.

She hadn't packed much in the way of formal clothing but pulled together a respectable-enough outfit thanks to the one decent blazer she owned, plus a plain T-shirt in a bold blue, and a pair of black trousers. Finally she selected a pair of earrings artsy enough to add a little pizzazz without being too outrageous. If the mirror wasn't lying to her, her hair was behaving, and in general she looked much less of a fright than she had the previous day.

Armed with directions from Mrs. Tate and an assurance that the distance from Dawson House to the Hall was no walk at all, Alex set out for Highgate in reasonable spirits. By the time she was—she sincerely hoped—halfway there, her respect for Mrs. Tate, and for Artemisia, who by all accounts had made the trip on a daily basis whenever Lady Melissa was in residence, had considerably increased. The walk was certainly a long one and felt like it was mostly uphill. At least the path was well marked and in good repair, but Alex was glad she had chosen a sturdy pair of shoes.

She didn't have much of a view of Highgate Hall until she was almost right on top of it, since whoever built it had clearly valued the comfort of a situation somewhat sheltered from biting winter winds over a more impressive but far less practical hilltop perch. As the path wound around the back of the hill and approached the front entrance, she got a better look.

The well-proportioned structure of local stone, long-since weathered to an indeterminate dark hue, nestled into a slight dip between two folds of rising ground, with the two lower floors backing into the hill itself, leaving only the two upper levels with what were probably spectacular views in all directions. Being no architecture expert, Alex couldn't begin to guess at its history, but its strong, clean lines gave it a solid, homey feeling.

The wide-open gates that had doubtless given the Hall its name were suitably impressive, being almost twice Alex's height and sporting a profusion of decorative ironwork and even a few touches of gilding. However, they were just as clearly ceremonial, there being no wall or barrier of any kind around the property, not even a hedge. Still, it didn't seem right to bypass them, certainly not on her first visit. Alex strode through the gates and crunched up the curving gravel path to the front door.

A tasteful placard informed her of the hours that the museum was open to the public, concluding with a request to ring for admittance. Alex did so, enjoying the feel of the old-fashioned bellpull and the joyful clanging it produced. The signal was answered promptly by a smiling and efficient man of middle years and first-class tailoring who ushered Alex into an entrance hall that was surprisingly light and airy, given the sturdy feel of the building's exterior.

When she had introduced herself and stated her business, his welcome changed from professionally to genuinely friendly. He offered her a seat, which she accepted, and tea, which she declined, before ascending the grand staircase in pursuit of whichever official was responsible for dealing with all things Brockenbridge.

Returning a few minutes later, he led the way up to the third level and down several corridors until they reached a door marked *Liaison* in gleaming brass. He knocked, and upon hearing a brisk "Come in!" in a female voice, he pulled the door open and waved Alex into the room.

Alex stepped inside and stood there stunned, barely registering the faint closing of the door behind her and her guide's retreating footsteps. The woman seated at the desk before her was unbelievably lovely, a fall of shining red hair framing her patrician features in perfect counterpoint to her smooth, creamy skin. Alex had no idea what color the woman's eyes were since she was focusing on the computer in front of her, giving Alex a moment to close her mouth and try to recover.

But that effort was wasted when the woman glanced up and Alex felt herself falling into a pair of the greenest eyes she had ever seen. For the first time in her life, she understood what breathtaking beauty really meant.

The woman started to laugh, a charming peal. "You're Alex Petrocelli?" She laughed again. This time it was a bit less charming. As she stood and walked around the desk toward Alex, she said, "I can see I should have read that memo from the trustees more carefully."

She smiled, inviting Alex to join her amusement. Alex attempted to comply, but her features felt stiff. She was used to being dismissed— or worse, ignored—by women as clearly out of her league as this one was, but this was a new low. She fought down the urge to run a hand through her hair or otherwise check for blemishes. Instead, she stiffened her spine and stuck out her hand.

"Yes, I'm Alex Petrocelli. How do you do."

"Rosamund Camberwell." Rosamund shook her hand, but didn't let go of it. "You must pardon me, really you must. When I read the announcement that our new Brockenbridge Scholar was named Alex, naturally I assumed it was short for Alexander. We get so few women as fellows, you see."

Alex supposed she did see. Withdrawing her hand, she said, "I'm very glad to be here, as you can well imagine, Ms. Camberwell."

"Rosamund, please. And an American, as well. How lovely!"

Apparently, Rosamund, *please,* hadn't bothered to learn even the most basic information about her, despite whatever responsibility she had for the Brockenbridge program. Alex took a moment to wonder just who had arranged her ride from the train station. She smiled thinly.

"As you can imagine, I'm anxious to get started. Is there anything I need to take care of before I begin?"

"You mean paperwork and so on? Oh, reams and reams, I'm sure. Let me put you on to Nicola. She'll soon get you sorted out."

Alex found herself being shepherded out of Rosamund's office and into a much smaller one next door, inhabited by a very blond, very pale woman of about Alex's age who turned a vivid, rosy red the moment she laid eyes on Rosamund. It was all too obvious Nicola had a huge crush on her boss. Not that Alex blamed her; Rosamund was certainly pretty enough to devastate women made of sterner stuff than this one seemed to be. Given the look on Rosamund's face, it was just as evident that she knew exactly how the woman felt and found it more amusing than otherwise. Alex, on the other hand, saw nothing entertaining about the situation.

"Nicola, darling, this is Alex Petrocelli, our new Scholar. Can you see that she signs all her forms and gets her ID card and passwords and so forth?"

Poor Nicola, apparently too flustered to speak, simply nodded.

Then it was Alex's turn. Standing closer than was strictly necessary, even given the office's tiny dimensions, Rosamund took Alex's hand in both of hers.

"Alex, it's been a pleasure. You must come by again soon so we can have a proper chat about your research."

Alex extricated her hand. "I'll, ah, be sure to do that, Ms. Camberwell." Oh, very smooth.

Pausing in the doorway, she favored Alex with an impish grin. "Rosamund."

And with that, she was gone. Alex took a moment to give herself a mental shake before turning back to Nicola.

Freed from Rosamund's distracting presence, her assistant proved to be efficient, friendly, and genuinely interested in Alex and her work, flatteringly so. Nicola had even read Alex's proposal, which came as a pleasant shock, especially given Rosamund's obvious lack of interest. Nicola made a number of helpful suggestions about Foundation resources that might be worth exploring for Alex's research, in addition to providing all manner of practical information about the museum and the Brockenbridge program.

When Nicola suggested a tour, Alex accepted with alacrity, declining the offer of an official guide in favor of Nicola herself. It turned out to be an excellent decision. While they didn't cover the entire building, which would have taken the best part of a day, if not longer, they went well beyond the standard stately-home areas open to the public, like Lady Melissa's suite and the ballroom. Nicola showed her various nooks and crannies where materials were archived, workrooms where artifacts were restored and maintained, and study areas for visiting researchers, including an office set aside for the Brockenbridge Scholar's exclusive use. When Nicola handed over the key, Alex couldn't help doing a little happy dance, which surprised a friendly chuckle from her guide.

"I've saved the best for last—or at least, I hope you'll think so. If Madame will kindly step this way…" Nicola ushered her into the library with a sweeping gesture and a full bow.

"Oh, I'm sure I'll—Wow."

It was certainly a grand room, with floor-to-ceiling bookshelves in rich, dark wood interspersed with huge arched windows, but it was the painting over the fireplace that had surprised the exclamation from her.

Artemisia's Farewell—there it was. Although Alex had seen prints of it, the reality was nothing like she had expected. For one thing, the painting was huge. Even a full-page illustration in a book could not possibly convey the in-person impact of a work of art of this size. It had to be a good eight feet wide if it was an inch, and proportionally tall—at least six feet. Clearly Smithson hadn't lacked confidence.

Nor had he lacked skill. The colors, the composition, the use of light and shadow all combined to tell a powerful story, one that in lesser hands might have come across as saccharine or silly.

The scene portrayed was a darkened room, mostly in shadow, with a few key details picked out by warm candlelight. In the left foreground, almost tumbling out of the frame, was Artemisia, her face etched with pain and privation. She had clearly been ravaged not just by the fever that was killing her, but by years of sorrow. Her dark hair hung loose and lank, and she was clad in some sort of nightshirt, pulled askew to bare her shoulder and the upper part of her chest on the left side, an almost toga-like effect.

She was half lying, half sitting on a narrow, disordered bed, leaning with her head thrown back against the headboard and supported on the side farthest from the viewer by a woman—some sort of servant or nurse—who bent over Artemisia with an arm wrapped around her shoulders from behind. The woman was looking down at Artemisia, her face turned almost completely away from the viewer.

In the center of the painting, but equally in the background, were two male figures, one in rolled-up shirtsleeves—presumably the doctor—and the other the vicar, Bible in hand. Both were gazing over at Artemisia with mournful yet reverential expressions, as if aware that they were in the presence of something both sacred and mysterious.

Which clearly they were, for Artemisia's own face, despite being marked by past sufferings, was transfigured, transformed by what could only be described as ecstatic joy, the candlelight touching her in such a way that she seemed suffused with inner light. Her right hand lay across her chest, resting against the bare skin over her heart. Her left arm was lifted and extended, her hand outstretched as she reached toward something in the upper right of the painting, a vision that apparently only she could perceive.

And here Smithson had truly excelled himself. The object of Artemisia's heartfelt desire and her last, dying utterance was not presented as an actual portrait of Lady Melissa. No—this apparition was barely worthy of the term, a mere suggestion, a thing of gossamer and moonbeams that hinted at golden hair and beautiful features but might have been only a trick of the flickering candlelight. Might have been, except for the joy and certainty on Artemisia's face. Clearly, she had been given a precious gift in her last moments on earth—reunited, however tenuously, with the one she had lost so long ago and had thought never to see again.

Alex gazed at the painting, helpless to do anything but feel the emotions coursing through her—sorrow for Artemisia's lonely years of grieving, regret for the premature loss of her poetic voice, and a strange mixture of joy and heartache for her last, poignant moments: hallucination, dream, perhaps even reality. Who could say?

Nicola had come to stand beside Alex, and she began to recite Artemisia's final words in a not-quite-steady voice. *"Death may have parted us, O my Heart, but Love will reunite us.* Do you think it really could have been true, Alex?"

Alex blinked her tears away and turned to meet Nicola's earnest gaze. "Do I think what really could have been true?"

"You know, Artemisia and Lady Melissa." The blush was again in evidence, but she soldiered gamely on. "I've always thought it was so romantic, the two of them. Being so in love with someone, for years and years, even long after they were gone. And then, the *Farewell.* I know people say she wasn't really talking about that kind of love, not that way, but I can't help hoping…" She was blushing even harder as her voice trailed away.

Ah, yes, the old love-isn't-actually-love approach to erasing lesbians from literature and history. Just look right at some inconvenient fact and pretend it isn't there, or if that fails, claim it can't possibly mean what it so obviously does mean. It's passionate friendship or chaste devotion or two lonesome single gals sharing expenses, or whatever. Sometimes she just laughed at the ridiculousness of it all, but not this time. Nicola looked upset, and Alex realized she was probably scowling.

Consciously rearranging her features, she gave Nicola what she hoped was an encouraging smile. "I think Artemisia meant exactly what she said. Just because I don't have enough evidence to publish in a peer-reviewed journal—or win the Prandall Prize—doesn't make their love any less real."

"The Prandall! Lord, the bane of my existence." Before Alex could pursue this interesting remark, Nicola glanced at her watch. "I'm off any moment now. Do you fancy a coffee? There's a café a short walk from here. I often stop in on my way home."

"Sounds good to me. I could use a change from all the tea."

"Sacrilege! Nothing like a nice cuppa." She lowered her voice to a stage whisper. "Actually, I much prefer espresso—but please, don't tell anyone."

"Your secret's safe with me—I'd hate to be responsible for you being shunned or deported or whatever it is they do to coffee lovers over here."

Laughing, Nicola hurried off to grab her things. Not long afterward, they were seated in a relatively quiet corner of a bustling café—one that even offered Wi-Fi, Alex noted.

After the first few sips of a most acceptable cappuccino, Alex's thoughts returned to Nicola's exclamation. "What did you mean when you called the Prandall Prize the bane of your existence? Are you hunting for evidence?"

"Heavens, no! My bailiwick is strictly administration, thank you ever so much. I leave all that researchy sort of thing to you scholar types."

"Really? You seem pretty knowledgeable to me."

"Thank you. Once someone else has sifted through the detritus of the ages and sorted it all out, it makes for fascinating reading. I just don't like to do the actual sifting and sorting myself. Much too dusty, for a start."

"Not even for the Prandall?"

"Especially not the Prandall! I swear, half my job is spent dealing with all the letters the Foundation gets from loonies trying to win the seven hundred thousand pounds."

"Is it that much now? Last I heard it was only five hundred thousand or so." She laughed. "Only! So now it's what, about a million dollars? A million and a half?"

"Something like that. Hard to believe it started with a mere thousand pounds, isn't it? The magic of compound interest."

"But why does all the mail come here? I thought the Foundation was London based."

"Oh, it is, but most people can't be bothered with that. They just slap Artemisia and Bramfell on the envelope and hope for the best. Sadly, it works, because the letters keep arriving. Sometimes I have dreams where I'm being buried under a pile of Prandall correspondence, never to be seen again. Last time I woke up screaming. Just as well I'm between girlfriends at the moment."

"You, too? What, are all the women around here blind? If you're single, clearly there's no hope for me at all." Nicola colored prettily but looked rather alarmed. Alex realized she must sound like she was either flirting or fishing for a compliment—and maybe she was, on both counts. She seriously needed to get out more. "I can see how that could give anyone nightmares. But why do you get saddled with it all?"

"Because I'm the most junior member of staff, of course. No one else can bear to deal with it."

Nicola seemed to have recovered her equilibrium, so Alex decided to stick with the topic. "You know, I've never understood the point of the prize—I mean, the reason why Prandall set it up. He's always described as an admirer of Artemisia's, so you'd think he'd want to discourage the rumors about her and Lady Melissa, not wave money in people's faces asking for proof they were lovers."

"Oh, that's just typical Victorian logic. He was throwing down a gauntlet—daring people to provide proof, because he was sure it didn't exist."

"Sort of put up or shut up. Yeah, that does make sense. Only it didn't shut anyone up."

"Too right. All it did was encourage people to manufacture evidence in hopes of winning the money. And the paper avalanche has never stopped."

"What on earth do you do with the letters? Do you have to answer them all?"

"Oh, I just send off a response our solicitors drafted—Thank you for your inquiry, we regret to inform you, etc.—and then I box it all up for storage. Unfortunately, I have to read each one first, on the off chance there's something that ought to be passed on to London."

"Anything promising?"

Nicola grinned. "No, not even once in the entire time I've been here." She sighed. "I suppose it wouldn't bother me so much if it weren't all such pathetic rubbish. Most of the forgeries are so obvious even I can spot them—half of them are in ballpoint, for heaven's sake."

"Well, maybe Artemisia was ahead of her time—an inventor as well as a poet."

"It's astonishing, the lengths to which some people will go for money."

"While the rest of us toil for our daily bread." Alex looked up at the sound of Cam's voice. "Evening, Nicola. Hello, Alex."

Nicola spun around in her seat to greet the newcomer, a delighted smile on her face. "Cam! I haven't seen you in ages. Do join us, please."

Cam didn't immediately accept Nicola's offer, meeting Alex's eyes with an inquiring, mildly amused look on her face. Suddenly there was a lot less air in the general vicinity, although Nicola didn't seem to have noticed.

Clearly there was no way out of this without being completely rude. Alex managed to mumble something that could charitably have been considered an invitation. Cam wasted no time setting down her mug and pulling over a chair, turning it backward and straddling it. She casually crossed her arms along the top—a move that just happened to show off the well-developed forearms revealed by her rolled-up shirtsleeves—and smiled at both of them. Doubtless it was Alex's imagination that the look directed her way contained just a hint of smugness.

Nicola said, "So where have you been hiding, Cam? I haven't even had a chance to properly thank you for giving Alex a lift from the train station. Alex, I'm so sorry I couldn't meet your train, but something came up last minute that I truly wasn't able to avoid. I do so appreciate you coming to the rescue, Cam."

Cam's hazel eyes were fixed on Alex even as she answered Nicola. "Always glad to be of service to a lady in distress."

Said the Goddess's gift to women. Alex nearly choked on her coffee when Cam winked at her, for all the world as if she'd heard her. *Either she's a genuine mind reader or I have whatever the opposite of a poker face is. Just as well I don't gamble.* "Thank you, Nicola. I had a feeling you must be the one responsible for that arrangement. Somehow I can't picture the fair Rosamund going to so much trouble. I can't say I envy you working for her."

Nicola seemed a little uncomfortable. "Oh, Rosamund's all right. Certainly better than my last boss—even after three months I'm still grateful for the change"—Nicola glanced aside for a moment—"mostly." Looking back at Alex, she continued, "She's just not much on details. More of an idea person, you might say."

"She's lucky she's got you, then."

"Kind of you to say so." Nicola looked sideways again and this time Alex followed suit. Cam was staring into her coffee, cradling the mug in both hands. A working woman's hands, sporting a few scrapes and scratches. Strong, capable hands.

It took a moment to realize that Nicola had asked her a question. Fortunately, she repeated it. "So has Aunty Elspeth been taking good care of you?"

"Aunty Elspeth? Mrs. Tate is your aunt?"

"Actually she's a sort of cousin, but we were always taught to call her Aunty."

"Does everybody in town—" She glanced over at Cam, who had emerged from her brown study and was shaking her head at Alex in mock disappointment at her inability to remember something so simple. Alex rolled her eyes. "I mean, does everyone in the *village* work for the Artemisia Foundation?"

"Not really," said Nicola, "but between the Foundation and the tourists, most of us owe our living to Artemisia in some form or fashion."

"And I suppose I do too, or at least, I will once I get my dissertation written and use it to land a job."

Cam said, "What sort of work are you after, then, lass? Sorry, I mean, Alex." Not sorry at all, if the cheeky expression was anything to go by.

"Well, nothing's certain these days in academia, but I'll be looking for a tenure-track job—preferably at a halfway decent university. Thanks to the Brockenbridge, I might even get it."

Nicola seemed taken aback. "Might get it? Are things really so bad in the States?"

"A lot of my friends from graduate school are working as adjuncts." She looked over at Cam as she explained. "Small salary and no benefits, no office, no respect, almost no hope of a permanent job. Universities claim they can't afford to hire full-time faculty, but they're happy to churn out bushels of new PhDs, year after year. Apparently in their minds there's no connection between the graduation glut and the hiring dearth, so if you can't find a real job, it's just your own fault." Her companions were staring at her. "Sorry for speechifying, but the whole thing makes me crazy."

"No need to apologize, Alex," said Nicola. "I just didn't realize things were so bad." She looked at her watch. "Oh, Lord. I must dash."

As if by mutual agreement, they all three stood up and moved to the sidewalk just outside the café door. Nicola took her hand to say good-bye, but unlike Rosamund's farewell gesture, it felt friendly and natural.

"Alex, I hope to see you back at the Hall very soon." As she walked away, she kept talking over her shoulder. "Cam, drop round anytime. And you know Mum wants you for Sunday dinner next week."

"Tell her I'll be there. And yes, I'll help the lads finish the repairs to the garden wall." Turning back to Alex, she said, "Good sorts, her brothers, but hopeless at anything practical. Good job the lot of them went to university like Nicola, or they'd have starved by now."

Alex couldn't think of a response, nor did one seem expected. "I'll be going now. It was, uh, nice to see you again."

"Not as bad as you imagined, you mean?" Alex could only stare at her. Cam smiled back, clearly amused at the effect of giving voice to feelings Alex hadn't realized were quite so obvious. "Let's get you home."

"Really, that isn't necessary. I'd have to try very hard to get lost in a place this size. Good night." She started walking away, striding boldly and hoping Cam would take the hint.

Instead Cam fell into place beside her and had no trouble at all keeping up. Finally Alex gave in and slowed to a normal speed. When she did, Cam smiled at her but didn't say anything, simply continuing beside her at the new pace. Alex felt no need for conversation either, and the walk passed in silence that was surprisingly comfortable.

When they reached the gates of Dawson House, they stopped. Alex suddenly felt awkward. She wasn't sure what she expected, or wanted, from Cam. A handshake? A kiss? Nothing at all?

For her part, Cam seemed to feel neither expectation nor uncertainty. She just pushed the gates ajar for Alex to walk through, then pulled them shut, watching as Alex walked to the front door and unlocked it.

When Alex turned back and lifted a hand to say good-bye, Cam called out, "Chin up. I have a way of growing on folk. And not like fungus, either."

Laughing, Alex went inside and locked the door.

Once she had switched on the light, she noticed that the sitting room door was open—wide open. Curious, she went inside. When she'd glanced at the room the day she arrived, she hadn't noticed much beyond some under-upholstered chairs and a couple of spindly occasional tables. Now that she was actually standing in the room, she could see that there was a portrait of some kind over the fireplace. After turning on all the lamps, she looked back at the painting. Her breath caught in her throat.

It was *Romantic Poet*. She'd seen prints of it many times, of course, but this was different. The painting looked as if it could come to life at any moment. This couldn't be just a reproduction—it had to be the original. The artist was unknown and the identity of the subject disputed, but it had long been rumored to be a portrait of Artemisia herself. Now that Alex could finally see the real thing, she was sure it was her.

As the first overwhelming rush of shock subsided, she began to focus on details. The sleek, dark hair, gathered in a neat club at the back of the neck. The carefully tied white cravat adorning the throat. The smoothly fitted jacket and trousers molded to a trim figure, one that was subtly—but, to a careful eye, definitely—female. Small, deft hands, one holding a quill and the other a piece of paper inscribed with a few lines of verse.

And those eyes, always those eyes. Dark, deep, intense. Gazing out at her as if the woman were about to speak, but only to her, one soul to another. She was truly, truly beautiful.

And so young—painfully young. What a contrast to the tormented martyr of Smithson's painting. That had been a meditation on sorrow and suffering leavened at the very last by a moment of redemption. This was a paean to the promise and joy of youth with all its glorious, hopeful possibilities. It was heartrending to know what the future held for this radiant young woman.

The portrait must have been made when Artemisia first came to London, barely seventeen, an orphan raised in provincial obscurity by an eccentric uncle, yet already a published poet, trying her wings in the great metropolis. Somehow she had found the courage to live life on her own terms, demanding to be seen and known for who she truly was, refusing to hide or dissemble.

Daring to love and be loved. And what a price she had paid.

No wonder Lady Melissa had fallen for her, fallen so hard that she ignored all the gossip and scandal to spend the rest of her tragically short life with Artemisia by her side.

Alex wondered how anyone could have doubted for a moment that this was Artemisia's likeness. Why, off to one side the artist had even provided some rather obvious hints, the marble bust of a woman in Grecian headdress and drapery displayed on a short pillar and backed by a small tapestry. In prints and even reproductions that part of the painting was usually dark and indistinct, but here it was sharp and clear, the crescent moon and arrow design on the tapestry glinting with strands of silver, and, for those who couldn't work out even so strong a clue, the artist had helpfully labeled the statue *Sappho*, albeit in Greek. How could anyone viewing this painting have possibly misunderstood?

At the doorway, she turned back to the portrait, gazing deep into Artemisia's eyes. She found herself speaking out loud.

"I will find out the truth, I promise you. And I will tell your story."

She hardly expected a reply, but just for a moment everything went perfectly still. It felt like the moment after an indrawn breath, or right before a kiss. It was almost as if the house itself had heard her and, somehow, approved.

Shaking her head at her own imagination, Alex closed the sitting-room door behind her and headed for the kitchen.

CHAPTER FIVE

Alex spent the following morning gleefully exploring the materials in the Dawson House archive room. So absorbed was she that Mrs. Tate actually had to call her for lunch. If Grace hadn't happened to slink into the archive room, plopping herself down in typical feline fashion right on top of what Alex was reading, she might never have come up for air, and Mrs. Tate would have actually had to leave the kitchen a second time instead of merely being on the point of doing so when Alex hurriedly presented herself.

The days began to settle into a pattern. Exploring the archives after breakfast, then a chat with Mrs. Tate at noon. Alex had managed to persuade her to pause then for a cup of tea, which did much to alleviate the master/servant feeling of eating lunch alone while Mrs. Tate worked. Her afternoons were devoted to leisurely walks, either up to the moor or around the village, and the evenings she spent quietly reading at home.

She saw no signs of Cam on any of her excursions—not that she was looking for her, of course. She stopped in at the museum a couple of times to chat with Nicola and locate materials for further study. Rosamund was not in evidence, having been called back to London, no doubt on a matter of importance.

Alex did little else for the best part of a week, barely firing up her laptop except to send an occasional e-mail to her mom. More often than not when she was in the house, she had company in the form of Grace, who always seemed to put in an appearance when Alex was least interested in paying attention to her, a problem that Grace solved by merciless harassment until Alex obliged with petting and praise. Scapegrace indeed.

Alex had no idea how the cat was making its way in and out, since she never seemed to use the doors. But in a house as old as this one, there were bound to be nooks and crannies that a determined searcher could ferret out—or in this case, cat out. And since Alex never saw any sign of mice or any other unpleasant visitors, she assumed Grace must be doing something to earn her keep.

The only difficulty that Alex had was she was still waiting for her boxes to arrive, and she didn't feel like she could get down to any real work until she had all her books around her, safe and sound. Repeated calls to the Leeds office of the shipping company only yielded mysterious mumbles about customs and complications, her interlocutors' accents becoming increasingly broad and decreasingly intelligible in direct proportion to the persistence of her demands for explanations and action.

Even when at long last she got the news that her books had emerged from quarantine, things still weren't right. She was able to arrange for the boxes to be sent through to Dunheath railway station, but that was as much as the company could or would do, regardless of reasoning or pleas. She was on her own to get her things from the station to Dawson House.

Which was annoying, of course, but not a serious problem. Or at least, it shouldn't have been. It should have been a simple matter to get a local firm to fetch them for her. She knew of at least one right there in the village that could almost certainly do it, although now that a little time and distance had given her a chance to reflect on a certain party's officious ways, she was determined to avoid that particular option.

But try as she might, she could discover no alternative. Mrs. Tate, overhearing her on the phone for the third morning in a row trying to locate someone—anyone—to transport her books, barely waited for her to hang up before snapping a business card down on the desk in front of her. The very same business card Alex could have sworn she'd thrown away the day she arrived.

She looked suspiciously at Mrs. Tate, but the woman just stared at her until she began dialing, then walked off shaking her head.

Cam answered on the second ring.

The conversation that followed amply justified Alex's misgivings. The woman just would not be cooperative. Alex wondered if Cam was always like this. If so, it was a wonder she managed to stay in business. Which paradoxically was apparently booming, since that was the reason she gave for not being available to pick up the boxes for at least two more days.

Alex wanted to just hang up on her, but she was desperate. According to the people in Leeds, her boxes should actually be at the station by now. So Alex gritted her teeth and carried on, determined to make the best of what was already a bad job.

"There's naught breakable in the boxes, is there?"

"What?"

"Well, if they're as heavy as you say, I might drop one when I'm shifting it. But books and such can stand up to a bit of rough handling, I should hope."

"Rough handling? Listen, you, you…there is no way I'm letting you throw my precious books around like a, like a—"

"Right you are. No telling what mischief I might get up to on my own. Best if you come along and supervise."

"If I come along? Oh, all right."

"I'll drop round at two on Thursday to fetch you, then. And don't worry about your things in the meanwhile. No one's like to bother them. Stands to reason—what would folk want with a bunch of old books? It's not like they're worth anything."

Cam held the receiver away from her ear just in time to avoid being deafened by Alex's slamming down the phone. She grinned to herself. She really shouldn't tease the woman, but it was so easy to get a rise out of her, it was irresistible. Unfortunately, doing it over the phone meant she missed seeing the way Alex's eyes flashed when she got really worked up.

Lovely eyes she had, a deep blue that seemed to change color depending on the light. Unusual, that, especially with that dark hair. Alex's was such a rich, deep brown. Not like her own mousey brownish blond that was neither fish nor fowl, as her mum used to say, having been cursed with the exact same shade.

And those curls. She wouldn't mind a chance to find out if they were as soft as they looked. Just to run her fingers gently through them for a bit and—No. No, no, no. She would not go down that road. Yes, it had been a good while since she'd been out with anyone. But she had sworn off posh types for the best of reasons, and she hadn't yet broken that rule. No reason to start now.

Especially not with an American who would be on her way and gone in a few months. Not that she had anything against something casual. Which might be just the ticket to getting her mind off Alex. Next chance she got, she'd head into Leeds and go round the pubs. Bound to be someone interesting, and even if not, she'd have a good time catching up with her mates.

Still, no harm in having a bit of fun with Alex in the meantime. *I might drop one.* Ha! That was her best yet. Pity she'd had to miss the look on Alex's face at that moment. Silly thing—as if she'd ever treat a client that way.

Come to think of it, perhaps it wasn't quite so funny that Alex had fallen for the country-bumpkin act so easily. Probably thought she really was that thickheaded. Oh, well, nothing for it now.

Sighing at her own foolishness, Cam hunted up the number for Dunheath Station so she could ring Seth and make sure he had someone get Alex's boxes locked away safely until Thursday.

Whatever else might be true about her, at least Cam was punctual. When Thursday afternoon rolled around, Alex decided to simplify matters by waiting just outside the Dawson House gates, and the bizarre-looking vehicle that apparently comprised the entirety of the Carter's Contracting motor pool made its appearance promptly at 2:00 p.m.

Of course, the woman couldn't just pull over and let her get in. No, Ms. Impress the Ladies had to make a production out of getting out and sauntering over to open the door for her. Alex gave her an overly bright thank-you smile but decided not to go all out and bat her eyelashes—too much risk of Cam missing the sarcasm, she figured. However, when she realized that the passenger seat belt was back where it was supposed to be, untangled and ready for use, she did actually feel a little grateful.

And the interior of the vehicle was so clean it was practically gleaming—not that it had been really dirty before, but still, it looked like Cam had found time in her busy schedule to spruce things up for her—at least, she assumed it was for her. Alex risked a sideways glance as Cam pulled back onto the roadway. Was she really trying to impress her, or did Thursdays just happen to be her spit-and-polish day?

The trip to Dunheath proved to be relatively painless. For some reason, Cam was in what for her was a talkative mood, occasionally pointing out landmarks and natural features as they drove along. When they finally reached the station, she backed the van up to the edge of the sidewalk outside the front entrance.

Alex tried to hop right out, but somehow Cam anticipated her, rushing around before she'd even gotten the seat belt unfastened to open her door with a grand flourish, then slamming it shut behind her before racing ahead with exaggerated eagerness to jerk open the station door.

For a moment Alex just stood there, arms akimbo, glowering. But then Cam gave her an exaggerated bow before straightening up with a grin to wave her inside.

Alex couldn't stop herself from smiling back. Oh, the hell with it. She bobbed a little curtsy and swept into the station, nose in the air. Cam followed, laughing.

The sight of Seth staring down at them from his stool behind the counter sobered them immediately. Alex felt like a naughty schoolgirl, and from the look on her face, Cam was feeling something similar. As Seth disengaged himself from his perch and shuffled toward them, ring of keys in hand, Alex could hear him muttering to himself. She couldn't understand most of it, but she was able to catch "that Cam" and "full of mischief." It made her wonder what else Cam could possibly have been up to.

He unlocked what was apparently a storeroom, and Cam slipped inside. She emerged a few minutes later, box in arms. Despite being the smaller of the two, it really was quite large, Alex realized to her chagrin. Maybe she should have split the books up into three crates after all, but at the time it hadn't seemed worth the extra expense.

Fortunately, Cam didn't appear to be having any trouble with this one regardless of its size and weight, although she was moving rather slowly and carefully. Alex raced to open the door for her, which earned her a terse "Ta," followed by a warning growl when Cam almost tripped over Alex's foot. Alex scrambled out of the way as Cam regained her balance and clomped across the sidewalk to drop the box into the back of the van.

It landed with a crash that made Alex wince before rushing over to inspect for damage. None was apparent from the obstructed view she had around Cam's shoulder. As she watched her maneuver the box—none too gently—farther back into the vehicle, Alex realized the woman wasn't even breathing hard. Damn. With a mental shake, she refocused on more pressing matters.

"You know, the other box really is a lot heavier. Don't you think you should get some kind of cart?"

"No."

Cam made as if to head back inside but Alex remained firmly planted between her and the door, crossing her arms and giving her what she hoped was an intimidating stare.

"And why not, pray tell?"

"Don't need one."

"Seriously? Could you maybe just drop the macho routine for five minutes?"

Now it was Cam's turn to stand with arms crossed, glaring.

"Look, I know exactly how heavy it is—I packed the damn thing myself. It took both Mom and me plus my next door neighbor to get it into the car, and two guys at the shipping office to get it out of the car. And they used a cart."

Still no response, other than a raised eyebrow.

"Why don't you at least let me help you with it? Listen, if anyone finds out and tries to revoke your butch card, I'll swear you only did it under extreme duress." Was that a hint of a twinkle in her eye? "I'll say I used the ultimate weapon." She sniffled and wiped away an imaginary tear.

Cam's mouth was definitely twitching. She glanced over Alex's shoulder, no doubt wondering what Seth was making of all this.

Alex said, "Don't worry—I'll take care of him." In her best fake pirate voice, she added, "*Arrr*. Dead men tell no tales, me hearty."

Cam gave an exaggerated sigh of surrender. "Can't let you do that. Without Seth, I think the station would just fall to bits."

"I suppose you're right. I'd hate to be responsible, so I guess we'll just have to hope for the best."

Cam laughed. "Right, then. Let's get that box sorted."

Even with their combined efforts, it wasn't easy hauling the other box up off the floor, but eventually they managed it. Without any prompting, Cam took the more difficult position, walking backward, which Alex was grateful for, except that it meant she was responsible for navigating. Progress was slow.

As they worked their way carefully out of the storeroom, Cam said, "Bloody hell, lass, what have you got in here—paving stones? Anvils?"

Alex waited until she was through the doorway before replying. "No, just a bunch of dead people's heads." Cam stopped abruptly, her eyes flashing a moment of panic. "Gotcha. But I'm not really kidding. It's my research materials—history, philosophy, literature, women's studies. Historical documents, sources of inspiration."

Cam started moving again, a little faster this time. "Surely you might have been a bit more sparing. We do have the odd library, even this far north."

"It's not the same—for the most important stuff, I want my own books. They're like old friends. Besides, I need to be able to write in them."

"What? In books?"

"You know, making notes, underlining someth—hey, watch out for the door. A little to the left. No, not your left, my—"

Too late. Somewhere between Alex's mixed-up directions and the distraction of their conversation, Cam caught a foot wrong and tripped, falling backward against the station door and pushing it open in the process. Her momentum and the weight of the box carried her out through the doorway. She missed her footing again on the sidewalk and fell down smack on her butt. Fortunately, mostly thanks to Alex's attempt to tilt the box away from Cam even as it slipped from her grip, the thing landed not on top of her but right next to her, splitting open with a resounding crash and scattering books in all directions.

"Oh my God! Are you okay? Did you hurt anything?"

"Naught but my pride, and that should heal right enough." One of the books had ended up in her lap and she picked it up, a strange expression on her face as she looked at the cover. "Inspiration for your research, you said? Maybe it's a pity I didn't stick with school longer than I did. Seems I might have missed a fair bit." She handed the book to Alex, who had a pretty good idea of what to expect even before she looked at it.

And so it proved. Naturally, it couldn't have been a feminist treatise, or a lesbian romance novel, or even some halfway-respectable erotica. No, of course it was one of her collection of classic pulps— and not even something reasonable, by, say, Ann Bannon. Nope, it was *Satan Was a Lesbian* in all its gaudy scarlet glory, featuring a leather-clad, whip-cracking brunette menacing a not-at-all-unhappy looking blonde in black underwear while Satan himself looked down approvingly. She felt her face turning as red as the cover.

"Thank you," she said dryly before helping Cam to her feet, which surprisingly she tolerated without comment. Maybe she was more shaken up than she let on.

Clean up took a while, but that didn't really bother Alex at first. The box was pretty much a total loss, so they ended up stacking all the books in the back of the van, a few at a time. However, the sky, which had merely been cloudy when they set out from Bramfell, was looking more and more menacing every moment, and Alex found herself growing anxious as the rising wind made it obvious a storm was on its way. She started racing around and just dumping books into the back of the van any old way.

Finally Cam laid a hand on her arm. She tried to pull away but Cam's grasp, though gentle, wouldn't budge. Cam drew her closer.

"More haste, less speed, lass. Just breathe."

Which Alex suddenly found herself completely unable to do. Wind, books, anxiety all vanished as she gazed deep into the golden brown eyes that were mere inches away. The moment seemed to stretch on forever.

Cam abruptly released her and took a quick step back. Alex found herself looking around, suddenly very interested in anything but Cam. Somehow, they managed to finish the rest of the job without ever actually coming near each other again.

When they were finally done, the entire back was piled with books. It wasn't going to be much fun unloading, but at least they had beaten the rain.

CHAPTER SIX

A s Cam drove away from the station, the first drops of rain hit the windscreen. She started thinking ahead to the unloading, thankful for the porte cochere at Dawson House. Anything to get her mind off the woman sitting beside her and what had almost happened in the station car park. She'd almost kissed Alex—right in front of Seth, for God's sake! Poor old gaffer would have had heart failure, and then she'd have had to tell his great-granddaughter how he ended up in hospital because Cam couldn't be trusted within arm's reach of a pretty girl. Of course, Seth's great-grand wasn't bad looking herself, so—

Bloody hell, she was babbling. She never babbled, ever. What was wrong with her?

The question naturally made her glance sideways at the answer. The sound of a horn tore her attention back to where it should have been all along, and she swerved just a bit to get back to her side of the road. She heard Alex swear under her breath and didn't blame her in the least.

Bloody flaming hell. She hadn't been this distractible in a long, long while. Not since—automatically her mind shied away from that very sore spot. Maybe she should take her own advice and breathe.

A few minutes into the drive, visibility had dropped so far it was all she could do to concentrate on the road just ahead of her. Thankfully she had taken this route so often she could just about drive it blindfold, because matters were rapidly reaching that very point. God only knew what somebody would do who wasn't as familiar with—

The answer came tearing at her around a blind curve. *Bleeding bloody tosser.* She didn't waste time or effort on her horn, just changed gear and whipped out of the way onto the shoulder, leaving the fool in possession of the roadway and his worthless life. Ignoring Alex's cry of distress, she focused on maintaining—regaining—control of the van as they flew around the corner. Now she just had to slow down a bit more, try a touch of brake so she could steer back—

Thump. Thump, thump, thump. Damn. Damn, damn, damn. Those sounds and the feel of the wheels bumping along that way could mean only one thing. She slowed to a complete stop and put on the hand brake for good measure. The pounding rain sounded even louder now that the engine was off. Or maybe it was just coming down harder. This was going to be loads of fun.

Alex, of course, was already talking. Probably going to tear a strip right off her. But then she realized Alex didn't sound angry at all.

"…amazing. I mean, you were so calm—I would have been a wreck. And then we'd probably have ended up in one—a wreck that is. Goddamn fool—too bad it happened so fast I didn't get his license plate. I'd be on the phone to the police right now. If I had a phone. Bastard."

Cam smiled at her fierce tone. "You mean to say you really don't have a mobile? I thought you were just trying to warn me off asking for your number."

"I really don't have a mobile. As for the rest of it, though, I'll have to take the Fifth."

"Sorry?"

"I'm refusing to answer on the grounds that it might incriminate me." Alex really had an adorable smile.

"Oh, right—like on *CSI.*"

She suddenly looked rueful. "I screamed like a girl, didn't I?"

"I'll, uh, take the Fifth." Cam felt herself grinning like a fool. "Unfortunately, we've got a puncture."

"A flat tire? Seriously?"

"I'll just nip out and deal with it…" Cam looked over her shoulder at the big box wedged just behind the seats, and all of the loose books beyond it, no longer stacked in neat piles but flung about every which way.

Alex must have been looking at the very same thing, because she said, "Please tell me that the jack and spare tire aren't where I think they are."

"Fifth." It didn't feel so funny now. "Right, I guess I'll have to start by shifting some of the books—"

Never in her life had she seen anyone race out of a vehicle so fast. Lord knows the woman was usually in such a hurry, but this was just ridiculous. Bracing herself, she opened the door and jumped out. She was instantly soaked, and the ground was already a mire. She felt her boots sink in and dampness seeping into the top of her socks. No help for it. She trudged through the muck to the back of the van.

There stood Alex, her hair plastered to her head and her T-shirt plastered to her body. Cam didn't mind taking a moment to admire the view, but she needed to sort out whatever was going on with Alex so she could get on with repairing the puncture. The sooner she could do that, the sooner they could both get out of the bloody weather and be on their way.

Cam moved closer, and Alex threw herself back against the van, her arms flung out to block the doors. The look on her face was so ferocious Cam took a step back before she even realized she was frightened. Startled. Just a bit surprised, is all.

When Alex spoke, her voice was low and menacing. "You are not going to open these doors."

"I'm just going to repair the puncture. I'm not going to hurt anything."

"You are not going to open these doors." This time it was little more than a growl.

"Now then, Alex"—Cam focused on keeping her voice calm and slow—"I've got to repair the tire. I need the things from the van so I can—"

"I said, you are not going to open these doors. Period."

"Be reasonable."

Big mistake. Alex flew forward, and Cam took another step back, but not fast enough. Alex was right up in her face, yelling and waving her arms about.

"Reasonable? Reasonable! If you open those doors, do you know what's going to happen? Well, I'll tell you—every single one of those books is going to come falling out into the rain and the mud. Didn't you see how they were all piled up in the back, right against the doors? And then they will be absolutely, one hundred percent ruined. And that is not going to happen."

"But, Alex—"

"I am paying you, goddamn it. I hired you to transport my books safely to Dawson House, and that is what you are going to do. Is that clear?"

Cam blew out a soundless whistle. "Yes, miss. Perfectly clear." She stepped to one side, putting some distance between them. Alex moved to stay between her and the van, clearly still prepared for battle. Which should have been funny, since the idea that Alex could do anything to stop her physically was ridiculous. But that possibility should never even have arisen. Alex was absolutely right. She was a client.

Cam began a careful study of the toes of her boots and the surrounding mud. She never behaved like this with a client, even the thickheaded, unreasonable, insulting ones. So. No puncture repair. But in that case, what the bloody blazes was she going to do?

"Cam, I'm sorry."

Cam looked up, surprised at Alex's change in tone. Alex reached out a hand as if to touch her arm, then dropped it. She really did look apologetic.

"I didn't mean to imply that you, that I—oh, the hell with it. What are we going to do?"

"Well, I'd say we've two choices. We can stand about in the rain and hope for rescue. Although they do say this stretch of road gets its share of elves and whatnot roaming about, on the lookout for unwary folk."

"That doesn't sound encouraging."

"Not to worry. Apparently they're mostly after naughty children. At least that's what Mum always used to say."

"So what's our alternative?"

"Ring for AA."

"A what? Oh, I bet that's a tow truck. That's my choice."

"I agree. Let's get back inside and I'll ring a garage." Sitting in the van, wet through, was almost worse than being out in the rain. Cam took out her mobile.

"Any luck?" said Alex.

"No joy, I'm afraid. No signal."

"Of course not. That would mean an end to our perfect run of luck. Bad luck." She smiled, and Cam smiled back. "What now? Wait for the elves?"

"I don't fancy sitting here doing nothing, elves or no elves. There's a pub down one of the side roads a mile or so that way." She gestured with her thumb. "I can ring from there." Alex was frowning. "I'll be back before you know I'm gone. Stay in the van—I'll make sure the doors are locked."

"Oh no, you don't. I've read that story. I'm not staying here waiting for the Elf Queen to spirit me off and have her wicked way with me."

"Not to worry—I hear she only fancies boys. Besides, you don't want to be trudging miles through the wet."

"I'm not made of sugar—I won't melt. And I'll probably be warmer walking in the rain than just sitting here shivering."

Trust Alex to carry on being stubborn. Shaking her head, Cam climbed out of the van. Once Alex had stepped out as well, she locked up and they started down the road.

❖

By the time they finally reached the pub, Alex was thoroughly over whatever silly scruples had led her to insist on accompanying Cam, even though the rain had tapered off and finally stopped, considerably reducing the misery factor. Cam seemed unfazed by any of it, striding along, never flagging, but even with all the walking Alex had been doing on the moors and around the village, she had trouble keeping up. Still, she refused to say anything and stringently stifled any sounds that might have come across as unspoken complaining. After all, she was responsible for the situation—well, not as responsible as that idiot who ran them off the road, but still.

Alex was so engrossed in putting one foot in front of the other that she barreled right into Cam, having completely missed it when she came to a stop. After a bit of confusion, Alex somehow found herself with both of Cam's arms wrapped around her waist. Cam was holding her so close their faces were practically touching. Alex had just enough time to register a mixture of embarrassment and excitement before light flooded them from a suddenly opened doorway and they sprang apart. Clearly they had arrived at their destination.

In a short while they were inside and seated at a table near the fire—blessings on whoever had decided to light it despite the date on the calendar—and they had ordered, at Cam's insistence, food as well as hot drinks. While Cam went in search of a phone, Alex looked around the room.

The pub exhibited a certain rustic charm, heavy on the rustic. Dark wood, low ceilings, a few scattered customers who would have been right at home in a Hammer Studios vampire movie. By the looks of it, this could well have been the spot where Branwell Brontë came to drink away his broken heart.

Cam was back not long after their meal was served, reporting that rescue was on the way but unlikely to arrive for a while yet. At first they ate in silence. Cam had been absolutely right about the food, and Alex told her so. Her shepherd's pie was savory and delicious and would probably have tasted just as good even if she hadn't been trekking through the rain.

"The place isn't much to look at, but they lay on fine grub. Don't overwater the drink, either."

"What is this again? It's really good—although I think I'd better ease up on it. I'm not much of a drinker."

"Hot gin punch. Not sure what all they put in it, but theirs is better than any I've had elsewhere, even in London."

"Oh, do you go down to London a lot?"

"Up to London. At least, that's what London folk'll tell you."

"They do think a lot of themselves, don't they? One of my friends lives in London, but he was raised here in the North. It's not exactly the same."

"Too right, it isn't."

"I spent a year in London while I was at university. I enjoyed it at the time, but I don't think I'd want to live there again."

"Why not?"

"I just don't like the way it feels—too much hurry, too big, too anonymous. A short visit is about as much as I can stand. How about you?"

"I don't go there at all, not anymore. But I did live there for a while."

"Really?" Somehow, she couldn't picture Cam among all the chrome and glass and bustle. Or the filth and decay and despair. "When was that?"

"It's been a good few years."

"How did you end up there?"

"I wanted a go at the bright and shiny, a chance to meet folk that hadn't known me since I was in nappies. Old story, isn't it? Leeds was too close, and Manchester was, well, Manchester. Never did fancy it. So London." She smiled, but it didn't touch her eyes.

"But then you came back here." Something wasn't right, but Alex didn't want to push too hard.

"Aye. Mum wasn't well, and so I came home. After she died, I saw no reason to go back."

"I'm so sorry. How old were you?"

Cam looked off to one side, thinking. "It's been, what, four years? No, five. So twenty-nine." She looked back at Alex. "I can't say I think much about the time going by. She was here, and now she isn't. That's what matters."

After a small silence, Alex said, "So you were exactly the age I am now when she died." She shook her head sympathetically. "It must have been awful. I can't even imagine what I'd do if I lost my mother. It's been just the two of us for so long."

"Is your father dead, then?"

"I'd like to think so."

"What?"

"Well, maybe not exactly dead. But I hope he's at least got some kind of painful, disfiguring disease. The rat bastard finally left for good when I was eleven, but not until he'd put Mom through all kinds of crap. He used to try to get me to cover for him. You know, the last woman he was cheating on her with was pretty nice. I hope she wised up quickly and left him. How's your dad?"

"Car crash. I was sixteen."

"Oh."

"Just as well I was done with school by then—or school was done with me. Went to work for my uncle and never looked back."

"Sorry. That wasn't very sensitive of me."

Cam laughed, a little bitterly. "No need to be sensitive. No great loss, as far as I was concerned."

"Then I really am sorry."

"It was a lot harder on Mum. He and I used to have epic rows, and she loved both of us."

Alex felt her stomach twist. "Did he hit you?"

"He came close once or twice. I think I could have stood it better than some of the things he said. Seems I wasn't enough of a son or a daughter to suit him."

"Ouch. So he couldn't handle you being a lesbian?"

Cam's expression went completely blank. She looked at Alex in utter shock. "A lesbian? What on earth are you talking about?"

Alex felt her jaw actually drop as her mind furiously replayed various scenes—Cam asking for her number, giving her those flirty looks, almost kissing her...

Cam guffawed. "Oh, you should see your face. I should snap a picture."

Alex tried to speak but could produce nothing but incoherent spluttering.

Cam continued to laugh. "I swear I've never met anyone so apt to swallow whatever nonsense is on offer. Perhaps next time I'll take you to see the fairies at the bottom of the garden."

Alex finally found her voice. "Oh, very funny. Just too goddamn hilarious. Cameron Carter, you are just—"

"Not Cameron." Cam's eyes flashed a moment of dismay—clearly she'd spoken without thinking.

Alex scented revenge, if only she could run her prey to earth. "What is it, then?"

"Couldn't say."

"What, is it one of those tell-you-but-I'd-have-to-kill-you things? For a spy, you give away your secrets way too easily."

Cam remained silent. She did not look at all happy.

"Hmm. Cam, but not Cameron. Campbell?" No response. "Camilla?" A nervous twitch. Getting warmer. "Camille?" The expression of horror on Cam's face signaled bull's-eye. "Camille? Seriously? Oh my God—Camille!"

Cam leaned in and hissed, "Keep your voice down." She glanced around furiously as if to see if anyone was listening. "Bloody hell, I've been trying to get folk to forget that blasted name these thirty years."

"I can see why. Nothing wrong with the name, but you, my friend, are most definitely not a Camille."

"Tell me something I don't know."

"How on earth did you ever get stuck with it?"

"Mum just loved going to the cinema. Every Friday, there she was, rain or shine. She was especially fond of old American films— *Casablanca* and so on. She named me in honor of her favorite film star."

"Camille? Oh, you must mean Greta Garbo."

"No, Bette Davis."

"Camille? Bette Davis? Oh, right. *Now, Voyager*. It's been a while since the last time I watched that one. Ever seen it?"

"No, I've refused on principle. Blasted film almost ruined my life."

Alex thought for a moment and started to giggle. "You're luckier than you know. Your name could have been a lot worse."

"Worse than Camille? The mind boggles."

"She could have named you—wait for it—Fifi."

"What, like a bloody poodle? Pull the other one, it's got bells on."

"No, I'm serious. It's the part of the movie where Bette Davis is on a cruise to South America to finish recovering from a nervous breakdown—"

"And what, she falls overboard and gets rescued by a poodle?"

"No, silly, Charles Boyer. Or maybe it was Paul Henreid. Anyway, some Continental guy, super suave. And she doesn't fall overboard. They run into some people she wants to conceal her identity from— don't ask me why."

"No fear on that score."

"Anyway, her real name is Charlotte but he introduces her to them as Camille. Afterward she asks him why Camille, and I think he points to a camellia plant nearby or something. I'm not really clear about that part, but for sure then he tells her it had to be Camille because the only other French name he could think of was Fifi." Alex smiled, savoring the moment. "Fifi Carter. I like the way that sounds. Maybe I should start calling you that."

"Try it on even once and I swear they'll never find the body."

A shadow fell across the table. "Temper, temper." The voice was young, obnoxious, and male. To Alex, he said, "Evening, love. Don't waste your time on her. Whatever you need, I've got it and to spare." Just the slightest movement of his crotch, which was at eye level.

Alex smiled sweetly. "Going spare, is it?" She was careful to keep her tone bland. "How tiresome for you. But don't fret, I'm sure you'll get someone to take it off your hands eventually." Just the slightest emphasis on *hands*. His face darkened as her implication registered.

Cam snickered. "She's got you there, mate." She stood, and Alex followed suit. "Right, you lot, fun's over. Let's get on with it."

CHAPTER SEVEN

Much, much later, after they had mended the tire, returned to Dawson House, and unloaded all the books, Cam accepted Alex's invitation to step into the kitchen for a cup of tea. The cat was very much in evidence and, to judge by her complaints, clearly on the verge of starvation.

Spotting a plate of biscuits on the table, Cam sat down and helped herself to one, breaking off a corner and reaching down to offer it to the cat.

She was on it like a shot, but instead of tucking in right away, she looked back at Alex, for all the world as if she were checking to make sure she wasn't being watched. Then she looked Cam dead in the eye.

"Not to worry," Cam murmured. "I won't tell." Something must have communicated—probably the tone—because Milady was now willing to accept the tidbit, which disappeared in short order. Keeping a wary eye on Alex, Cam offered two more morsels, which likewise vanished. The cat scarpered just as Alex turned to bring the cozy-covered teapot to the table.

Alex looked after the disappearing streak of orange fur, shaking her head. Then she sat down, smiling at Cam as she did so. "Mrs. Tate's gingersnaps are wonderful, aren't they?" She took one and set it on her saucer. "I can't decide which I like better, these or her shortbread."

Cam concentrated on maintaining an innocent expression as she ate what was left of her biscuit.

Alex took the cozy off the teapot. "I don't know about you, but I'm absolutely exhausted. I hope you don't have anything too taxing planned for tomorrow."

Cam smiled. She was tired, but it was a pleasant sort of tired. "Just a bit of electrical work out Haworth way. A good night's sleep and I'll be right as rain."

Alex paused before pouring Cam's tea. "Milk in first or after?"

"After, please." Not bad for a Yank. "How about you?"

Alex handed over Cam's cup and poured her own. "Well, you've seen what my tomorrow's going to be—book organizing galore. I just hope I finish in time to get some actual work done."

"Just what are you working on?"

"I'm not really sure yet. I've got a general approach in mind, but a lot depends on what information I can find in the files here in the house and in the museum archives. I'm hoping to discover something new—something about Artemisia no one else has spotted yet."

"That's important, then, that it be brand new."

"Oh, yes. The terms of the Brockenbridge award are very clear. They want something original, which of course is tough to do after a hundred and fifty years of Artemisia scholarship. But what I really want is to find a way to prove that Artemisia and Lady Melissa were more than just soul mates or devoted friends or some other platonic euphemism."

"Fancy your chances for the Prandall Prize, do you?"

"Hardly. I just think it's time the truth was told."

"And you're sure of the truth."

"Oh, please. It's so obvious they were lovers. Can you imagine anyone writing those poems for someone they weren't sleeping with?"

"Well, now…"

"Oh—I'm sorry. Here I am assuming you're interested in Artemisia and her work. Occupational hazard, I'm afraid—imagining that the whole world shares my obsession." She smiled ruefully. "I do realize that just because you live here, it doesn't mean you have her every syllable memorized."

Cam grinned. This should be fun. Taking a deep breath, she began to recite. "*Dare I with impious hand profane thy golden tresses pure? Might I those sacred precincts rove…*"

Alex's eyes got bigger and bigger as she carried on, line after line, word perfect to the very end. "*Grant mercy to thine acolyte.*"

"How on earth did you do that?"

"Not such a numpty as you thought, am I?"

"I never thought you were a—what the hell is a numpty?"

"Clot, pillock, charlie, nit. My granny always used to say it."

"Oh—doofus, ding-dong, schlub, chowderhead."

"Wazzock, prat, gooseberry gatherer."

"You made that last one up, I know you did."

"Damn. What gave it away?"

"The look on your face. Never play poker, you'll lose your shirt."

"You as well. Although that might not be such a bad thing from where I'm sitting." Had she actually said that out loud? Alex was blushing. Best to change topic. "When I was about fourteen, the teacher made us learn a whole raft of poems off by heart, and I was class champion. Mum always said my memory was my best feature."

"I'll take the Fifth."

"Ha-ha. 'Dare I' was my favorite because it was so over the top. I remember asking why this Artemisia person was rabbiting on about touching some other woman's hair. She just about turned purple. I thought I'd embarrassed her, but looking back, I can see she was trying hard not to laugh. She said I'd probably figure it out when I got older."

"Which I assume you did."

"The very next month, as it happens. I got quite a nice Christmas kiss from a sophisticated older woman."

"Oh?"

"She was eighteen. Pretty little blonde. She was older, but I was taller. That made it seem more equal, somehow."

"Your first kiss?"

"Aye. You could say I was a bit of a late bloomer."

"If you were a late bloomer, then what does that make me? I didn't get my first kiss until two years ago."

"Two years ago? Have all the women in America gone mental? A looker like you ought to have them queued up out the door and round the corner."

Alex was blushing again. "Thank you for saying so, but it's my own fault, really. I'm hopeless at chatting people up. I'm shy."

Cam couldn't stop the laugh that burst out, mentally kicking herself at the change that came over Alex's face in response. "I'm sorry, but you're about the least shy person I've ever met."

"Oh, but you haven't seen me around an attractive woman."

"Now that's let the wind out of my sails."

"Oh, my God! I'm sorry—I didn't mean that you aren't attractive, of course you are—really attractive. That is, I'm not saying that I'm attracted to you myself, even though you're very good looking, although I'm sure I would be, in the right circumstances. What I'm trying to say is that you're just not the kind of woman I usually... Okay, I'm going to go into that corner right over there and curl up and die." She buried her face in her hands.

Cam was really laughing now—a big, hearty belly laugh that shook her all the way down to her toes. It took a solid minute to finally die down. "Oh, that was champion. Thank you, Alex."

Alex peeked out between her fingers.

"Really." She reached out and gently drew Alex's hands away from her face. "I haven't had a laugh that good since, since...I don't know when. Since before Mum died, I think." She looked down at their clasped hands and gave Alex's a slight squeeze before letting go. "Perhaps I'd better go now."

"Please do, before I say something even worse."

"I'm almost tempted to stay, just to see what you could come up with."

Alex walked with her as far as the front door. About halfway to the van, Cam looked back. Alex was leaning in the doorway, arms crossed, her head resting against the frame. The porch light played over her face. She was smiling gently at Cam.

Without letting herself think about what she was doing, Cam went back and kissed Alex on the cheek—her lips barely brushing the skin. Then she walked to the van and got in. As she started the engine, she looked over and saw that Alex had a hand pressed against that cheek, as if she could still feel the kiss.

Or at least, that's what she assumed it was, because that's the way her own lips felt.

CHAPTER EIGHT

Alex didn't see much of Cam for well over a week. She didn't think they were actively avoiding each other—at least, she wasn't trying to avoid Cam—but they never seemed to be in the same place at the same time. One afternoon when she was out for a walk around the village, she caught a glimpse of Cam's van—no mistaking that thing for any other vehicle—as it pulled around a corner. Twice she dropped into the café with Nicola, only to be told by the barista that they had just missed Cam, who had apparently been looking for Nicola.

Not that there was anything surprising about that, really, since it was obvious the two were old friends. Assuming that was all it was. Alex finally asked Nicola about it one day over coffee. She gave Alex the most peculiar, penetrating look.

"Me? And Cam? Lord, no—whatever made you ask that? It would be like kissing my sister. If I had a sister. Regardless, too much chance of hurt feelings all round. It was bad enough that time I let her set me up with one of her friends and it didn't work out."

"What happened?"

"She was nice enough, but she just about drove me daft. Sport mad—worse than my brothers. And not even football like a normal person—all the woman wanted to talk about was cricket. I mean, I ask you."

"That's too bad. But what happened with Cam?"

"Oh, she didn't say much—she wouldn't, would she? But just for a moment, I caught this look on her face. She was so disappointed.

I felt worse about letting her down than I did about the date going wrong."

"It meant that much to her?"

"I know she doesn't seem like it, but Cam really takes things to heart. Plus she's dead romantic."

Alex smiled to herself, thinking about the way Cam had kissed her. Just the slightest contact of Cam's lips against her skin, but the very softness of it had utterly charmed her. It had been completely unexpected, but somehow just exactly right.

Nicola sighed. "She wants everyone else to be happy, even if she can't be." She looked very uncomfortable all of a sudden.

Alex was dying to ask what that meant, but she realized Nicola had probably been entrusted with a confidence she didn't want to share. Wishing she had less integrity, or enough deviousness to dig for dirt without being obvious, Alex switched gears.

"So, how long have you two been friends?"

"Oh, yonks. She was at school with my oldest brother, plus she's some sort of a cousin, so she was always around when I was growing up. Of course, she's a fair bit older, so we weren't all that close at first."

"What changed?"

"What do you think? I developed a huge crush on her when I was thirteen or so. She was really sweet about it, you know. When I finally got up the courage to tell her how I felt, she said she was flattered. And what's more, she didn't make a big speech about how I was too young to know what I was feeling or she couldn't take advantage of me or some such rubbish."

Alex winced, but Nicola didn't seem to notice. "Then she managed to work the conversation round to whether there were any girls at school that I might want to ask to the cinema that weekend. That's how I ended up with my first girlfriend."

"That was kind. At least she didn't kiss the hell out of you and then dump you like a used tissue right afterward. Sanctimonious speech included, no extra charge."

"Oh no. What was her name?"

"Barbara. My dissertation director."

"Oh, Lord. That can't be good."

"You said a mouthful, honey." Alex shook her head at her own foolishness. "It's really my own fault. I wasn't as sensible as you were. For starters, it took me forever to come out, even to myself."

"That's hardly your fault."

"Right. It's not like I had any clues to help me figure things out. Just because I wasn't interested in boys at all, ever. And kept getting crushes on the girls in my classes all through middle and high school."

"I think you're being rather hard on yourself."

"Maybe. But I did finally figure out what was what, at university. Unfortunately, I spent a long time crushed out on Barbara. We're talking at least a couple of years. It's kind of tricky trying to connect romantically with people when your emotions are already focused on someone."

"Don't I know it."

"Rosamund, right?"

"That obvious, is it? The sad thing is, I don't even like the woman all that much. But that doesn't stop my heart pounding and my face flaming whenever I'm near her. It's like being thirteen all over again."

"Well, she is gorgeous."

"That she is." Nicola waved a hand as if banishing the apparition of the lovely Ms. Camberwell and her manifold charms. "But let's get back to your romantic escapades. Apart from this Barbara person, what have you been up to?"

"Not much. The only kind of luck I ever have is bad."

"Oh, surely not."

"Seriously. I always seem to go for the wrong women—either they're not interested, or already in a relationship, or some damn thing. It never fails."

"Never? Wait just a minute. Do you really mean to say that you've never—"

"Not so loud. My lousy track record isn't exactly something I want to advertise."

"Well, color me gobsmacked. Try to look on the bright side—at least you can still lure unicorns."

"Thanks, but I'm not quite as pathetic as that. No unicorns for me—I did manage to get my virtue duly sullied." Alex mimed checking off an item on a list.

"What, just the one time?" It came out much too loudly and Alex shushed her. Nicola leaned closer, speaking more softly. "Sorry, it's just that you seem so…"

"So…what? Well, whatever it is, it's just a facade, believe me. Anyway, after the big fiasco with Barbara, I got really mad. At myself, that is. Once the worst of the humiliation wore off, I decided I was through wasting time and waiting for The One, assuming she even existed. So I went to a bar and picked someone up. Well, let her pick me up."

"And?"

"And what? We had sex."

"And?"

"And it was fine."

"Fine? That's it? Just fine?"

"If you must know, it was mostly kind of awkward. Not the sort of thing you want to rush right out and do again."

"That's awful."

"Oh, it wasn't that bad. I certainly don't regret doing it. At least I won't have to die wondering."

"I feel dreadful hearing you talk that way. Alex, with the right person it can be amazing. It can be…everything."

"So they tell me. Starlight, moonbeams, blah-blah-blah. And with the wrong person, it can be hell. Just ask my mom. Actually, you won't need to ask. She'll be happy to fill you in without any prompting."

"Oh, dear."

"Yeah. It's not like I've completely given up hope or anything, but it's not something I spend a lot of time worrying about. I'd rather just get on with my life. I'm happy enough."

"If you say so."

"Tell you what—I'll make you a deal. You stop beating yourself up over Rosamund, and I'll try to do something about my romantic ineptitude."

There was a brief lull in the conversation, and Alex's mind wandered, recalling a few of her more disastrous dates. For some reason that made her think of Cam.

"You know, you never did finish telling me how you and Cam got to be friends."

"Not much more to tell, really. I got over my crush, she went off to London, and I went to university. Then when I got the job with the Foundation and came back to Bramfell, here she was. She had moved back to the village to take care of her mother, and after her mum died, Cam stayed on."

"Yes, she told me about that."

"Did she? That's odd. Usually she won't talk about it at all. At any rate, I'd see her round the village, and we'd have chats over coffee and so forth. Mum's always having her over for dinner, as well. I think she's secretly hoping the two of us will make a go of it."

"Your mother is trying to set the two of you up? That must be kind of weird."

"It is, a bit. But that's just Mum. She wants me to settle down with someone. She's been keen on that for all of us since Richard— that's my oldest brother—got married. Keeps telling me I should find a nice girl so I can start giving her grandchildren instead of wasting my best years behind a desk."

"Fortunately, I don't get that routine from my mother. Maybe it's because she's a professor herself, so she understands what it's like. It's not that I like doing research, or want to do it—I have to do it. I have to find out things and answer all those questions that keep coming up. It's like they're haunting me—worse than Grace when she wants some love."

"What does your mother teach?"

"History. So like I said, she really gets it about my work. But mostly she's in no hurry to see me pair up because my dad was such as asshole. She keeps telling me not to make the same mistakes she did. As if I need to be reminded, after seeing what she went through." She looked at her watch. "I think it's time I headed home."

"Me as well. Thanks for the coffee. My shout next time. Tuesday?"

"Works for me. I'll meet you here."

All the way home, Alex replayed the conversation in her mind. Given Cam's apparent lack of interest in pursuing her, not to mention whatever lay behind Nicola's cryptic comment about Cam's inability to find happiness for herself, it didn't look much like her streak of romantic bad luck was in any danger of ending. So much the better. She'd have nothing to distract her from her work. Which was, of course, a good thing.

CHAPTER NINE

One morning Alex came downstairs to find Mrs. Tate in the midst of baking bread. That was definitely unusual, since bread was one of the very few foods she *didn't* insist on making herself. It was clear that Mrs. Tate must have started her work at an absolutely ungodly hour, because she was now in the midst of cutting, rolling, and shaping the dough into loaves of various designs, getting ready for the final rising before they went into the oven.

Alex was so surprised that she asked Mrs. Tate if she wanted some help without pausing first to consider whether the offer might be viewed as disrespectful. Fortunately Mrs. Tate took in it in the spirit in which it was intended.

"Thank you, Alexandra. Before you wash your hands, could you please check the back door? I could have sworn I shut it properly but I can feel a draft. The last thing I want is to have that animal underfoot or worse."

"Worse?"

"Waving her tail in my face, leaving paw prints in my dough."

"You're right, it was ajar. Well, it's closed tight now. Does she really do that?"

"She would if ever I gave her half a chance. Always up to mischief, is our Miss Grace."

"Would you like me to do the dishes, Mrs. Tate?"

"I should say not. What I'd like you to do is come help me with this loaf. It's a four-strand braid and it really needs an extra set of hands to do it properly."

Alex spent a delightful half an hour or so assisting Mrs. Tate. By the time they were down to the last of the dough, the number and variety of loaves was a little overwhelming.

Mrs. Tate gestured toward the remaining bits and scraps. "The last one is for you, Alexandra."

"For me?"

"You must gather and shape it by yourself. It's the Maid's Loaf."

"Maid as in housemaid?"

"And why would I be having *you* do it if that were so? You don't celebrate Lammas in the States, do you?"

"That's a harvest festival, right?"

Mrs. Tate nodded, seeming pleased to find that she was possessed of at least that much information.

"No, we don't. I guess Thanksgiving would be the closest, although when you think about it as a harvest festival, it seems silly to have it in November when the crops have already been in for months. I do remember my grandparents talking about Ferragosto and the fireworks they used to have when they were kids back in Italy. That's a harvest festival, too."

She looked around at all the loaves, covered in tea towels and waiting to be baked. "Oh! That's why you're making all the bread. Now I remember—my friend Fiona told me once about Lunastal in Scotland—I suppose it's the same holiday—and how you take bread to church to be blessed. Are you going to take all this to church on Sunday?"

"And why would I be baking on a Friday for that? All this will be fit to pound nails with by Sunday."

Alex doubted the strict truth of that statement, but Mrs. Tate did have a point.

"Besides, we don't take Lammas loaf to church in Bramfell. Had a vicar once with odd notions—new to the village, of course. Family had only been here, what, fifty years? Proud of his book learning, that one, but not so much good sense that he could afford to spare any."

Ouch. That one hit a little too close to home, although she doubted Mrs. Tate meant for her to take it personally.

"So what does he do but decide that Lammas loaf is too pagan for Sunday worship and not to be brought into church for blessing anymore, the way it had been since time out of mind. Pagan!"

"What happened?"

"Oh, folk just moved the blessing to the party instead, as you'll see tonight. I'm not sure what else went on—I was only a bit of a thing at the time—but I do know that by May Day, we had a new vicar, and he led the maypole dancing himself. Somehow, though, we never changed the loaf blessing back."

One word registered. "Party?" Oh, dear.

"Dancing at the village hall starts at sunset, right after the blessing." Her tone made it sound more like an assignment than an invitation.

"I wouldn't want to intrude. Parties aren't really my thing anyway." *And that's the understatement of the year.*

"Nonsense. The whole village attends, including the Brockenbridge Scholar. It's tradition." She looked Alex right in the eye, and any hope of avoiding her fate disappeared. "It's expected."

"Yes, Mrs. Tate."

She looked Alex up and down. "Don't own a dress, do you?" Alex shook her head. "Sometimes I despair of the younger generation. It's not nearly so much fun dancing in trousers, plus there's nothing to catch a lad's interest like the odd glimpse of paradise whilst you're twirling about. You might not think it to look at me now, but I did quite well with the lads in my time."

"No, Mrs. Tate. I mean, yes, Mrs. Tate."

"Well, what can't be cured...Wear that blue blouse of yours, the one that's a match for your eyes."

"Yes, Mrs. Tate."

She cocked her head to one side, considering. "And put your hair up. Have you got some earrings, at least?"

"Yes, Mrs. Tate."

"Good. No makeup, though. Skin like yours shouldn't be mucked up with that rubbish."

"No, Mrs. Tate."

"Now let's get on with the Maid's Loaf. Haven't done one of these in years—not since Lucy's youngest got married."

"What exactly is a Maid's Loaf?"

"Making it is a task that falls to the eldest single woman in the house, until she marries, and then it passes to the next."

"Oh, of course—single, maiden. What is it I'm supposed to do?"

"It's always made with the last of the dough. You gather up all the leftover scraps—be sure to get every last bit—and make a ball. Form that into a loaf and say the rhyme that goes with it. Say it three times."

"Third time's the charm?"

"Yes, exactly." She didn't sound like she was joking.

"Okay. Sounds easy enough. What do I say?"

Mrs. Tate cleared her throat and chanted in a sing-song rhythm:

"If you seek a true love you can find them.
Gather up the fragments and combine them.
Think about your true love as you shape it.
Share it with your true love when you've baked it."

"What is that? It sounds like a spell."

"Of course it's a spell. What would be the point, otherwise?"

"Oh. As you say, what would be the point? And what is the spell supposed to do, exactly?"

"Get you a husband, what else? Hopefully by May Day. That's what the Maid's Loaf is for. You just need to be sure all the lads in the village have a taste of it before sunrise—or if you've someone particular in mind, you offer it only to them. The right lad'll want more than just a taste, if you catch my drift."

"But the thing is, I'm not exactly in the market for a husband."

"Don't be silly, Alexandra. The rhyme says *true love*. There's no reason you actually have to marry them. Not that we ever point that out to the menfolk, mind."

"Yes, I see, but regardless, I'm not...I don't want..."

"You young people can be so squeamish, it's a wonder you ever manage to have sex at all. How can you expect to get what you want if you can't even say it out loud?"

Alex opened and closed her mouth a couple of times without managing to get any sound to come out.

"Really, Alexandra, if it's a woman you want, then that's what you focus on as you make the loaf. I should have thought a girl as smart as you could work that out for herself."

Alex managed to croak out, "I'm sorry, Mrs. Tate."

"It's not as if you're the first lesbian on earth, Alexandra. Not by a long chalk—and not in the village, either, nor even in this house. Which you, being the Scholar, should know better than anybody. Well, don't just stand there looking like you've swallowed a frog— the loaf isn't going to make itself, is it?"

"No, Mrs. Tate."

The rest of the morning was something of a blur. Making the Maid's Loaf in strict accordance with instructions, helping to get all the loaves in and out of the oven, and finally, retreating to the study after a belated breakfast to just sit, letting Mrs. Tate's words run around and around in her head.

Eventually Grace came to find her. She was unusually calm, perhaps sensing Alex's mood. The cat leaped gently into her lap, kneading Alex's belly a few times before settling down, and stayed there, purring contentedly, while Alex absently petted her.

After lunch, she helped transfer the bread into a car driven by one of Mrs. Tate's many nephews for transport to the village hall—all except the Maid's Loaf, which she promised faithfully, despite her misgivings about the entire procedure, to bring along herself, since apparently no one else was supposed to touch it until after the blessing. Finally, she saw Mrs. Tate off to supervise the people setting up for the party, all of whom were doubtless in dire need of her guidance.

That left seven hours until sunset. Alex decided to take a nap.

❖

Just before sunset, Alex dutifully made her way to the village hall, attired as instructed and loaf in hand. Based on the number of people assembled in the yard and crowding up and down the street, the entire village had turned out. Most of them were holding baked goods, although it was quite a mixture, with cakes, cookies, and sandwiches in evidence as well as loaves of bread. Apparently the line between Lammas offerings and party refreshments was a fuzzy one, no doubt yet one more sign of the modern decline in standards that Mrs. Tate so deplored.

Looking around, she saw a few people she knew—shopkeepers, the village librarian, some of the staff from the museum, and of course Mrs. Tate. She was standing at the top of the steps outside the entrance to the hall with a group that appeared to consist of the oldest villagers, all holding loaves, plus the vicar looking very smart and ceremonial in her vestments embroidered in golden yellow, flame orange, and mahogany.

Alex spotted Nicola on the opposite side of the crowd and beside her a head of familiar-looking golden-brown hair. She couldn't see Cam's face, but she knew it was her. Alex's stomach gave a little flip. She waved but they didn't acknowledge her, apparently too immersed in conversation to notice.

Her attention was claimed by the vicar's call for quiet. The ceremony that followed was brief, co-led by the vicar and one of the elders, probably the oldest person in the village judging strictly by her appearance. The old woman's voice was steady, though, as she led the crowd in a call and response chant that Alex couldn't understand a word of it. It might just have been heavy Yorkshire dialect, but it felt like something more—the sort of words that would have been spoken when the weathered carvings up on Bram Tor were sharp and fresh.

At least the very last line was clear. Everyone raised their offerings high and chorused, "Lammas blessings on the bread, Lammas blessings on our heads," then repeated it. The third time, Alex joined in. After that, it was over and everyone went inside.

In the resulting bustle of friendly mingling, instrument tuning, and refreshment organizing, Alex found herself marooned in the midst of the cheerful, chatting crowd. A familiar voice from just behind her made her turn around.

"There you are! I had you spotted early on, but then you vanished. Lord, what a mob. I swear it's worse every year."

"Hello, Nicola. Don't you look nice." And indeed she did, wearing a drapey dress of dark rose that picked up the tone of her lips. No doubt she'd have lots of fun twirling in it and flirting the night away. Speaking of which, where was Cam? Alex tried to look around for her but Nicola reclaimed her attention.

"You as well. I like your hair that way—it's quite fetching."

"Thanks. I guess I clean up okay. Listen, didn't I see—"

"What do we have here?" She took the plate from Alex to examine more closely. "Is this a Maid's Loaf? Oh, damn!"

"Mrs. Tate insisted. Shouldn't I have brought it?"

"No, no, of course you should have. It's just that I promised both Mum and Aunty Elspeth I'd make one myself and I clean forgot. The last few days at work have been absolutely mad and I've dragged home every night completely shattered. You know how it always is right before a Bank Holiday. I don't know what it is about a Monday off that suddenly converts everything to a crisis. Oh, well, no sense letting yours go to waste."

Nicola helped herself to a tiny piece. "Yummy. Maybe you'll let me have more than just a taste." She winked at Alex.

"Nicola! You don't seriously mean that." No way. Talk about kissing your sister.

She grinned. "So Aunty Elspeth did tell you what it's really for. I just wanted to be sure. Not to worry—I've no designs on your virtue as yet. But the night is still young, so—*oomph!*"

The person who had backed into her turned out to be the very apologetic, not-at-all-bad-looking vicar, now in civilian clothes, who dismissed Alex with a pleasant smile before giving Nicola a careful once over, lingering in certain strategic spots. Interesting.

Nicola seemed oblivious, holding the bread out to her. "No worries, Sarah. Here, taste a bit of this."

"It's quite good—even better than last year's, I think."

Nicola laughed. "Probably because I didn't make this one. It's Alex's." The vicar stopped in mid-chew, her panicked eyes darting over to Alex. Clearly she knew all about the Maid's Loaf.

Alex did her best to pretend she had no idea what was going on, keeping her tone casual. "I'm afraid I can't take much credit for it either. Mrs. Tate is the one who made the dough. I just baked it."

The poor vicar's face was turning the color of Nicola's dress. She looked like she wanted to spit out whatever was left in her mouth, and then dig a very deep hole to crawl into. Taking pity on her, Alex murmured something about finding a place to drop off the loaf and moved away, choosing a direction at random.

Apparently her instincts were pretty good, because the crowd got thinner as she proceeded. She eventually reached a mostly clear area, obviously intended to serve as the dance floor, right in front of the stage where the musicians were setting up. A familiar-looking woman with tawny hair seemed to be doing most of the actual work. Cam was wearing delightfully form-fitting dark trousers and a crisp white shirt, the sleeves rolled up enough to showcase a respectable set of muscles. Draped on a chair nearby was the matching jacket and a tie in a dull gold that would probably do wonderful things for her eyes.

Cam got down off the stage and the musicians began tuning, or possibly rehearsing. By the time Alex reached her, Cam had her jacket back on and was starting on her tie. Any apprehensions about Cam avoiding her on purpose disappeared when Alex saw the welcoming smile that burst out the moment Cam spotted her.

"Alex! I was hoping you'd be here." She let go of the tie, leaving it hanging around her neck with the ends loose. The color did look amazing on her. "Sorry I've been out of touch, but this last job ran me ragged."

"Been busy, have you? Here, let me help you with that." She set her plate down on a nearby chair and took hold of both ends of the tie, adjusting the length before starting on the knot.

"Ta. It's that hard to manage without a mirror. Been up to my eyebrows in it and no mistake."

Alex was barely listening. This was so not a good idea. Standing this close to Cam, it was all she could do to keep her hands moving in some kind of coordinated way. If she didn't look up, if she didn't think about the warmth she could feel right through the layers of cloth…If she didn't think at all, then maybe, just maybe, she could get the damn knot over and done with so she could step back out of range and start breathing normally again.

For her part, Cam for once could not seem to stop talking, just a bit too loudly.

"Some fool over to Ilkley left a tap running in his holiday cottage, flooded the whole place. Needed new flooring, and that was just for a start. Owner was beside himself, what with the Bank Holiday coming. Morning, noon, and night job, that one. Wasn't even sure I'd make it to the party."

"I'm glad you did." *And I'm even more glad to be done with the damn tie*—although she does look really good in it. Alex put a little distance between them, surveying Cam up and down. "You look very smart, Ms. Carter."

"You as well, Ms. Petrocelli. That color really suits you."

"Thanks." Alex picked up the plate again. Cam spotted the bread and pounced, helping herself to a sizeable piece and wolfing it down before Alex had time to blink.

"Sorry—I'm famished."

"It's fine, really."

"Never did get any dinner, or tea either, I was so keen to finish in time." Alex held out the plate and Cam broke off another chunk, devouring it like it was going out of style. "Mind if I finish it?"

Either Cam had no idea what she was eating, or she was so hungry she didn't care about the consequences.

"Please, help yourself."

The rest of the bread disappeared. "Champion, that was. One thing there's no shortage of at Lammas is good bread. Who made it, or do you not know?"

"Mrs. Tate made the dough, but she had me shape and bake it by myself."

Cam went very still. Alex was pretty sure what that meant: Cam was well aware of the Maid's Loaf tradition but, like Nicola, wasn't sure how much Alex knew. Which presented certain possibilities.

She gave Cam what she hoped was a friendly, innocent smile as her mind raced. Should she go there? Oh, why not. "You know, Mrs. Tate said a funny thing—not funny ha-ha, funny peculiar. That I should be careful who I let taste it. Do you know what that was about?"

Cam shook her head, unwilling or perhaps unable to speak.

"And she said something even stranger—you know how you just ate the whole loaf, or close to it?"

Cam nodded. She didn't look happy. Good.

"She told me anybody who did that would want more than just a sample of my cooking." Cam's eyes flashed for a moment, but she stayed silent.

"I'm not sure what she meant by that, but she said if I couldn't figure it out, I should ask them."

She stepped a little closer. Cam's eyes darkened.

"So, Cam, what do you want?"

A beat. Two beats. Alex felt something shift. This wasn't a joke anymore. She felt herself being drawn into that steady gaze.

A voice intruded. "Just look at the two of you, standing about with nothing to say for yourselves." Nicola had most definitely arrived, with the vicar in tow looking less than thrilled to see Alex again. "I see your Maid's Loaf has gone, Alex. That was quick work. Did you manage to find that special someone already?"

"Well, Mrs. Tate was careful to point out that even if the loaf does its job, I don't have to get married, do I?" She smiled sweetly at Cam. "There's nothing wrong with just having a good time, is there?" If looks could kill, Alex knew she would now be pushing up daisies. "And as you said yourself, Nicola, the night is still young."

"I hope you got a taste at least, Cam. Aunty Elspeth really excelled herself this year. Sarah thought so, too."

As Nicola rattled on obliviously and the vicar appeared to have discovered something fascinating on the floor, Alex leaned over and hummed a few bars of "There are Fairies at the Bottom of Our Garden" in Cam's ear.

Cam let out a burst of laughter, hastily disguised as a coughing fit. Alex helpfully pounded her on the back a little harder than was strictly necessary. Nicola looked at them strangely.

"I swear, I don't know what's got into you two. Well, I want to dance. Come on, Sarah."

The two of them vanished onto the already crowded floor. Alex had been too preoccupied to notice the music starting. Whatever it was, she didn't recognize it, but it definitely had a solid beat. She could feel the floor vibrating.

Cam just stood there a moment, shaking her head and grinning at Alex. "Well done. You've got a bit of your own back." She offered her hand with a fancy flourish. "If Miss would care to join me?"

Alex batted her eyes and delicately clasped the proffered hand. "Miss would indeed."

Cam drew Alex smoothly into her arms and glided with her into the midst of the dancers.

❖

One dance became half a dozen. Alex didn't consider herself much of a dancer, but Cam made it so easy, she forgot everything except how much fun she was having. Even when the band switched from contemporary to more traditional dance tunes—which they played surprisingly well—she and Cam never even paused.

Cam led her effortlessly through a lively number that might have been a polka. Alex enjoyed whirling around the floor but decided Mrs. Tate was absolutely right; it would have been even better in a skirt.

The next dance was something slow and Latin, and Cam took full advantage of it, holding Alex close and leading with her body as well as hand pressure. Alex let herself drift into a pleasant daze, floating through the moves of the dance without conscious thought, imagining it was just the two of them alone, swaying together on a deserted beach under a tropical moon. Wishing it were true.

It took a moment for her to realize that the music had stopped completely. Probably the band was taking a break.

Cam was still holding her. Alex opened her eyes and looked up. Cam smiled gently.

"Fancy a walk, lass? Somewhere quiet?"

"Yes, I'd—"

"Cam." Nicola's quiet voice shattered the moment. Again. She seemed to be making a habit of it.

Cam dropped her arms and Alex stepped away. She looked at Nicola, wondering what on earth she was up to. Nicola was ignoring her completely, standing so close to Cam she was practically touching her, staring at her grimly.

"I'm sorry, Cam, but I thought I'd better tell you…" First she and then Cam focused on something over Alex's shoulder. Cam's face turned to stone. Her whole body stiffened.

"Nicola, darling!" Alex recognized the voice instantly. "Where have you been hiding yourself, you naughty girl? I've been searching for you in this wretched crowd for simply ages."

Nicola said, "I'm sorry, Rosamund. I didn't realize you'd be back in time for the party."

Alex turned to see the self-same Ms. Camberwell standing just behind her, exquisite in a clinging emerald sheath whose slit skirt and plunging bodice saved observers the bother of having to imagine very much. Alex, for one, certainly appreciated this thoughtfulness. Rosamund's flaming hair spilled negligently over one shoulder in a charmingly natural way that must have taken at least an hour to perfect.

"Never mind, darling, you'll just have to make it up to me later." She gave Nicola's hand a quick squeeze, in the process easing her to one side and stepping forward to stand between Nicola and Alex.

Letting go of Nicola's hand, Rosamund lasered Alex with those too-green eyes.

"And here's the other one I've been hunting for."

Now why does that make me feel like a rabbit being spotted by a kestrel? Alex put a smile on her face, hoping it looked genuine.

"Alex, darling, you're even lovelier than when I saw you last."

Of course, that wasn't quite the compliment it might have been, considering Rosamund had only seen her once before, which weighted the odds pretty heavily in favor of improvement.

"Thank you, Ms. Camberwell."

Rosamund placed a casual hand on Alex's shoulder, and all rational thought vaporized.

"Now, Alex, you know better. It's Rosamund." The hand squeezed slightly for emphasis on the last word.

Alex made no response, being incapable of doing anything at all except gaze into that beautiful face while continuing to absorb the warmth of the contact that somehow spread from her shoulder all the way through the rest of her body.

Rosamund paused, her hand still in place, and looked past Alex. Her smile tightened just a fraction. "Cam. It's so good to see you again."

"Rosamund. Not backward at coming forward, as per usual."

Rosamund laughed, a tinkling bell only slightly out of tune. "Darling Cam! Always so colorful!"

Cam turned and she looked at Alex, never meeting her eyes but staring for a long moment at Rosamund's hand on her shoulder. "I'm off, then." And just like that, she was gone.

Rosamund removed her hand from Alex's shoulder. "Nicola, do be an angel and fetch me a drink. This instant, darling, before I utterly perish from thirst."

"What would you like, Rosamund?"

"Why champers, darling! Whatever else?"

"There won't be any champagne, I'm afraid. They do have beer and cider, or I could get you a fizzy drink."

Rosamund shuddered delicately. "Now, darling, do be sensible—how can I possibly be expected to get through the evening without alcohol? I suppose cider will have to do—but only if it's decent stuff and not that horrid scrumpy."

"Certainly, Rosamund."

As Nicola went off in search of acceptable refreshment, Rosamund turned to face Alex. "Alone at last!" The bell-like laugh seemed to be back in tune. "Alex, darling, I know I've neglected you shamefully. Do please say you'll forgive me."

Another casual touch. This time the hand was on Alex's elbow, and equally effective at depriving her of the ability to form sentences.

"The Foundation summoned me to London, as they so frequently do, you know. And as usual by the time they finally thought to call me in, things had already reached a critical stage. Sorting out all the wretched details took simply forever. And here you were the entire time, having to manage all alone." She leaned forward, gazing deep into Alex's eyes. "I do so hope you'll let me make it up to you."

Alex managed to dredge up a murmur of assent, to what she wasn't at all sure.

"Marvelous! Dance with me, darling." Rosamund grabbed Alex's hand and dragged her back onto the dance floor, right past the returning Nicola. Alex barely managed to avoid tripping over her feet, but even so Nicola ended up spilling the drink she was carrying, most of which seemed to end up on her dress. Alex called an apology over her shoulder as the oblivious Rosamund pulled her away.

Dancing with Rosamund was quite an experience. Rosamund closed the distance between them and put her arms around Alex's waist. When Alex reflexively reacted by grasping Rosamund's shoulders, she pulled Alex right up against her.

The full-body contact zinged through Alex so sharply that it took a moment for her to realize that Rosamund wasn't moving. Not wanting to just stand there, and not knowing what else to do, Alex started swaying from side to side, hoping the movements didn't feel as awkward to Rosamund as they did to her. Cam had made it all seem so easy and natural, Alex had forgotten what a bad dancer she usually was.

She must have been doing something right, however, because when the next song started—another slow one—Rosamund rested her head against Alex's shoulder. Alex forgot everything except Rosamund, the feel of her body, the scent of her hair. She floated on a cloud of sensation until Rosamund stopped moving and pulled back a little, taking Alex by one hand. The music had stopped, so the band must have decided to take another break.

That thought led inevitably to another one. Alex glanced quickly around the room but saw no sign of Cam anywhere. She did see Nicola leaning against the wall, arms crossed, looking miffed. As she had every right to be.

Feeling ashamed that she had allowed herself to be distracted for so long, Alex made a beeline for Nicola, pulling Rosamund along with her. When they finally reached Nicola, Alex stammered out an apology for the mishap, offering to pay for having her dress cleaned. Nicola stared down at their clasped hands for a moment before coldly thanking Alex and making herself scarce.

Alex felt awful. It's not as if she had planned to—What? Well, to do whatever you would call what had just been going on between her and Rosamund. Flirting? Something more? In any case, surely her reaction to Rosamund's obvious interest had been just as much of an accident as her near-collision with Nicola. It's not that she had ignored Nicola's feelings, exactly, let alone deliberately set out to snatch Rosamund away from her. In actual fact, she hadn't been thinking about anything at all. Didn't that mean that whatever had happened wasn't really her fault?

Unfortunately Alex's guilt over the hurt and anger on Nicola's face refused to diminish, despite this supremely logical self-justification. She wished she could talk the whole thing over with someone—along with whatever the hell was going on with Cam, as well. Ironically, the person she most wanted to discuss it with was Nicola herself.

To make things worse, Rosamund was asking questions, obviously mystified by the entire exchange, and not exactly pleased that Alex wasn't really answering her. Alex could hardly explain that the real reason Nicola was so angry was because she had a crush on Rosamund and was jealous. Still, by not saying anything, Alex was making it seem that Nicola was throwing a hissy fit over her dress, which made her look petty, not a nice impression to give her boss.

She finally settled for saying that she'd had words with Nicola earlier, being as vague as possible while trying to make it sound like it was all her own fault rather than Nicola's, and could she get Rosamund something to drink?

It seemed that she could. Unfortunately, the line at the bar was long, and by the time she had managed to acquire two glasses of cider and return, Rosamund had vanished. When Alex finally spotted her, she was chatting animatedly with the slightly dazed-looking vicar while resting one delicate hand on her arm.

Alex downed both ciders and stomped home.

Cam wasn't quite sure how she had ended up outside Dawson House, sitting on the waist-high wall beside the gatepost, telling her troubles to the ginger cat that was always hanging about the place. One minute she was storming out of the village hall, wanting to smash something, determined to walk and keep walking until the feeling went away. The next thing she knew, she was sitting here in the moonlight, petting this ball of fur that purred like a motorbike with a bad silencer and complaining about women. And life in general, and the high price of petrol, and the blister she was getting from her new pair of shoes. But mostly women.

"You're not a bad listener, are you, cat? Cheaper than a therapist, that's for certain. And less gossipy than a bartender."

The cat jumped up and scurried off.

"What, you don't fancy compliments?"

Then she heard the footsteps coming toward her. It didn't take psychic powers to predict that they belonged to the one person she least wanted to see.

Sure enough, it was Alex, and by the way she was striding along, ever so slightly out of step, it was obvious she was both quite unhappy and somewhat tipsy. Cam momentarily considered beating a strategic retreat, deciding against it mostly because she didn't think she was likely to escape unobserved, and she refused to be seen sneaking away like a thief. Especially when, unlike some people, she hadn't done anything wrong.

Too soon, Alex caught sight of her. She came to a dead stop, swayed just a bit, then marched right up to Cam. "So, what, are you stalking me now?"

"Nice to see you, too. Got a right monk on, haven't you?"

"What's that in English?"

Cam opened her mouth to translate but Alex cut her off.

"Forget it—don't try to change the subject. What are you doing here?"

"Minding my own business, not that it's any of yours."

"And you just happen to be doing it on my doorstep at midnight. What's that you said the other night—Pull the other one, it's got bells on? So what the hell do you want?"

"Not a bloody thing. It's a public thoroughfare." She took a closer look at Alex, whose eyes were a little hazy. "Just how much have you had?"

"About as much as I can take, thank you very much. What is it with you people around here, anyway, dancing with a person and then running away or—"

"I didn't run off, I left. Just because I didn't care to stand about watching you and Rosamund carrying on—"

"What, did Nicola come crying to you about how I broke her heart? Where is she, hiding in the bushes? Come out, come out, wherever you are! Don't be a fraidy cat—I won't bite. Unless you ask nicely."

"You broke Nicola's heart? Well that's just famous, that is. How'd you manage it, if I may be so bold as to inquire?"

"All I did was dance with Rosamund a couple of times. Okay, maybe it was more than a couple of times, and maybe I was holding her kind of close during those slow numbers…"

Cam could feel a ball of fury forming in the pit of her stomach. Alex just kept right on talking, as usual.

"But seriously, I don't understand why she's so mad. It's not like I was kissing her in the middle of the dance floor or anything."

"Wait—you and Rosamund were kissing on the bloody dance floor? Or was that you and Nicola? Christ, maybe you should give out numbers, like a bakery."

"Says the woman who practically inhaled my Maid's Loaf. Fat lot of good that did me. I just said I wasn't kissing anybody, you idiot. Try listening to somebody else for once—you'll enjoy the change."

"Oh, that's rich coming from you, that is."

"Besides, what do you care who I kiss?"

"I don't care! Why the bloody hell should I?"

"Good. I'm glad to hear it. I don't care who you kiss either. Anyway, it's not my fault that Rosamund barely knows Nicola's alive. If you ask me, Nicola should stop wasting her time mooning over her boss and hit on the vicar instead. Chat her up. Whatever."

"Nicola? And the vicar? You can't be serious."

"I know, right? But you should have seen the way the vicar was looking at her—like she'd be happy to have her for lunch. Not that Nicola noticed. I swear, for such a tiny little village, you people have more dyke drama. I can't wait to get back to the States."

"That can't happen soon enough to suit me."

"You, Cam Carter, are not a nice person. And if you don't mind, I'll thank you to leave me the hell alone."

"With pleasure. You're no great prize yourself, you know."

"Thank you so very much. Permit me to remove my offending presence."

Cam watched Alex stomp over to the gate and try to pull it open, unsuccessfully of course. Once. And then twice. Before she could try again, Cam went over and pushed on the gate. It swung open.

Alex glared at her as she swept through the gap. Cam slammed the gate shut, pausing just long enough to watch Alex get safely indoors before heading for home, swearing under her breath.

CHAPTER TEN

The next morning, much too early, Alex staggered into the bathroom. She squinted at herself in the mirror and shuddered. Patriotic marbles, again. At least it was Saturday, so she had almost two whole days before she had to face Mrs. Tate, or anybody else. After splashing water on her face, she dragged herself downstairs to brew some tea that she sincerely wished were coffee.

She took a sip and winced when the too-hot liquid burned her tongue. Putting down the cup, she just sat there, wishing her headache would go away. Why the hell did she feel this bad after only two glasses of cider? She knew she was a lightweight, but this was ridiculous. Maybe the local brew was extra strong.

She took another cautious sip of tea. People always said that drinking too much made you forget things. Unfortunately, she remembered far too much of her conversation with Cam. Not exactly her finest hour. Hell, she'd had more mature exchanges on the elementary school playground.

Of course, some of it was Cam's fault, but reminding herself of that didn't make it any better. At least Cam had done her the courtesy of being honest about her feelings—or rather her lack of them. She supposed it was better than being strung along and then dumped. So her pathetic streak of failed attempts at romance remained unbroken.

She raised her teacup in a grim toast. "Here's to women, and my lack of success with them. And Cam Carter, my latest imaginary girlfriend."

Just as she lifted the cup to her lips, a door slammed somewhere in the main part of the house. She started, spilling most of the tea, and swore. Putting the cup down untasted, she got a cloth and wiped up the mess. It really wasn't like her to be so jumpy. Dawson House certainly offered odd noises galore—creaks and moans and rattles at all hours of the day and night—although it could also be eerily silent, no doubt depending on which way the wind was blowing, and of course, whether the Divine Miss Grace was lurking indoors or out.

Not until she had poured a replacement cup did her thoughts drift back to the previous evening. Just as well that Cam had set her straight—ha-ha—about their non-relationship before she wasted any more time barking up that particular tree. But was that really all there was to it?

There had been times, more than a few, when she could have sworn there was something going on between her and Cam. Especially during the dancing. She shut her eyes and drew a slow breath in, remembering Cam's arms around her, holding her close. There really had been something there—something romantic, magical almost, if only for a few moments. Had she been the only one to feel any of it?

She sighed. No point in wasting time wondering now. Cam had been clear—much too clear—about her lack of interest in Alex. No doubt she'd do them both a favor and keep her distance in the future. Bramfell might be a small place, but she'd seen so little of Cam since she arrived, maybe they could just keep on avoiding each other.

And then there was Nicola. Not exactly someone she could avoid, given all the ways Nicola had been helping with her work. And even if she thought she could get away with it, she wouldn't try—it wouldn't be right. She had hurt Nicola's feelings, and she owed it to Nicola to face her and let her say whatever she had to say about it. That was definitely not going to be fun, but she'd just have to deal with it.

Of course, Nicola might refuse to forgive her. Nothing Alex could do about that, except try to make things right between them and hope that they could still be friends.

And that left Rosamund—which was probably exactly what she should do: leave well enough alone and stay as far away from her as possible. She sighed again, thinking of Rosamund on the dance floor, shimmering like a fairy princess in her emerald gown, glorying in the music. She doubted she'd be able to avoid Rosamund completely, given her position at the Foundation, but so far they'd had very little to do with each other. There shouldn't be a problem keeping it that way. She hoped.

Maybe she should eat something, not that she had any appetite. Something plain, toast, maybe. No, she thought, shuddering, not that. After yesterday, she wouldn't care if she never saw another piece of bread as long as she lived. She got herself some cereal instead.

Afterward she poured another cup of tea to take with her to the study. Maybe she could force herself to get some work done. As she walked down the hall, she noticed the pile of mail on the table by the front door. In all the upheaval of the previous day, she had forgotten about it completely. She was delighted to discover a letter from Ian—a nice long one. Taking it into the study with her, she sat down and began reading eagerly.

Ian's rational, amiable voice came through every line, soothing her ravaged nerves and quieting her mind. Most of what he had to say was family news, along with friendly encouragement for her work. He'd heard from Fiona, who was doing well and sent her best. Alex made a mental note to e-mail her later.

But then came a sentence that drove everything else from her mind: *I've had a good rummage through the attic as promised and I've located a packet of letters from Oona.*

Alex's heart started to pound. This was it—the key, the clue, the magic spark she needed for her work. She could feel it.

Aging eyes and fading ink make for a bad combination, but so far I've managed to decipher one item that might be of interest, and I am taking you at your word and sending it along straight away. It is enclosed, transcribed as faithfully as I am able. I have engaged a documents expert at the Foundation to prepare a facsimile and will send that along as soon as I may.

Alex's hand started to shake so badly that she had to put the letter down on the desk. Moving aside the top sheet, she looked down at the next one, also covered in Ian's neat, old-fashioned handwriting.

As she started reading, she realized that Ian hadn't just pulled out a few random quotes. He had copied over the entire letter, word for word, so she could see everything in context. Bless the man! She started skimming excitedly but realized she wasn't comprehending the words, just running her eyes over them.

Taking a breath, she started again, doing her best to focus. Finally she resorted to reading aloud, and that seemed to help. Under other circumstances, the letter would have been fascinating, a time capsule giving a glimpse of life in a bygone era as well as insight into Ian himself. But now it was all she could do to make her tedious way through the mild gossip and affectionate advice that lay between her and her quarry like jungle vines obscuring the trail to a lost city.

The phone rang, jolting her back into the present. She automatically picked it up, mentally kicking herself as she did so. She added silent curses to the kicks when she heard the voice on the other end.

"Alex, darling! You are such a naughty little thing."

"Hello, Rosamund. What can I do for you?"

"Is that any way to greet me? And after the way you treated me last night."

"Sorry." Her eyes drifted back to the letter.

"Really, darling, you don't sound very sorry. And you should be, you know, after abandoning me that way."

It took a moment for Alex to realize Rosamund had paused. "I am sorry. Very sorry." Sorrier than Rosamund could imagine, but not for leaving.

"One minute you were there, and the next minute you had vanished. No one knew where you had gone."

"I…wasn't feeling well. I didn't think you'd miss me." That last was certainly true.

"Well, I did. Very much. But I'm willing to let you make it up to me."

Oona's letter had moved on from current news to memories of the past. She was getting warmer.

"I said, you can make it up to me."

"Yes, sorry, Rosamund. How can I do that?"

"Have dinner with me, darling."

"Sure, that'd be great. How about next week sometime?"

"Next week? Darling, if I didn't know better, I'd think you were trying to put me off."

"Okay, what about tomorrow night?"

"Well, I suppose I could try to wait that long, but honestly darling, I know I'll just die of screaming boredom. It's Saturday! Can't we go tonight? Do say yes, darling."

"Of course. Tonight will be fine."

"Brilliant! Pick me up at eight."

"I don't have a car, Rosamund."

"Of course not—how silly of me. I'll pick you up, then."

"Sounds great. See you then."

She hung up absently, returning her full attention to the letter. After all the anticipation, the actual information was kind of a letdown.

Sandwiched in between Oona's account of a bad storm that had hit the village during the twenties and her mother's recipe for something called black bun, which sounded delicious, was one short paragraph: *As you've asked me for more stories about Artemisia, I mind me that Mam used to tell of how our Miss Thompkins (as she always called her) was ever a great walker. By the hour she'd walk the moors, in all weathers, and always alone. Pining for Lady Melissa, folk said, and thought it right touching. More often than not, she'd take a servant along for propriety—Mam said it was the only time she ever did anything the way folk expected. I asked Janet about it once, and she laughed and said it was the exception that proved the rule.*

That was it—Artemisia went for walks. A lot. Alex reread it several times, silently and out loud, hoping to see something in it beyond the obvious. Well, the part about how the villagers were sympathetic about her being in mourning for Lady Melissa might count for something—there wasn't a lot of contemporary information of any kind about Artemisia from working class sources, and nothing at all about her relationship with Lady Melissa. And the letter did provide her with quotations—albeit indirect—from two people who had actually known Artemisia.

The more she thought about it, the better she felt. Surely she could make at least a couple of decent bricks from this tiny morsel of straw. And that might be enough, if she was very, very lucky, to build something worthwhile. She headed for the archive room to see what she could find in the files.

❖

By the time eight o'clock rolled around, she'd been at it for hours and her brain was fried. She had barely managed to throw on some decent clothes and run a brush through her hair when she heard a horn tooting impatiently. She hurried out to the street, only to stop dead at the sight of Rosamund behind the wheel of a yellow Porsche convertible, top down, her glorious hair glowing in the fading light.

Rosamund laughed, clearly noting, and liking, her stunned reaction. "Do hurry, darling. I'm simply starving!"

Alex had barely sat down and closed the door when Rosamund peeled out. It took a few minutes of fumbling for Alex to locate and engage her seat belt, but Rosamund seemed not to notice. Unlike some people, Rosamund did not appear to have a safety fetish.

It didn't take Alex long to discover just how true this was as they whipped through the narrow village streets with little regard for speed limits or blind curves. Alex realized that she could either hyperventilate all the way to the restaurant—or, as seemed equally likely, the crash site—or she could unclench her fingers from the dashboard and try to enjoy her last moments on earth. She took a deep breath in a vain attempt at relaxation, only to swallow some kind of bug and succumb to a coughing fit.

Apparently the sight of her choking to death was what it took to finally get through to Rosamund, who actually slowed down, all the way to a stop, right in the middle of the lane. Fortunately, gasping pleas and frantic hand gestures from Alex convinced her to start up again before anyone came along and rear-ended them.

Mentally cursing herself for not thinking to jump out when she had the chance, Alex considered the bright side: if they survived the journey, they should arrive at their destination, whatever it was, in record time.

It turned out to be Leeds. Rosamund screeched to a halt under an awning in a brightly lit downtown neighborhood, smiled at the valet who helped her out of the car, and swept into the restaurant, leaving

Alex to scramble after her. She didn't catch the name of the place, but everything from the ostentatiously minimalist décor to the carefully distressed faux-bohemian designer wear sported by the clientele shrieked Chez Trendy. Alex hoped the limit on her credit card would be high enough to cover whatever passed for food in this joint.

Sadly, her fears were justified. Along with being overpriced, the dishes were exquisitely presented and uniformly inedible. At least the portions were small.

Rosamund was the only pleasant surprise. She proved to be a charming dinner companion, full of amusing stories and easy chatter. And she was certainly no hardship to look at, her eyes glinting like jewels in the candlelight, her blaze of hair flowing over pale shoulders left bare by a deep blue dress that clung in all the right places. Every so often she would touch Alex's hand or arm to emphasize a point, and each time, Alex felt a little jolt that zinged right to the pit of her stomach—and lower. Alex was careful to stick to one glass of wine, but even so, but the end of the meal she felt light-headed.

Unfortunately, the size of the bill was enough to sober her up. The look on her face must have really been something, because Rosamund snatched the check out of her hand and refused to give it back, laughing when Alex tried to protest. "But darling, I chose the restaurant. It's only fair that I pay."

"Then next time, I'll choose the restaurant."

"Of course you will, darling." Rosamund smiled archly, and Alex realized she had just agreed to a second date before she had even survived the first.

While they waited for the valet, Rosamund informed her that they couldn't possibly go back to Bramfell yet, darling, not on a Saturday night, for heaven's sake. Alex, who would have been just as happy to go straight home, reluctantly agreed to visit a club that was "simply too hot for words."

When they got to the club, Rosamund pulled into the dimly lit parking lot, turned off the engine, and then just sat there. After a moment, she gave Alex an expectant look along with a tilt of her head toward the driver's side door. Alex, recalling Cam's relentless courtesies, realized that Rosamund expected her to do the honors.

She got out and walked around to open Rosamund's door. Rosamund held out a hand, and Alex, feeling foolish, took it and guided her to her feet. As she did so, Rosamund seemed to catch a glimpse of something behind Alex, but before she could turn and see what it was, Rosamund was on her, pushing her back against the car next to theirs and kissing her, full force.

At first Alex was so shocked she could only stand there woodenly, arms at her sides, feeling the surprising strength of Rosamund's hands pressing against her shoulders and the even more surprising enthusiasm of Rosamund's lips on hers. What the heck? Maybe Rosamund was drunk—she'd certainly had more than her share of the wine at dinner.

Alex lifted her hands to Rosamund's shoulders, trying to ease her back a little, but to no avail. Rosamund never paused, just varied her technique, nibbling on Alex's lips and tracing them with her tongue.

Alex's mind slammed shut and her body took over. She closed her eyes and began kissing back. Nothing existed but the feeling of Rosamund's mouth on hers, the trail of heat that raced through her, the ache that had started between her thighs. She parted her legs and eased her hips to one side, trying to center herself on Rosamund's leg, seeking the pressure she needed.

But Rosamund surprised her again, easing back a fraction, never breaking off the kiss but spinning them around so that Rosamund ended up with her back against the car and Alex was the one on the outside. During the maneuver, Alex's eyes came open, purely by reflex, and as the kiss continued she let her eyes roam around, her brain too fogged to fully take in what she was seeing.

Still, a warning bell chimed somewhere deep in her mind, something about one of the nearby vehicles. And people—other people standing there. Watching them? Something wasn't right. She pulled away from Rosamund, ending the kiss but still clutching her, her knees so weak she was afraid if she let go she'd fall down.

"Someone's…someone's over there."

Rosamund laughed. "But that just makes it better, darling. Don't tell me you're shy." She reached for Alex to pull her into another kiss, but Alex stepped away, letting go of Rosamund and swaying slightly. Maybe she was the one who was drunk. She certainly felt woozy.

As she looked around, trying to figure out what was wrong, she spotted a vehicle farther down the row. The bottom fell out of her stomach and she put out a hand, automatically holding on to Rosamund's arm for support. With all the cars in the way, she couldn't read the writing on the side of the van, but she didn't need to. There couldn't be two monstrosities like that running around the North.

For just an instant she allowed herself the utterly irrational hope that it would turn out to be someone else standing there next to the van, but that vanished as soon as she forced her eyes to focus. Of course it was Cam. And just to make things completely perfect, Nicola was there as well. Cam's arm was around her shoulder, holding her close to her side. How sweet.

Evidently the relationship between them had progressed somewhat beyond the innocent friendship Nicola had been at such pains to reassure her about. Not that she actually had any excuse for getting upset, given the way she had behaved toward both of them lately, not least the lovely exhibition she had just provided. The light was too dim to really make out the expressions on their faces, but by posture alone she could tell that Cam and Nicola had seen more than enough.

As she stood there, frozen to the spot, staring at them, her view was obscured by Rosamund leaning over to claim another kiss. Alex pulled away.

"Rosamund, would you take me home, please? I've got a really bad headache."

"Oh, my poor darling. Of course." Surprisingly, she didn't sound disappointed.

Cam stared at the Porsche as it pulled out of the parking lot, tires squealing. Rosamund's driving certainly hadn't changed, nor had her taste for public warm-ups before more private activities, something Cam had never really managed to enjoy. She preferred to keep private things private. It had been something she had gone along with to please Rosamund—just one more thing on a very long list.

At the time, all those compromises had seemed like a ridiculously small price to pay. She had thought of them as a kind of tax she owed the universe for the unbelievable miracle that had brought Rosamund into her life. Gorgeous, glamorous, fun-loving Rosamund had somehow chosen to love her dull, plain, common-or-garden self, like a fairy queen falling for a mortal in one of the ballads her mother had taught her.

Cam had been so head-over-heels that keeping Rosamund happy had seemed like the most important thing in the world. She never stopped to consider the way all the little things added up, the times she would bite her tongue, or do without something she wanted, or agree to something she really wasn't comfortable with. Each time had seemed so unimportant that she hadn't realized until it was too late that she had really been giving up parts of herself.

And when everything had come crashing down, and she found herself facing the awfulness of her mother's death alone, she had barely recognized the person she had turned into. Just like in the old songs when the mortal is finally exiled from fairyland, only to find that a hundred years have passed and everything they once knew was gone.

She smiled grimly. She knew exactly what this little trip down memory lane was in aid of, and it wasn't working. Nothing could drive out of her mind the sight of Alex and Rosamund kissing. She finally gave in, letting the image replay, feeling the roiling in her gut again.

And it hadn't been just a little kiss, either, some quick brush of lips against a cheek. Even from a distance, it had been obvious that Alex could barely contain herself. Flipping Rosamund around like that and shoving her against the car—somehow she hadn't pictured Alex being so aggressive. Rosamund must be over the moon. No doubt she'd thoroughly express her appreciation once she got Alex into bed. If she hadn't already.

Her gut twisted again. What was it she had said last night about not caring what Alex did? One of her mother's favorite sayings came back to her: Lie to others if you must, but only fools lie to themselves. She'd turned out to be a bloody great fool, then, hadn't she?

And working overtime at it. How else could she seriously have thought that the reason she was so angry last night was because of Rosamund, when it was Alex all along? Alex with Rosamund's hand on her shoulder. Alex going on about dancing with Rosamund, holding her, kissing her—or not kissing, she claimed. Well, she'd gone and kissed her now, hadn't she? And plenty more besides, if Rosamund had had anything to say about it. Rosamund always got exactly what Rosamund wanted, and heaven help you if she didn't.

Cam cursed herself for her stupidity, and rotten timing. Five minutes here or there, and she'd have completely missed the show. Learning about the two of them some other way surely couldn't have been as bad as seeing that.

And if she hadn't been so intent on trying to cheer Nicola up, they wouldn't have been here at all. But Nicola had seemed so down, and after what Alex had said about Nicola fancying Rosamund, she'd thought a trip into Leeds would be just the ticket. Drop round a pub or two, look up some of her mates, give Nicola a chance to meet some new people. It had seemed too good a chance to miss.

"Sorry, Nicola. Me and my bright ideas."

"Let's just go home, shall we?"

"Right."

CHAPTER ELEVEN

Alex managed to avoid everybody for over a week—except for Mrs. Tate and, of course, Grace. Apart from a brisk walk on the moors too early and much too bright every morning, she stayed hunkered down in the house all day. Whenever the phone rang she ignored it, letting it go through to voice mail that she never checked. Mostly she buried herself in her work and tried hard not to think about anything but Artemisia.

Fortunately, perhaps, when Mrs. Tate was around, she didn't offer her usual friendly chatter. Alex knew she wasn't exactly in disgrace, since her meals continued to display the heights of Mrs. Tate's culinary talents. But their interactions had a formal tone that hadn't been there before. While Alex welcomed the breathing room this new distance gave her, she hoped it was only temporary. She had a sense that Mrs. Tate was not so much disapproving as disappointed in her. No big shocker there, since she was pretty disappointed in herself, not to mention confused, shaken up, and a few other things besides.

At first she was surprised that Mrs. Tate seemed to know what had happened—or at least, that something had happened—without Alex having said a thing, but the gossip here in Bramfell was bound to be even worse than it had been in the English department back home—which had certainly been bad enough. And her being a stranger would multiply everyone's interest exponentially.

Not that she thought for one minute that Cam would say anything, but Nicola might have told her troubles to someone—maybe even Mrs. Tate. Now that was an embarrassing thought. And Rosamund would have no compunction about blabbing everything far and wide. Certainly to her London pals—over dinner, she had been emphatic about how close they all were—plus anyone in Bramfell she deemed worthy of her friendship.

"Maybe I should just save everyone the time and trouble and embroider myself a scarlet letter. Probably *D* for dingbat." Grace, who was sprawled in her lap generously permitting herself to be petted, flicked an ear. "What do you think, huh?"

Whatever opinion the cat might have offered vanished along with the rest of her when a knock sounded at the front door. Alex had little hope that it would turn out to be a welcome visitor, like the postman or maybe the Angel of Death. Well, she couldn't hide forever. Worse luck.

It was Nicola. Alex diffidently offered a cup of tea, which Nicola calmly accepted. God bless British sangfroid. Tea having been duly brewed and poured, they sat for a while in silence.

"Look—"

"I say—"

They both laughed—just a little, but it was enough.

"Nicola, I'm so sorry. I really didn't mean to hurt you. I don't know what came over me the other night with Rosamund. I don't usually do my thinking with my—"

"Lady parts?"

"Oh, Goddess, just shoot me now and put me out of my misery, why don't you?"

"Too easy. I prefer to have you alive and suffering. Which, I take it, is what you've been doing, shut up here in durance vile, subsisting on bread and water and avoiding the phone."

"Not bread—I've given it up after last week's fiasco."

"Your loss, then. Don't blame the medium for the message."

"The message being, I suppose, that I'm a lousy friend. If you never talked to me again, I'd understand."

"Over Rosamund? Just because she makes me blush and stutter like a schoolgirl? Please. I can hardly lay claim to her because of that. She has the same effect on every woman she meets—including you, I'd say. Actually, I should thank you—I think seeing the two of you going at it finally cured me of my infatuation."

Alex winced. "I'm really embarrassed. I don't usually do stuff like that in front of God and everybody." *I don't usually do stuff like that at all.*

"Yes, well…I just wish Cam hadn't been there. She was pretty upset."

"How come? She made it pretty clear to me she's not…I mean, why would she care?"

"You really don't know?"

"Wait—was it because of what I told her about you liking Rosamund? I'm sorry. I never would have said anything if I'd realized how things were with the two of you."

"What are you talking about?"

"I know you said you and Cam were just friends, but, well, the two of you looked pretty cozy standing there that night with your arms around each other and I just assumed…" Nicola was looking at her like she had three heads. "Feelings can change," she finished lamely.

"Not in this case. Honestly, I don't know what you thought you saw, but the whole reason we were there at the club was because Cam was trying to help me meet someone—someone available. Which, apart from anything else, Cam most definitely is not."

"I don't understand."

"So you really don't know about her and Rosamund? For some reason I thought…never mind."

"Cam and Rosamund? They're together?" A series of mental pictures flashed past, each worse than the one before, all of them featuring Cam with Rosamund, Cam holding her, kissing her, touching her. She felt queasy. Cam hadn't given her any reason to think she was currently involved with anyone, let alone Rosamund. Quite the opposite. Had she really misread Cam so badly?

"Not anymore, not for years. But she broke Cam's heart. I don't think Cam has ever recovered. You should have seen her face the other night, watching the two of you. I thought she was going to be sick."

"I really didn't know. Thank you for telling me." Why didn't Cam? *She must be so hurt by what I did. But how was I supposed to know?* "I guess I'm the only person in Bramfell who isn't clued in to what's going on with everybody's love life. Anything else I should know about, while we're on the subject?"

"Let's see. Jim up at the Hall—that's the tall guide with the moustache—sees quite a bit of my uncle Derek. And Aunty Elspeth has been keeping company with the village librarian for donkey's years—ever since his wife died."

"Mrs. Tate? Wow. Good to know."

"At least, folk say that's when they stopped trying to keep it quiet."

Carefully casual, she said, "What about the vicar? Is she seeing anyone?"

"Sarah? Not that I know of. Very discreet, is Sarah. But she has to be, doesn't she, what with being the vicar and all that. Why do you ask?"

"No reason, really. You two just seemed to hit it off so well at the party, that's all."

"I should hope so—we've been friends since primary school. I lost track of her when we both went off to university, but since she got assigned to Bramfell, it's been like old times."

"She seems nice."

"Yes, she's very sweet." She paused. "She really is."

Nicola sat there looking thoughtful, while Alex tried to keep the grin off her face.

After a moment Nicola glanced at her watch. "I must push off— duty calls, and all that."

"On a Sunday?"

"We've got a drinks do laid on for some major donors up at the Hall. Fair warning—I'm organizing one in October called Meet the Brockenbridge Fellow."

"Oh no."

"I'm afraid so. Speaking of which, you need to get back to work."

"But I have been working—all day, every day, it feels like."

"All I know is, your office up at the museum is starting to collect cobwebs. And for God's sake, start answering your phone before a certain party sends me over with a billet-doux."

"What?"

"I'm serious. Since you've been dodging her calls, she's been after me to bring you little notes—God knows what's in them."

"I'm not sure I want to find out."

"So far I've managed to put her off but that can't last. She is my boss, after all."

"I'm sorry she's been trying to drag you into this."

"I really don't mind, you know, about you seeing her. You can't help yourself, can you?"

"I don't suppose I can. Rosamund is just so...Rosamund." *And unlike some people, she, at least, is interested in me.*

"Don't I know it. But I've got to draw the line somewhere, and I will most definitely not be your go-between."

"Message received and understood. You know, if things go the way they usually do for me, this thing with Rosamund will probably just turn out to be *Th'expense of spirit—*"

"*—in a waste of shame*? Oh, surely not. At least try to enjoy the ride while it lasts."

"Don't say ride—I'm still having nightmares about her driving. Wherever we go next time, we're definitely walking."

After seeing Nicola out, Alex reluctantly sat down to check her messages. Twelve from Rosamund. Nothing from anybody else. Not that she was expecting there to be, of course.

She picked up the phone and dialed Rosamund's number.

She must have had caller ID, because Alex didn't even hear it ring before "Darling!" came over the wire so loudly she had to hold the receiver away from her ear.

Somewhere upstairs a door slammed.

Chapter Twelve

Back to her more usual routine, and with a date with Rosamund to look forward to on Friday, Alex started to feel much better. Things with Mrs. Tate gradually returned to normal, and she and Nicola managed to meet up for coffee a couple of times. As if by unspoken agreement, they avoided touchy subjects, so she had no idea how Cam was doing, but hoped no news was good news. Best of all, she was finally making some progress with her dissertation.

And not a moment too soon—nine months had sounded like forever, until the days and weeks started slipping away.

Otherwise she would have been just as happy to ignore the calendar. She really did love it here in Bramfell. The scenery was gorgeous, the people were friendly, even the tourists were tolerable, and—certain unfortunate episodes notwithstanding—the place was remarkably peaceful. She could imagine staying here for a long, long time—possibly even the rest of her life.

What a pity there wasn't a university nearby where she could work once she had her doctorate. She suspected that not even the Brockenbridge would be able to open those doors for her, an American studying British literature, however well her dissertation was received.

She sighed. Best to enjoy her time here while it lasted, and focus on getting her work done so she could apply for Stateside jobs and start the long, soul-wearying struggle for tenure. If she was lucky enough to ever even have that problem.

Enough. Carpe diem. Time for breakfast.

As she came down the stairs she heard singing coming from the kitchen. It sounded beautiful. What it didn't sound like was Mrs. Tate. If she didn't know better, she'd swear it was—

"Cam!"

"That it is." She was up to her elbows in the stove, the various innards of which were scattered around the counters and the floor.

"What are you doing here? And where's Mrs. Tate?"

"And a very good morning to you as well." She stepped away from the stove, wiping her hands on a rag.

"Sorry, you surprised me. Good morning." Searching Cam's face for some sign of what she was thinking or feeling, Alex could read nothing but pleasant neutrality. Which was good, right? "Is Mrs. Tate okay?"

"That depends on what your definition is. She was as angry as I've ever seen her, but she looked to be in good health when I left her."

"Where is she?"

"Over to young Lucy's to cook up your dinner."

The nickname sounded funny coming from Cam, since the person in question had at least two decades on her, but Alex had discovered that the entire village used it to help distinguish the three possessors of that name.

"She said to tell you it would be ready at the usual time, but you'd need to get your own breakfast."

"Oh. Right."

Alex looked around, a little thrown by having to deal with the unexpected so early in the morning, and with no likelihood of any help from caffeine, given the stove's condition.

Cam gestured toward the table. "Since I was told you'd be up along about now, I popped out and fetched you a coffee. Reckoned you'd need it, with the cooker on the blink and no way to brew yourself a cuppa."

"Oh. That was really kind." She sat down and took a sip. Ecstasy. And it wasn't just coffee—it was her usual, a cappuccino. She could practically feel the magic molecules swarming through her bloodstream and revving up her brain. "Bless you for this." She took another sip. "But I'm still puzzled about why Mrs. Tate called you in.

She gave me the strong impression that the Foundation had someone officially on retainer for repairs, and bringing in anybody else was sacrilege or something."

"And who do you suppose it is that has the contract, and has had since 1963?"

"Pretty impressive, getting the contract almost two decades before your birth."

"So I couldn't possibly have taken over the business from Uncle Reg when he finally retired, could I? Have some more coffee—I think your brain's still lying in bed where you left it."

"Oh, excuse the hell out of me." The hurt that flashed over Cam's face and just as quickly vanished was like a punch in Alex's gut. She put down the coffee and got to her feet. "Look, I'm sorry." She reached out a hand toward Cam, who just stood there, stock still, the few inches between them an unbridgeable gap. Alex let her hand drop. "Really, I don't know what's gotten into me lately. And I haven't even properly apologized to you for the dance, and the night after."

Cam summoned up a smile that didn't touch her eyes. *"Least said, soonest mended,* Mum always used to say, and I reckon she was right."

"But I really feel like I should try to explain—"

"Leave it." Her tone was so harsh, Alex involuntarily backed up a step. "Sorry, lass."

"It's all right." Cam's eyes were searching her face, so she planted on a smile, hoping it was convincing. "Really, it's fine. You're right—it's best if we just let it go." For now.

Cam went back over to the stove. "I'd better get back to it. Aunty Elspeth will be cross if I don't have everything back in trim by the time she turns up."

"Aunty Elspeth?"

"She really is my aunt—my great-aunt, actually."

"Is everyone in the whole village related to each other?"

"Huh. I never really thought about it, but I suppose you're right—except for the Foundation folk, of course. And we do have a few new families."

"That have only been here what, a hundred years?"

Cam looked up and smiled at her. "Something like that."

Alex sat down and finished her coffee while Cam worked.

After a while she put down her tools and sighed in frustration. "I've never seen the like. Been at this a solid hour or more, and I've yet to find a thing wrong with it. I'd swear everything was fine, except that Aunty Elspeth says that when she tried to turn it on first thing this morning, she couldn't get it to work for love nor money. Nor, for that matter, could I."

Alex got up and came over. "Maybe it was some kind of clog or kink somewhere and just by taking everything apart you got rid of the problem. Have you tried putting it all back together to see if it will work now?"

Cam started to reply—and from the look on her face, the response would have been a sarcastic one—but she stopped dead, obviously thinking over what Alex had said. "Why not? I'm blessed if I can think of anything else to try."

Cam went back to work with renewed energy. Alex got herself something to eat and by the time she was finished, so was Cam.

As Cam reached over to try the stove, Alex said, "Just a minute."

She picked up the teakettle, emptied it and refilled it with fresh water, then set it on a burner. "For luck," she said.

"Right. You do the honors. It was your idea, after all."

Alex turned on the burner and it worked perfectly. Her eyes met Cam's and they grinned at each other like they'd just won a prize. The look went on just a fraction too long. Cam turned away.

"Would you like a cup?" Alex said to the teapot as she measured out the leaves.

"Ta very much, but I've got to be getting on." Cam's voice was muffled, and Alex glanced over to see her with her head down, very busy stowing away her tools. She stood up, case in hand. "Tell Aunty Elspeth if this happens again, we may have to get someone in."

"Considering how upset you say she was that it broke in the first place, maybe I'll just let you be the one to mention that possibility. I'd hate to be responsible for giving her a catastastroke."

Cam chuckled. "Aunty Elspeth's tougher than you think. She's more likely to just toss the thing out of doors and cook in the fireplace."

"Is that even possible, or safe? It must be two hundred years old."

"And still in good working order—I make sure of it. Aunty Elspeth says there's nothing like an open fire for certain things."

"You don't say."

After Cam left, Alex poured herself some tea and sat drinking it, staring into the fireplace and imagining what you could create with it, if only you knew how.

❖

Fortunately the Dawson House cooker remained in working order, and there were no more indignant phone calls from Aunty Elspeth. And no more encounters with Alex, either, complete with offers to explain all about her and Rosamund, as if Cam needed, or wanted, to be told. Or to tell her how she was sorry but she really did *like* Cam, just not in that way, and could they still be friends. Or whatever it was she thought needed saying that Cam couldn't figure out right well on her own, thank you very much.

Of course, not seeing Alex didn't stop Cam from thinking about her all the time, wondering what she was doing, missing her, kicking herself for her own foolishness. But there was no help for any of that, was there?

At least work was all right. Just some easy jobs round the village, and a few past due accounts that needed chasing after. Things were going so well, in fact, that on Friday Cam decided to treat herself to a night out at her local. A pint or two and a friendly game of darts sounded like the perfect way to end the week.

When she got there, she discovered she was in luck. Vera was tending bar instead of her husband. Aside from being easy on the eyes, she was always good for a bit of fun. Cam had been practicing her chat-up skills on Vera since forever. And Vera, despite being at least a couple of decades older—not to mention resolutely straight and happily married—had taken it all in good part, never making her feel awkward or unwelcome even early on when she doubtless had far more enthusiasm than appeal.

As soon as she managed to make her way through the crowd to the bar, Vera brought over her usual. "Evening, love."

"Gorgeous as ever, Vera. Please tell me you've given Stan his marching orders and can finally make me the happiest woman on earth."

Vera grinned and gave her a friendly rap on the arm. "Clear off. Can't you see I've no time for your cheek?"

The bar really was quite busy, so Cam found a seat in a quiet corner. As she sipped her cider, she thought about those early days. Looking back, she suspected that she had borne a closer resemblance to a golden retriever puppy than the suave charmer of her teenage ambitions. She had to smile as she pictured her younger self, sauntering in with a casual slouch copied from some film star, trying her best to look and act confident, all the while secretly terrified that she was doing it all wrong and no girl was ever going to want her.

And here she was back again, almost full circle. Older certainly, and without the desperate need to rush down the road of life that had driven her then, all the way to London. And Rosamund. Painful memories began to surface but she pushed them away. She was definitely in no hurry now.

And in many ways that was a good thing. Bramfell suited her. The easy pace, the rhythm of a life that was still in touch with the land and the seasons, the beauty of the countryside that both stirred and soothed her, like the old songs that she loved. As much as she had enjoyed London, there had always been a sense just under the surface that something wasn't quite right, although it had been so overshadowed by all the excitement that she hadn't paid it much mind. She hadn't realized what she really needed, deep inside, until she found herself alone and in pain and far from home. As horrible as losing her mother had been, she was grateful to be back where she now knew for certain she belonged.

And yet she had apparently learned very little from that experience, because somehow she had managed to make the exact same mistake again. Not paying attention to what she was feeling, not realizing what it was she really wanted, needed. But this time, she had come to her senses too late. Alex was with someone else. That the someone was Rosamund was just salt in the wound.

Why had she been so blind? Thinking back, it should have been obvious what was happening between them—or had it been happening only to her? All those little moments, the accidental touches, the uncomfortable silences that seemed to mean something, could have been nothing at all to Alex.

And Alex had certainly had plenty to say about not liking the way Cam did things—or Cam herself, half the time. For her part, Cam had found herself opening up to Alex, sharing things that she rarely talked about with anyone. But what Cam had taken for a growing understanding between them, Alex might have seen as just friendly conversation, a way to pass the time.

Even their physical closeness, the way it had felt holding Alex in her arms, falling under her spell on the dance floor, could have meant little or nothing. After all, based on what she had seen that night outside the club in Leeds, Alex wasn't the least bit shy about acting on her passions. That she had never done anything remotely like that with Cam ought to be the clincher, surely—Alex just wasn't attracted to her.

That ought to make sense. Except that her gut was telling her something different. Well, not her gut, perhaps. Possibly something a bit lower down. And that might just be because she was lonely.

Wait—she wasn't lonely, was she? Was she?

True, she hadn't been with anyone for a while, but that hadn't seemed like a problem. Really, until she had started to recover a bit from losing her mum, she'd been in no fit state to be with anyone, and instinctively she'd known that. She had needed to be by herself for a time, to deal with the pain and learn how to be in the world in a different way.

But the worst of that had long since passed, and she still hadn't done much about finding someone. Someone who wasn't Rosamund. Losing her had been painful, but looking back it was clear that having her had hurt even more.

If she'd ever really had her at all. She had thought Rosamund was the love of her life, worth any sacrifice. But the more she thought about what happened, whatever their relationship had been, it wasn't that.

When she'd truly needed Rosamund, Rosamund had called her selfish. *Selfish.* She hadn't expected Rosamund to actually do anything to help take care of her mother. She had wanted Rosamund herself, for her to just be there. To come with her to Bramfell, to help her get through the worst thing she had ever had to face. Not forever. Just for a while, just until she could get her feet back under her.

But Rosamund had reacted as if Cam was demanding that she give up her entire life, and everything that mattered.

And just what had mattered so much? Rosamund hadn't spelled it out, but Cam knew. London, of course, and her posh friends, and the parties and clubs, and a hundred other things. Rosamund had actually offered her money. She said she'd pay to have Cam's mother put somewhere, tidied out of sight like a shabby bit of furniture you didn't want to show to visitors. Taken away from home to some cold, bare place where she could be seen to by strangers, because that would be easier. Easier for Rosamund, no doubt.

And when she had refused, trying to explain that what her mother needed now was her, the way she needed Rosamund, Rosamund had walked away—but not before laying into her right and proper, the cruel and bitter words cutting more deeply than any knife could have.

It wasn't so much what Rosamund had said, or even that she was so angry. After all, as time went by and Cam was able to think more clearly, she realized that in some ways she had hurt Rosamund. Since she was the one who left, it was she who was abandoning Rosamund, and not the other way around.

Of course, even knowing that didn't lessen the pain of being called stubborn, uncaring, cold, unfeeling, and all the other things Rosamund had thrown at her. Not least of which had been common, low class, ignorant, uneducated, and obvious—apparently that meant butch, a word Rosamund could never bring herself to say out loud. Not that Cam had ever denied being any of those things. They were honest descriptions, if harshly worded, and how could the truth be an insult? Cam knew who and what she was and had made peace with it long ago.

No, it was the way Rosamund had flung the words at her, like drops of poison she wanted to burn into Cam's skin. It was the nastiness of it, the desire to injure and damage her, that had taken everything that had ever existed between them and made it into a lie. Rosamund didn't actually say, *I never loved you.* She didn't have to.

That's what had finally turned Cam's heart to ashes—realizing that she had given herself body and soul to something that had never been real.

It had taken a long, long time to recover from that, but she'd been so certain that she was past all of it. That she was ready to move on, to try again, to welcome someone into her life. It was just that she wasn't in any great hurry. When the time was right, when the right woman turned up, it would happen.

Except that the right woman had finally come along, and it hadn't. And she had no one to blame for that but herself.

Staring down at her now empty glass, she decided she wanted another. Getting to her feet, she looked around. The room was full of people—people she had known all her life. Laughing and joking, or just sitting quietly together, mostly groups of three or four, with a few courting couples here and there. She was the only one on her own. Of course, she could easily have joined up with some of the others, but just at the moment that held less than no appeal.

Drinking alone didn't sound much better. She'd never been one to look for her solutions in the bottom of a glass. Maybe she should just go home and try to get some sleep. At least that way she could forget about everything for a while—especially Alex.

As if she had conjured her up, the door from the restaurant side opened, and there she was. So pretty. Smiling at her companion— Rosamund, of course. They were arm in arm and both looked happy. Obviously they had just enjoyed a pleasant meal and now were moving on to the next stage of their evening. They paused in the doorway, surveying the room as if looking for a place to sit.

Cam knew she should do something other than just stand there staring at them, but she felt frozen. Both of them spotted her at almost the same time. Rosamund's smile grew wider, a bit spiteful, but Cam didn't waste more than a fraction of a moment on her. Alex, on the other hand, captured and held her gaze.

Cam felt her heart race and her stomach flip-flop. Seeing Alex like this, on top of everything else, something inside of her snapped. She wanted to rush over and grab hold of her, tell her something, that she had made a mistake, that she was sorry, if only Alex would listen, would just give her a chance. In front of Rosamund, in front of everybody—it didn't matter so long as she said yes.

Alex's smile disappeared in an instant. She looked stricken, almost horrified. Cam couldn't imagine what she had done to put that look on Alex's face. Then Alex turned away, saying something to Rosamund, and they left.

Cam sat back down, stunned. Whatever had just happened, it was clear that Alex wanted nothing to do with her. Pain rolled through her like a wave. Clearly she had to stay as far from Alex as possible and hope that, in time, the need and the hurt would both go away.

❖

Alex walked along, only half listening to Rosamund's chatter. She kept seeing the look on Cam's face, the pain and the longing as she stared at her and Rosamund together. Nicola was absolutely right. Not only had Rosamund broken Cam's heart, but she was clearly still so deeply wounded that just the sight of Rosamund with someone else was enough to tear her apart, so badly that she couldn't even try to hide it.

Cam had looked like she was about two seconds away from rushing over and pouring out her soul, begging Rosamund to take her back, in spite of all the people around, in spite of Alex herself standing right there. *Face it. Cam is still in love with her. You never had a chance.*

How ridiculous her little twinges of jealousy about Cam and Nicola seemed, now that she knew the truth. Everything finally made sense. The way Cam had seemed interested in her, but never followed through. She was so naturally charming, she probably flirted with every woman she met. It didn't mean a thing.

And the times Cam had been so angry, like that time after the dance. Alex remembered that she had been talking about Rosamund, about dancing with her, about Nicola's crush on her. Talking and talking and talking, and every word must have been like nails on a chalkboard. No wonder Cam had lost her temper. Or the other morning when she had tried to apologize, and Cam had just about bitten her head off for even going near the subject.

Seeing her with Rosamund must be torture, and Alex hated the thought of what she was doing to Cam. Whatever else might be going on, she felt connected to Cam in a different way than with most people. She really liked her—despite her many shortcomings—and she hated, hated, hated that she was hurting her. If just seeing her and Rosamund standing together in the pub had put that look on her face, watching them kissing that night must have just about killed her.

Oh sweet Goddess, Cam probably thought she and Rosamund were already sleeping together. She came to a dead stop, a feeling of dread coursing through her. Before she could try to analyze exactly what it meant, Rosamund cleared her throat loudly, reclaiming her attention.

"You know, darling, for the past five minutes I've been reciting nursery rhymes, just to see if you would notice. A person could begin to get just the teensiest bit peeved, you know."

"Oh, Rosamund, I'm so sorry."

"Did I do something to upset you? Did something happen over dinner, or perhaps afterward?"

She didn't look or sound angry. If anything, the look on her face was one of amusement.

"No, no. Absolutely not. I'm having a lovely time. I've just got a lot on my mind, I guess."

"Hmm. Well, all I can say is that I hope one of the things you've got on your mind is me."

"Oh, definitely. Believe me." She smiled, trying hard to recapture the way she had felt earlier sitting in the restaurant, enjoying the plain but delicious food and the pleasure of being in Rosamund's company.

"Well, that's certainly a relief. Come on, darling, I can't wait to get you home." Laughing, Rosamund took hold of Alex's arm and began rushing along, not a great idea in darkness even on the sidewalk, and an even worse idea once they turned off onto the drive that led up to Highgate Hall. Fortunately, the steepness of the incline took its toll even on Rosamund's high spirits, and they eventually settled down to a more sedate pace.

As they made their way across the grounds, headed for the cottage that was one of the perks of Rosamund's job, Alex tried to figure out what was wrong with her. She was strolling in the moonlight with a captivating, beautiful woman who gave every indication of being seriously interested in her, and not just platonically. Rosamund had been dropping not very subtle hints all evening, and now the woman was practically dragging her off to bed.

Alex should have been happy—hell, she should have been ecstatic. So why did she have a lump of lead in the pit of her stomach? Maybe it was nerves. Rosamund was definitely out of her league.

Much too soon to suit Alex, they arrived at their destination. Rosamund let go of Alex's arm to get out her keys. She opened the door but didn't switch on a light, taking Alex's hand to draw her inside.

"Wait, Rosamund." Alex stayed where she was, standing on the threshold.

"But, darling, I've been waiting." She stepped close to Alex and touched the index finger of her free hand to Alex's chin. "All evening," she purred, drawing her finger slowly down the center of Alex's throat, pausing at the notch in her collarbone to trace a small circle before slipping lower, stopping at the last spot of bare skin above the V where her shirt was buttoned. "Haven't we both waited long enough?"

Alex tried to say something, but all that came out was a very unsexy squeak, mostly because of what Rosamund was doing with her finger, slipping it just under the edge of her shirt and sliding it back and forth inside the fabric over the tops of her breasts.

Alex put her hand over Rosamund's and moved it away, holding it down by her side. "Rosamund, I'm sorry. I just don't think this is a good idea. Not yet."

"Why ever not? We're both adults, and it's not as if either of us is involved with anybody else. We don't have to think of anything but our own pleasure."

Alex didn't answer, trying to think of a way to explain about Cam.

"Right, darling?" Rosamund was gazing at her wide-eyed, her innocent expression tinged with just a hint of concern.

"It's complicated."

"What do you mean?"

Alex realized there was no way she could say anything. She couldn't talk about her concern for Cam without bringing up what she knew about Cam's own feelings, and there was no way she would share any of that with Rosamund. It would be an enormous betrayal. But Rosamund deserved some sort of explanation. So she'd just have to tell her the other part of the truth, as embarrassing as it was.

"I know it sounds stupid, but I'm scared. I don't have a lot of, well, experience. I'm afraid you'll be disappointed."

Rosamund laughed. "Is that all that's worrying you? I've got the perfect cure for that—a little champers, a bit of slow dancing. Soon you'll be so relaxed you'll just float. Leave everything else to me. I'll be more than happy to take care of it, believe me."

"I don't think champagne would be a good idea on top of the wine we had with dinner."

"Darling, you can't be serious. You Americans can be so prim about the strangest things. There's no harm in a glass of champagne. Or several glasses, for that matter."

"It's not that—I just think I've had enough for one night. Any more will put me right to sleep. And that wouldn't be fair to you. Anyway, I think it's best if I go home."

"I can't believe this. You're really turning me down. I'm so disappointed." Rosamund was pouting, but her eyes were dancing. "Say you'll make it up to me, darling."

"Oh yes. Yes, I will. I promise. I just think I need a little time. Like I said, I'm pretty new at all this."

"Ooh—if there's one thing I love, it's a challenge."

She leaned over and kissed Alex, long and slow, her tongue probing languidly. Alex felt the heat of it all through her. Just as she was seriously considering changing her mind, Rosamund pulled away.

"That's to give you something to think about in the meanwhile. Until next time, darling." She darted inside and closed the door. Alex heard her laughing.

Well, that went well.

Alex turned away and started trudging home.

CHAPTER THIRTEEN

Monday morning brought with it another breakdown at Dawson House—the washing machine this time. Cam walked round to the back entrance, tool case in hand and a false smile planted on her face, ready, she hoped, to face Alex. What she wanted was to whip in, do the job, and whip out again with a minimum of fuss. What she got when she stepped into the kitchen, however, was a good half a stone of furry body, paws, and tail coming down on her head from the shelf above the door.

Fortunately, the wretched animal somehow had sense enough to keep its claws in during the rumpus that followed, so Cam came through without any major damage or important bits missing, and so did the cat—at least as far as she could tell before it ran off. Of course her case burst open when she dropped it to pull the beast off her, so her tools ended up all over the room, and Alex, who had been standing about in the kitchen talking Aunty Elspeth's ear off instead of being off wherever it was she was supposed to be, doing whatever it was she was supposed to be doing, had insisted on helping pick them up.

That would have been all right, probably, only Alex insisted on trying to put them away as well, which meant that the whole blasted process took twice as long as it should have, since Cam ended up having to undo most of Alex's help. Aunty Elspeth meanwhile stood by pointing out items they had missed. For some reason, she seemed to find the whole thing vastly amusing. Especially when Cam and Alex managed to bump heads under the kitchen table.

What with the delay and all, she wasn't able to finish the repair before dinnertime—not that there was actually anything to repair, just as she had suspected. Aunty Elspeth insisted on feeding her along with Alex. Not that Cam didn't appreciate her kindness—or her cooking—but the last thing she wanted was to sit across from Alex trying to make small talk, something she wasn't much good for at the best of times. Fortunately, she was spared the worst of it when her aunt sat down with them for a cup of tea and a nice little chat, as she called it.

Things were still rather awkward, though, since Cam really wasn't up to making conversation and it seemed Alex wasn't either. At least Aunty Elspeth had plenty to say about the weather and the harvest and the various ailments of assorted family members, so the meal didn't suffer from long stretches of silence. Cam knew she really should be doing more to hold up her end of things, but she spent most of the time looking down at her food, stealing an occasional glance at Alex's dark head bent over her own plate.

Unfortunately, during one of those times Alex happened to look up, and before Cam could look away, their gazes locked. Those lovely blue eyes were clouded with concern, but Cam couldn't properly read her expression before Alex glanced down again. At least Alex didn't look like she was angry at her.

When the meal was finally over, she gratefully escaped to finish her work. When she walked back into the kitchen, Aunty Elspeth wasn't there, but Alex was, still sitting at the table, staring into space and turning her teacup round and round in its saucer. She looked sad.

For a moment, Cam thought about trying to say something to her—not the desperate pleading she had almost given way to in the pub, but something—but then Aunty Elspeth came back and the moment was lost.

She'd have a try some other time. After all, she could hardly mess things up between them worse than they already were, could she, and at least she'd not have given up without even trying. The thought made her feel considerably better. And even if she made a right fool of herself in the process, well, Alex was worth it, wasn't she?

Cam realized she'd been staring at Alex for a while, and now Aunty Elspeth was staring at her. But instead of making any sort of comment, Aunty Elspeth said, "All quiet on the western front, is it?"

"Aye. I reckon it should be fine now, just like the cooker. But if it's not, or anything else gives you trouble, you'll have to get on to Uncle Eric or one of the lads from Brewer's, at least for the next few days. I'm off to Scarborough."

She looked at Alex, who was now staring at her intently, but it was Aunty Elspeth who responded.

"Oh? Left it a bit late for a seaside holiday, haven't you? Whole place will be nothing but tourists."

"I won't be on holiday, just helping out a mate on a big job. Paying back a favor. I should be home Saturday, or perhaps Friday if it goes well. I'll ring once I'm back, or I'll drop round."

"See that you do. Our Eric's all right for simple repairs, but I don't fancy letting him muck about with anything complicated, let alone that gormless lot from Brewer's."

Cam gave her a kiss on the cheek. "Cheers, Aunty."

Alex said, "Have a safe trip." Her voice had regained a little of its usual sparkle, and her smile was as sweet as ever.

Cam decided she wasn't going to wait. She'd talk to Alex as soon as she got home from Scarborough. Hopefully by then she'd have figured out what on earth to say. She smiled back at Alex. "Ta, I'm off, then."

Alex watched the door close behind Cam, glad she had finally left. This had not been the most comfortable morning she had ever spent, having Cam here but not being able to talk to her. Not that Alex had any idea what she would have said to her. "I'm planning to sleep with the woman you love, so please accept my condolences"? Still, she wished she could have at least tried.

That moment at the table when their eyes met, what she had seen in Cam's face had been awful. It had made her want to go over and hug her—Mrs. Tate's presence notwithstanding—and tell her how sorry she was, how she wished she could make everything all right between them, how much she cared about her. All of which would doubtless have done less than no good. Very likely it would have just made her angry.

Of course, Cam had looked a bit more like her old self when she was talking about her trip. Even if it was for work and not a vacation, she seemed to be looking forward to it. Maybe being away would help her. At least there'd be no possibility of her bumping into Alex and Rosamund for a few days, and Alex wouldn't have to worry about tormenting Cam.

All in all, it was probably just as well that Cam was going to be gone for a while—and definitely good that she was going to be away over Thursday night. Rosamund, ever persistent, had talked her into another date and hadn't been willing to wait for the weekend, so they had agreed on Thursday. Rosamund had also been pretty clear that she had her sights set on breakfast as well as dinner.

Alex supposed she should find all this attention hugely flattering, but mostly she just found it puzzling. Women, let alone women like Rosamund, never pursued her. She couldn't imagine what it was about her that drew Rosamund so intently. Well, she had said she liked a challenge, so maybe that was it.

Besides, did it really matter? Rosamund wasn't in love with her, any more than she was with Rosamund. This was a fling, not a romance, or even a grand passion. It was probably better that way anyway—fewer complications, and no heavy hearts when she and Rosamund inevitably went their separate ways, returning to the places where they really belonged. Back to reality, after a brief but pleasant dream.

When she thought about it that way, it didn't really make sense for her to keep taking things slowly with Rosamund. Besides, it wouldn't make Cam feel any better if she waited a day, or a week, or a month. Cam probably thought they were already lovers, so really, what was the point?

And who had any guarantee of the future anyway? Happiness postponed could easily turn into happiness missed—perhaps forever. She thought about Artemisia, bereft by Lady Melissa's death, alone for all those years.

She'd decided: after their dinner on Thursday, she would invite Rosamund to come back here to Dawson House. For the night. Then she got up and headed for the study. Time to get some actual work done.

It seemed to take a lot longer than four days to get there, but Thursday evening finally arrived. Alex had considered making dinner for Rosamund but ultimately decided against it. She was nervous enough to begin with, and had been having trouble concentrating for days. It certainly wouldn't help matters if she made some major goof during the meal prep.

On the other hand, going out to eat instead of cooking dinner would have its own drawbacks. Even if everything went reasonably well during the meal, Alex figured there was too much chance of her getting cold feet during the transition between the restaurant and home. Probably the best option would be to pick up something and bring it back to eat at Dawson House. Then if things went according to plan, it would be easy enough to just go upstairs.

Only one small problem. Somehow she didn't think champagne-loving Rosamund would respond well to a suggestion that they pop round to the takeaway. Well, if she was too offended, Alex would just have to think of something else.

In the event, however, Rosamund surprised her. Perhaps it was the way Alex explained her idea, starting by stressing how much fun it could be for Rosamund to try something new for a change, something out of the ordinary for her. Fortunately Bramfell boasted several carryouts that were a step or two up from a basic chippy, so Alex was able to suggest something that wouldn't unduly strain Rosamund's refined sensibilities.

Then she clinched things by mentioning how cozy it would be eating at Dawson House with just the two of them alone. If the look on Rosamund's face was anything to go by, they might not even make it through dinner.

As it happened, they made it to and from the restaurant in record time, but once they got back to Dawson House, things didn't go quite so smoothly. For some reason, Alex couldn't get her key to work on the front door, so she left a slightly less than pleased Rosamund standing there in the dark while she stumbled around to try the back door. This was a little tricky because she was carrying both their dinners, since Rosamund had made it clear that, while she might have to stand there waiting in the dark being attacked by insects, she certainly wasn't going to do it while holding a hot, greasy sack.

Of course, having both hands full made it somewhat harder for Alex to manage when she discovered that, despite the fact that the back door hardly ever shut properly and could usually be opened with a simple push, this time—naturally—it was firmly latched.

Juggling two very full bags while trying to operate the key at the same time didn't work very well, so Alex set the food down. However, her next attempts were no more successful, even though she turned the key slowly and carefully each time. She was starting to wonder whether she had the right key.

There were all sorts of keys lying around Dawson House, the majority of which Alex had never seen used. Most of them looked pretty old, and she had no idea if any of them even matched an existing lock, rather than some ancient door that had been replaced back when England was still being ruled by the House of Hanover.

Alex had a hard time seeing how she could have ended up with the wrong key, though, because hers was on a cord. Usually she wore it around her neck, and even when she didn't, she was hardly likely to mistake it for some other random key. Besides, she had been wearing hers all day today and she was sure she hadn't ever taken it off. Well, pretty sure. Today had been a little stressful.

She tried again, still without success. In frustration, she pounded on the door with her fist. "Open up, damn you!"

She heard something click. Maybe the door was actually unlocked but stuck. She tried rattling the door. "I said, open."

Finally she kicked it. "Will you open already, for Pete's sake?"

There was another clicking sound and the door swung ajar, just a fraction but that was plenty. Alex hit the light switch, reached down, and grabbed the food. She dumped it on the kitchen table as she raced by, running down the hall to pull the front door wide open.

Rosamund did not look happy. She didn't say a single word, just stalked past Alex into the hall. As Alex closed the door, Rosamund turned around to face her.

"Well?"

"Uh, I'm sorry, Rosamund."

"Of course you are. What I meant was, are you just going to stand there staring at me, or are we going to eat? I'm starving."

"The food is in the kitchen."

"Well, fetch it then. Where's the dining room?"

"There isn't one. We're going to eat in the kitchen."

Rosamund rolled her eyes and gave an exasperated sigh. "Then where is the kitchen?"

"This way, Rosamund."

Somewhere upstairs, a door slammed. "What the bloody hell was that? I thought you said we'd be alone."

"We are. That just happens sometimes. Doors slamming, or swinging open. It's an old house."

"How simply marvelous."

When they reached the kitchen, Rosamund sat at the table and crossed her arms, making no attempt to help as Alex dished out the food. Alex suddenly realized she didn't have anything to offer Rosamund to drink. Despite all her nervous planning, she had forgotten all about getting something special, like a bottle of wine. When she confessed her lack of foresight, Rosamund just shook her head. Alex got them both glasses of water and sat down.

Of course by now the food was barely lukewarm. Alex offered to heat it up, but when Rosamund discovered that would mean twenty minutes in the oven rather than twenty seconds in the microwave, she stiffly declined.

They ate in silence. Alex had absolutely no appetite and mostly pushed her food around on her plate. Finally Rosamund put down her fork.

"Well, darling, I must say this wasn't one of your better ideas." She said it with a smile but the tone made Alex wince. "I think perhaps you should try making it up to me."

Her voice was slightly more pleasant, and maybe she intended to sound flirtatious, but it came across a lot more like a demand. Alex sighed and looked away, trying to remind herself that Rosamund had doubtless been looking forward to this date as much as she had, and must be really disappointed that their evening had so far featured more discomfort than romance. After all, she was pretty disappointed herself.

However, if Rosamund had managed to roll with the punches a bit more, this all could have turned into a shared adventure instead of a source of misery and friction. Alex thought about standing in the pouring rain, absolutely soaked to the skin, while Cam made jokes about predatory elves, her hazel eyes twinkling.

Oh, so not good thinking about Cam right now.

She felt a touch and looked down at Rosamund's hand on her arm. Not so long ago, the excitement of the contact would have shot right through her, but just at the moment she didn't feel anything at all.

"I'm sorry, darling." Alex looked up. Rosamund did look contrite. "I really didn't mean to be sharp with you. It's just that I've been looking forward to this evening for so long. Say you'll forgive me."

"Of course, Rosamund. Let's just go upstairs."

"Oh yes, darling. Please."

Alex took Rosamund by the hand and led her to the staircase. As they reached the top of the stairs, Rosamund paused and shuddered. "Ooh, what a simply ghastly draft! I swear, darling, I don't know how you can stand living in this place. It's positively medieval."

Alex didn't bother to reply. When they reached the doorway of her bedroom, she stopped and turned to face Rosamund. "Kiss me. Maybe that will help."

Rosamund didn't waste any time on subtlety. In an instant her mouth was on Alex's, her tongue probing and demanding. Her hands roamed over Alex's back and shoulders, then lower to clasp her bottom, holding her in place while she ground her pelvis against Alex's.

And it was working. Alex felt her excitement rising as Rosamund stepped forward, moving them both backward into the room. Alex felt the back of her knees hit the edge of her bed. She let herself slip backward as Rosamund leaned forward, easing them both down.

As Rosamund's weight pressed her flat, Alex's back came down squarely on top of a large lump. A screeching, squalling, fur-covered lump. Rosamund instantly let go of her and sprang away, screaming, as Alex rolled to one side and leaped up.

Rosamund was out in the hall now, still screaming. And Grace was still on the bed, howling and hissing, her claws fully extended. Her back was arched and all her fur stood out. Her ears were pressed flat to her skull and her mouth was wide open, her lips drawn back and all her teeth on full display. In the dim light from the hallway, her eyes glowed like something out of a cheap horror movie.

At first Alex was too terrified to move, afraid that the moment she did, Grace would attack her. But then she realized that Grace wasn't even looking at her. All her attention was focused on Rosamund.

And Rosamund knew it. Her screams had degenerated into whimpering as she slowly backed away, her arms wrapped around her shaking body.

Keeping a wary eye on Grace, Alex eased her way out of the room, pulling the door closed as she did so. She rushed over to Rosamund and tried to put her arms around her, but Rosamund pushed her away. Before Alex could do or say anything else, Rosamund raced down the stairs. Alex heard the front door slam behind her as she ran out.

For a moment, Alex just stood there stunned. She had never seen Grace act like this. Hell, she had never seen any cat act like this, ever. Maybe she was sick. Oh my God, maybe it was rabies. But they didn't have rabies in England, did they?

She walked over and put her ear to the door. Grace had stopped howling. In fact, she could hear nothing at all—no sounds, no movement.

She turned around, leaning her back against the door as she tried to think. What was she going to do? She should call someone. There was probably some kind of animal control service she could call, but she had no idea what they'd do to Grace. Maybe a vet?

She knew who she really wanted to call. The one person she couldn't, because she wasn't here. Cam was in Scarborough.

She let herself slide down until she was sitting on the floor, her back against the door. She started to cry. After a while she wiped her eyes with the back of her hand and tried to pull herself together. This wasn't helping.

All of a sudden she felt something poking at her butt and she shifted away, squealing in alarm. She looked down and sure enough, there was a paw sticking under the door, sliding around as if trying to find her again. If Alex hadn't known better, she would have assumed Grace was playing. Then the paw pulled back inside and she heard what sounded a lot like Grace scratching the floorboards, the way she did when she ended up on the wrong side of a closed door and she wanted you to do your job and open it for her.

A heart-rending meow rang out, proclaiming its piteous tale of a pathetic, suffering creature heartlessly neglected by cruel, uncaring humans. In other words, Grace sounded absolutely fine. And 100 percent normal.

Alex knew she shouldn't open the door. She should do things the way you were supposed to, let them take Grace away to be caged up and poked and prodded and maybe even put down. But she just couldn't do that. Not to Grace.

Muttering "What's a little rabies between friends?" she eased the door open a fraction, prepared to slam it shut at the first sign of Satan Was a Feline. But Grace just sniffed delicately at the opening and looked up at her, as if puzzled. Alex opened the door all the way and Grace strolled calmly out into the hallway.

Alex walked into her room and flopped down on the bed. She'd just take a minute to recover before she went downstairs to call Rosamund and make sure she was okay. Alex rolled over and curled up on her side. A moment later, Grace leaped up onto the bed and lay down next to her, kneading Alex's belly a few times before she settled. Alex stroked Grace's head, listening to her purr. Within minutes, she was asleep.

CHAPTER FOURTEEN

Friday was pretty much a lost cause. Fortunately Alex woke up early enough to clean up the kitchen before Mrs. Tate arrived, but that was about the only thing that went well. She made several attempts to contact Rosamund, none of them successful, so she left messages at all her numbers, hoping at least one would get through.

Then she called Nicola, whose response to Alex's tale of woe was rather disconcerting. She seemed to find the whole thing hilarious, and although at first she made appropriately sympathetic noises when Alex tried to explain how upset she had been about Grace, Nicola proceeded to spoil it by interrupting.

"Wait, you let Rosamund leave, and you didn't go after her, because you had to stay and take care of Grace?"

"She ran out so fast I couldn't possibly have caught up with her. And Grace really did need me."

"Oh, my goodness. The lady or the tiger? My cat—or my girlfriend!" She dissolved into a fit of the giggles.

"That's not fair. I was concerned about Rosamund as well," said Alex.

"Oh, obviously *as well*. That's my point." Another giggle.

"You know what I mean. It's just that Grace was an emergency and I was so worried and…oh, never mind."

Nicola then informed Alex that Rosamund had called in sick that morning but had not sounded particularly traumatized—if anything, she sounded angry. She had also left strict instructions not to be disturbed by anyone for any reason and had mentioned Alex specifically, which had puzzled Nicola at the time but now made perfect sense.

After finally getting Nicola off the phone, Alex went in search of the other person she needed to talk to. As she neared the kitchen, she heard Mrs. Tate say to someone, "It's no good, you know. She isn't back yet. Best to save your antics for another time and let me get on with my work."

But when she walked in, Mrs. Tate was alone.

"Who were you talking to just now?"

"Oh, nobody. The oven wasn't heating properly. But it's fine now."

"You know, I find it helps to talk to machines as well. For me it usually works best on printers and photocopiers. It seems to keep them from jamming."

Unlike Nicola, Mrs. Tate did not find her heavily edited account of the events of the previous evening in the least amusing, if her expression was anything to go by. She made no comment, however, beyond tersely thanking Alex for letting her know about Grace.

"I've always said that animal is far more trouble than she's worth. Still, I can't bear to see any creature suffer if it can be helped. I'll keep my eye on her." She concluded by looking pointedly at the mantel clock, so Alex left her to her work and tried to get something accomplished herself.

That, of course, turned out to be a total waste of time. The events of the previous night kept chasing each other around and around in her head. Finally she gave up and went for a good long hike across the moors, which didn't provide any solutions but at least left her with a bit of appetite for supper and enough restored calm to get some sleep afterward.

Saturday started out as mostly a repeat of Friday, except that Alex left a message only at Rosamund's office number and didn't try Nicola at all. She went for another long walk between breakfast and lunch, and in the afternoon found she was able to focus on her work for the first time in days, even when Grace turned up to help her by walking all over her desk. She seemed to be perfectly fine but didn't stay long—almost as if Alex was the one who had needed checking on.

In fact, as the hours went by, Alex grew so absorbed in what she was doing that she almost didn't register the knocking at the front door. She was overwhelmed with a sense of dread. It had to be Rosamund, come to yell at her—although showing up on the doorstep didn't quite seem her style.

The knocking sounded again. Well, no sense trying to put it off. Rosamund's temper wasn't going to get any better by her being made to wait.

Just before she pulled the door open, Alex stiffened her spine and drew a deep breath in, only to let it out in a gasp of joy when she saw who it actually was.

Cam stood there on the doorstep holding a grocery bag in her arms, the early evening light touching her hair with a golden glow. She was smiling, a little tentatively—almost shyly.

Alex gave her a big hug, grocery bag and all, and dragged her inside. "You have no idea how much I've missed you."

The front door swung closed with a decided clank.

Cam was gratified by the big welcome, but so surprised that she didn't even get a chance to properly enjoy the hug before Alex dropped her arms and took a step back—though only a little one, she was pleased to note. Just seeing Alex standing there, eyes alight with happiness, made her feel warm inside. For the first time in far too long, Cam felt herself settle. Everything was all right now.

"I've only been gone three days. What would you do if I were away for a week?"

"Pine away and die, of course." Alex grinned at her.

Cam knew she was joking, but that didn't stop the little zing in her stomach. "Then let's hope it doesn't come to that. I'd hate to be responsible." Cam spoke lightly, but as she said the words she realized she meant them absolutely. Never, never did she want any harm to come to Alex, least of all through anything to do with Cam herself. Of course she never would hurt anyone if she could help it, but this felt different—something deep and lasting, like a vow.

Alex led the way back to the kitchen. Cam had come prepared with what she hoped was a plausible excuse for dropping by—several, in fact—but found she didn't need one. Alex seemed to accept her presence as perfectly natural, and in the bustle of dealing with the food Cam had brought they fell into easy conversation. So far, so good.

"Why did you bring all this over?" Alex had both hands in the sack, doing more rummaging than unpacking. "Did Mrs. Tate ask you to go shopping?"

Anxious not to have her surprise spoiled by overeager exploration, Cam held out a hand. "No, she didn't." Just as she hoped, Alex responded to the unspoken request by getting down to business, pulling things out and passing them to her, starting with the milk bottle.

"I had a fancy for some proper Yorkshire grub, is all. You know how it is, cooking for yourself—you always make too much, and end up eating whatever it is for days on end until you're sick of the sight of it."

Alex paused, an onion in each hand. "Wait—you cook?"

"I think I ought to be slightly offended by that remark. You know, just because I'm beautiful doesn't mean I can't boil water."

Alex threw first one onion at her, then the other, both of which she caught easily. When Alex followed with a third, she bobbled all of them for a moment before getting them under control. She juggled for a while, grinning at Alex before tossing all three of them back at her, one right after the other.

Alex caught them, but just barely, dropping them onto the counter with more speed than grace. "Quite the Renaissance woman, aren't you? You juggle, you cook, you dance, you recite poetry, you can fix things, you're really good at scattering random objects all over the place—"

"Ooh, now I'm blushing."

"Quiet, you." Alex kept unpacking as she talked, and Cam started getting out mixing bowls and pans. "You sing like an angel. You really do, you know. How did you learn?"

"Mum taught me. Said she'd learned the songs from her gran, and I should keep them safe and pass them on."

"With all those sterling qualities, it's a wonder some woman hasn't snapped you up long ago." Her smile collapsed. "Oh." She put down the carton of eggs she was holding. "Cam, I'm sorry. Listen, Nicola told me about…that is, I really didn't know that you and Ro—"

"Nicola should keep her nose out of what doesn't concern her." Cam looked down at her hands, which were clenched on the edge of the counter, the knuckles white.

"She was only trying to help. I just wish…anyway, I'm sorry." She put her hand on top of Cam's fist and gently tugged at it. Cam loosened her grip and let Alex take hold of her hand. She turned to look at Alex. Her temper vanished in the shock of seeing Alex's eyes swimming with tears.

"Cam, I never, ever meant to hurt you. When I see the pain on your face, it just kills me, knowing I'm the one that put it there." Tears spilled over and rolled down her cheeks.

"What's all this, eh?" Cam carefully, tenderly, brushed away a tear. "We can't have all this salt water about. It'll ruin the food."

It was a pathetically feeble attempt at a joke, but Alex smiled anyway. She let go of Cam's hand and turned back to the sack of food, clearing her throat.

"So, what exactly are we having for dinner, anyway?"

"Don't go all posh on me. Dinner's what folk eat at midday."

"Yeah, yeah. What exactly are we having for the evening meal?" She took out the flour and set it on the counter next to the milk. "Something good, I hope."

"Only the best thing on the planet, Toad in the Hole."

"Please tell me no amphibians will be harmed in the preparation of our meal," Alex quipped. She'd seen it on menus but never tasted it herself.

"Ha-ha. Yorkshire pudding and sausages. Proper English ones, not that spicy rubbish."

"Oh, I love Yorkshire pudding, but I've only ever had it with roast beef. Which goes in the pan first, the batter or the sausages?"

"Neither. The pan needs to be smoking hot when you clap in the sausages and pour the batter over, but first the batter needs to sit awhile."

"How long?"

"At least thirty minutes or so, but the longer the better, Mum always said."

"Okay, so what do we do while we wait? Make the gravy?"

"We can do that while the pudding cooks." She grinned mischievously. "I've something better in mind."

Cam reached deep into the bottom of the bag and pulled out a DVD.

"You didn't! *Now, Voyager*? I can't believe it. I thought you said you couldn't bear the thought of watching it."

"I reckoned it was high time I faced up to a few things, and I thought I'd start with this."

"All I can say is, I'm honored that you decided to share the moment with me. But where can we watch it? I don't usually watch TV, but I think there's one in Mrs. Tate's room. I don't know if there's a DVD player, though."

"There is—I set it up myself."

There was only the one easy chair in Mrs. Tate's room, not that Alex had ever seen Mrs. Tate using it, since taking it easy was apparently not something she believed in, and Cam insisted that Alex sit there. Cam brought in one of the kitchen chairs for herself and set it beside Alex's seat, then started the movie and turned off the overhead light.

Two hours later, they were holding hands and Alex, at least, had to wipe her eyes. She cast a sidelong glance at Cam, whose own eyes were suspiciously moist.

"What are you looking at?" Cam said, letting go of Alex's hand. "Only silly folk cry over soppy films."

"Humph. It's just as well you didn't bring *Dark Victory*, then. You could have done an even better job of showing me how you don't cry over sappy movies." In a mock dudgeon, she got up and flounced into the kitchen.

Cam was right behind her, falling all over herself trying to apologize.

"I'm not really mad, silly. It's just that you're so funny when you try to act all tough. It's really cute." Cam looked a little stunned. Alex smiled at her. "Now, what do we need to do with this batter?"

Half an hour later, *tea* was ready. As they were dishing out the food, Cam cut a tiny piece of the main course and speared it with a fork. She blew on it carefully. When she finished, she stepped closer. Alex reached for the fork.

"No, lass. Open your mouth."

Something in her tone shot through Alex all the way down to her toes. She stood there just looking at Cam for a moment while Cam gazed back at her. Her eyes looked enormous.

Alex parted her lips and very slowly, very gently, Cam slipped the food into her mouth. Alex closed her lips, offering just enough resistance to keep hold of the morsel as Cam eased the fork back out. Never taking her eyes from Cam's, Alex carefully nibbled the food, rolling it around with her tongue as if sampling a fine wine before she finally swallowed it. It was probably delicious, but she couldn't even taste it. All she was aware of was Cam.

Cam set the fork down, her gaze locked with Alex's. Stepping closer, she took Alex's face between her two hands, as delicately as if she were made of spun glass. Then she brushed her lips softly against Alex's. Once, then a second time.

When Cam pulled away just a bit, putting a tiny fraction of air between them, Alex made a little sound of protest and reached for her, grabbing Cam by the back of the head with both hands and pulling her in for another kiss, a lingering one this time.

She fisted her hands in Cam's hair—silk—as she kissed and kissed her, their lips gently mingling and caressing. But it wasn't enough. It wasn't nearly enough. She slid her tongue along the lush inner edge of Cam's lower lip, tracing back and forth until Cam opened for her. Slipping her tongue inside, she began to explore, shivering at the pleasure of Cam's heat. She pressed herself against Cam, pushing her into the counter. She couldn't get close enough. She couldn't get deep enough.

Cam slipped her fingers through Alex's curls—so soft, softer even than she had imagined they would be, holding Alex's head with gentle firmness as Alex's tongue danced in her mouth. She wanted more. She needed more.

She let her own tongue dance back, playing with Alex's for a while before thrusting into Alex's mouth. Alex moaned and opened wider, crushing her whole body against Cam's as the kiss went on and on and on.

From somewhere in the distance, the sound of an animal yowling intruded itself into her brain.

"Really, darling, I thought you had better taste." Cam froze at the harsh, mocking, all-too-familiar voice.

Alex broke off the kiss and whirled around.

Cam looked up. There was Rosamund, standing with her arms crossed just inside the back door. Cam froze, too stunned to speak.

"Rosamund—what the hell?" Alex had crossed her own arms and positioned herself in front of Cam, as if protecting her.

"Not exactly the welcome I was hoping for, Alex darling. Although somehow I can't say I'm surprised." She looked past Alex, addressing Cam. "I should have known when I saw that van of yours out front. I suppose this is your idea of revenge. It wasn't enough for you to leave me the way you did, just because I wouldn't do what you wanted? No, even after all these years, you've got to try to ruin my happiness. You make me sick."

Cam tried to say something but could manage only a strangled sound.

"Just how long has this been going on, anyway?"

"There's nothing going on, Rosamund," Alex answered.

Cam flinched. Nothing?

Alex uncrossed her arms. "Look, I know you're upset." Her tone was calmer now. "We need to talk, but this isn't really a good time."

"Oh, don't worry, darling, I'm not here to ruin your little tête-à-tête. By all means, carry on. I'll just—"

A streak of orange fur zoomed in, sliding to a halt on the floor in front of Alex, hissing and snarling at the interloper. The look of withering contempt on Rosamund's face changed to one of terror. She fled, the door slamming behind her.

Surprisingly, Grace transformed from Demon Kitty to Angel in the House in scarcely an eyeblink. After taking a moment to smooth down her fur, she sauntered over and rubbed against Alex's leg, then did the same to Cam before going about her business.

Alex stared mutely at Cam, who could only look back, her mind reeling. Finally Cam broke the silence. "I'm sorry. Those things she said…"

"Yes, about those things she said. Rosamund and I aren't exactly married, but you know we're going out. Just why did you come over here tonight, anyway?"

Cam was shocked, and a little ashamed. "Like I said, I didn't fancy cooking alone, so—"

"Oh, come on. You show up on a Saturday night with dinner for two and a romantic movie and expect me to believe it was all by chance? That kiss didn't just happen, did it? You planned it. You planned all of it."

"That's not the way of it at all."

"Not at all? Really? Not one little bit?"

"All right, I was hopeful, I'll admit, but not the way she made it sound. Rosamund's got a way of twisting things round that you wouldn't believe. Please, Alex." How had things gone pear-shaped so quickly?

"I can't help it—I just don't know what to think. Right now, I'm not even sure what my own name is. I think you'd better go."

"Aye, I think I'd better had." And she did, her heart in her throat.

CHAPTER FIFTEEN

The next morning Alex staggered around cleaning up the kitchen, feeling cold and empty inside. She hadn't been able to face doing any of it the night before, barely managing to even put away the food. She'd wanted to pitch all of it—pots and pans included. But food wasn't something you wasted. It was life—it was sacred. Her mother and grandmother had taught her that.

Not that she could face the idea of eating much of anything at the moment. She made do with a piece of toast and a cup of tea for breakfast, trying not to think about the ugly things that Rosamund had said. She didn't believe Rosamund, couldn't believe her, however plausible she had sounded, so full of injured innocence as she hurled nasty accusations at Cam.

Alex knew better—Cam wasn't like that. But Rosamund had caught her off balance, and the words had seeped into her like drops of poison, working their way through her, damaging everything they touched.

Worse, she kept seeing the way Cam had looked when she walked away—like something inside her had died. And that was Alex's fault, not Rosamund's. She shouldn't have sent her away like that, no matter how upset and confused she felt.

Especially not after what she and Cam had shared. Those moments with Cam, touching her, kissing her, had completely overwhelmed her. Alex knew all the pretty phrases from poems and books, but nothing had prepared her for the way Cam's tenderness had seared right through her, the way her own passion had blazed up in response.

But then Rosamund had turned up to spoil everything, like a bird of ill omen croaking death and disaster. And Alex had let her.

She had to make it right. She needed to find Cam, talk to her, figure out a way to fix things. But first she needed to pull herself together, somehow, and get Rosamund's whispers out of her head. Maybe if she could fill her mind with something else, it would help her get a grip. She decided to try working for a while.

As she walked through the foyer, she noticed that the mail had piled up again. When she forced herself to go through it, she was rewarded with the discovery of another letter from Ian. He reported that he hadn't been able to find anything else related to Artemisia in his great-aunt's letters, which of course was disappointing. On the other hand, he had started writing down what he could recall of the stories she used to tell him, and he had enclosed the first installment.

It was quite a mixture. Some of the information didn't appear to have much to do with Artemisia, or even with Janet, but Alex was glad he was apparently passing on his recollections unedited, since that seemed more likely to be effective in the long run at helping him remember as much as possible. And even the most apparently peripheral things might turn out to be important later, or at least spark her own thinking in helpful ways.

So she read and reread what Ian had sent, silently and aloud, trying to just let it all sink in without prejudging any of it or closing off any ideas. After a while, she started noticing certain passages in particular. Ian had included a fairly long section describing Oona's criticisms, handed down from her mother, of Smithson's painting, and the more times Alex read it, the stranger it seemed.

She had always assumed the painting in the Highgate Hall library was a somewhat romanticized version of Artemisia's death, but apparently a better description would be completely fantasized. The supposedly candlelit scene had taken place midafternoon on a sunny day, and the doctor, far from being present, had been sent packing days before by Janet when he tried to insist on continuing to bleed the weak and clearly failing Artemisia. And yes, Janet had been present, along with a number of other people Smithson hadn't bothered to portray, including the vicar's wife, a couple of village women who had been helping to nurse Artemisia, and, of course, Oona's mother herself.

Alex realized she shouldn't be quite so surprised. History had a way of leaving out the so-called unimportant people.

The other passage that struck her had to do with Artemisia's visits to Highgate Hall after Lady Melissa's death. When she first began her study of Artemisia's life and work, Alex had been surprised to learn that even after Lady Melissa's death, Artemisia had continued to be a regular guest of Mr. Dawson, and not just at social events. Apparently they were personal friends, and Artemisia would often call on him, and vice versa. After his death, in fact, he had left her the ownership of Dawson House.

All of those things Alex was already familiar with, and although the situation had puzzled her at first, she had decided that the two of them must have bonded through their shared grief over Lady Melissa. The new information in Ian's letter was brief but rather strange. According to what Oona had told him, Artemisia would never set foot in the Highgate Hall library. No one knew the reason, although since this behavior started after Lady Melissa's passing it was assumed to be somehow connected.

Alex wondered why this particular fact had never before come to light. Perhaps it had been such a minor eccentricity amid so many greater ones that no one had considered it worthy of remark. Thinking about Smithson's painting, she realized how ironic it was that the one room in the house Artemisia had religiously avoided was also the one where she was now on display in all her—albeit fictitious—glory.

Even though it was almost lunchtime, Alex decided to head up to the Hall and take another look at the painting. Maybe seeing it again, or just being in the library, would inspire her.

Once she reached the Hall grounds, she headed for the back door that gave access to the kitchens. She preferred not to use the front entrance on Sundays when no one was around. Her route took her past Rosamund's cottage, but fortunately there was no sign of her. She knew she would have to deal with her sooner or later, but the very last thing she needed right now was to see her.

Taking out her set of museum keys, she unlocked the door, carefully relocking it behind her, and made her way through the servants' hall and into the main part of the house. When she opened the library door, the curtains were all drawn and the room was in darkness. In trying to locate the light switch, she managed to catch her foot on the edge of a carpet. Her keys flew out of her hand and as she fell sprawling, she heard them hit the floor.

Fortunately she wasn't hurt, just shaken up. She got slowly to her feet and let her eyes adjust. Then she turned the lights on and started looking for her keys.

She found the key chain near the bookcases to the right of the doorway. The ring had snapped open and the keys had scattered. The front- and back-door keys, being so large, hadn't gone far, and after a little more searching she found the archive-room keys as well. But her office key was missing.

After going around in circles for a while without success, she went back to the spot where the key ring had landed and stood there, looking slowly in all directions. There weren't any places that she could see where the key could have ended up. The bookcases were sitting directly on the floor, not raised on feet, so there would be no way for the key to have slipped under them. Their sides were pushed up against one another and appeared at first glance to be perfectly flush.

But when she took a closer look, she discovered that there was a tiny little gap between two of the cases. It seemed hard to imagine that her key could have gone in there. And the gap wasn't wide enough for her to slide her fingers into. Or was it?

She lay down on the floor and looked carefully at the gap. Up close, it did seem to be a tiny bit wider at the bottom. She wasted a moment wondering why. Maybe the floor was warped. Maybe the planets were properly aligned.

Keeping her hand relaxed and moving slowly, she was able to ease her fingers between the two bookcases just a little way, then a little more. And then she felt it—something small and metal. Hooray. She started flexing her fingers to draw the key toward her.

But then she felt her fingertips brush against paper. A fairly sizeable sheet. Excitement raced through her. Who knew what it might be, or how long it had been there? Maybe it was something important. Something about Artemisia.

Or maybe it was something to do with the hundreds and hundreds of other people who had lived in and worked at and visited Highgate Hall over the centuries. Like a grocery list, maybe, or a thank-you note, or somebody's random doodling. Maybe it was blank. Maybe if she stayed like this long enough her hand would swell and she'd be caught like an animal in a trap without any hope of rescue until Monday.

Taking a deep breath and letting it out, she tried to calm herself. Then she spread her fingers and reached forward again, oh so delicately, afraid of pushing the paper farther in instead of drawing it out. The tips of her index and middle fingers closed around the barest edge of the paper and she tugged back a fraction. The paper slipped free and she swore.

Then she tried again. This time, she got a better grip and felt the paper slide toward her just the tiniest bit. Afraid to breathe, she continued easing it along, managing to use the edge of one finger to slide her key as well. Finally, she was able to claim both her prizes. And the paper did have writing on it—cursive writing.

She stood up. The key went into her pocket and she took the paper over to a desk, setting it down on the blotter. Then she sat down and switched on the lamp.

At first she couldn't decipher the old-fashioned handwriting, even though it looked familiar. Then something clicked. The handwriting was Lady Melissa's.

She thought she was going to faint. *Breathe*, she told herself.

Glancing over the whole thing, she saw there was no signature or salutation. That might mean many things, but her gut told her it was because the letter was highly personal, so personal the writer didn't want to risk identifying herself or the recipient in case it fell into the wrong hands. Was she writing to Artemisia?

After your disgraceful exhibition yesterday—

That did not sound at all good. Alex forced herself to start over and concentrate on the words.

After your disgraceful exhibition yesterday, it should come as no surprise that I find it impossible any longer to continue our association. That you should make such a ridiculous and imprudent suggestion beggars belief. That you could believe me so lost to all propriety and common sense as to consider giving assent to such a scheme is beyond insulting.

I shall never be able to look upon our association with anything other than disgust. That I allowed you those freedoms that should have been reserved for the marriage bed will never be sufficiently regretted.

You will not see me again. Should you attempt to call, I have left instructions that you are to be denied admittance, and you will likewise find no welcome among my acquaintance, should you be so foolish as to importune them. Any correspondence will be returned unopened.

Alex could picture it as if she had watched it happen. Artemisia arriving at the Hall, a place she was used to treating as a second home, but this time finding herself escorted not into Lady Melissa's presence, but to the library, as if she were a mere business appointment. Left to cool her heels there until a servant, most likely Lady Melissa's maid, delivered this cruel dismissal. Trying to control her reactions and retain some dignity as her whole world came crashing down. Letting the letter fall from nerveless fingers, never noticing as it slid between the bookcases. Stumbling, half-blind with unshed tears, out of the room, out of the house. Feeling the door close behind her, forever.

Alex was horrified. It sounded as if Artemisia had proposed that she and Melissa run away together instead of continuing to live a lie. She had dared to ask the woman that she loved for what she wanted and needed. And Melissa, concerned only with preserving a façade of respectability to maintain her social standing, had responded with singular harshness. Artemisia had taken a huge risk, and she had paid a heavy price. No wonder Artemisia had stopped writing poems about Melissa.

She checked the date on the letter. Melissa had died less than a week later, struck down by a lung infection, probably pneumonia. Alex shuddered.

The sound of the door opening behind her was like a gunshot in the silence.

"Alex darling, what on earth are you doing in here all by yourself?"

Rosamund. Perfect.

Rosamund walked over to the desk. "Really, after last night I should—Why, you're as white as a ghost. What is it?"

Alex didn't trust her voice. She just pointed to the letter. Rosamund came and stood beside her chair.

She read slowly through the letter, muttering the words to herself under her breath. Alex just sat there, waiting for her to finish.

"Darling, what is this?"

"Lady Melissa wrote it." Her voice sounded as dead as she felt. "I recognize the writing."

"But I don't understand. I've never seen this before. Is it from the archives?"

Alex shook her head. "I found it. In here."

Rosamund gasped. "Wait—do you mean to say you found this? Just now?" She bent over the letter again, eagerly rereading. "*Allowed you those freedoms...marriage bed*—Darling! You do realize what this means, don't you?"

"Melissa didn't love her. Not really."

"The Prandall, darling. The Prandall—seven hundred thousand pounds! I can't believe it. Darling, you've done it!"

"I suppose I have. It doesn't seem to matter much. She didn't love her."

"You're not making sense. You must be in shock. Well of course you are, anyone would be. I'll see if I can find something in the kitchen that will help."

Alex sat there staring at the letter, not really seeing it. What a betrayal. The pain must have been indescribable.

Rosamund was back almost immediately, carrying—what else?—a bottle of champagne and two glasses. She opened the bottle, laughing as the foam sprayed over the carpet, and poured a glass for each of them.

Alex took hers, staring at it as if she'd never seen anything like it before in her life. Everything seemed a little unreal. Maybe she really was in shock.

Rosamund laughed again. "Now let's make a toast to all that lovely money. To seven hundred thousand pounds." She clinked her glass against Alex's before drinking.

Alex lifted hers mechanically and said, "Artemisia." Then she took a sip. It was cool and sweet and felt wonderful going down her throat. She hadn't realized how thirsty she was. She took another sip, and then another one. Before she realized it, her glass was empty.

"Thank you, Rosamund." She put the glass down and looked at the letter again. Something about it nagged at her, something that didn't make sense. But whatever it was, it eluded her.

Her glass was full again so she took another sip. Looking up, she focused on the painting over the mantel. The reason she had come to the Hall today in the first place.

She thought about what Ian had written, about everything that was wrong with the painting, and everyone who was missing from it. Had that only been this morning? It felt like a thousand years ago. She was so tired. Her body felt like lead.

She sat staring at the painting, sipping her drink and letting her mind wander. She wondered how Artemisia had ever managed to recover from what Melissa had done to her. But recover she must have, somehow. Otherwise, how could you explain her dying words?

Death may have parted us, O my Heart, but Love will reunite us.
It seemed almost unbelievable, but according to Ian's letter, that was exactly what Artemisia had said, right before the end. At least that much of the legend was apparently absolutely true.

So somehow, Artemisia must have found a way not just to tolerate the pain Melissa had caused, but to forgive her. More than that, Artemisia had been able to reclaim the love that she had felt for her—a love that Melissa herself had denied, repudiated, reviled. Alex had the proof of that right in front of her.

Looking up at Artemisia's face on the canvas, transfigured in the glow of Smithson's imaginary candles, she hoped that the end of Artemisia's life really had been touched by some measure of joy, that at least that much of Smithson's art was truthful. Turning the mystery over in her mind, she let her eyes drift closed.

At some point she slipped into sleep. When she woke up, she was alone.

Rosamund was gone. And so was the letter.

CHAPTER SIXTEEN

Cam walked down the path that led to the back of Dawson House, still trying to figure out exactly what she was going to say to Alex. Somehow she had to get her to listen, to undo the damage Rosamund had done last night. She had been walking the moors for what felt like hours, hoping to get things straight in her mind, but she couldn't settle on the right words.

She kept going back to the feel of Alex in her arms, the wonder of that kiss, the remembered heat of it burning all the thoughts from her head. And then she would flash on the moment when everything had turned to ashes. The look on Alex's face, the tone in her voice when she had sent her away. She could feel the chill of it all the way through her.

And so it had gone, back and forth and back again, with her in no better state now than she had been when she first set off that morning. So much for taking a good long walk to sort things out.

She went up to the kitchen door. She'd delayed long enough. She'd just have to fumble through as best she could. She knocked, and when there was no answer, she pushed at the door. As expected, it swung right open.

The kitchen was dark, which was a little surprising. She switched on the light, giving a quick glance up at the overhead shelf to check for lurking cats as she stepped inside. She shut the door and looked around, calling out to Alex as she did so.

She heard a strange sort of noise from over by the fireplace, but the high back of the bench blocked her view. She came round the side of it only to stop dead.

Alex lay on the floor, curled up in a ball, sobbing.

For a moment, she froze. But only a moment. Then she was kneeling on the floor, pulling Alex into her arms. "Alex, love, what is it? What's wrong?"

Alex clutched at Cam's shirt and burrowed against her. At first all Cam could think to do was hold her tighter, stroking her back and arms. She was so cold. She was trying to talk, but all that came out was incoherent sobbing.

Cam's stomach was churning and she felt herself starting to breathe too fast. No, none of that, not while Alex needed her. Ruthlessly she clamped down on her own reactions, forcing herself to think. Whatever had happened, all that mattered now was getting Alex better. And that clearly wasn't going to happen if she stayed there on the bare floor.

Shifting gently, Cam got her feet under her, slid her arms under Alex's shoulders and knees, and picked her up. Alex stopped sobbing and put her arms around Cam's neck, resting her head on Cam's chest. Where to set her down? Not the bench—too narrow. Going all the way upstairs would take too long. But there was a bed in Aunty Elspeth's room—that would do.

Cam carried her in there and sat her on the side of the bed, keeping one arm around her while she got Alex's shoes off. Then she eased her under the covers, pulling them up around her neck. When she turned to go, Alex whimpered.

"I'll be right back, love."

She hurried out into the kitchen and put the kettle on, then started opening cabinets, looking for something stronger than tea. She found a bottle of brandy and poured a generous tot into a glass, then took it in to Alex. Cam lifted her head, supporting her neck, and held the glass for her to drink. But at the first sip, Alex twisted her head away, making an angry sound. All right, no brandy. Cam eased Alex's head back down.

After considering a moment, Cam drank it off herself and took the glass out to the kitchen. The instant the tea was ready, she stirred in plenty of sugar and grabbed a few biscuits from the table for good measure before going back to Alex.

Alex accepted the tea without protest. When she had drunk a bit and seemed a little better, Cam helped her to sit up. Alex took the cup but needed both hands to keep it steady. Cam sat on the edge of the bed and put her arm around Alex's shoulders, holding her gently as she sipped.

When Alex finished the tea, Cam took the cup and set it aside, then handed her one of the biscuits. As if on cue, the cat appeared, leaping up onto the bed and mewing pitifully.

"Sorry, she needs it more than you do. I'll open a tin for you later."

The cat looked at her dubiously—apparently she was wary of empty promises. Smart, that one.

"I don't think she believes you." Alex's voice shook a little but she sounded calm.

Cam closed her eyes, relief flooding her, before opening them again to glare at the cat. "Doesn't matter what she believes. I keep my promises."

The cat picked her way delicately up the bed until she reached an acceptable spot, turning this way and that until she had positioned herself with her body curled up to one side of Alex and her head on Alex's leg, within easy petting distance. Alex obliged and the motorboat purr started up.

After a while, Alex sighed. "Oh, Cam…"

"Don't try to talk yet. Have another biscuit."

Once all the biscuits were gone, Alex wiped a hand over her face, obviously trying to pull herself together. "Where do I start? I went up to the Hall, I guess around lunchtime, only I never did eat lunch, did I? That's probably why…Oh, Cam, she stole it!" Alex buried her face in her hands and started to cry.

"Rosamund." The word was like a curse in her mouth. Of course. Cam had known, instinctively, who was responsible the moment she saw Alex lying there. Alex cried out, and Cam realized that she had tightened her hold on Alex's shoulder to the point of hurting her. Silently swearing at herself, she eased her grip, making soothing circles to rub away the pain.

As Cam tried to comfort her, Alex leaned back and settled her head into the curve between Cam's neck and shoulder. Cam held her close, stroking her hair and her back. After a while Alex stopped crying. Eventually she fell asleep. At some point, Cam did, too.

Alex awoke to the unfamiliar sensation of Cam's arms around her. Unfamiliar, yet absolutely right. She felt warm and safe encircled by her strength, listening to her soft breathing. Dimly she knew something awful was lurking just at the edge of awareness, waiting to claim her, but not yet. In this moment, everything was right.

She burrowed against Cam, trying to get closer. Slight as the movement was, Cam stirred. She kissed Alex on the forehead, soft and lingering, and seemed about to kiss her lips, but something made her stop and pull back. Alex felt a twinge of disappointment.

Cam let go of her and eased away. She got to her feet slowly and stiffly, taking a moment to stretch before turning on the bedside lamp.

Even that little bit of light made Alex cringe. Things were starting to come back to her—a few fragments, none of them good, and an underlying sense of desolation.

Meanwhile, Cam hunted through Mrs. Tate's chest of drawers and located a cardigan and a thick pair of socks, both of which she insisted Alex put on before helping her to her feet. She wouldn't let Alex walk into the kitchen on her own, either, and at first Alex was inclined to protest, but she decided she liked having Cam's arm around her waist. And maybe she did still feel just a little shaky.

Alex sat at the table, feeling completely drained, while Cam busied herself making tea, heating soup, and toasting bread. Alex's mind was clear and her memories by now were all too distinct. And yet having Cam there, just doing ordinary things, not even saying a word, made her feel better.

Once they started eating, she found it possible to talk about what had happened, in bits and pieces at first. Cam didn't say anything, but her face looked grimmer and grimmer. Finally Alex was all talked out.

"So, what do you want to do?"

"You mean you believe me?"

"Believe you? There's nothing to believe. I know what happened because you told me. That's good enough for me."

"Thank you. That means a lot." She reached out and took Cam's hand. Cam gave it a gentle squeeze, then released it. Alex pulled her hand back.

"But I can't prove any of it. I can't even prove I was at the Hall today, let alone what I did there. The whole place was completely empty. It's my word against hers. And she has the letter."

"There's that. But you have the truth. That's got to count for something."

"Not without evidence."

"Where do you reckon she is now? Never mind, I know the answer: London. Where else would she be?"

"She probably floored it all the way down the M-1. I hope nobody got in her way."

"Too right. For seven hundred thousand pounds that one would run down her mother—and her grandmother as well. For a good deal less than that, in fact."

The bitter tone surprised Alex. Cam didn't sound much like a woman in love, although given the things Rosamund had said to her—had it only been last night?—it made sense.

Alex said, "I'm sure she went straight to the Foundation—she's probably been with them for hours by now. God only knows what lies she's told them."

"Is there anyone on staff there you could ring? Maybe Nicola knows someone."

"I can call Ian. He's on the Board. Maybe he can help me. And even if he can't do anything, he's my friend. I want him to know the truth."

Alex called Ian, and with her hand safely cradled in both of Cam's, poured out the whole story in what she hoped was a coherent fashion, then waited apprehensively for Ian's reaction.

"I'm very glad that you called me, Alexandra. Pity it couldn't have been a bit sooner, but that can't be helped. Sadly, I can't say I'm entirely surprised by what you've told me."

"Really? Why not?"

"Something about the whole thing just didn't smell right, especially considering the source. Ms. Camberwell has always been inclined to burnish her own image at others' expense. Not a case of *beauty is truth, truth beauty*, I'm afraid."

Alex silently concurred.

"Besides, quite a few things made me wonder. Too many details, for one, and too much talking in general. Always a bad sign, in my experience. And such insistence that we needed to ring the media right away, despite the document not having been properly authenticated. Which, of course, now makes perfect sense. And then there's what she said when I mentioned you."

Alex felt the bottom drop out of her stomach. "What did she say?"

"It was very peculiar. I started to ask, quite naturally, whether she had spoken to you about the letter, but I only got as far as saying your name when she interrupted me and said, 'She's lying.' Really quite extraordinary. If I hadn't been suspicious before, that alone would have done it."

"What happened then?"

"I think she realized she'd made a mistake, because at that point she stopped talking."

"What do the others on the Board think?"

"From what I could tell, most of them had reactions similar to mine, though not all. Ms. Camberwell does have her admirers. In any case, based on what you've told me, Alexandra, I shall go back to my colleagues and insist that we adjourn until you can join us."

"Oh." She sighed. "Yes, I guess I do need to go down there."

"I know this hasn't been easy for you, my dear. How soon do you think you'll be up to traveling?"

"I'll be on the first train tomorrow, Ian."

"Bravo, Alexandra. Never fear, we'll get this sorted out."

CHAPTER SEVENTEEN

Cam spent most of the next day trying not to worry about Alex, who of course had been set on going to London by herself. She supposed that was a good sign. After all, Alex hadn't uttered a word of protest the night before when Cam had informed her she was staying over in one of the spare rooms, within easy calling distance, as she tucked Alex into her own bed, the cat eyeing her the entire time from her post at the foot of the bed like a suspicious chaperone.

As if she'd try anything when Alex was in such a state. Of course, when they'd woken up together from that nap earlier in the evening, she hadn't been able to stop herself from kissing her. But she'd been pretty groggy then, and for a long, wonderful moment she hadn't been aware of anything but Alex, the warmth and softness of her, the scent of her hair and her skin. She'd come back to herself right quick, though, before she'd done more than kiss her forehead just the one time.

Which had been a good thing. Of course it had.

Letting go of Alex and moving away from her in that moment had been like tearing off a limb, but she had managed it. Perhaps one of these days she'd surprise herself and not actually do the thing that was right and proper and best for all concerned. And probably give herself heart failure from the shock.

Of course, it wasn't always so easy to know what the right thing was. Last night it had been obvious Alex wasn't fit to be left on her own, the fact that she hadn't argued the point being all the more proof, as if Cam had needed any. She had found Alex's meekness worrisome enough that she ought to have been delighted when it became clear Alex's willingness to cooperate hadn't survived the night.

Cam hadn't known what to think. On the one hand, it was good to see Alex back to her old stubborn self, insisting that she was fine as she rushed about preparing for her trip. But Cam hadn't been the least convinced that she was truly up to the journey, physically or emotionally. Not that her concerns had mattered in the end. For while Alex had accepted a ride to the station as well as Cam's offer to explain things to Mrs. Tate and Nicola, she had refused to let Cam go with her to London.

Despite all attempts to make Alex see reason, she had remained obstinate, saying that she needed to face the Board on her own. Not much of a surprise, that, and though Cam would never admit it aloud, in spite of her worries she was proud of Alex for standing firm. What had surprised her was the other reason Alex gave for wanting Cam to stay behind.

"When you don't work, you don't get paid. Besides, you must have a huge backlog of jobs from your trip to Scarborough, and losing another day or two will only make it that much worse. You'll end up working so much extra time you'll half kill yourself, just so you don't disappoint people."

Most folk had no idea what it was like to be self-employed. They reckoned she had loads of free time or expected her to just drop everything to do them favors because she didn't have a real job. And very few of them seemed to understand the pride she took in her work. But somehow Alex did. She really did.

So now Cam was waiting and wondering and trying to concentrate on what she was doing. Just as well she hadn't had anything especially hazardous on her schedule today, since she'd already managed to bash one finger, plus she'd acquired a good few scrapes, scratches, and bumps—more than an ordinary week's worth in just a few hours. Not that she would have done much better just sitting about, going slowly mad waiting for her mobile to ring.

As the hours went by with no word, Cam finally gave up and went home. Once she got there, she wasn't able to do anything much besides drink endless cups of tea and pace, but at least she wasn't injuring herself. Close to nine, she finally heard from Alex.

"How did it go?" Cam listened for clues in the silence, trying to imagine Alex's face.

"All right, I guess." She sounded so far away. "The whole thing is kind of a blur. Ian says I came across as sane and sensible, but you can't prove it by me."

"How did they take it?"

"I couldn't really tell. I thought they all looked pretty grim, but so did Ian and I know he believes me. Maybe they always look like that during an interrogation." She laughed, but it sounded forced. "I suppose it could have been worse. At least they skipped the rack and the iron maiden. Anyway, it's over. They said they'd let me know, so now I guess I just wait."

"Did you see her?" The question slipped out and Cam silently cursed herself.

"No. Which is probably just as well." She sighed. "It wouldn't have helped much if I'd started yelling or burst into tears. And if she had been there, I'd probably have done both." She was trying to sound lighthearted, but Cam could hear the hurt just below the surface.

She clenched her jaw, imagining the pain Alex must be going through, pain she herself was only too familiar with. As much as Rosamund's involvement with Alex had torn at her, she could have wished for it to last forever rather than see Alex hurt like this—well, she could almost have wished for it. She was human enough that she was glad Alex was free, pain or no pain, especially knowing that Rosamund would have shown her true colors in the end.

"When are you coming home?" Even to her own ears, she sounded slightly pathetic. She ached to see her, to hold her.

"Midday tomorrow. I'll stay overnight with Ian and take the morning train. Nicola's going to meet me, so you won't need to interrupt your work."

After she rang off, Cam tried to tell herself it was just as well Alex was putting a bit of distance between them. As much as she longed for her, she knew she was not someone Alex likely wanted hanging about just at the moment. Even if Cam could actually manage to get through a conversation without bringing up Rosamund's name, the very sight of her must be a constant reminder of what that woman had put her through.

Cam wanted to comfort Alex, but honestly, how would she go about it? Offer to share tips for getting over Rosamund, drawn from her own experience?

Of course, what Cam really wanted to say to Alex was the one thing she couldn't give voice to: *Let me help you forget her.* The last thing Alex needed right now was Cam coming on to her. Not that she'd ever do anything so low as to try and take advantage. But even the most honorable intentions didn't change the fact that this was the wrong time.

And especially not when Alex needed all her energy and focus to fight for what was rightfully hers. Alex's work mattered so much to her—she was so passionate when she talked about Artemisia and how she wanted to tell her story to the world. The letter she had found should have been a triumph and a joy, but Rosamund had ruined that.

And yet, despite what Rosamund had done, Alex hadn't abandoned her mission. She had made it clear that, even though the reality of Artemisia's life hadn't turned out to be the romantic ideal she had expected, she was still absolutely dedicated to pursuing and publicizing the truth. Cam envied her that sense of purpose, something she herself had never experienced. And she truly admired Alex for holding fiercely to it even in the face of disaster.

Especially given the anguish she must be feeling at being so betrayed by the one person she should have been able to trust. Cam prayed that Alex hadn't been deeply in love with Rosamund, and not just for selfish reasons. But even if Alex hadn't had her heart broken all to pieces, to have a lover turn on you like that, after you had welcomed them into your life and opened yourself up to them, even in the most casual, physical way, was horrible. She must be hurting so badly.

And the only cure for that was time. However much Cam wanted to be with Alex, she would just have to be patient. If she really cared about her, how could she do anything else? She would respect her feelings. She wouldn't pressure her. She would wait as long as she had to, for Alex's sake.

So what kind of awful person was she that all she could think about was how much she wanted Alex, right now?

❖

The next few days brought Cam neither clarity nor peace of mind. Alex rang to say she was back in Bramfell, but the conversation was brief. Other than that, Alex might as well have been on the moon for all Cam saw or heard from her. If it hadn't been for Nicola, she would have had no idea at all what was happening.

It sounded as if Alex was doing reasonably well, and however much Cam might have preferred to judge that for herself, she was grateful that the news was good rather than otherwise. Nicola was a bit vague about specifics, but she and Alex were clearly working together to deal with Alex's discovery and minimize the damage Rosamund had done. Apparently Alex's friend Ian had some sort of plan of his own and was doing everything he could as well. Cam had of course offered to pitch in, in the unlikely event that she could somehow help, and Nicola had promised to call on her if there turned out to be something she could do.

Meanwhile, Cam was throwing herself into her work as if her life depended on putting in the longest, hardest, roughest days possible, with the result that once in a while she was able to lose herself in the task in front of her for short periods, and at night she couldn't help but sleep thanks to sheer exhaustion. The rest of the time she spent thinking about Alex, wanting to be with her, and wishing that Prandall and his wretched prize and even Artemisia herself had long since been forgotten by one and all.

Cam tried to tell herself that perhaps it was better this way. Better for Alex, at least. She eventually worked her way around to the idea that what Alex really needed was not to see her at all, until Alex herself decided the time was right. So even when her schedule eased up a bit, she started deliberately trying to avoid Alex. That meant not walking about the village the way she usually did, and staying away from the café in case Nicola and Alex were there.

One evening she almost ran into them at the pub. Fortunately she spotted them the moment she walked in, so she was able to turn around and head right back out again before they saw her, but it had been a bit too close for comfort. After that, she went straight home at the end of every day. When the time was right, Alex would ring her. She hoped.

But she hadn't factored in her Dawson House responsibilities. One morning the inevitable happened. Aunty Elspeth reported that this time, it was the hot-water heater that had stopped working. Unfortunately, Cam didn't get the message until she was on the way to Haworth for a job that was going to take the best part of a day. Much as she hated to do it, she had to beg off until the following morning. If Alex was half as unhappy about that as Aunty Elspeth sounded, Cam reckoned she was going to have an interesting time of it when they finally did meet up.

❖

Alex was not pleased. In fact, she was pretty damn grumpy. Two mornings in a row without hot water did that to a person. She glared at herself in the bathroom mirror. Yup, her hair looked even worse than yesterday. *Explosion in a Curl Factory*, artist unknown.

Grace was watching her through half-closed eyes from a perch on the edge of the tub, some instinct having informed her that she could sit there without fear of being disturbed.

"What are you looking at?" Grace gave her a slow blink, clearly not the least perturbed by her tone.

Alex turned back to the mirror, despite knowing it was pointless. It was scrunchie time. Which was always so flattering.

Not that it made any difference, since nobody who mattered was going to see her like this. People who disappeared for days on end with no explanation did not matter. Especially if when you finally ran into them, they turned tail and ran the minute they caught sight of you.

"What is her problem anyway? I thought we were past all that."

Grace tilted her head to one side and mewed inquiringly.

"Cam, of course. Maybe the woman has an evil twin. Or maybe she's the evil twin, and it was the good one who was over here when we—goddamn it." Yet another scrunchie had bitten the dust. Tossing the broken elastic into the trash can, Alex tried again with another—which she was pretty sure was her last one. She wished, not for the first time, that they came in industrial strength.

"I'll tell you one thing, though, when she finally deigns to show up and fix the damn water heater, she's not getting out of here again until I've had a chance to give her a piece of my mind. And then some."

Once Alex had finally wrestled her hair into submission, she splashed her face with icy water—icy being, of course, the only option. She must have been too enthusiastic with it, because a yowl from Grace was followed by sounds of a rapid feline retreat for parts unknown. Great. Now they were both having lousy mornings.

By the time she clomped downstairs, she had decided that she wasn't going one more day with her hair like this, water heater or no water heater, even if it meant she had to do things the old-fashioned way and boil water in a soup pot, the way Mrs. Tate had yesterday for doing the dishes. Maybe she should go old school all the way and use the kettle in the fireplace. Regardless, hauling all that water upstairs was going to be a huge pain.

But as she walked through the kitchen doorway, she remembered the scullery. She could wash in there, assuming—

"Ouch!" Something small and hard bounced off her skull just above her right ear and fell to the floor with a clank. "What the hell? Sorry, Mrs. Tate."

She didn't receive a verbal reply, just a raised eyebrow and an admonitory headshake before Mrs. Tate returned her attention to her work.

Alex knew that whatever it was that had hit her, there was only one possible explanation. Sure enough, when she turned around, there was the culprit sitting on the shelf above the doorway—heaven only knew how she managed to get there—looking down at her. If cats could smirk, Grace was definitely smirking.

"Payback, huh? Very funny."

Apparently satisfied that her point had been made, Grace leaped down with her usual nonchalant elegance and pranced over to the stove. She sat herself near Mrs. Tate's feet, not quite in the way, and began delicately washing one paw, the picture of well-bred feline innocence. As if.

So just what had Grace hit her with? Alex looked around and finally spotted something under the table—one of the myriad keys that were scattered throughout Dawson House. This one was more ornate than most and attached to a cord rather than a ring, just like her house key. Something about it looked familiar, but before she could focus her thoughts, Mrs. Tate had her breakfast ready, so she stuck it in her pocket to deal with later.

Just as she was finishing her meal, Cam came in through the back door. The sight of her apprehensive entrance, scuttling sideways with her head turtled protectively into her neck as she cast a wary glance at the shelf above the doorway, was too much for Alex to withstand. She burst out laughing. But then she remembered that she was angry and made herself stop.

Cam cringed as three pairs of eyes bored into her. She had a pretty fair notion why Alex and Aunty Elspeth were unhappy with her, but what the bloody hell had she done to upset the cat? She'd fed it the last time she'd seen it, hadn't she? And proper tinned food, not just table scraps. There was no pleasing some folk.

Squaring her shoulders now that she had no fear of a surprise attack, she decided the best course was to ignore the storm clouds and carry on.

Her far too cheerful "Morning, all" earned no response other than glares, the cat accompanying hers with an ear flick. "I'll just get right to it, shall I?"

"That would be best," said Aunty Elspeth dryly before turning her back to busy herself at the sink, filling a large pot. "And in the meanwhile, I'll just set this on to boil so I can do the washing up with it. Again."

Crikey.

Alex said, "When you've finished, Mrs. Tate, would you mind putting some water on for me?" She crossed her arms and looked Cam dead in the eye. This wasn't going to be good. "I've decided I can't bear to wait any longer to do something with my hair."

For one insane moment, Cam considered telling her that her hair looked adorable, which of course it did. It always did. But Alex narrowed her eyes, as if daring her to give voice to what must have been a far too obvious thought. Being possessed of a healthy survival instinct, Cam settled for beating a hasty retreat in the direction of the airing cupboard.

When she set down her tools and opened the door, she noticed that the cat had followed her upstairs. "What, have you come to tell me you've been waiting on me as well?"

The cat rubbed against her leg and started purring. It occurred to her that the airing cupboard had to be one of the warmest places in the house, and given what she knew of Aunty Elspeth, doubtless it was strictly off-limits to anyone with four feet. Even as she formed the thought, the cat leaped up onto a high shelf and settled herself atop a stack of blankets.

The cat sneezed once and closed her eyes, her purr fading away as she fell asleep.

Well, at least someone in Dawson House had forgiven her. The sooner she repaired the water heater, the sooner she'd be back in everyone's good graces. She hoped.

She'd been at it a good while with little success when she heard footsteps on the stairs. Moments later, Alex was standing in the hallway. The expression on her face was difficult to read. She certainly looked far less hostile than she had before, but Cam reckoned she was in for it regardless.

The funny thing of it was, she didn't even mind. Anything, even a row with Alex, was better than not seeing her. She had gotten so used to not being around her that she'd stopped noticing how much it hurt.

Alex paused a moment to just look at Cam. It had taken a long time to calm herself down enough to be fairly sure she wouldn't just march up here and yell her head off—not the best way to open a conversation. Now she was really glad she had gotten her temper under control. The way Cam was looking at her, her eyes so soft and sad, made her feel all twisted up inside.

"Cam, what's going on?"

"I don't really know. I haven't been able to find a thing wrong with—"

"I don't care about the stupid water heater. What's going on with you?"

"Not a thing. I'm all right."

"If that's supposed to be funny, it isn't. I'm in no mood. Tell me what's wrong."

"I'm not being funny. And there's nothing the matter with me."

"Then there must be something wrong with me. Because I can't think of any other reason why you're suddenly so set on avoiding me that you run away the minute you see me."

"Saw me that night at the pub, did you? Sorry. Thought I was fast enough."

"But why did you do it? I've been racking my brain trying to think what I could have done or said that—wait." Horror shot through her. "Oh my God. You've changed your mind, haven't you? You think I'm lying about what happened with the letter."

"No, lass, no. Never that." Cam stepped forward, closing the distance between them.

"What is it, then?"

"I just thought it would be better if I kept away for a bit."

Alex searched Cam's face, trying to make sense of what she was hearing. "Away from me? Better how? I don't understand."

"I reckoned you'd need time, after what happened. Time to get it all sorted. And you'd find it easier without me underfoot."

"It's true I've been really busy. Even with Nicola helping, I haven't had much time for anything besides the letter and everything that goes along with it. I'm sorry—I know I should have called you. It's just that everything has been so crazy." She reached out and took Cam's hand. "I've missed you."

"And I've missed you." Cam stepped closer. Only a whisper of air separated them. "So much."

Alex gazed into Cam's eyes. She felt herself starting to drown in them. When Cam reached up and rested her hand gently against Alex's cheek, the touch was so light it seemed barely there, but it sent a bolt of heat right through her.

As Cam began to glide the tip of one finger softly over her skin, Alex closed her eyes. When she felt Cam draw the finger, oh so gently, over her mouth, she parted her lips. Cam continued to trace slowly back and forth along her lower lip. It felt so good Alex tried not to move, not to breathe.

The moment was shattered by the sound of a feline body landing plop on the floor nearby, followed by the scrambling of paws over wooden floorboards as Grace ran off down the hall. Alex's eyes flew open as she heard Mrs. Tate's energetic footsteps on the stairs. Cam sprang back, a look of chagrin on her face. She was actually blushing. It was really cute.

Checking to make sure the coast was still clear, Alex gave her a quick peck on the cheek—which made Cam blush even harder—

before rushing into her room and shutting the door, smothering a fit of the giggles as best she could.

After she'd gotten herself more or less sober, she eased her door open a crack and listened. Cam was talking to Mrs. Tate. She sounded like she had recovered her own equilibrium fairly well.

"I reckon it's just like the cooker and the washing machine. No reason I can see for it stopping working, and when I put everything back together it's right as rain."

"Oh, there's reason enough, dearie, and we both know what it is."

"You-know-who up to her usual tricks. Though I've never known her to mess about thus much, least of all in such a short span of time."

"I've only seen it this bad once before, when that so-called appraiser was making off with bits and bobs from the attic to flog on Portobello Road at the weekends. You could tell how angry she was—and a good job, too, since it was thanks to her we caught him. Long before your time, that was."

"Uncle Reg told me all about it when I first went to work for him. He wanted to be sure I knew what was what at Dawson House. So what do you reckon she's on about this time?"

"I think you can answer that question better than I can, dearie."

Alex couldn't contain herself any longer. She burst out of her room. "Do you mean someone's been deliberately causing all these breakdowns?" She looked first at Cam and then at Mrs. Tate, but neither answered. "And it sounds like you know the person who's doing it. Why don't you call the police and have them arrested?"

Cam smiled at her. "I reckon they'd find that a bit difficult to manage. The Bramfell constabulary does well as a rule, but it's not so easy to lay hold of a dead person."

Mrs. Tate gasped, but Alex didn't really pay attention, being too focused on letting Cam know that this time, she wasn't falling for her nonsense.

"Dead person? Like what—a zombie? A vampire? Are they down in the bottom of the garden keeping the elves and fairies company? Come on, quit kidding—what's really going on?"

But Cam wasn't smiling. In fact, she had a hand clapped over her mouth, as if she'd let something slip that she shouldn't have. And

Mrs. Tate was glaring at Cam as if she had indeed revealed some deep, dark secret.

Alex looked back and forth from one to the other. "Wait, are you actually trying to say…Oh, you have got to be joking." They both just stared back at her. "You can't possibly believe there really is a dead person hanging around? Like, a ghost or something?" Neither of them looked the least bit amused. Worse, they didn't try to deny it. "Are you seriously trying to tell me you think Dawson House is haunted?"

"Of course it's haunted," Mrs. Tate snapped. "The whole village knows it." She sighed. "Though we generally don't speak of it, and certainly not to outsiders. As this one here well knows."

"Sorry, Aunty."

"Too late to be sorry now." She looked at Alex. "Well, I suppose you're not quite such an outsider as all that, under the circumstances."

"Thank you, Mrs. Tate." *I think.* Alex was about to ask her what she meant by under the circumstances when a thought struck her. "It's not just the breakdowns, is it? There's all those noises, and the doors always opening and closing, and the cold spot that sometimes shows up on the stairs. And that's all because of a…a ghost?"

"More or less." Cam grinned at her. "Janet lives here, just like you do."

"Thanks a lot. That will help me sleep at night. Wait a minute—when you say Janet, do you mean our Janet? Janet from the photo downstairs?" Suddenly she made the connection that had eluded her before. "The photo downstairs!"

She raced down to the kitchen, coming to a stop in front of the photograph of Janet and the children. She pulled the key that Grace had hit her with out of her pocket and held it up to the photo to compare it to the key Janet was wearing. They were identical. Even the cord was the same.

She let out a whoop of joy and started jumping up and down. Cam came racing in, fear on her face. Unable to produce anything but squeals, Alex ran up to her and dragged her over to the photo, waving the key and gesturing wildly.

"It's the same key. Yes, I see that." Cam was speaking slowly and soothingly, clearly trying to talk Alex down from what she saw as a fit of hysteria, but Alex didn't care.

Finally she was able to form sentences. "This is so amazing! I've got something in my hands that belonged to Janet, that was important to her."

Cam still looked less than comfortable, but Alex couldn't seem to stop bouncing around and babbling. "It must have been, right? Otherwise why would she have been wearing it in the photo? Photos were a big deal back then, so she would have carefully chosen whatever was included. I wonder what it's the key to? Oh, who cares!" She did a little pirouette. "It's her key—her very own key! And now I've got it. It's almost like she gave it to me."

"If you say so." Cam put a hand on Alex's arm. "Are you sure you're all right? Finding out the truth about Dawson House must be a bit of a shock."

"I'm more than all right. I'm fabulous. We should celebrate! How about tomorrow night? Tell you what—I'll make dinner and we can watch another film. Maybe you can get *Dark Victory* this time. How about it?"

"Sounds lovely, only I've got a big job set for tomorrow and I can't be sure what time I'll finish up. Why don't we say the following night instead?"

"Sounds great. That'll give me more time to shop and get everything ready. I know just what I'm going to make, too."

"So what are we having, then?"

"You'll see. I want it to be a surprise. Now go away and fix the water heater or something. I have a dinner to plan." Alex sat down and started making a list.

Chapter Eighteen

Very bright and more or less early the next morning, Alex headed for the grocery store. As expected, they didn't carry most of what she needed, but she found a nice piece of local beef and had the butcher grind it for her instead of having to make do with a package of generic mince. Her grandmother would have insisted on the sauce having at least three kinds of meat, but Alex preferred using just beef and, if she could find any, pancetta. Of course, her grandmother would also have been scandalized that she was planning to serve a pasta dish as the main course at dinner. Oh, well.

Right after lunch, Nicola picked her up for a trip to Leeds to visit a store that supposedly carried genuine foods from Italy. It lived up to its reputation, and Alex was able to get almost everything on her list, including both pancetta and a can of San Marzano tomatoes. Unfortunately the store was out of tagliatelle, but since they did have fresh fettuccine she wasn't really disappointed.

Their next errand was for Nicola, who claimed to be in desperate need of a new dress but was being rather vague about the reason why. After they had scoured two stores without finding anything she liked and were rapidly working their unsuccessful way through the offerings in a third, Alex pulled her into a quiet corner and demanded more information.

"All right, if you must know"—Nicola started to blush—"Sarah rang me a few days ago."

"Sarah? You mean your friend the vicar? What did she want?"

"That's just it. I'm not quite sure. That is, I know what she said. She wants to have dinner with me tomorrow night."

"Okay. So what's the problem?"

"She sounded, well, strange. Sort of nervous, like she was worried about something. But when I asked her about it, she just laughed it off."

"Maybe she's got something she needs to talk to you about, but she didn't want to say so on the phone."

"That's what I thought at first. But ordinarily she would have just told me that straight out. And there's something else." Instead of continuing, Nicola started fiddling with her watch.

"Come on. Spill it."

"Well, you remember that conversation we had a couple of weeks ago, just after the Lammas dance? We were talking about who was dating whom, and you asked me about Sarah?"

"I'm unlikely to forget it. That's when you told me about Cam and Rosamund."

"Oh, right. I did, didn't I? Well, in any case, I've known Sarah for years and years, and I really like her, but I never thought of her that way before. But what you said got me thinking, and I started noticing things."

"Like what?"

"Oh, just little things, like the way she looks at me sometimes, or how whenever we're out somewhere together she's always checking that I'm comfortable, making sure the waiter is attentive, that sort of thing. Taking care of me."

"Right, so what's the problem?" Didn't seem like a problem to her.

"She's never actually said anything. But I think maybe tomorrow night is supposed to be a date."

"That's great! At least, I hope it's great."

"No, it's terrible. What if it isn't a date, and I end up embarrassing both of us?"

"You could play it by ear. You know, just be cool about it and see how it goes." What was she missing?

"But what if it really is supposed to be a date, and she thinks I'm not interested?"

"Are you interested? Do you want it to be a date?"

"Yes. No? I don't know. I think so."

"I'm starting to see the problem. Why don't you talk to her about it? No, that's a terrible idea. If she's been beating around the bush this long, the direct approach will probably scare her and she'll end up denying everything just by reflex."

"Oh, Alex, what am I going to do?"

"You know, if I were a gambler, I'd bet on its being a date. You must have picked up on something that made you think it might be, so why not trust your instincts? And maybe you could give things a push in the right direction." Alex started looking through the dresses on a nearby rack.

"What do you mean?"

Alex pulled out one of the dresses and held it up. "How about a little cleavage?"

"More like a lot of cleavage. I don't think I could wear a bra with a neckline that low."

"And that would be a problem…why, exactly? At least try it on. Like the song says, *Faint heart never won fair lady*."

"All right, I will. Now what about you?"

"What about me?"

"You had me drive you all the way out here to buy a bit of bacon and a tin of tomatoes. Just so you could make dinner for Cam. They sell bacon and tomatoes in Bramfell, you know."

"Not the right kind."

"And it's got to be the right kind, because…"

"Because I take my cooking very seriously."

"Alex."

"All right. I want dinner tomorrow night to be special."

"So is it a date?"

"I certainly hope so."

"Do you think she thinks it's a date?"

"Well, the last time she came for dinner we ended up kissing."

"What? When was this? What happened?"

"Rosamund happened. It was last Saturday, and Cam was kissing me, and then she showed up, and…and I do not want to talk about Rosamund."

"No more do I. Let's talk about Cam instead. So she kissed you, did she? Was it wonderful? Never mind, don't tell me—my thirteen-year-old self will hate you forever."

"All right, I won't tell you it was wonderful. And fabulous. And amazing." Nicola smacked her on the arm, and Alex grinned. "She's wonderful. I just wish I could be sure."

"About what?"

"Whether she's really interested in me. I keep getting these mixed signals. I wouldn't have wasted so much time on what's her name otherwise."

"That doesn't sound like Cam. I should have thought she'd be absolutely the last person to play games."

Alex, thinking of some of the stunts Cam had pulled, rolled her eyes.

"You know what I mean. She'd never hurt somebody's feelings, not deliberately."

"Yeah, I get that. I think she'd sooner chew her own arm off than see me hurt. Maybe she's just scared. Has she said anything to you?"

"About you? Not a whisper. She doesn't kiss and tell, not our Cam."

"Unlike me, you mean? Don't answer that. You've known her a lot longer than I have. What do you think is going on?"

"At a guess I'd say she's more likely unsure of you than herself. She hasn't been involved with anyone since Rosamund—I was going to say not seriously involved, but I doubt she's been involved with anyone, full stop, in all that time. How would you rate that kiss?"

"What, on the steam scale? Well, if one is *I've enjoyed our evening* and five is *Come for dinner, stay for breakfast*, it was definitely bacon and eggs."

Now it was Nicola's turn to roll her eyes. "Quite the romantic, aren't you? I think perhaps you need a bit of help in that department." She pulled out a dress. "How about this one?"

"It's pretty. But I can't get all dressed up like that for a casual dinner. She'll get the wrong idea."

"Don't you mean the right idea? You want her to kiss you again, don't you? At the very least?"

"I guess when you put it that way..." Alex grabbed the dress from Nicola. "Let's hit the fitting room."

❖

Alex spent all of Saturday morning cooking. As she chopped up the pancetta and the vegetables for the soffritto, she thought back to her conversation with Nicola the previous day. Maybe Nicola was right, and she was the one who had been driving Cam to distraction, and not the other way around. In either case, a little clarity was long overdue. Well, they would have plenty of time to talk over dinner.

If she could get up enough nerve to broach the topic. She should take her own advice. She went to get the meat out of the refrigerator and happened to glance over at the photo on the wall. She smiled at Janet's image.

"So we're sharing Dawson House, are we?"

As she started browning the meat, it seemed natural to just keep talking. "I know I should be weirded out by the whole ghost thing, but I'm actually kind of glad you're still around. Or sort of around. Whoa!"

She should have been expecting Grace to show up, drawn by the cooking aromas. If she had, she wouldn't have jumped half a foot and splattered herself with olive oil just because Grace rubbed against her leg. The cat was now busy devouring the shreds of meat that had ended up on the floor.

"Helping clean up, are you?"

Having finished providing this valuable service, Grace was now licking her whiskers and gazing up at Alex, clearly hoping that further assistance would be required. Alex resolved to frustrate that expectation, keeping a careful eye on Grace's meanderings to avoid any additional accidents.

Finally it was time to add some liquid to the sauce, starting with a little wine. While the alcohol cooked away, she opened the can of tomatoes and paused to consider. She had bought the smallest can they had, but it still looked like too much. In the end she used about half the can and put the rest in the fridge. Last of all, she stirred in some milk—another of her grandmother's secrets.

Now all she had to do was let the sauce simmer for three or four hours, throw together a couple of salads, boil up the pasta water, and set the table. And try not to lose her mind waiting for seven o'clock.

❖

Precisely at seven, Cam gratefully stopped pacing about in the back garden and knocked at the kitchen door. She knew you were supposed to be right on time for a dinner invitation, but she had arrived far too early, despite having changed her shirt three times and her trousers twice, and by now was chilled right through. She should probably have stayed in the van.

It took a few moments before the door opened. Alex was much more dressed up than she was. Perhaps she should have worn a jacket and tie after all.

Alex seemed a little flustered. "Sorry, I wasn't expecting you so soon. I forgot. Americans aren't usually quite this punctual."

Alex accepted the bottle she was holding out and gave her an awkward little one-armed hug. "Oh! You're frozen." Alex jumped back as if in dismay, but then grabbed her hand to lead her inside.

Just as well, because it was pitch dark. She couldn't see a thing.

"Come over to the fire. It got so chilly that I went ahead and lit it. First time so far this year. At least for me. I'm sure Mrs. Tate had the fire going all winter for last year's Scholar." Alex sounded nervous. Relieved that she wasn't the only one, Cam found herself able to relax for the first time all day.

Once they reached the hearth, Alex let go of her hand. Cam stepped closer to the fire and held both hands to the flames. "Oh, that's lovely." She rubbed her arms, feeling warmer already.

"What's this you've brought?" Alex tilted the bottle to read the label by the firelight. "Perry? What's that?"

"It's just like cider, but it's made from pears."

"That makes sense. Should we have it with the meal?"

"It might be better to save it for afters—I don't think it would go so well with tomatoey garlicky things."

"How do you know what we're having? I so wanted to surprise you."

"If you wanted to keep it a secret, you should have done the cooking elsewhere. I knew the moment you opened the door—the smell's a bit hard to miss."

"Oh, of course. I've stopped noticing after being around it all day. For a minute there I thought you had X-ray vision or something."

"Why is it so dark in here, anyway?"

Alex smiled at her. She had done something with her hair that was really pretty. "Why does anything ever go wrong at Dawson House?"

"Oh, no—not our friend?"

"That's my guess. Everything was fine until about five minutes ago, and then the lights went out. But only in here. The lights in the hall are still on."

"That is peculiar."

"More than you know. It isn't even all the electricity that's out in here, just the lights. I checked and the refrigerator's still working. I'll bet the TV isn't affected either."

"Bloody hell. I must be going soft in the head. I forgot about the DVD. I'm sorry."

"Don't worry about it. I'm not really in the mood for tragedy tonight anyway."

"Neither am I, as it happens. Well, looks like it's a busman's holiday for me. I'll just get my kit from the van."

"No, don't. After Janet's gone to all this trouble, it seems a shame to spoil it."

"I'm afraid I don't follow."

"Think about it. What do people do when their lights go out?"

"Swear? Hunt for a torch, discover the batteries in it have gone dead, and swear some more?"

"No, silly. They light candles."

"Oh. Oh! You mean she wants us to have dinner by candlelight. Sorry, I seem to be a bit slow tonight."

"That shouldn't be a problem. From what I've seen of your slow setting, it suits me just fine." Alex reached out and slid the tip of one finger gently across Cam's lower lip for a brief moment, then stepped back and shot her a mischievous grin. Caught off guard, Cam's brain seized up completely.

"Why don't you find us some candles while I put the finishing touches on the meal?" Alex walked away, stopping to put the perry in the fridge before going over to the stove.

Cam managed to start breathing again. Candles. She could do that. Probably.

❖

Alex clutched the edge of the stove to try and steady herself. She could hear Cam moving around near the fireplace and she was very glad for the concealing darkness. She was sure her face must be as red as the dress she was wearing. What the hell could possibly have possessed her just now? She never did things like that.

Time to get a grip. She needed to finish getting dinner ready. As she peered through the dimness to start the pasta cooking, a thought struck her. Maybe it was the dress.

The minute she had tried it on yesterday, she had felt different. Something about the way it was cut, the way it hugged her curves on top, the way the skirt flared out around her legs, made her want to move, to dance. Almost without realizing it, she had started to shift and sway, rocking her hips to a slow beat pulsing somewhere in her imagination. And that of course had made her think of Cam—dancing with her, holding her, kissing her. It gave her the shivers, but in a good way. A really good way. Even Nicola had been a little affected by the way it looked, if her blushing face was anything to go by.

So anyway, here she was, all decked out in soft, silky crimson and behaving completely out of character. It was like a fairy tale featuring some kind of magical clothing—like a pair of slippers or a cloak— something that casts a spell on anyone who wears it, transforming them, rendering them unrecognizable. Although with most such stories, ultimately the enchanted garment ends up revealing the truth rather than concealing it. So maybe this was the real her that the dress had unleashed.

Well, at the very least it was practical, since the red color would conceal any sauce-related mishaps. Hopefully Cam's white shirt would survive unscathed. It looked so good on her, it would be a shame if it got stained. Of course, if that happened, she could always offer to wash it for her—right away, naturally. She smiled, wondering what Cam was wearing under it. It would be very, very wrong of her to hope for the worst just so she could find out.

By now the room was much brighter. Cam had managed to locate and light several candles and was moving around the room positioning them on the counters and the table. Meanwhile Alex drained the pasta and transferred it to a large bowl. She mixed in parmesan cheese and, after giving it a moment to melt, added a ladle of sauce and tossed the pasta enough to lightly coat it. She served up two generous platefuls, added more sauce to each, and picked up both dishes, intending to carry them to the table.

But when she turned around, Cam was standing there, practically right on top of her. She hadn't realized Cam was so close. For a moment it looked like disaster was about to strike.

But Cam reached out and put both hands on her waist, steadying her so she could move the plates out to either side, out of range. Then she took a good look at Cam's face and forgot all about the food, and everything else.

Cam stood still, gazing at Alex, feeling her warmth right through the thin fabric beneath her hands. She took a moment to regret having startled her, but she hadn't been able to help herself. When she'd looked up from setting the last of the candles in place, she had really seen Alex for the first time that evening and had watched, captivated, as she moved back and forth, lifting and pouring and stirring, one motion flowing into the next, the shimmering fabric of her dress catching the flickering candlelight with every movement.

Cam couldn't help herself—she was drawn to Alex, almost in a trance. She wasn't thinking, only feeling. She had to get closer, had to touch her.

And now that she had her hands on her, she needed more. She opened her mouth to apologize for the near collision but all that came out was, "So beautiful." She closed the fraction of distance between them and kissed her. Gently at first, but then with more passion. She loved the feel of her, the taste of her. She became aware that Alex was pulling back, pulling away, and reluctantly, she broke off the kiss.

Alex said something. She looked upset. Worried, Cam studied her face, wondering what she had done, but a beat later the words

"I'm going to drop them" finally penetrated her brain and she kicked into gear, grabbing both plates just in time.

A moment of frantic juggling later, she had them balanced just enough to get them onto the table, more or less intact. A little sauce had spilled over the side onto her hand and reflexively she licked it off.

And groaned. It was that good.

CHAPTER NINETEEN

Alex, grateful for Cam's dexterity in rescuing their dinner, was almost as delighted by Cam's obvious pleasure in her cooking as she had been by the kiss that she'd unfortunately had to break away from.

"Come sit down and eat before it gets cold."

Cam started to sit, only to stop and go over to the counter near the stove, opening first one drawer, then another.

"What are you looking for?"

"A spoon, of course. Ah, here were are."

"Put that back this instant."

"Why? How else am I going to eat my pasta?"

"That sound you hear is my grandmother rolling over in her grave. Spoons are for soup. You eat pasta with a fork."

"Maybe you do, lass. Us ordinary folk need a bit of help."

Alex crossed her arms and gave Cam a fake-serious glare. "Come and sit down and I'll show you what to do." When Cam didn't immediately comply, she added, "At least try it. Someone as good with her hands as you are shouldn't have any trouble."

Cam shot her a grin and sat. "When you put it that way, how can I refuse?" She picked up her fork. "All right. How do I eat my spaghetti with just this?"

"This isn't spaghetti. It's fettuccine. When a sauce is this thick, you have to eat it with flat pasta. If you use spaghetti it just falls off." Cam gave her a look. "Sorry. I'm only slightly obsessed." She picked up her own fork. "Okay. The first thing you do is catch a little of the pasta with your fork—just a strand or two—and lift it up a bit, away from the rest. That's it. Then you put the tines down on a bare spot—try the edge of the plate. Okay. Now slowly start to twirl it, keeping the tines in contact with the plate the whole time."

By the time Cam had finished laboriously twirling, she had a mound of fettuccine the size of a Ping-Pong ball on the end of her fork. She held it up like a pasta lollipop and looked dubiously at Alex, who couldn't help laughing.

It took a few more tries, and a lot of laughter, but eventually Cam got the hang of it.

"Now you can add regulation pasta eating to your catalog of impressive accomplishments. Be sure to update your social media profile—what woman could resist?"

"I don't have a profile. Besides, there's only one woman I care about impressing. And I don't need to go online to find her."

The look that accompanied this statement made Alex stop breathing for a moment. She blinked, suddenly very nervous. Trying for a casual tone, she said, "If that's supposed to mean me, you don't need to bother trying to impress me."

"It's a hopeless cause, then, is it?" Cam's tone was light, but her eyes were wary.

"You know that's not what I meant. I think by now I have a pretty good idea of what kind of a person you are."

"Do you? And what kind am I, then?" This time the tone wasn't light at all.

"The right kind. The best kind. The kind worth hanging on to."

Cam looked rueful. "Not everyone shares that opinion."

"Rosamund is a goddamn fool."

"What?"

She took a deep breath. "Look, I'm sorry. I know it's hard for you to talk about her. It's hard for me, too. But I think we need to."

Cam didn't say anything, just nodded. She pushed away from the table, leaned back in her chair, and crossed her arms. Her face was expressionless—the same blank look Alex had seen whenever Cam had come face to face with Rosamund.

Alex sighed. "Damn, this is hard. I don't even know where to start. All I can think about is how much she hurt you. And it just makes me crazy to think that I helped her. I can't believe what a fool I've been."

Cam leaned forward. "What do you mean, you helped her?"

"After what happened with the letter, I've been doing a lot of thinking. I've gone over and over things in my mind, trying to figure out how I ended up in this mess, what I could or should have done differently."

"You can't be blaming yourself for what she did. That's just not right."

"But I'm not blaming myself, not exactly. I want to understand how it happened, what clues I missed. That way next time, if there is a next time, I won't repeat the same mistakes."

"And what have you figured out, then?"

"I keep coming back to those things she said that night when she barged in here. The things she said about you." Cam stiffened, but Alex didn't stop. "Of course I realized it was a total bunch of crap as soon as I thought about it carefully. I just wish I'd done that right away, instead of kicking you out like I did. I'm really sorry—there's no excuse for that."

Cam's face softened. She reached out a hand and Alex grasped it. "No, it's like I said. You mustn't blame yourself, not one bit. She's got a way of twisting things until you don't know what to think. She used to do that to me all the time—make me feel as if anything that made her unhappy was my fault somehow, that if I disagreed with her there was something wrong with me. It took me a long time to get my head back on straight afterward."

"After you broke up, you mean? She made it sound like you dumped her, and for no good reason, but I'm willing to bet that's not what happened at all." Cam's mouth twisted. "I'm right about that, aren't I?"

Cam didn't say anything, just nodded.

"But that's not the only thing she said that didn't make sense. All that stuff about you wanting revenge and trying to destroy her happiness by going after me, that didn't sound anything like you. But you know who it does sound like? It sounds like Rosamund."

"My God." Cam's eyes were darting back and forth, as if she was thinking rapidly. Then she looked back at Alex, wide-eyed. "My God."

"You see, the one thing I could never figure out was why Rosamund was pursuing me so intently. I'm not exactly a ten, unless your scale goes up to fifteen."

"Now that I can't agree with." Cam lifted Alex's hand and kissed it before lowering it gently back down to the tabletop.

"You're sweet. But you know what I mean. So why was she after me? I thought maybe she was just bored and I was handy. But think back. She started it at the Lammas dance—after you and I had been dancing together. I bet she saw us and realized that you…that we…" Suddenly she felt shy.

Cam smiled at her gently. "That I had found someone."

Alex smiled back. "Yes. And then there was the way she pounced on me in the parking lot outside that club in Leeds. At the time I had no idea why she was doing it—it came out of nowhere—but she must have seen you standing there and decided to put on a show. Damn. She really played me, didn't she?"

"Let it go."

"I'm trying to. But it's not easy." She shook her head. "Oh, and then there was the time I saw you in the pub where she and I had just had dinner. After we left she was sort of strange—like she was upset and amused at the same time. She must have realized that I was thinking about you. I was so worried about you."

"About me? Why?"

"The look on your face just tore at me—so much pain—and all I could think was how I was hurting you, how awful it was for you to have to see us together because…Oh, my God. I thought you were breaking your heart over her. But you weren't, were you?"

"Not over her, lass."

"Oh. Oh! I really am an idiot. I'm surprised you're even still talking to me. I've just been so clueless. Well, at least I never actually slept with her, thank God." Too late, she clapped a hand over her mouth. "Damn. I'm sorry. That was tacky. Not something you needed to hear about."

But Cam just laughed. "I could almost feel sorry for her. Almost. I'd say that's enough time wasted on her. Let's talk about something else. What do you hear from your friend Ian?"

Alex was grateful for the change in subject. "He says he has a plan. He's going to research the specific terms of Prandall's bequest. Apparently no one's clear on the actual wording—everyone talks about the prize, but they never quote from the document itself. It hasn't even been taken out of the vault in decades. He's hoping there will be something in it he can use. For example, if it says something like the prize winner has to discover evidence and provide it to the Foundation he could argue for splitting the award since I did one of those things."

"That sounds promising."

"I think it's a long shot, even if he does find something. I'm sure there's a flock of lawyers involved by now and I doubt I'll ever see a penny. But I do want credit for the discovery, and Ian has promised to fight for that. Anyway, he's doing his best, and that's all I can ask for." She stood and began to clear the dishes. "How about a cup of tea?"

Cam stood as well and carried her plate over to the sink. "I'd love one."

Between the two of them, they soon had the table cleared, the leftovers put away, and the tea made. They worked efficiently together, maneuvering easily around one another, coordinating tasks with little need for conversation. Toward the end of the cleanup, Grace arrived, complaining loudly of suffering and starvation.

Alex hardened her heart. "Don't even try it. I already fed you today. Twice, if you count those scraps you tricked me into dropping on the floor."

Grace tried Cam next, rubbing against her leg and mewing pitifully. "No chance. All the food's packed up. Why don't you go for a ramble and see if you can find a nice juicy mouse?"

Apparently Grace thought the suggestion had merit, because she pranced over to the back door, then cast an expectant glance over her shoulder. Cam responded to the unspoken command, shutting the door firmly once the cat had exited.

Alex carried over both cups of tea and handed one to Cam. "Why don't we sit by the fire?"

Cam smiled. "I'd like that."

❖

They went over to the fireplace and Alex sat down on the bench. Cam knelt beside her, set her tea down on the stone hearth, and added more wood to the fire. Alex watched as the flames seemed to all but disappear, only to flare up strongly as the fire worked its way into the fresh fuel, claiming and consuming it.

She shifted her gaze to Cam, enjoying the way the flickering flames made patterns of shadow and glowing light across her hair and the side of her face. Cam was looking at her steadily. Alex couldn't look away, didn't want to look away. She could feel Cam's gaze like a caress, warm honey gliding and spreading all the way through her, into her flesh, into her bones.

Cam finally broke eye contact, grabbing the cup from Alex's hand and putting it hurriedly down somewhere on the floor. Then she reached for her, one hand on the back of Alex's neck and the other at her waist, drawing her into a hot, hard kiss. Alex opened her mouth and Cam's tongue plunged inside, claiming and taking. Alex grabbed Cam by the shoulders, trying to pull her closer.

The kiss went on and on. She never wanted it to end, but she needed more and she needed it now. She laced her fingers through the softness of Cam's hair and tugged.

At first nothing happened. Cam was devouring her mouth so intently that she probably didn't even notice. Alex pulled harder, then harder still, and finally she was able to gain a tiny fraction of air between her lips and Cam's. Eyes closed tight, Cam groaned and buried her face in the hollow between Alex's neck and shoulder. She started nipping at the bare skin with her teeth.

In spite of the shudders this was sending through her, Alex managed to turn her head enough to whisper fiercely in Cam's ear, "Let's go upstairs."

"No." Now Cam was sliding her tongue along Alex's collarbone.

Alex whimpered. "Please. You're making me crazy."

"Can't." She started moving her mouth over Alex's throat, kissing and teasing with tiny flicks of her tongue. "Can't wait that long."

"Then do something, damn it. I need you to touch me."

Cam raised her head and grinned. "Always glad to be of service to a lady in distress."

Alex froze.

For a moment Cam was afraid that Alex was going to give her a clout round the ear.

But then Alex laughed. "You wretch. Come here."

Not wanting to waste another second, Cam moved to sit beside Alex, slipping her arms around her and lifting her carefully so that Alex was sitting sideways across her lap.

Before Cam could do anything else, Alex planted a kiss in the hollow at the base of her throat and began slowly unfastening her shirt, pausing in between buttons to kiss the bare skin she was gradually revealing. Cam gasped at the surprise and pleasure of it, hesitating for a few crucial moments.

Not long, but long enough for Alex to get her shirt all the way open and push it back, tugging the sleeves down to her elbows, exposing her completely and effectively immobilizing her. Then Alex started sliding the fingers of one hand slowly over her skin from her waist to her neck and back again. The sensation, combined with the feeling of helplessness, was scary and exciting and really, really good. She couldn't take her eyes from Alex's hand.

"You know," Alex said conversationally, "I've been wondering all evening what you were wearing under your shirt." She rested her palm in the center of Cam's chest for a moment, then spread her fingers and began making slow circles, slipping lightly over the tops of her breasts, never quite touching the nipples. Cam kept watching, her breath coming faster.

"It didn't look like you had a bra on, but I thought maybe a tank top." Alex was still using the same matter-of-fact tone. She stopped moving her hand and Cam looked up to meet her eyes. Alex grinned. "I'm glad I was wrong."

Alex looked down again and Cam followed her gaze. This time, Alex was using both hands on her, fingertips circling around the outside of her nipples, right at the border where the darker and lighter skin met. Her touch was so light it was maddening.

Cam could barely breathe. Her nipples were hardening, but Alex just kept circling them, feather light. "Thought...you said...you wanted me to touch you."

"I guess something must have changed my mind." Alex's palms had replaced her fingertips, still circling, but she was holding them just a little above where they needed to be. Any contact was random, glancing, and never enough.

Cam clenched her teeth, trying without much success to keep from whimpering. She knew she could ask Alex to stop. Or she could just shift a bit and pull her shirt all the way off. She should definitely do that. In a minute.

"I wonder what it was that did it. Oh, well. These things happen, don't they? Now let's see…" Alex pressed her palms down against Cam's nipples and rubbed them—hard—and then she pinched them, not at all gently. The pleasure-pain shot right between Cam's legs, and she threw back her head and howled. Alex leaned over and captured Cam's mouth with her own, still tugging at her nipples.

Then Alex leaned back and looked her dead in the eye. "It sounds to me," she said, far too sweetly, "as if you might be in some distress. So tell me, lady, is there any way that I can be of service to you?" On the word service Alex ground her hips down against Cam's lap, sending another burst of heat through her.

Cam growled and tore against the cloth around her arms, ripping the shirt like it was made of paper, freeing herself instantly. Alex squealed and tried to move away but Cam was too fast, grabbing her around the waist and holding her easily even as she squirmed, despite the effect those movements were having on her ability to focus.

"Oh, no you don't, lass. Not just yet." Torn between anger and amusement, for a moment she stared at Alex, who was now sitting quietly, caught in the circle of her arms and regarding her with some apprehension—as well she might—but absolutely no repentance. Eventually amusement won.

Alex relaxed a fraction when Cam finally smiled at her. She had known she was playing with fire, but once she'd started, she hadn't been able to stop. The look on Cam's face, the way she was breathing, the sounds she was making—Alex had loved every second of it. "I'm in trouble now, aren't I?"

"Probably." Cam's smile had a touch of devilment in it.

Alex found herself grinning back. "Let's make sure," she said, resting her palms against Cam's stomach and lightly massaging the bare skin, enjoying the feeling of smoothness over the firm muscles below.

Cam made a sound of appreciation, halfway between a sigh and a moan. Encouraged, Alex lowered her hands a fraction, slipping her thumbs just inside the waistband of Cam's trousers, gliding them slowly back and forth over the skin beneath the fabric.

Between one heartbeat and the next, Cam tightened her hold, pulling Alex close, trapping her hands between them. Alex gasped. She knew Cam was strong, but she had never realized just how much. She could feel it now. The arms enclosing her were so powerful. Cam holding her like this made her feel completely claimed and utterly protected all at once. It felt so good she was almost light-headed.

Cam brought one hand up to cradle her head, keeping the other arm securely around her. For a long moment Cam held her like that, eyes locked with hers. Any trace of humor was gone. All Alex could see was hunger. She felt the heat of it all through her.

Cam's eyes grew cloudy and she lowered her gaze to Alex's mouth. Alex's lips tingled as if Cam were already touching them. She sighed, letting her own eyes close.

Then Cam finally kissed her—not slowly, but steadily, thoroughly, as if nothing existed but this moment, and the moment never had to end.

When Cam eased back from the kiss, Alex gave a little cry of protest.

"Sh, love," Cam whispered. "I'm right here." She caught Alex's lower lip lightly between her teeth, worrying at it for a moment, sending a dart of pleasure through her.

Eyes still closed, Alex felt Cam tilt her head back before pressing her lips tenderly against her neck, moving lower with each soft kiss. Alex felt herself floating, her mind adrift. Being held like this, she was free to let everything go. Cam wouldn't let her fall.

Keeping her hand carefully cupped around Alex's head to hold her steady, Cam trailed her mouth down Alex's throat, taking her time, loving the scent of Alex's skin, the silky feel of it. When she reached the hollow at the base she lapped at it with her tongue, then blew on it lightly, making Alex gasp. Then she eased her mouth along Alex's collarbone until she reached the point where it vanished under the fabric of her dress, lingering a moment before starting to work her way down, kissing along the bare skin just above the neckline, over the tops of her breasts, following the edge all the way around, then back to the center, planting kisses along the cleft between her breasts, teasing with her tongue. Alex's breathing was broken now with soft little gasps of pleasure.

Cam wanted her so badly she felt dizzy. She slid her free hand from Alex's waist up the back of her dress to fumble with the zipper. Somehow she managed to slide it down in spite of the way her hand was shaking. Raising her head, she twined her fingers deeper into Alex's curls and kissed her mouth again as she slipped the dress off each of her shoulders in turn, sliding down the straps of her bra with it.

Then she eased her hand between their bodies and grabbed the dress at the center of the neckline, along with the bra behind it, and pulled it down to Alex's waist before embracing her again. She pulled her close, groaning into Alex's mouth at the pleasure of feeling their naked breasts pressed together.

Cam felt Alex free her arms from the dress and slip them around her neck.

Alex turned her head a little to the side, breaking away from their kiss. "Touch me," she whispered. "Please. I need you to…please."

Alex started kissing her neck, still murmuring *please* in between kisses. Cam slid her hand down Alex's side, enjoying the smoothness of the fabric beneath her fingertips, on fire with the awareness of how thin the barrier was that was keeping her from the soft warmth of Alex's body underneath.

She drew her hand past Alex's waist, over her hip, and along the outside of her leg until she reached the hem of the dress. She pushed against the edge of the cloth, drawing it higher until it was gathered just above Alex's knee. She could feel Alex kissing down the center of her chest as she slipped her hand up under the dress, letting it rest on the bare skin of Alex's leg for a moment before trailing her fingers slowly upward along the inside of her thigh.

She told herself to take her time, not to rush this. Just touching Alex like this felt so amazing, so—a blast of white heat flared through her as Alex's mouth closed over her nipple and sucked it, hard, then began to circle around it with her tongue. She had Cam's other breast in her hand, fondling it and rolling the nipple between her finger and thumb.

Cam growled, her brain wiped clean of everything but hunger. She pushed her hand all the way up between Alex's legs. Some thin bit of fabric was there but it only took a moment to pull it down and away. Then there was only flesh, velvety soft and so wet, like silk under her fingers. She couldn't wait, couldn't think, she had to touch her everywhere, everywhere, it felt so good, so perfect.

Alex's mouth was on her neck, kissing her and raking her teeth over her skin, making moaning, pleading sounds. Less frenzied now that the first sharpness of her need had passed, Cam teased her fingers through Alex's silky wetness, playing with her, searching out the places that made her cries louder, more desperate.

Alex thought she was going to die if Cam kept her teetering on the edge much longer, but she couldn't bear it if she stopped. It was so good it was almost like pain. But she needed more. She needed— "Inside me, please. Please, I need you inside...Yes, like that. Just like that. Oh, please don't stop."

"Hush, love. I've got you. I've got you."

Alex was grinding her hips now, rocking back and forth on Cam's hand, feeling Cam take her. It was so good, so good. And then Cam's thumb was stroking her in just the right spot, just there, but so lightly, too lightly. Alex reached down and put her hand on top of Cam's, pressing down hard, the way she needed it, yes, harder, just like that, just—And then Cam captured her mouth again, tongue thrusting inside her, taking her completely as she came and came.

CHAPTER TWENTY

Alex felt utterly content as Cam held her gently, stroking her hair and kissing the top of her head. She hugged Cam lightly around the waist, wanting to stay just like this, forever.

Or maybe not. As a matter of fact, she had a much better idea. She eased one hand upward, rubbing slow circles along Cam's side before moving to cup her breast.

Cam gasped. Delicate strokes of her thumb on Cam's nipple made her gasp again. Alex lifted her head and kissed Cam lightly, then whispered in her ear, "That feels good, doesn't it?"

"Uh."

"I guess that means yes. I like making you feel good." She tugged on Cam's earlobe with her teeth, drawing another inarticulate sound from her.

Alex moved her hand to the waistband of Cam's trousers and undid the button.

Leaning back just enough to look into Cam's eyes, now half-closed and heavy with need, she said, "I hope you don't mind too much if I enjoy myself just a little bit more."

A ghost of humor surfaced amid the wanting in her eyes. "Suit yourself."

Alex smiled, ready to indulge herself fully. "Oh, I plan to." Alex slid the zipper down very, very slowly, keeping her eyes locked on Cam's the entire time.

"Now let's see. What would be fun?" She placed her hand flat on Cam's stomach and spread her fingers, rubbing lightly. When she moved lower, slipping just inside the waistband of her underwear, still circling slowly, Cam made a strangled sound. Then she slid her hand all the way down. When she touched her, Cam groaned.

"You're so wet. Oh, my God." Suddenly she didn't feel like playing.

She eased her hand away and quickly stood up. Her dress bunched around her waist was a distraction, and she impatiently pulled it off and tossed it aside. Cam sat there watching her, uncertainty on her face.

"Take your trousers off—and your underwear. Do it. Do it now."

Excitement flashed in Cam's eyes and she hurriedly complied.

When Cam was naked, Alex knelt in front of her and rested her hands on Cam's knees, forcing herself to pause a moment before gently moving them just a little apart. Cam let her legs fall farther open, inviting her closer. She leaned forward so their bodies were finally together, skin against skin, and took Cam's head between her hands, holding her tenderly as she kissed her, taking her time. Cam embraced her, lightly stroking her back and shoulders.

Alex kissed her way down the center of Cam's body, eyes closed, tasting her skin, feeling her breath quickening, listening to her sighs and gasps, letting her hands trail down Cam's neck, over her breasts, and down to rest on the tops of her thighs. She spent a long time kissing Cam's belly, teasing her tongue around the edge of her navel, before moving to kiss the insides of her thighs, each in turn, and to rub her cheek against the soft skin there.

Cam's hands were on hers now, gripping tightly. She looked up and saw that Cam's head was thrown back and her eyes were closed. She looked like she was holding her breath.

Alex eased her hands free. With gentle fingers she parted Cam's folds. She was wet and swollen and so beautiful. Alex lowered her head and kissed her, then opened her mouth to take her in, moaning at the incredible taste and feel of her. That was her last rational thought. She gave herself up to Cam completely, feasting on her. She couldn't get enough of her.

Cam's hands were tangled in her hair, pulling her closer, showing her where she needed more, and still more. Cam's breathing was faster, harder, and she was making desperate sounds.

Alex was nothing but feeling, nothing but need, silently begging Cam to take her pleasure, not to stop, not to let her go. Suddenly Cam's hands tightened, holding Alex's head completely still as she thrust against her mouth hard and fast and came in a long, shuddering wail.

Alex stayed where she was, teasing with her tongue until Cam pulled her head gently back.

"Can't." She panted. "Can't…no more."

Alex rested her head against Cam's thigh. Cam's hand was twining lazily through her hair, fingers moving slower and slower. Alex smiled to herself and looked up. Cam's eyes were closed and her breathing was deep and slow.

"Cam?" she murmured. "Cam, honey?"

"Mmph."

"Wake up, sweetheart."

"Am awake." Cam's eyes were open now but she still didn't exactly look alert.

"That's good, sweetie, because I'm awake, too." She trailed her index finger up and down Cam's stomach lightly enough to tickle. Cam made an annoyed sound and clamped a hand over hers, stopping the movement.

Now her eyes were focused. Alex smiled sweetly at her.

"I'm also a little chilly and kind of stiff. This floor isn't exactly the most comfortable place to spend time." She got to her feet and took Cam by the hand, tugging slightly. "Do you think maybe we could go upstairs now? I know it's a long way, but I promise to make it worth your while." Her mind was already conjuring up ideas, and she looked Cam up and down, trying to decide where to start first.

Cam stood, grinning at her. "Can't wait."

❖

Cam plummeted out of a dream of suffocation and torment to find the cat treading frantically all over her body, yowling desperately. Awareness shattered through—she was naked, Alex was lying beside her, also naked, and the room was full of smoke.

Roughly, she shook Alex awake, yelling, "Fire! The place is on fire. Get up!" Even as she said it, she tumbled off the bed, grabbing Alex by the arm and hauling her up as well. The cat ran away, howling.

"Oh, my God!" Alex was resisting Cam's effort to pull her forward, looking wildly about. "Wait—let me grab some clothes."

But Cam just pulled harder, dragging Alex with her. "No time! With fire, there's never time. Come on."

She stopped in the open doorway, Alex just behind her. Looking rapidly in both directions, she could see that the hallway was full of smoke but she could neither see nor hear the fire.

Alex coughed. "What do you think?"

"The stairs should be clear. Let's go."

Bending double to keep below the worst of the smoke, together they ran to the staircase, both of them coughing now. Cam paused to look down.

"I don't see any flames," said Alex.

"Neither do I. Come on."

They ran down the stairs and headed for the front door, barreling through it out into the morning sunlight.

The door slammed shut behind them as Alex threw her arms around Cam and hugged her fiercely, the feeling of skin on skin and the solid warmth of Cam's body easing the terror. Cam returned the embrace with interest, holding her so tightly it was almost painful.

"Oh, sweetheart, I was so scared."

"Me as well, love. Thank God the cat woke us."

"Grace! I didn't see her. Do you think she got out?"

"I shouldn't worry. Likely that cat has ninety lives. She'll be fine."

"I hope so."

As the adrenaline rush subsided, Alex's conscious mind kicked in and registered that they were both standing naked outdoors in broad daylight. Which felt wonderful, of course, pressed up against Cam and holding her so close, but then again, she was suddenly very grateful for the concealing shrubbery.

Perhaps sensing the change, Cam eased away from the embrace, keeping an arm around Alex's waist as she turned to study the house.

"Funny sort of fire, this. All that smoke everywhere, but no flames. I wonder where it's burning."

"Probably the kitchen—oh Goddess, it must be from the fireplace. We didn't bank the fire before we went upstairs. I forgot all about it."

"Likewise. Had a few other things on my mind."

"Somehow I don't think it was your mind that was the problem."

"True enough. Or yours, I'd say." She smiled.

"Point taken," said Alex. "What now?"

"You know, something's not quite right. Let's get a look at the back of the house, shall we?"

Standing in the backyard, Cam stared at the house, a puzzled expression on her face. Alex looked, too, but there was nothing to see—no smoke, no flame. If you didn't know better, you wouldn't think the house was on fire at all.

Alex was still puzzling over this when Cam started toward the kitchen door. "I'll just take a quick look inside."

Alex moved to block her. "Like hell, you will. That's how people get killed, going back into a burning building after they've gotten out safely."

"I'm not going to get killed. I'm only going to pop my head in for a minute."

"You don't have to be such a goddamn hero. There is not a single thing inside that house, or even the house itself, that's worth your life. Let's just call the fire department."

"Just call them? And just exactly how do you reckon we should just do that, eh? I don't know about you, but I don't fancy strolling stark naked through the village."

"A little embarrassment is a small price to pay for safety."

"I have to live with these people. You don't."

"What the hell is that supposed to mean?"

"You know bloody well what I mean. You'll be going back to the States in a few months, but I'll still be here. Or are you planning to pitch a tent out on the moor when your grant's done?"

Alex winced at the derisive tone, but she sensed the fear underneath and her own anger melted away. Cam had given voice to something she herself had been studiously avoiding thinking about.

She took Cam's hand, clasping it in both of her own. "I'm worried about that, too, sweetheart. I don't know what I'm going to do—what we're going to do—when the time comes. Hell, I don't even know what we're going to do tomorrow, or five minutes from now. And unless you've got second sight, you don't either."

"True enough, love—although I do know what I'm set on doing at the moment, and that's checking on the state of things in the kitchen."

Alex sighed. "Obviously I can't stop you. But there's no way you're going back in there by yourself. If you go in, I'm coming with you."

Cam snatched her hand back. "I don't think so."

"Fine. In that case, you go right ahead." She made a sweeping gesture in the direction of the back door. Cam didn't move, giving her a suspicious look.

"Right then, what's the catch?"

"Catch? There's no catch. You want to do your superhero routine, please feel free." She paused for effect. "Meanwhile, I'll be around front getting my laptop from the study. I'll only be a minute, just like you."

Cam grabbed Alex's arm, her face a thundercloud. "Try again."

"The way I see it, you've got some choices. You can stand here holding on to me—which is absolutely fine with me. We can stand here till doomsday or the house burns down, whichever. Or you can let go of my arm, and we can each go inside by ourselves, as you're determined to do. Or—"

Cam suddenly looked much less unhappy. "Or nothing. You're not going in there, with me or on your own, and that's final." Surprisingly, she let go of Alex's arm. "You've forgotten one thing— the front door's closed, and you've no key. Unless you've managed to hide it somewhere…?"

She grinned, damn her, giving Alex an appreciative once over. But then Alex remembered the other time she'd been locked out, and she grinned back. "Not to worry. I'll get Janet to open the door for me. I got her to do it once before—at least, I'm pretty sure I did." She took a step backward, then another.

Cam started to lunge for her but caught herself in midstride. "Janet! That's it! The flaming bloody damn place isn't on fire at all."

❖

Alex felt instinctively that Cam was absolutely right. So when Cam ran to the back door, which—no surprise—was helpfully ajar, and disappeared into the kitchen, Alex just followed her inside, barely even apprehensive. There was smoke everywhere, which did seem to be originating from the fireplace, but there was no fire to be seen, there or anywhere—not even a single glowing ember.

Alex grabbed a couple of dish towels and ran water on them, handing one to Cam and putting the other over her nose and mouth. Cam did likewise, then went over to the fireplace, fumbling with something. Alex heard clanking, and then the smoke near the hearth seemed to lighten a little.

Despite knowing it wasn't necessary, Alex filled a pot with water and carried it over, poured it on the ashes, then went back for more. She wanted to make absolutely sure there was no danger. Cam followed her example, and by the time they were done the whole bottom of the fireplace was a soupy black mess of half-dissolved ash and scraps of unburned wood.

"Let's go outside for a bit."

"Yes, I'd like to try breathing again."

Once they were outdoors, Cam said, "So. Flue was closed up tight. What do you reckon?"

"There aren't a whole lot of possibilities. Somehow I doubt Grace could have managed it. But someone certainly did, and it wasn't you or me."

"Which pretty much leaves our departed friend."

"I wonder why she did it—it's not like she needed to, this time."

"What do you mean?"

Alex smiled. "Just something that occurred to me when she arranged for the candlelight last night. A few things fell into place. Ian told me once that Janet was known in the village as a matchmaker. Stands to reason that wouldn't have changed."

"Matchmaker? Wait a bit, all those breakdowns…?"

"Every single one of which meant that you had to come over here and fix them. I overheard Mrs. Tate once telling Janet there wasn't any point in causing another one right then, since you were out of town. Of course at the time I thought she was just talking to herself."

"So all this while—"

"We've been set up. By a ghost." Alex put her arms around Cam and hugged her, loving the feel of her skin. "I suppose it ought to give me the creeps, but I think it's kind of sweet."

Cam kissed her on the forehead. "As do I. I wish there was a way I could thank her somehow." She glanced at the open doorway. "Sadly, I'd say it's time we got back to work."

"I suppose we should open every single window."

"If a job's got to be done, best to do it right."

By the time they had finished, and Cam had double-checked that they hadn't missed even one window anywhere in the entire house, the air inside was much clearer, but enough smoke still lingered that they decided to go out for breakfast while waiting for it to dissipate completely. Cam grabbed her clothes from the kitchen and they hurried up to Alex's room to get ready.

It only took a moment for Cam to pull on her trousers. Her shirt was another matter, of course, but as there wasn't much to do about it, she just left it lying there. She sat on the bed to put her shoes on. Watching Alex dress, she wondered what she was feeling, and whether she was hurt by the harsh way Cam had spoken to her earlier. She thought about asking but decided to wait. She had surprised herself with her own anger, and she wanted to try and work out what was going on first.

Of course the knowledge that Alex would be going away much too soon was never far from her mind, but she certainly hadn't been thinking about it last night, not one bit, nor this morning either, not in the midst of all the rumpus.

And if you had asked her, she would have said that she didn't want to discuss it with Alex, not for a good long while—let alone throw it in her teeth the way she had. And definitely not on their very first morning together.

She coughed once, the smoke still lingering enough to be irritating, and met Alex's concerned glance with a smile she hoped was free of shadows. How could they be together at all if she spent every moment imagining the time when Alex would be gone? Whatever time they did have was too precious to waste. Alex was here, now, right in front of her. Somehow she had to make that be enough.

Alex soon finished dressing, crossing her arms and smiling at Cam, an expression on her face that would have held interesting possibilities if the house weren't quite so inhospitable at the moment. Cam hoped that by the time they got back from their meal, conditions would have significantly improved. She leaned back on her hands and arched her back, enjoying the way Alex's eyes flashed as she flaunted herself.

Alex was breathing a little harder. "As much as I like that look on you, I don't think they'll enjoy it quite as much at the café. In the US, some restaurants even put up signs: No shirt, no service."

"Get a lot of topless women roaming the streets, do you? Must be quite a hazard."

"Sorry to disillusion you, but it's not a major problem, at least not in Boston." She picked up the remains of Cam's shirt. "You looked so good in this. It's really a pity."

"Don't suppose you'd fancy trying to mend it."

"Not a chance." She smothered a cough. "I'm hopeless at sewing. I think it's probably a lost cause anyway." She balled up the shirt and tossed it into a corner, then gave Cam a considering look. "The T-shirts I sleep in are pretty loose on me. They'd probably fit you all right." She pulled two from the drawer and held them out. "Teddy bear or kittens?"

Cam froze. Then she took a good look at Alex's face. "Very funny, ha-ha." She chose one at random, checking just to be sure. No picture at all, just an Artemisia Foundation logo. The shirt was a little tight in the shoulders and arms, but wasn't a bad fit otherwise.

"Right, then." She held out a hand to Alex and off they went.

❖

They got their food to go and brought it back to Dawson House. Alex was glad—it was much more fun lounging on the grass in the backyard with Cam's arm around her, the two of them feeding each other morsels of pastry in between kisses, than sitting in the café trying to be decorous.

Trying being the operative word—not that it would have mattered much either way. Judging from the sidelong glances and whispers, everyone present had been well aware of how things stood between them. Probably something to do with the way Cam kept a hand on the small of her back the entire time, which had interfered somewhat with her simultaneous efforts to open doors and carry all the food for both of them. Alex had worked very hard at keeping a straight face during the more awkward moments. Truth to tell, she was beginning to get a sneaky little thrill every time Cam went out of her way to do something for her.

No, sitting here alone like this, in their own private space, safe from prying eyes and interruptions, was definitely a much better idea. Gradually, between the warmth of the sun and the comfort of Cam's presence, Alex grew drowsy. She rested her head on Cam's shoulder and let her eyes drift closed, thoughts roaming through her mind and starting to slip away.

No doubt the news about the two of them would be all over town and halfway to Leeds by noon. Alex smiled softly to herself. Who needs the Internet when you have village gossip? She wondered what it had been like for Artemisia, living out her days in a place where all the details of her life—painful or joyful—would have been considered public property, part of the fabric that knit the community together. Had she kept any of her secrets? Had she even tried?

From far away, she heard Cam's voice. "Now that's peculiar."

"Mmph?"

"I could have sworn we opened all the windows."

Alex kept her eyes closed. "We did. You checked."

"Then why is one of them still closed?"

Reluctantly, Alex lifted her head and opened her eyes. "Where?"

"One floor up, in the center."

Alex looked carefully. "Huh. One of the windows is closed. You're right, that is strange. I wonder which room that is."

"One way to find out. Count over from the end and let's go inside and take a look."

It was an excellent idea, except for the fact that it didn't work. They tried it a couple of times, counting from both ends of the hall, but the windows in every single room were open.

Cam sighed in frustration. "What do you reckon? Could she be playing with us, opening and closing the windows?"

"I suppose so, but it seems unlike her, somehow—causing trouble with no purpose. How about this: one of us stays inside and leans out, while the other goes outside to see where the closed window is relative to that room."

"Great idea. You stay here and I'll go out."

A few minutes later, Cam looked up to see Alex waving from an open window. The closed window was next to the one where she was standing.

"It's just to your left." Cam pointed. "Go next door and see."

But when Alex did, she stuck her head out of another open window, and this time the closed window was to her right.

"Stay there, I'm coming back up."

Once Cam had rejoined Alex, she quickly explained what she had seen. The two of them were standing in the hall in between the two rooms. They were right at the top of the stairs, facing a set of shelves built into the wall.

Cam looked at them carefully. The shelves were covered in fancy carving and were just barely deep enough for the few bits of bric-a-brac they held, including a small vase and a couple of tiny figurines. She had walked past the shelves hundreds of times, of course, but never paid them any mind. Now it was obvious that something about them wasn't right. For one thing, they were far too shallow to be of much practical use. Why go to all the trouble of building shelves like that?

And there was something a bit off about the wall on either side. It was hard to put her finger on just what was wrong, but something definitely was.

Standing in the open doorway of the room Alex had just been in, she started to work it out. To be sure, she checked the room on the opposite side of the shelves.

"These rooms are too small," she said to Alex.

"What do you mean?"

"These two rooms on either side should each be at least a foot or so wider than they are. There's a good three feet or more of missing space in between them, right behind these shelves."

"You mean there's something back there?"

"Exactly. This isn't a bookcase. It's a door."

CHAPTER TWENTY-ONE

A door!" Alex said. "And somewhere back behind it is that closed window. You're right—it's the only thing that makes sense. But if it's a door, how do we open it?"

"Well, with no doorknob ready to hand, I'd say we look for a catch or a button or some such." Cam removed the things that were sitting on the shelving, then reached up and started running her hands over the wood, both the shelves themselves and the carving surrounding them. However, she found nothing, even after going over the whole area several times.

She stepped back and stared at the decorations, wondering what she was missing. But all she could see was a load of fruit and flowers mixed together. Pretty enough, if you liked that sort of thing, but otherwise not very helpful.

Alex came to stand beside her, humming under her breath, and slipped a hand around her waist.

"It's a pity there aren't any books on the shelves," she said "Not that they'd fit, of course. But in the movies, it's always moving one of the books that opens the secret passage. Unless it's moving an ornament. But you've already taken everything off."

Cam put a hand on the back of Alex's neck and began playing with her curls. Maybe they could take a break.

Alex smiled at her. "Oh, well. Guess this isn't the movies."

Then she started humming again—the same few notes over and over. It was getting just a bit annoying. "What is that song?"

"Just some silly thing from a kids' TV show. I'm looking for something here that doesn't fit, that's not like the others—something that breaks a pattern." She let go of Cam and stepped forward, scanning the carving intently. Suddenly she stopped. "Oh, please. It can't be that easy."

"What can't be?"

"Everything on the decoration is in multiples—there are three apples and two lilies, and so on. Except for the rose. There's only one rose. Of course."

"Why of course?"

"There's a Latin phrase that's used in English: *sub rosa*. Literally it means *under the rose* but what it really means is keeping something secret. So the secret to opening the secret door is—"

"Under the rose. Well, go on, then, give it a try."

Alex fumbled with the carving for a few minutes. Cam heard a small but definite click.

Alex stepped back and gestured triumphantly. "Ta-da!"

The carving of the rose was pushed in and sideways, revealing a small slot. "Um, congratulations and all that, but I don't see how that helps us. That looks to me like a keyhole."

"Yes, it certainly does. And I know exactly where the key is." She ran to her room and came back a moment later grinning broadly, swinging a key back and forth on the end of a cord.

Cam recognized it immediately. "Don't tell me that's the key the cat hit you with?"

"The very same. I told you then it felt like Janet had given it to me. I guess she really did, and now I know why."

Alex slid the key into the slot and tried to turn it. "Huh. It doesn't seem to be working. Maybe I was wrong."

"More likely the mechanism's just a bit stiff. Stands to reason after a century or so. Let me fetch my tools."

Once Cam had oiled the lock and made a few adjustments, the key turned easily. The shelving unit swung slowly open with a terrible creaking worthy of any horror film, revealing a dark recess behind it. Cam took a light from her tool case and played the beam over a small, narrow room, not much bigger than a wardrobe, with what looked like a desk, a couple of chairs, a few bookshelves, and on the wall at the back, a set of shutters, closed tight.

She would have insisted on going in first, just to be sure it was safe, but Alex had already rushed past her to throw open the shutters, flooding the space with light through the—yes—closed window.

Cam stepped inside, surprised that the air seemed fresh and cool, not musty as you would expect of a space so long closed up. And there was no dust anywhere to be seen. She smiled to herself. Janet's doing, most likely.

A gasp from Alex claimed her attention instantly. "What?"

"That notebook. The one on the desk with the marbled cover and the tiny gold rose stamped in one corner. I recognize it. It's the one Janet's holding in the photo downstairs. That means Janet was in here. She was in here the day she died."

"What? How can you possibly know that?"

"Ian told me the photo downstairs was taken the morning of her birthday, and she died that afternoon or evening. Ian's great-aunt Oona was the one who found her the next morning. She was lying at the top of the stairs, right over there. Right outside this room. I think she must have come in here, and after she'd stepped out again and locked it up, she collapsed and died. And I think the reason she came in here in the first place was to hide this notebook. I wonder why."

Alex sat down at the desk, and Cam took the other chair.

Alex set her hands flat on the desk on either side of the notebook, not quite touching it, as she stared down at the cover. "When I first saw the photo, I assumed this was a book of household accounts, or something similar, and that she had included it in the photo as a token of her professional responsibilities. But that doesn't make sense—if that's all it is, why keep it locked away in here?"

"One way to find out, Alex. Open it."

Alex turned to look at her. "I'm almost afraid to. There's something about it—can't you feel it? It's like the whole house is holding its breath."

Cam reached out and took one of Alex's hands in hers. "Go on, love. It'll be all right."

Alex slowly, carefully lifted the cover. Cam could see that the first page had something written on it in ink, but it was too far away for her to read. "What does it say?"

"It's a dedication. *For My Dearest Love*. It looks like…it can't be. Sweet holy Goddess. It's Artemisia's writing."

The face she turned toward Cam was a mixture of wonder, excitement, and fear. Cam felt her own breathing quicken. Something really was happening—she could feel it, too. "Don't stop now."

With just the tip of one finger on the edge, she turned the page. *"On the occasion of the anniversary of your birth, please accept this fair copy of the verses which you have inspired*. And she signed it."

"I can read it from here. That says *Artemisia*, right enough."

Alex turned another page, and then another, scanning quickly. "These aren't the poems she wrote for Lady Melissa. I've never seen any of them before. 'The Moor at Sunset, Hand in Hand.'" She went on to the next page. "'With My Body, I Thee Worship.'"

"That one sounds nice."

Alex shot her a look but made no other comment. She turned one more page and stopped dead. "'When My Lovely…'" She gasped and looked up at Cam. In a trembling voice, she whispered, "This one is called, 'When My Lovely Janet Smiles.'"

In the next moment, it sounded like every door in the house slammed shut, one after another, then flew open, then slammed shut again. They both leaped to their feet.

Alex was terrified. She threw herself into Cam's arms. Cam turned her against the wall and held her tightly, as if she was trying to shield her with her body from whatever was happening. The front doorbell started ringing, a continuous clanging. A howling like a small whirlwind came rushing down the hall toward them, then went racing down the stairs. The sound of doors opening and slamming again, this time in unison, filled the air and made the whole house shake.

And then everything fell absolutely still and silent.

Alex tried to slow her breathing. "What the hell just happened?"

Cam eased her hold but kept her arms around her. "I'd say our friend was a bit excited by what you found."

"What *we* found. You're the one that got us in here—you spotted the window, and the door, and you got the key to work." Alex leaned back a little so she could see Cam's face more easily. "I was afraid that we were having an earthquake or something, but I think you're right about what was really going on. I just wish she hadn't been quite so vivid about it."

"Can't rightly blame her, though. If I'd held on to a secret for a good hundred and fifty years or more and finally been able to tell it, I'd be a bit vivid myself."

"Isn't it amazing? Just think—the two of them were in love, and all this time nobody knew it. And it sounds like they were really happy, too. Those poems, I can't wait to read them. Oh, and we've got to tell people. We've got to tell everybody right away."

"Steady on. Why don't you just sit down a minute and catch your breath."

"You're right, you're right. I think I'm just overreacting because I was so scared." She sat down again, and so did Cam. "Okay. Breathing now. But isn't it wonderful? Oh, sweetheart, I can't even believe it."

Cam was still looking a little concerned. "Tell you what, I'll just ring Nicola, shall I? After what happened before, you'll want this handled properly, and I think she'll know what's best to do."

But she couldn't reach Nicola, either at her home number or on her cell. "That's odd," Cam said. "She's usually home this early on a Sunday, and she always leaves her mobile on."

Alex thought for a moment. "Try the vicarage."

"At this hour? Services don't start until—wait a bit." She gave Alex a strange look. "You reckon…Ha!"

"What's so funny?"

"Nothing. It's just that when I was over there a few days back giving Sarah a hand with some wiring, I remembered what you'd said about her fancying Nicola."

"But that was weeks ago."

"What can I say? I've a memory. Anyway, I gave her a bit of encouragement. Seems she took it to heart."

"Did she ever. She called Nicola up for a date—from the sound of it, probably right after you talked to her. They were supposed to go out last night. That's why I suggested you try the vicarage, just in case things went really well."

Cam grinned. "Let's find out." She was already dialing.

It took a while to get an answer, and from the half of the conversation Alex could hear, it was clear that the timing of the call was…inopportune. However, eventually Nicola came to the phone, and Cam handed her cell to Alex.

"This had better be good, Alex. No—it had better be utterly, blindingly brilliant, and even then I may never speak to you again."

"I'm assuming dinner worked out well, then."

"Yes, it did. But since we're no longer friends, I don't see why you should care. Any more than I care about you and Cam. Not that you'd bother telling me anything, I suppose."

"How could I, since we're no longer on speaking terms? I guess you'll have to die wondering just how big a grin I have on my face." Alex wrinkled her nose at Cam and blew her a kiss. Cam reached for her hand and kissed it.

"You're enjoying this, aren't you, you wretch?" Nicola mock-accused.

"Guilty as charged." Cam was now working her way around Alex's wrist, kissing lightly, and it was getting too distracting. Reluctantly, Alex drew her hand away. "Seriously, though, I'm really happy for you. And I truly am sorry about the bad timing. But I think once you hear the reason we called, you may even consider forgiving me."

It took only a few sentences to bring Nicola up to speed. Fortunately, Alex took the precaution of holding the phone away from her ear in time to avoid serious hearing damage from Nicola's shrieks of joy and amazement. These were followed, quite naturally, by several moments of confusion on the other end of the line. Sarah's concerned tones demanding to be told what was wrong came through loud and clear, along with Nicola's attempts to explain, which she alternated with rapid-fire appeals for further information that Alex made no attempt to respond to. She simply continued to hold the phone and wait.

The time didn't go entirely to waste. As the distant sounds of chaos continued, Cam beckoned her over. She straddled Cam's lap and put her arms around her neck. One kiss led to several more, until at first Alex barely even noticed the sound of Nicola calling her name. Reluctantly, she eased her head back.

Cam moved on to kissing her neck. "Just ring off," she murmured.

Alex sighed. "Duty calls, I'm afraid." She held the phone to her ear again. "What can I do for you?"

"You called me, remember? What on earth is going on over there?"

"Sorry. I got sidetracked." Cam nipped at her skin. "We were having ourselves a little snack." Cam chuckled and ran her tongue over the spot she had just bitten.

"How can you think of food at a time like this? Don't go anywhere. We'll be right over."

"Take your time. We won't mind." She dropped the phone on the desk before reaching down to pull Cam's shirt free from her waistband.

CHAPTER TWENTY-TWO

Nicola, showing a previously unsuspected aptitude for command, took charge the moment she arrived at Dawson House with an adoring Sarah floating dreamily in her wake. Upon viewing the secret room, she issued her first decree, which a hugely disappointed Alex tried to argue with: they must leave the notebook where it was and close up the room without touching anything else.

Logically, Alex knew Nicola was absolutely right, and that a find of this magnitude needed the most careful treatment to document, protect, and preserve it, but her heart ached at being parted from Artemisia's words and she protested vehemently.

Even worse was Cam's reaction, because it was so unexpected. When Cam spoke up, Alex was sure she would support her, but she actually said that she agreed with Nicola. It hurt Alex's feelings quite a bit when Cam shooed her out of the secret room after volunteering to close the shutters.

Alex was so busy making her case to Nicola for why they should at least make a copy of the newly discovered poems before resealing the room that she barely noticed how long it took Cam to join them in the hallway. Nicola looked a little suspicious when Cam finally emerged, shutting the door behind her, but let it go after hearing her explanation about problems with the catch on the shutters. As Nicola moved on to other concerns, Alex thought she caught a flash of devilment in Cam's eyes, but her bland expression was back in place so quickly that Alex decided she must have been mistaken.

Then it was on to the next task, which was to summon the head of Highgate Hall's conservation department. As soon as he arrived, Nicola insisted on swearing them all to secrecy, Sarah included. The conservator, a heavily bespectacled, serious man, cardigan clad and a touch underfed, was reluctant at first to make any promise before receiving an explanation, but all it took was the mention of Rosamund's name for him to hurriedly agree. In a gesture that reminded Alex of the scene where Hamlet has everyone touch his sword and vow silence, Nicola had them put their hands together and recite an actual oath.

Alex wanted to laugh but her friend was so deadly serious about the whole thing that she didn't dare. The only thing missing was a ghost under the floorboards yelling *Swear!*—which was ironic, under the circumstances.

Once they had duly pledged, they adjourned to the kitchen to confer over a pot of tea. As Alex, with occasional help from Cam, recounted the tale of their morning's adventures, Nicola's eyes grew wider and wider, and as for the conservator, his hands started trembling so much he had to put his cup down rather precipitately to avoid dropping it. Sarah congratulated them heartily, then announced it was time for her to head over to the church, promising to rejoin them later.

After the vicar had left, Alex, Nicola, and the conservator discussed next steps, with Cam offering to contribute in any way that she could. They soon concurred on a basic plan of action for securing and investigating the find. Their only major disagreement was about the key to the secret room. Alex was adamant—she would not give it up. None of the arguments the others could marshal moved her, and this time, Cam backed her up.

Cam also came up with a solution, offering to make copies of the key so they could all have access to the room while Alex kept the original. This was reluctantly accepted by the other two, so Cam and the conservator each went off to fetch what they needed for their respective tasks while Alex and Nicola called Ian to tell him the news.

After his exclamations and congratulations subsided and normal conversation was possible, Ian absolutely agreed on the need for secrecy. He was dismayed to learn that five people were already aware of the find and insisted that no one else be told. Alex pleaded to be allowed to inform her dissertation director, at least in general terms, and eventually she wore him down.

"But not one other person, Alexandra. Negotiations with Ms. Camberwell are at a critical stage, and if she gets even a whiff of your new discovery, matters could get quite nasty, I fear."

"The only thing that surprises me about that is that they haven't gotten that way already. How soon do you think you'll be able to come up here and take a look for yourself?"

"Not until we've settled things over the Prandall, I'm afraid. But the minute we've concluded, I'll be on a train headed north. Just see if you can keep me away."

"I wouldn't dream of trying. I'd only end up crushed and trampled into the dust."

Alex then put in a quick call to Barbara, having forgotten the time difference in her enthusiasm. After apologizing for rousting her out of bed at such an early hour on a Sunday, Alex quickly filled her in. She was a little surprised by how dispassionately Barbara reacted to the news. She sounded intrigued, but she didn't seem very excited over something that was bound to revolutionize the field she had been part of for so many years. She spent more time asking about Alex's research plans and the likely effect on her dissertation schedule than she did about the details of the find.

Her response to the request for secrecy was also disconcerting. At first she refused to agree, citing the importance of the find and the need to capitalize on the associated publicity for the sake of department and university prestige, as well as Alex's career. Even when Alex made a personal plea, asking Barbara to go along for her sake, she still said no. Racking her brain for an effective argument, Alex finally countered with vague references to a confidentiality agreement and legal issues with the Foundation. That seemed to do the trick, but she could tell Barbara wasn't very happy with her.

After the conversation ended, Alex felt a little disoriented. She had spent so many years fascinated by Barbara as a woman and in awe of her as a senior scholar that she had never really considered how little she and Barbara actually had in common. She had never expected that Barbara would allow PR to take precedence over scholarly considerations, let alone their friendship. Or what Alex thought of as their friendship.

She sighed. Looking up, she could see both Nicola and Cam looking at her with troubled expressions. However, only Nicola said anything. Cam simply returned to her work.

"So. That was Barbara, was it?" It was clear Nicola was less than impressed.

"Let's just file it under *Too soon old, too late smart* and move on, shall we?"

"I suppose we'll have to. Cam, how are you coming with the key?"

Cam held up the wax impression she'd made. "I'm done with what I can manage on my own. Do you reckon your conservator friend can finish this at the Hall?"

"Perhaps, but I'd rather not do that, in case anybody notices and starts asking questions. I'm not sure what alternative we have, though."

"Not to worry. I've a mate over in Dunheath who runs an ironmongery out of an old blacksmith's shop, makes door knockers and authentic old whatnot for tourists." She handed the original key to Alex, who stowed it safely back in her pocket. "I use her when I need a bit of work done for a restoration. I'll speak to her tomorrow about casting the new keys for me. I doubt she'll be the least bit curious, and I know she'll do a first-rate job."

"That sounds perfect," said Nicola. "Cam, I don't know what we'd do without you."

"Cam has lots of talents," said Alex. Although she had been careful to keep her tone completely neutral, Cam shot her a look that made her wish Nicola would go somewhere else for a while. Quite a while.

But then the conservator returned with his equipment and supplies and everyone trooped upstairs, each with appointed tasks. The conservator's job was to explore, measure, and describe the room and its contents while Cam assisted him and Nicola supervised and documented everything. Because the room was so small, Alex, after unlocking the door, had to content herself with standing outside trying to see over people's heads and asking questions which for the most part no one bothered to answer.

She tried very hard not to be jealous of Cam's practical skills that were making her such a valuable member of the team at the moment. She would be able to make her contribution when it came time to analyze the writings that were at this moment only a few tantalizing feet away, just sitting there unread, in a notebook that she had been holding in her hands only a short time ago. Somehow, that didn't help.

❖

Cam heard the edge in Alex's voice when she announced that she would be downstairs making a pot of tea if anybody needed her and decided the moment had come to reveal her surprise. Briefly excusing herself to the others, she headed down to the kitchen.

Alex was sitting at the table, arms crossed, looking grim. Cam fished her mobile out of her pocket and went over to stand beside her.

"I've a few photos on here that might interest you, seeing as you've nothing else to do."

"Rub it in, why don't you? Sorry, but I don't think your vacation pictures are going to cheer me up. I'm just kicking myself that I didn't copy down one or two of the poems when I had the chance."

"It's a shame not to have thought of that—you being the Scholar and all." Cam reached over to hold the phone in front of Alex and tapped the controls. Up popped the first of the photos that she had taken of the notebook in the secret room while she was supposedly wrestling with the catch on the shutters. "A pity."

Alex took one look at the page of poetry filling the tiny screen and gave a delighted shriek. "You didn't! Oh, Cam, you're amazing." Alex grabbed her around the waist and gave her a quick, fierce hug before snatching the phone and scrolling through the other shots. "I think you got every single page. Oh, sweetheart, thank you."

"I reckoned it would kill you, being so close to those brand-new poems but not being able to read them."

Alex tore her eyes from the screen and flashed her an adoring look. "I don't know how you do it, but it's like you can read my mind. I really was just about ready to die."

Cam brushed her fingers gently through Alex's hair. "Wouldn't do to be left with a corpse on my hands, now would it?"

Somewhere nearby, a door closed firmly—not quite a slam, but with a decided clank. Alex murmured, "Yes, I think one dead woman in the house is plenty." Cam saw Alex sneak a glance at the poem before looking guiltily back at her. "I'm sorry, it's just…"

"Not to worry. I know the fever's on you." She kissed Alex on the top of the head. "I'll leave you to it, then."

Cam turned back in the doorway, watching Alex for a moment. Her head was bent over the screen and she had a look of such fierce concentration on her face it was almost frightening. And yet she seemed utterly happy. Something washed over Cam, a feeling of tenderness and longing that she was afraid to try to grasp hold of. Instead, she headed upstairs to get back to work.

CHAPTER TWENTY-THREE

For Alex, the next few days were a crazy mish-mash of frenzied activity and heady delight. The secret room and its contents yielded quite a few surprises, including a dozen or so densely written volumes penned entirely in some sort of code. She and Nicola were both convinced these were Artemisia's journals, but of course nothing could be proven until someone figured out how to decipher them. They had already unearthed enough material to keep a whole department's worth of graduate students busy for years, and it felt like they were just getting started.

The moment Alex caught sight of Mrs. Tate on Monday morning, she recognized that, given how intertwined that redoubtable woman's life was with every aspect of Dawson House, letting her in on the secret would not violate her promise to Ian. Now Mrs. Tate was in her element, cooking hearty dinners for the conspirators and baking all sorts of delightful things for their afternoon tea breaks. Grace was also very much in evidence, seeming not the least perturbed by the commotion but rather determined to profit by it, prowling and meowing and demanding affection and treats, although she never once tried to enter the secret room.

The house was overrun with people at all hours, and although everyone promised to be discreet about their comings and goings, it was obvious from the start that rumors would be flying around the village concerning the unusual activity. And as Nicola pointed out, anything that the whole village was talking about was bound to travel farther in very short order, perhaps all the way to London to the ears of a certain dishonorable redhead.

Cam was the one who came up with a way around the difficulty. All it took was her dropping by the café and casually mentioning to the barista how upset the Foundation people were about the damage a burst pipe had caused at Dawson House, and how hard they were working to rescue the old papers stored there.

As Cam herself said, returning triumphantly from her mission laden with coffee for everyone, "You could hear the change in the talk even while I was standing there. It was like I'd flipped a switch." Alex accepted the cappuccino Cam passed her. "Why pay any mind to a raft of waterlogged old paper, when you can enjoy a proper chin-wag about the way certain people are carrying on in front of God and everybody? That would be you, Vicar—you ordered the latte, right?" She grinned at the furiously blushing Sarah as she handed her the drink. Alex tried to hide her own guilty amusement, but apparently not very successfully, since Nicola put a reassuring arm around Sarah and scowled at both of them.

"I'd say you've provided them with more than a bit to chat about yourself lately, Cam."

"I do my poor best," she replied, giving Alex a quick kiss on the cheek as she sat down.

"God bless village gossip," said Alex, lifting her cup in a toast that everyone heartily joined in.

Unfortunately, there wasn't quite enough carrying on to suit Alex. The one thing she truly regretted was that all the goings-on at Dawson House meant that she and Cam had very little time to themselves. Fortunately, Cam turned out to be quite good at maneuvering them into a temporarily empty space to snatch a few private moments while the others were occupied elsewhere. Alex felt like a cross between a teenager sneaking around and a B movie femme fatale carrying on an illicit affair. Mostly it was just fun; having been such a Goody Two-Shoes all her life, she'd never had any reason to sneak around before. And she and Cam certainly made up for lost time at night.

But the one thing they never seemed to do was talk. Not that they were silent around each other—far from it—but they never had any kind of serious conversation. Which was fine, really, since what did they have to discuss? Being with Cam was wonderful, and Alex could tell that Cam felt the same way about being with her. Some things didn't need to be put into words.

Of course they were going to have to discuss what would happen at the end of her fellowship, but there was plenty of time to figure things out. They'd work out something, somehow. Why borrow trouble?

As the days went by, matters calmed down slightly. The conservator at last pronounced himself satisfied and took himself, along with his notes and charts and diagrams, back to his office at the museum to prepare his report, although not before turning over several pages worth of instructions. Nicola promised to follow the entire protocol faithfully, and based on the way she had been acting from her very first moment on the scene, Alex knew that she absolutely would.

The decision had been made, after long and thorough discussion, that the newly discovered books and papers were for the moment best left in situ, rather than risking possible damage by moving them. The crucial factor as far as Nicola and Alex were concerned was the protection that Janet's continuing presence would presumably provide, although naturally they did not share this information with the conservator, who having settled in Bramfell a mere dozen years ago, and being of a scientific bent besides, was unlikely to appreciate this vital point.

The main beneficiary of the decision was Alex, now that she was finally granted grudging, carefully supervised access to the poetry notebook by a hovering Nicola. It didn't get much more convenient than having your research material housed a few steps from your bedroom door, and she took full advantage of her opportunity, poring over the notebook, sometimes skimming quickly to let the magic wash over her, sometimes scrutinizing each word syllable by syllable, searching for nuances and hidden connections.

In a way she was glad for Nicola's gatekeeping, since she knew that, left to her own devices, she would have a difficult time keeping her hands off the notebook. She was of course very careful with it always but was glad she didn't have to depend on her own self-restraint to avoid the possibility of damaging it through too much handling. Thanks to Cam's foresight, she always had access to the words of the poems, but there was no substitute for holding the book itself, feeling the paper slide under her fingertips, aware each moment that Janet had touched these same pages she was touching, that Artemisia had inscribed them with her own hands, etching the paper with these words that had flowed from her innermost being, from the love she and Janet had shared.

Gradually Nicola stopped insisting on sitting beside her every single minute that she spent in the secret room, only stopping in periodically to check on her. That definitely made it easier to focus, and Alex was able to accomplish much more as a result. Finally it got to the point where Nicola only came in to tell her that her time was up.

During one of these solitary sessions, Alex glanced up to see Cam standing quietly in the doorway. She felt the tiny burst of joy that always seemed to hit her when she caught sight of Cam unexpectedly. Now that Cam was back to her normal work routine, Alex rarely saw her during the day, yet here she was.

Cam's eyes shone with affection that was both gentle and intense. When Cam looked at her like that, it took her breath away, making her feel desired and cherished all at once. But now she felt something else as well, something she couldn't quite grasp.

A line from the poem she was working on echoed in her mind.

The poem was called "This Moment, Present" and, like all of the newly discovered works, it managed to be both a demonstration of technical expertise and at the same time an expression of intense feeling captured in deceptively simple, straightforward language. Compared to Artemisia's published work, the new poems were less ornate, more subtle, and more emotionally open—in other words, better. By several orders of magnitude.

Of course, her earlier work was wonderful; it had the noble beauty of a Renaissance fresco or Greek statue. But the new work went far beyond her previous achievements. The poems themselves varied, capturing different moods and moments. Sometimes they were deep and powerful, like the sea, or light and playful, like a spring breeze, or rich and peaceful, like the warmth of a late afternoon in summer. But always they spoke directly to the heart.

In her eyes, forever waits for me. Gazing at Cam, Alex felt the poem's final words sounding within her like the last note of a song after the bow has been drawn across the strings of a cello. Whatever this was between them, it wasn't light or casual. And it wasn't something she could analyze, or figure out, or control. It simply was.

And in that moment, the realization shot through her that for her, at least, it was forever.

Cam was smiling at her, so she fixed a smile on her own face even as her guts seized and her stomach turned over. She was in deep, deep trouble, and she hoped like hell that the fear didn't show.

Cam stood in the doorway, her eyes locked with Alex's. She had been watching Alex work, enjoying the play of light and shadow on her face from the window and the changes in her expression as she stared at the notebook in front of her, pausing every so often to write something down in a small spiral-bound journal.

Cam doubted that she would ever truly get what all the poems were about, not the way Alex did, but she could see the effect they had on Alex, the way they made her sparkle with excitement, the way they moved her. And when Alex read them aloud to her, Cam could feel the love that poured out of them, the love Artemisia had had for Janet. Still had for her—because that love was living on, somehow, in the poems themselves. You didn't need a university education to understand that.

As Alex looked at her now, Cam saw something in her eyes, something that she couldn't put a name to, something that shook her down to her core but that called to her nonetheless. It was like seeing thunderclouds race toward her across the moor, power and beauty and danger all at once, and wishing she were a hawk so she could ride the wind, despite knowing the storm might leave her battered and broken.

She couldn't make sense out of it, but she didn't need to. In that moment, she knew Alex was hers, she was Alex's. That was all that mattered.

She realized that Nicola was standing beside her, murmuring something in her ear. With an effort Cam refocused her attention. "Sorry, I didn't quite catch that."

"I said, are you all right? The look on your face…"

"I'm fine. Actually, I'm better than fine. I'm happy." She met Alex's eyes again and smiled at her. Alex's answering smile warmed her through and through. "Really, truly happy."

❖

That afternoon Alex got the phone call she had been hoping for and dreading. Ian invited her to London, along with Cam and Nicola, for the awarding of the Prandall Prize. The Foundation planned to announce the award at a combination celebratory banquet and press conference to be held later that week.

"Not that there may be much for you to celebrate, Alexandra, although no doubt your new find provides some consolation. In this case, however, I'm almost certain virtue will have to be its own reward."

"Probably no money for me, you mean? Well, I can't say I'm exactly surprised. Will I at least get a share of the credit, or is she still insisting on stealing that, too?"

"At the moment I'm unable to say anything specific, although I think I can safely promise you a certain measure of satisfaction by the end of the evening."

"I hope you're right, Ian. I'd hate for the three of us to drag all the way down there just to spend hours watching the smug expression on a certain person's face."

"I don't think you need worry about that, Alexandra." He sounded quite pleased with himself.

"Ian, you're up to something."

"Ask me no questions…"

"Don't worry, I won't. But I'm grateful for whatever it is you're trying to do, even if it doesn't work."

Chapter Twenty-four

All too soon, the three travelers found themselves on Ian's doorstep. They spent the afternoon relaxing and chatting with Ian in front of the parlor fire. Alex did her best not to pay attention to the clock and tried to maintain at least the appearance of calm.

Given the worried way Cam kept glancing at her, she realized she probably wasn't doing a very good job of it, but she did her best to preserve her composure for the sake of the others, most especially Cam herself. Her own wounds might be fresher, but they hardly compared to the way Rosamund had treated Cam. Alex had finally managed to get the story out of her one night; the rage that Rosamund's cruelty toward Cam had roused in Alex had blasted away any lingering feelings of shame or self-doubt about her own interactions with the woman, fueling instead a keen hunger for retribution.

Given Rosamund's endless craving for attention, nothing was likely to upset her quite as much as finding herself the object of no notice whatsoever, not even the negative interest of being shunned and glared at. It wouldn't be quite as satisfying to Alex as personally inflicting grievous bodily harm, but since Rosamund would doubtless find it excruciating to be treated like yesterday's news, it would do.

With that in mind, ever since receiving Ian's invitation, Alex had been secretly practicing in front of a mirror every chance she could, trying to achieve an expression and tone that combined bland courtesy with just a suspicion of boredom. She wasn't sure she'd be able to pull it off, but she was determined to try.

At last it was time to get dressed for the banquet. Naturally, tonight Alex was going to wear her dress. Cam hadn't seen her in it since their first night together, and apart from anything else, Alex was hoping that by wearing it she would give them both something to focus on that would counteract whatever unpleasantness the evening might bring. She shooed Cam out of the bedroom so she could dress without distraction.

Cam's reaction when Alex stepped out of the room to show off was everything she could have hoped for. The look in Cam's eyes was certainly gratifying, but even better was when Cam walked her back into the bedroom, closed the door, and started expressing her appreciation in more tangible ways, her mouth on Alex's and her hands roaming over her body. Had they been on their own, they might have skipped the banquet altogether, but far too soon Nicola was knocking on the door.

Nicola looked from one of them to the other as Alex adjusted her dress and Cam smoothed down her hair. She shook her head in what Alex hoped was feigned exasperation.

"Honestly, you two. It's bad enough Sarah couldn't arrange a substitute on short notice and I had to leave her behind. But do you have to rub it in?"

Alex started counting in her head—she'd only reached three when Cam piped up with, "We hadn't quite got round to that part yet, but apologies regardless."

"Don't look at me," Alex said to her friend. "You've known her a lot longer than I have. Don't you know by now what will happen if you feed her a line like that?" Nicola seemed slightly less than amused, so Alex hastened to add, "You certainly look very smart."

And she did—in yet another new dress, this one a sophisticated gray-blue shot with silver threads that subtly caught the light when she moved. There was nothing subtle about the cut of the dress, though, and Alex had no trouble deciphering the message: Eat your heart out, Rosamund. This is what you could have had.

"Yes, Nicola. That's a pretty color." Cam was clearly trying to sound apologetic, but her voice held an undercurrent that made Alex wonder if the message of Nicola's dress might have been meant for more than one person. She cast a sideways glance at Cam, who blushed rather guiltily but instantly moved closer, putting an arm around her waist. Alex let her body relax against Cam's.

Nicola looked mollified. "Thank you. You both look quite nice as well. You should wear a jacket and tie more often, Cam."

Alex noticed that the tie in question—the gold one Cam had worn to the Lammas dance, the one that made her eyes glow like warm honey—was askew. She adjusted it and was rewarded with a kiss. Maybe they'd survive the evening after all.

"Okay, troops," Alex said, stepping away from Cam's embrace, "*Once more unto the breach, dear friends*, and all that." She went out into the hall, closely followed by the others. Soon everyone was gathered in the parlor.

"You and Cam certainly look ready for a grand occasion, Alexandra," said Ian. "Seeing the two of you dressed up like this reminds me of when Oona and Flossie used to get ready to go out on the town." He smiled. "Oona was the one who taught me how to tie a tie, you know. That's quite an elegant dimple you have there in your Half-Windsor, Cam."

"Kind of you to say so, Mr. Montrose."

Alex only half noticed how genuinely pleased Cam seemed to be by the compliment to her sartorial skill, her attention having been caught by Ian's previous remark. "Oona and Flossie, Ian? Who was Flossie?"

"Oona's partner, of course. Funny, I could have sworn I mentioned her when I told you about my mother."

Alex took a moment to try to gather her wits. "You mean it wasn't just Oona who raised her after her parents died—it was Oona and her partner? Huh. So the two of them lived together in Bramfell…"

"Almost forty years."

"In Bramfell?" Nicola sounded just as shocked as Alex felt. "They must have been the scandal of the village."

"Hardly that," said Ian mildly.

Alex tried to imagine what the village would have been like back then. "But how did they manage? How did people treat them?"

"Treat them? Perfectly well, as far as I could see." Ian smiled wryly. "After all, they were just two spinster ladies keeping house together. Sad, of course, but still, it was nice that they had each other for company, seeing as how they were both alone." He shook his head. "None so blind. It was obvious to me, even as quite a young lad, how much they loved each other. But I suppose it was just as well for their sakes that they were able to hide in plain sight." He sighed. "They've both been gone a long time now."

Ian's words resonated with Alex. Something about being alone even with another person there. Something to do with Artemisia, and Oona, and one of Ian's letters. "Alone! Hah! Ian, that's it—remember the note you sent me about how Artemisia used to walk the moors alone, pining for Lady Melissa, and how pleased people were that she took along a servant for propriety, since it was pretty much the only respectable thing she ever did?"

"I certainly do remember. Oona even asked Janet about it."

"And I'll bet Janet had a hard time keeping a straight face when she did." She looked at the three of them, smiling at their puzzled faces. "Don't you see? Artemisia wasn't roaming the moors in forlorn solitude with some hapless servant stumbling along a few paces behind her."

Cam eyes glinted in sudden comprehension. "It was Janet, wasn't it?"

"Yes! She and Janet were out walking together, enjoying each other's company. Day after day, right under people's noses, and nobody noticed, because Janet was a servant, and therefore invisible. None so blind, indeed." Suddenly all her excitement drained away. "Day after day."

Cam looked closely at Alex. Her face was pale, and her voice trailed off as she said, "Year after year." She looked properly stunned, although neither of the others appeared to take any notice.

Ian said, "Bravo, Alexandra! Yet another mystery solved. I hope you're keeping a list."

"Even if she isn't, I am," said Nicola. "In fact, if you don't mind, Mr. Montrose, I'd like to borrow pen and paper so I can note this down straightaway. I find orderliness and precision so important in administrative matters, don't you?"

"I quite agree, my dear. I have what you need in my study, if you'll step this way."

❖

As the door closed behind Ian and Nicola, Cam stepped closer, resting one hand against Alex's cheek. "What's bothering you, love?"

Alex wasn't looking at her, her gaze fixed on something far away. "Forty years." She sounded horrified, and Cam's stomach curdled. "I can't even imagine it."

Cam tried for a light tone but couldn't manage it. "It might not be so bad with the right person." She dropped her hand and turned away.

Lately she'd started telling herself that it didn't matter that Alex never seemed to want to talk about the two of them, that it didn't matter that she'd never said she loved her, that she didn't need to hear the words out loud to know the truth. Maybe she'd been fooling herself. Just like before.

"Oh, sweetheart. That's not what I meant."

Cam felt Alex grasp her hand firmly in both of hers, and she turned back to face her, afraid of what she'd see.

Alex's eyes were full of tenderness, but so sad, and Cam was utterly confused.

"It's just such a long time. And Janet and Artemisia...Oh, hell"— Alex started tearing up—"I hadn't thought about the dates before. Everybody used to think Artemisia was alone all those years after Lady Melissa's death, but she wasn't. She was with Janet, probably for most of that time. Maybe they had thirty years together, maybe a bit more."

"That's a long time. But why does it make you sad?"

"Don't you see? Janet is the one who was alone. All those years and years and years."

"Oh, lass." A chill ran through her and she pulled Alex into her arms. The thought of losing Alex, whenever it happened, however it happened, was unbearable.

Alex turned her head so it was resting on Cam's shoulder. "One of their poems talks about forever. How can you dare to say forever when you might not even have five more minutes? And if you love someone, really love them, how can you risk putting them through that kind of pain?" She lifted her head and pushed away from Cam.

Cam let her go but kept hold of her hand. "I know I'm not making any sense. I'm just scared."

"So am I." She lifted their joined hands and softly kissed Alex's knuckles. "Nobody knows the future, love. All we have is right here, right now. It's got to be enough, because it's all we've got."

Alex pulled her hand free and started to pace. "And another thing. Why even think about trying to stay together when you know everything's going to change? I'm not the same person I was five years ago or even five months—who on earth am I going to be decades from now? Who are you going to be?" She wrapped her arms around her waist as if she were cold. "Or what if it all just goes wrong? My mother and father loved each other once. At least I think they did." She turned away. "How can you promise forever when you know it's a lie?"

Hearing the anguish in Alex's voice hurt, but even so Cam's heart felt lighter. Alex wasn't saying she didn't want them to be together; she was afraid they couldn't be. It wasn't much of a difference, but it was enough for hope.

She went over to where Alex was standing, gazing into the fire, and stepped up behind her, laying her hands on Alex's shoulders. "I don't think it's meant to be like that, exactly." Gently, she turned Alex around to face her. Alex's eyes searched hers, a silent plea for help. "It's not like swearing an oath on pain of death or signing your soul away to the devil." Alex smiled, a little shakily, but it was still a smile. "I reckon it's more like dancing."

And just like that, the shadows were gone from Alex's eyes, replaced with curiosity. Always the scholar. Her scholar. "What do you mean?"

"Well, when you step onto the dance floor with someone, you sort of know what you're doing and where you're going, but you have no way to tell what everyone else is going to do, so you know you'll have to adjust as you go. But as long as you hang on to one another and keep up with the music, generally it works out fine. And even with the odd misstep, it's still miles better than sitting on the sideline watching."

She drew Alex into her arms, into a ballroom hold, and led her through a couple of waltz measures, humming under her breath.

"Once you get used to the music, and each other, you can even throw in the odd flourish." She spun Alex gently into a turn, then drew her back into her arms and dipped her, not too wildly, but enough to make her gasp, and finally pulled her up for a kiss.

The sound of applause from the doorway brought her up short. Letting go of one of Alex's hands, she stepped to the side and turned to face Ian and Nicola, bowing as Alex curtseyed.

"What a pity we won't be having dancing this evening," said Ian. "You two would certainly bear away the palm. Well, my dears, I think it's time for us to depart."

CHAPTER TWENTY-FIVE

At first the banquet went pretty much as Alex had expected. The evening began with cocktails and canapés, which would doubtless have been delightful under other circumstances. Rosamund, resplendent in a strapless gold lamé gown that was camped right on the line between daring and déclassé, held court in one corner attended by a tall, dark, and trouser-suited type who was certainly impressive looking—if you liked your women handsome, sophisticated, and ice-cold.

Meanwhile, Alex stayed far away, glad of Cam's reassuring arm around her, chatting with her and Nicola and pretending to enjoy herself while Ian and the other Foundation members circulated, stopping by to exchange pleasantries while dividing their time between her group and Rosamund's so precisely she suspected they had a timetable.

Alex never really relaxed, but whenever someone from the press came over her insides congealed. Then she did her desperate best to be utterly boring, a bland smile fixed in place as she tried to say nothing at all in as many words as possible until they went away.

Cam whispered in her ear, "You're good at this. If I didn't know better, I'd swear there was nothing in your head but fluff and feathers."

"Thank you, sweetheart. I think."

Finally it was time for the meal. Alex noted with some amusement that, unlike most official dinners she had been to, the dais at one end of the room contained only a podium and microphone backed by a large poster with the Foundation's logo. There was no table elevating certain favored diners above the hoi polloi; instead, everyone was seated at round tables, with the press, her group, and Rosamund's rigidly segregated and Foundation representatives carefully sprinkled among them in equal numbers.

She was quite surprised that the meal was edible. It wasn't exactly gourmet, but it was definitely several steps above the under- or over-cooked shreds of defenseless vegetables and flavor-free chicken drenched in some gluey, over-seasoned sauce that was usually offered in place of food at a catered dinner. She was too on edge to do it justice, but at least she had an actual meal to push around her plate and make designs with.

❖

Cam was getting tired of watching Alex pretend to eat. She was on the verge of saying something when she noticed Ian headed their way, accompanied by a man who had lawyer written all over him. Something was up. She glanced around the room and spotted Rosamund standing by the door next to another solicitor type, the one who'd been at her elbow all evening. Probably her latest lover as well—Rosamund was never one to waste an opportunity. On the surface she looked tough, but Cam had seen the way she hung about Rosamund and recognized the signs—the poor woman was like a cat on hot bricks, in constant fear of Rosamund's displeasure.

Ian murmured something to Alex that Cam didn't catch, but when Alex rose, she did, too. Ian gave her an assessing look, then nodded as if in approval. Taking Alex's arm, Cam followed him and the other man over to the doorway where Rosamund and her companion were standing. Ian led the group out into the hallway and into a nearby meeting room.

❖

Alex looked around the room, noticing that the man with Ian had a portfolio under his arm that he placed in front of him on the conference table. As Ian invited everyone to be seated, Alex gave Cam's hand a quick squeeze, very glad for her company. Ian introduced the man, who proved to be the Foundation's chief legal counsel, and Rosamund introduced tall, dark, and glacial, who had been looking down her nose at Alex the entire time and who turned out, not surprisingly, to be Rosamund's solicitor.

Alex started to introduce Cam but found herself interrupted when Cam spoke up for herself.

"Ey up, all. Dead chuffed to make your acquaintance, squire, miss." Alex almost choked. Cam had a big, goofy smile on her face, and she sounded like she'd just stepped off the set of *Wuthering Heights* after playing Third Bumpkin from the Left in a crowd scene. All she needed was a piece of straw between her teeth and a five-bar gate to lean on.

Alex barely managed to keep a straight face. From Ian's expression, he was having a similar difficulty.

Still grinning, Cam turned to Rosamund. "Now then, Rosamund, keeping well, eh? Tha wert right mardy last time I saw thee, but now tha looks happy as a pig in muck. Nothing like the prospect of a bit of brass to cheer folk up, Mum always said."

Ian succumbed to a coughing fit, both lawyers looked as if they'd swallowed something unpleasant, and Rosamund was turning an interesting shade of puce that clashed wildly with her hair. Although Alex doubted Rosamund had understood Cam's exact words much better than she had, the gist was crystal clear.

Alex decided it was time to put her rehearsals to use. She took a moment to settle herself, hoping her expression was suitably nonchalant. "Yes, Rosamund, it's good to see you looking well." It sounded just right—perfunctory politeness with a hint of tedium. Now for the kill. She turned to Ian. "You said there was something we needed to discuss. I hope it won't take long—I'd hate to miss dessert."

"Aye, lass. Happen it'll be chocolate cake," Cam said.

She gave Cam a sharp, swift kick in the ankle. She knew what Cam was doing, but enough was enough. She was grateful, though. Whatever was coming next, she'd handle it. Her nerves were gone.

Alex focused as the solicitor took out a sheaf of official-looking papers and droned on about the Foundation's proposal for resolving her dispute with Rosamund.

Finally Alex said, "So let me make sure I understand what you're proposing. Rosamund and I would sign an agreement giving up our right to sue the Foundation or each other over anything to do with the prize. And in return, I would be recognized publicly for having discovered the letter."

The Foundation solicitor said, "That's accurate, Ms. Petrocelli."

"I don't have a problem with that. I'm not interested in wasting time in court."

"But what about the award itself?" said Rosamund. "What does the agreement say about that?"

Ian answered, "The agreement specifies that the entire amount of the Prandall Prize, in accordance with the terms of Josiah Prandall's bequest, will be awarded to you, Ms. Camberwell."

"The entire amount?" The raw greed on Rosamund's face made her look so ugly, Alex was shocked. "She gets nothing? I get every penny?"

"Yes, Ms. Camberwell," said the Foundation solicitor. "Every penny."

"What's the catch? There must be a catch."

"Please take all the time you need to look over the agreement," said Ian calmly. "In fact, if you would like to take a few days for your solicitor to review it—"

"But then I wouldn't get the award tonight. Isn't that so?"

The solicitor cleared his throat. "Our main concern is to avoid any possible negative publicity for the Foundation, so we are prepared to do whatever is necessary to achieve an amicable settlement among the parties involved."

Rosamund made a derisive noise. "In other words, I'll have to wait. Let me see it." She took the paper that the Foundation solicitor passed her and skimmed through it. "Very well. I'll sign it."

Her solicitor looked worried. "As your legal advisor, I'm afraid I cannot recommend—"

"Now, darling, I know you mean well"—Alex had heard that tone often enough to know the solicitor hadn't a hope—"but really, see for yourself. It says right here, *The entire amount of the Prandall Prize, in accordance with the terms set forth in attachment A*—that's a copy of the bequest, see?—*is to be awarded to Rosamund Camberwell.*"

"It does appear to be in order, but still—"

Rosamund snatched up a pen and signed the document. Then she handed it back to the Foundation solicitor and glared at Alex. Cam put an arm around her, murmuring in her ear.

"What do you reckon?"

Something about the whole thing felt a bit off, but Alex couldn't put her finger on exactly what it was. "It's fine. I didn't really expect to get any of the money. Don't worry." To the solicitor she said, "May I have the document, please?"

She paged through it quickly. "Ordinarily I wouldn't sign anything without reading it carefully, but you know what? I'm not going to bother. I just want to get this over with and move on." She looked at Cam, her eyes clear and calm. "We have better things to do, don't we?"

"That we do."

Alex signed the document and passed it back to the solicitor, then stood. "Is there anything else, gentlemen?"

Both Ian and the solicitor shook their heads. Alex turned to Cam and smiled. And she wasn't just putting on a brave face. She really was happy. "Let's see if there's any cake left, sweetheart."

Alex was delighted to discover that there was indeed plenty of cake, which turned out to be not only chocolate but several notches above the standard of the rest of the meal. So immersed was she in exploring the manifold pleasures of the chocolate experience as manifested in fudgy cake, creamy mousse, silky ganache, and warm espresso-tinged sauce, that she missed most of the speechifying. She had just savored the last decadent mouthful and chased it with a sip of reasonably good coffee when she realized silence had fallen over the room and everyone at the table was looking at her expectantly.

Cam whispered, "They've just asked you to say a few words about finding the letter. Best to get a move on."

Silently cursing herself for not having expected and prepared for the invitation, and mentally aiming a few choice expressions at Ian for not having warned her, Alex made her way to the microphone to the accompaniment of polite applause. As she looked out over the sea of faces, her mind came to a complete standstill.

Playing for time, she cleared her throat and said, "Thank you." She waited a beat, hoping to be struck either by inspiration or a falling object, anything to get herself off the hook, but the universe failed to oblige.

But then she caught sight of Cam smiling up at her, looking so proud of her and just so *Cam*. Solid and steady and everything she had never even bothered to imagine, let alone hope, could be hers. And just like that, the words were there.

"I feel unbelievably lucky, not only to be studying the work of a great poet, but to have been able to share with the world the truth about the love that inspired her most famous literary accomplishments. I never expected that to happen, just as I never expected to fall in love. But sometimes lightning does strike twice. I have no idea what the future will bring, but here, in this moment, I'm happy. And this moment is all that any of us ever have, isn't it? *In her eyes, forever waits for me.*"

The uncertain applause that followed her back to her seat was undercut by baffled murmurs, but Alex barely noticed. When she reached Cam, she took her hand and drew her to her feet before kissing her tenderly.

Cam embraced her, whispering in her ear, "Oh, lass, I do love you so."

Alex raised her head to meet Cam's eyes. "I love you, Cam. So much."

As they stood there gazing at each other, neither moving, Alex saw her own joy reflected in Cam's face.

Eventually Nicola's voice cut in. "Now that you two have given the press a chance to get plenty of snaps, what say we toddle on home?"

"It's best we go," Cam agreed but didn't stir.

"Sweetheart, I think she's right." Somehow Alex managed to get herself moving.

The three of them made it as far as the door when the sound of Rosamund's name echoed through the room. Alex looked at her companions.

"We've lasted this long. Why don't we see the damn thing through and watch the presentation?"

"Anything you want," Cam said.

"If you can stand it, I'll manage to endure," put in Nicola.

Strangely, even though Rosamund was onstage with Ian and several other Foundation members, the person at the microphone was the Foundation lawyer, who proceeded to read the entire text of Josiah Prandall's bequest, complete with every single whereas, subsequently, and heretofore.

Alex soon lost her way among the thickets of Victorian legalese, and so, she suspected, did everyone else in the room, with the possible exception of Rosamund's own solicitor, who was standing just behind Rosamund and looked horrified, although Alex couldn't imagine why. The Foundation lawyer had finished his recital and was now explaining the terms of the agreement that she and Rosamund had signed, which again struck her as very odd. Not that the document was confidential, but his explanation seemed out of place as a preliminary to the announcement of Rosamund's award.

At last he relinquished his place at the microphone to Ian, who addressed himself to Rosamund, asking whether she agreed that what the lawyer had said was accurate. As Rosamund headed toward the mic, her solicitor grabbed her arm and started whispering urgently in her ear, but Rosamund shook her off with an impatient expression and took her place beside Ian.

"Yes, Mr. Montrose, everything he said was correct." She was all smiles now.

"Is there anything you would like to add, Ms. Camberwell?"

"No, thank you."

"Nothing at all? I wouldn't want you to feel that we had rushed you."

This time her tone held a slight edge. "On the contrary, you seem bent on delaying me." Rosamund's lawyer put a hand over her eyes and turned away. "As you can imagine, I'm anxious to proceed."

"In that case, Ms. Camberwell, the Artemisia Foundation is pleased to announce that at long last, we are able to award the Prandall Prize to a worthy recipient. Allow me to present you with a check for the full amount of the prize, in accordance with the exact terms of Josiah Prandall's generous bequest."

Something in the tone of his voice made Alex glance at him sharply, and as he looked out across the room, his eyes met hers for a moment and she could have sworn he winked at her. He turned back to Rosamund and handed her the check as the audience clapped with somewhat restrained enthusiasm, which was not surprising considering the number of her former colleagues present.

Rosamund didn't even look at the check for a moment as she beamed for the cameras, which whirred and flashed. But then she looked down at the piece of paper in her hand, and her face froze. An instant later, a howl of indignation drowned out the applause, which faded and died.

Beside Alex, Cam muttered, half to herself, "I knew it. I knew he was up to something."

"But what could possibly be wrong?" said Nicola. "The solicitor just read us every bloody word of the bequest and it sounded all right to me. What I could follow of it."

"Look at her face," said Cam. "Here it comes."

"Where's the rest of it?" Rosamund gestured to the check. "Where's the rest?"

"Ms. Camberwell," Ian replied calmly, "you have in your possession a check for the entire amount of the one-thousand-pound prize. If for some reason that isn't satisfactory, I am authorized to provide the sum in cash."

"Not the thousand, you pompous old fool. The seven hundred thousand."

Ian's voice took on a flinty tone. "Ms. Camberwell, the Foundation solicitor just read the bequest aloud, and a copy is being made available to the press. The terms are clear. The amount of the prize is one thousand pounds. Precisely."

"Yes, yes, that's the original amount. But everyone knows how it grew over the years. The interest—"

"As I said, Ms. Camberwell, the terms are clear. No mention is made in the bequest of investing the original amount, or of what should be done with any interest it might or might not earn. So whether or not such interest exists, it is not part of the prize."

Rosamund lunged at Ian, and for one awful moment, Alex was afraid she was going to attack him physically. Fortunately she contented herself with screaming directly into his face. To his credit he didn't retreat or even change expression. Alex was reminded that he had spent many successful years in banking, which apparently had prepared him to engage in confrontations with people in an advanced state of rage.

"You tricked me! You cheated me and—"

Thankfully at this point someone had the presence of mind to cut off the microphone, so they were spared further details of Rosamund's meltdown, although the torrent continued to assault everyone's ears as Alex, Cam, and Nicola made their escape.

CHAPTER TWENTY-SIX

It took the better part of the night, several bottles of champagne, and a surprising quantity of snacks to talk through the events of the banquet.

By the time Ian finally managed to escape from the clutches of the press and his Foundation colleagues and return home to join the festivities taking place in his own parlor, Alex had begun to get seriously worried, despite Cam's and Nicola's and even Mrs. Glendale's attempts to reassure her. But arrive he eventually did, apparently no worse for wear, and proceeded to regale them with the entire tale of his now-successful quest to thwart the pretensions of the enterprising Ms. Camberwell.

Nicola still seemed concerned about future problems, raising pointed questions about possible complications long past the time everyone else had stopped asking.

Finally Cam said, "Give it a rest, can't you? Mr. Montrose has her boxed in as neatly as you could hope for. Even I can see that, though I didn't understand it at first." She turned to Ian, "You not only had her sign that bit of paper, which was beautifully timed"— she raised her glass, and he nodded in acknowledgment—"but you hit her with it just at the moment when she was least willing to listen to anyone trying to warn her to be careful. Even better, you got her to say in front of a roomful of people that she'd been happy to do it, so she couldn't claim she'd signed under pressure." She shook her head. "You could see from her solicitor's face that she knew what was going on, but Rosamund wouldn't pay her any mind." She paused and leaned forward, suddenly sober. "I wouldn't fancy being in her shoes right about now. Rosamund's no doubt blaming her because she couldn't stop her from doing the very thing she insisted on doing."

Cam shuddered and Alex put a hand on her back, moving it in slow circles as she imagined the ways Rosamund must have tormented Cam over the years.

Time for a change of subject. "What about the interest?" Alex said. "What's going to happen to it? If it even exists, that is."

"Oh, it exists, Alexandra. All seven hundred thousand pounds of it, safe in the same account where it has always been, quietly growing until such time as the Foundation decides what to do with it." He took a sip of champagne. "In fact, we have a board meeting set for first thing Monday to discuss the matter. I intend to propose that at least a small portion be awarded to you, in recognition of your more recent and most spectacular find."

"I appreciate that very much, Ian, but you know that I wouldn't have found anything at all without Cam. And Nicola was a huge help as well, not to mention what's his name from the museum conservation department."

"Alex," Cam said, "you know as well as me that it was really Ja—" Cam gave Mrs. Glendale a sharp glance. "I'm not looking to put myself forward or take what's yours by right, unlike certain folk who've already had more than their share of mention. I wouldn't have had any notion what to do with that pile of old paper in any case. You found it, because you were the one who was meant to find it, and if there's any reward coming, it should be yours."

"Your scruples do you both credit," said Ian, "but I think you can safely leave the matter in my hands. I intend to look out for everyone's interests, not excluding Nicola or what's his name."

"Nigel," said Nicola. "Poor fellow, I think I frightened him out of his wits with that secrecy pledge. Every time he sees me at work he drops his eyes and scuttles away. The money aside, Mr. Montrose, the Foundation really needs to make some decisions soon about the new find."

"I quite agree. Now that less pleasant matters have been taken care of, we can finally turn our attention to how best to present the world with—what did you call it, Cam? Oh, yes." He smiled at her. "With that pile of old paper that also happens to be the most significant discovery in English literature since Lavinia Dickinson stumbled across her older sister's poems."

Alex said, "I think you might be overstating things just slightly, Ian."

"Wait," said Nicola. "I just thought of something else. What if—"

"Now, my dear," said Ian, "I appreciate your concerns, which certainly do credit to your good sense and your devotion to the best interests of the Foundation, both of which I would love to see to the same degree in our senior staff. But at some point we have to be willing to let go and trust that the future will take care of itself." He smiled at Alex. "As you said so well, Alexandra, none of us can really know what lies beyond this present moment. It does seem best to enjoy what we can, while we can. A touch more champagne, Cam?"

"Just a drop, Mr. Montrose, if you please."

Alex finally let herself relax. Cam leaned back, wrapping an arm around her, and she rested her head on Cam's shoulder, feeling safe and at peace.

Gradually conversation gave way to yawns, and everyone staggered to their bedchambers.

"You look delightfully wide awake," Cam said once they were in their room, as she bent to remove her shoes and socks.

"Keep your voice down," Alex hissed. "And I'm glad to see you're not quite as sleepy as you were pretending to be."

"Who says I was pretending?" Cam pulled off her jacket and hung it on the doorknob before going over to where Alex was standing beside the bed.

"After the third yawn it was pretty obvious, at least to me. Just as well it's not your acting ability I'm in love with." Hearing the words come out of her own mouth so easily, feeling absolutely right, sent a thrill all the way through her.

"Now come here." She grabbed the knot on Cam's tie, dragging her closer. "I've been wanting to do that all night." She kissed Cam intently, already hungry for more.

Cam reached around her and pulled down the zipper on her dress, breaking off the kiss to murmur in her ear, "Speaking of things I've been wanting to do all night." Alex could feel Cam unfastening her bra, and then Cam's hands were on her shoulders, slipping the dress down her arms, the bra along with it, and sliding it lower, thumbs hooking the waistband of her underwear in passing. Cam leaned down to plant a kiss on her navel as she pushed everything to the floor.

Alex stepped away from the pile of clothing and stood naked, her breathing quickening as Cam straightened up, taking Alex's hands to gently hold her arms away from her body. Cam slowly looked her up and down, her eyes dark. Standing there like that, exposed and open, with Cam fully clothed, was unbelievable erotic. She could almost feel Cam's lingering gaze like a caress on her bare skin, and she longed for Cam to touch her.

"So lovely," Cam murmured, and her grip on Alex's hands tightened. When Cam released them a moment later, Alex closed her eyes, anticipating.

But all she felt was a kiss on her cheek, a tiny pinpoint of pleasure that sparked and vanished. When she opened her eyes, Cam was behind her, still not touching her.

Cam heard the whimper of disappointment that escaped from Alex and had to stop for a moment to get control of herself. She was determined to make this last as long as possible for both of them. Even if it killed her.

Alex tried to lean against her but she stepped back a fraction, placing one hand against Alex's head to keep a whisper of air between their bodies. Her fingers encountered a bit of metal among Alex's curls and she carefully teased it out. A hairpin. There were quite a few others, and she spent several minutes removing pins and combs, working slowly and delicately to avoid pulling Alex's hair even the slightest bit. Alex, apparently realizing how hard she was concentrating, took advantage of her distraction to close the space between them, pressing back into her. Cam let out a grunt of pleasure at the feel of Alex's body against hers. Clenching her jaw, forcing herself to breathe evenly, she returned to her task, quickly working out that last couple of pins before she completely lost her focus.

Alex wasn't helping matters, having started to move her shoulders ever so slightly from side to side, each slow shift dragging her body teasingly against Cam's breasts, just enough to drive her mad. The pleasure made her groan again, and she tossed the handful of pins and combs onto the bedside table so she could grasp both of Alex's shoulders, stopping the tantalizing movement. Cam tried to step back, but her legs hit the bed behind her. There was nowhere to go. The part of her brain that was still functioning tried to remember why that was a problem.

Alex realized that even though Cam's hands on her shoulders were firm, Cam's body was trembling. Alex smiled to herself. At least she wasn't suffering alone. The fabric of Cam's clothing, fine as it was, felt rough against the bare skin of her back and legs. Every part of her skin that wasn't touching Cam felt too cool. Cam's hands were warm, and she wanted them on her, all over her. She couldn't take the waiting much longer. Pretty soon she was going to start begging.

She felt Cam move a hand to the back of her neck, brushing her hair to one side and baring the nape. Alex held her breath, waiting for the kiss. Cam's lips scarcely grazed her skin, but she was so hungry for contact the pleasure of it made her gasp.

The next kiss was more lingering, and when Cam started flicking her tongue lightly over Alex's skin, she ground her lower body helplessly against Cam's.

Cam grabbed her around the waist with both arms, holding her tightly, all but stopping her movement.

"Please."

"Please what?" Cam's voice was a growl against her neck, right at the place where it met her shoulder. "Tell me what you want." But Cam began worrying at the spot with her teeth, and for a moment all Alex could do was whimper. "Tell me."

"Touch me."

Cam nipped at her earlobe. "Am touching you."

"Put your hands on me. Please. *Please,* I need you."

Cam couldn't take any more. The pleading in Alex's voice, the feel of her, the taste of her skin, the scent of her hair. She had to have her, had to have her now.

Quickly, she picked Alex up and turned to lay her on the bed. Then she climbed on top of her, one leg in between Alex's thighs, leaning most of her weight on one elbow while she cupped Alex's face with her other hand and kissed her. Alex's arms went around her neck, holding her tightly as she eagerly returned the kiss.

Cam drew her hand down Alex's body, roaming restlessly over her breasts for a while before moving lower. She couldn't wait any longer.

She slipped between Alex's legs, almost undone by how wet she was, and entered her, groaning against Alex's mouth at the unbelievable feeling of being inside her at last.

Alex was gripping her shoulders now, fingers digging into Cam's flesh as she moaned into her mouth. Cam started to stroke her, steady and firm, but holding back a little, letting Alex show her what she needed. When Alex curled one leg around hers and started moving against her, Cam matched her rhythm, faster and harder. It seemed like only moments before Alex started to come, and Cam finally let go, grinding against Alex's leg until the pleasure overwhelmed her.

Alex's voice roused her from a light doze. She was sprawled on top of her, probably crushing the life out of her.

"Sorry." She rolled to one side and then got to her feet.

Alex levered herself up on her elbows. "Where do you think you're going?"

"Not to worry, love. I'm just getting ready for bed." She took off her clothes and got under the covers, gathering Alex into her arms.

Alex settled herself into Cam's embrace, loving the warmth of her skin and the safe feeling of being held so tenderly. "I love you."

"And I love you." Cam kissed her.

Alex's head rode up and down on Cam's chest as she sighed, so she scooted up a little to rest her head against her shoulder.

"Oh, Alex. What are we going to do?"

Alex didn't have to ask what she was talking about. "I won't have to leave right away, you know. After the grant runs out, I mean. I don't have to start job hunting for a while. I've got a little money saved. I can stay a few more weeks, maybe even a month or two."

Cam tightened her hold. "A few weeks." Her voice sounded bleak.

Alex put a hand on Cam's cheek, turning her head so she could look in her eyes. "Who was it who was telling me to stay in the moment? You love me, right?"

"Aye." The fierce conviction behind that simple syllable was almost overwhelming.

"And I love you. And that's all we really need. We have time. Maybe not much time, but we'll find a way. We'll make it work, somehow."

"If you says so, love."

"I know so. Now stop thinking so hard. I need my beauty sleep." Cam shifted to one side and then got up on her hands and knees, straddling Alex's body. "You're beautiful enough already." She bent her head and kissed Alex, then started moving lower, kissing her neck and then her breasts.

"I think that's a compliment, so thank—Oh!" At that point, Alex stopped thinking for a while.

CHAPTER TWENTY-SEVEN

The journey back to Bramfell was a subdued one. Everyone seemed to be exhausted from operating on little or no sleep and dealing with all the emotional ups and downs of the banquet and its aftermath. When Cam followed Alex through the front door of Dawson House, set the bags down in the foyer, and shut the door, she took a moment to listen. The house was still as still—Sunday quiet, not even the odd creak or rattle. No Mrs. Tate, apparently no cat, maybe even no Janet, at least at the moment. Just her and Alex.

She opened her arms and Alex came to her, clasping her around the waist as Cam held her close.

"Oh, sweetheart," Alex whispered, "it's good to be home."

"That it is," said Cam, thinking not of the house but of the woman in her arms. "What say you make us a nice cuppa while I put the cases upstairs?"

"As long as you don't insist on putting them in the bathroom this time."

"You've only yourself to blame for that, as well you know." She kissed Alex. "Put them anywhere, she says, and then complains when I do just what she asked. If I live to be a hundred, I swear I'll never understand women."

Alex laughed. "So what does that make you, then, besides a stubborn—"

The list of her many virtues was cut off by the phone ringing. Alex went into the study to answer it and Cam followed her.

"I bet it's Nicola," Alex said as she answered. "Hello...Oh, hello, Barbara." Alex sat abruptly.

Cam's stomach clenched.

"No, this isn't a bad time." Alex caught Cam's eye and silently mouthed, "Sorry."

Cam sat as well, telling herself not to worry. After all, the woman was supervising Alex's research, so she might have any number of good reasons to ring her.

"No, I didn't realize you'd been trying to reach me."

Just because she'd upset Alex the last time they'd talked didn't necessarily mean she would this time.

"I'm sorry, I just never bothered to get one. I know everybody else on the planet has a cell phone, but I haven't needed one here. Things are different in Bramfell."

There was a long pause. So the woman was finally getting round to actually talking to Alex instead of rabbiting on about how upset she was about not being able to talk to her.

"No, I haven't seen the papers or been online. Yes, it was quite an eventful evening. The Arts section in the *Globe*? And the *New York Times*? Really? Did they spell my name right? Oh. Oh, well. Just a moment."

She put her hand over the receiver and said to Cam, "They quoted me in the paper. I think I'm almost sort of famous." She leaned over and gave Cam a quick peck on the cheek. To Barbara she said, "Well, I certainly appreciate you calling to tell me...Oh. Okay, so why did you...What? Are you serious? Oh...Oh, oh!" Grabbing Cam's hand, she murmured excitedly, "She's found me a job."

"That's wonderful," Cam whispered back, hoping the dismay didn't show on her face. If Alex had to start a job right after her grant ended, there wouldn't be any extra time for them to spend together. Still, that was months off.

Alex listened for another moment. "Wow, tenure track. That really is a miracle. How soon after the Brockenbridge ends would I need to...What do you mean now? Now, as in this week? You can't be serious. Oh, you mean for an interview. Wait...What? I don't understand. But how is that even possible? I'm barely halfway through my dissertation...Oh, okay."

Something was very wrong. The look on Alex's face, her voice, her body language. Cam's heart filled with dread.

"Oh. Yes, I understand...By Friday? Can I think about it and let you know?...Yes, by this afternoon...Yes, yes, of course I'm grateful. It's just so sudden and I need...You're right, it is exactly what I've been hoping for. Yes, it really is a dream come true. Thank you, Barbara."

She rang off and just sat for a moment, staring straight ahead. When she turned to face Cam, there were tears in her eyes.

Gently, Cam took Alex by the hand and drew her out of her seat and over onto her lap. For a while she just held her, rubbing her back softly as she cried. Cam herself didn't cry—she couldn't. It was like everything inside her was frozen.

Eventually Alex started talking, explaining what her supervisor had said about somebody's massive heart attack and how she had to get Alex hired to fill the post before someone else got back from a trip and interfered, but Cam just let the words wash over her, not trying to listen. She didn't need to know the details when she already knew the only thing that mattered. Alex was leaving—not in a few months, but in a few days.

And she wasn't just going to another place, she was starting another life. One that Cam wouldn't be part of, couldn't be part of. She'd put on the yokel act at the banquet for a laugh, but she needn't have bothered. She could have been her ordinary self and they'd have looked down their noses just as much. Not that she minded, really, not for herself, but they'd looked at Alex that way, too, just for being with her.

Cam knew that the longer the two of them stayed together, the worse it would get. And sooner or later, Alex might start thinking that way as well. Cam didn't think she'd be able to survive if she ever saw that look in Alex's eyes, the one that said *You are less than I am.*

Besides, Alex was a scholar, and thanks to the poems she had found, she was going to be a famous one—Ian had said so himself last night, though Alex hadn't seemed to realize what he meant. It wasn't so much the fact that she had found them—anyone might have done that. The poems spoke to her, called to something inside her, and Alex responded. When she talked about them, something special happened.

And if Cam could see that, could feel that specialness, others would, too. Alex was going to be teaching and giving speeches and writing books, and all the other things she was born to do, among folk from universities and museums and places like the Foundation. That was the world she belonged in.

But there was no room in that world for Cam.

She had known it all along, deep inside. Still, she had let herself hope that in time they would find a way, in spite of everything, to stay together.

But now they were out of time, and Alex had to leave.

Stubborn as she was, though, Alex was bound to fight against what was best for her. So it would be up to Cam to come up with a way to get her to do what had to be done. Almost by reflex, she tightened her hold on Alex, who had finally gone silent. How could she possibly let her go? Not just let her go, make her go?

Cam knew that if she succeeded, it was going to destroy her, but she could worry about that later. All she had to do at the moment was cut her own heart out without letting the wound show too much; she'd have plenty of time to bleed after Alex had gone.

Alex sat there wrapped in Cam's arms, but the solid warmth of her, the feeling of those strong arms around her, didn't comfort her. She might as well have been a thousand miles away, already across the ocean and gone. Everything inside her felt dead. But underneath the numbness, her mind was circling round and round like an animal in a cage, gone mad with trying to escape when no escape was possible. She wanted to howl, she wanted to throw things, but there wasn't any point.

Of course she could turn the job down. But academia was really a very small place. She doubted Barbara would be vindictive enough to badmouth her, but then again she wouldn't need to. Once word got around—and word always got around—that Alex had been offered a prime position and refused it, a lot of places would assume there must be something wrong with her, personally or professionally. With so many excellent candidates vying for every job, why take a chance on her?

The worst of it was that if she told Barbara no, she'd never know for sure what she had given up—what she might have accomplished, what she might have created and contributed. And she wouldn't only be letting down herself, but all the people who had helped her and believed in her—Janet not the least of them.

Not to mention Artemisia herself. There was something about the new poems that made Alex feel connected to her in a way that she couldn't explain or even really understand. She just knew that it was real. She couldn't imagine letting that go, actually choosing to leave the task of exploring Artemisia's best work to someone else.

But oh, sweet Goddess, she couldn't bear to lose Cam. Just the thought of it was tearing her apart. She felt Cam's arms tighten around her, and she buried her face in Cam's shoulder.

But she knew that even if she stayed with Cam, there were no guarantees. They were still discovering each other, still learning what it meant to be together. They'd hardly talked about the future in any serious way, just spun dreams of what might be. And there were so many practical issues to overcome if she did try to stay—getting official permission to remain in England, finding a way to earn a living, probably a lot of other things she hadn't even thought of yet.

If only she could just fall asleep now and wake up to discover it had all been a nightmare, that she didn't have to choose between the two parts of her life, the two parts of herself. She wasn't sure if she could survive losing either one.

❖

Cam felt the shudder rack Alex's body.

"Oh, Cam, what are we going to do?"

Cam braced herself. "We're not going to do a thing. You, on the other hand, are going to book a flight and pack your gear."

"The hell I am." Alex pushed away from Cam and got to her feet. "Sweetheart, you can't be serious. I can't just leave. I can't."

Cam stood as well. "Of course you can. You were going to leave from day one. We both know that. We've just been fooling ourselves, that's all, and fooling each other."

"What's that supposed to mean?"

"We've pretended that you wouldn't have to go—well, you've been pretending, and I've been letting you." Cam worked to keep her eyes hard and her tone flat—a little angry, but not too much. She needed to be convincing, which meant not overdoing it.

"That's not fair. I want to stay with you—I do. It's not my fault that I'm here on a grant. If I hadn't gotten the damn thing, I'd never have come at all. I'd never even have seen you."

"True enough, I reckon. And it's not as if you held a gun to my head to get me to climb into bed with you. That's my fault as much as yours."

"Fault? Climb into bed? What the hell is wrong with you? It hasn't even been a whole day since you were telling me how much you loved me and how we belonged together, and now you're talking as if all we have is some cheap, sleazy—damn it!"

Alex stalked out of the study and into the foyer, muttering under her breath. It didn't sound like English. Cam felt the ghost of a smile tugging at her, even though her stomach felt like she had swallowed broken glass. God, she loved this woman.

But this wasn't about what she needed. If she really loved Alex, she had to make this work.

Cam went as far as the doorway and stood with her arms crossed, watching Alex pace back and forth. "I'm not trying to insult you, Alex. I just think perhaps we got a bit carried away, is all." Alex glared at her and seemed about to launch into another tirade, but Cam didn't pause. "What with the excitement, and the goings on at the banquet, and then the champagne afterward. I'm sure at the time both of us thought we meant the things we said." That earned her a death glare. "But here, now, in this moment, can you honestly say you didn't go a bit further with it than you would have under normal circumstances? I'm not sure I can."

Alex came to a stop in front of Cam. She looked stricken. "Are you saying you don't love me?"

She wasn't strong enough to lie. "Don't make me answer that, Alex." The look on Alex's face was tearing her apart, but she couldn't let herself stop. "Oh, I'll hate to see you go. It'll hurt, and no mistake, just like it'll hurt for you to leave. But after a while it won't hurt so much, not for either one of us."

"I can't believe this. This is crazy."

"No, I'll tell you what's crazy." Something shifted inside her, and words came tumbling out, filled with unexpected heat. "Getting a chance at a job—and not just any job, a really good one, the sort you've said all along you barely had a hope of getting, and deciding to turn it down for no reason at all. That's not just foolish, it's bloody damn insane."

"No reason? I love you, goddamn it."

"Love won't keep a roof over your head or food on the table." She wasn't pretending now. She was angry—really angry. "I've been working day in, day out since I was so small I could barely hold a hammer, been the breadwinner since I was sixteen, and you know what I've got to show for it? These." She held up her hands and turned them back and forth so Alex could see the calluses, scars, and scratches.

"I don't understand."

Cam crossed her arms again. "I reckon you don't. No more should you, for all that. I expect you've never known what it's like to worry if the money will stretch another few days till the next bit of work comes along, or what it's like when it doesn't and you just have to do without." She laughed, but there was no humor in it. "You know, you and Rosamund make quite a pair."

"What?"

"The two of you last night—her screeching her head off over having a thousand pounds handed to her on a platter, and you waving away the very same thousand pounds because you couldn't be bothered to fight for it. Like it was beneath you to soil your hands over something so small."

Alex was staring at her in horror.

"Only it's not small, is it, not to someone like me. But I reckon I'm just too common and ignorant to know any better. Take the bloody job, Alex. Get on a plane and go back where you belong, and let me get on with my life."

Cam shouldered her way past Alex and headed out the front door, letting it slam behind her. From somewhere upstairs, an answering slam sounded.

Moving like a sleepwalker, Alex went up to the door and put her hand against the wood. It felt cold and solid and much too real. She bent forward and rested her forehead against it for a moment, pushing down the tears trying to force their way to the surface. She raised a fist and pounded against the wood, as hard as she could, over and over, until the physical pain finally broke through.

Spinning around, she set her back against the door and slid down to the floor. For a long time she sat there, cradling her throbbing hand against her chest. Her mind held nothing but the way Cam had looked at her just before she turned away, the sound of Cam's voice saying, "Go back where you belong."

At some point, Grace showed up, approaching cautiously and sniffing at her as if uncertain of her identity. After a while, she came closer. When Alex didn't immediately respond, Grace head-butted her and Alex absently began to stroke her and scratch under her chin. Usually this kind of treatment made Grace purr loudly, but she remained silent except for one or two inquiring whimpers.

Eventually Grace gave up and moved back out of petting range, giving Alex an unhappy meow before stalking away. Alex got to her feet and went to make her calls.

Chapter Twenty-eight

Somehow Alex got through what was left of her time in Bramfell, staggering around, only half aware. Throwing a few essentials into her carryon, then sleeping away most of Sunday. Dragging herself up on Monday, explaining things as best she could to Mrs. Tate, who visibly had to restrain herself from offering opinions or advice, merely promising to have the rest of Alex's belongings packed and shipped. Trying unsuccessfully to reach Ian, who was apparently sealed off from outside communication in his marathon of a meeting. But mostly searching everywhere for Cam, who was nowhere to be found and wasn't answering her phone.

And always, she was cold, so cold, deep inside where nothing could help.

She spent Monday afternoon on the moor, hoping she'd find Cam wandering somewhere along an isolated path, but with no success. The approach of sunset finally drove her back to the village. She headed up to Highgate Hall to see Nicola, who made congratulatory noises but was clearly appalled by the sudden change in circumstances.

"I still don't understand what it is your Barbara is doing," Nicola said.

"She's not my Barbara. Not anymore—if she ever was."

"Fair enough. Regardless, you won't have your degree for months yet, will you?"

"No, not until I finish my dissertation and defend it. Technically I'm not qualified for the position that opened up—and I'm not sure I would be even with a brand new Ph.D. But somehow she managed to convince whoever is responsible to finagle things based on—get this—the publicity that my new find will generate, and the need to snap me up while they have a chance, before some other school outbids them." Alex forced herself to unclench her jaw. "She told me all about it when I called her back to say I'd take the job. She actually told me to be sure I was ready for the press conference."

"Oh no."

"So much for her promise of secrecy. I've tried calling Ian to warn him, but I haven't been able to reach him. Can you make sure he gets the word in case my messages don't get through, so the Foundation can make the announcement before she does? I feel bad enough about what's happening without having to add that to it."

"Of course I will. Is that why she's in such a rush?"

"That, and the need to finish getting everything settled before some dean gets back from wherever he went and puts a stop to all of it. I hate politics."

Nicola sighed. "So you really are going through with this. I can barely believe it."

"I don't see that I have much choice." She knew her tone was bitter, but she couldn't help it. "Besides, if I don't do this now, I'll just have to go through it all later with some other school, except that the job offer probably won't be as good. Why put off the inevitable, as…as somebody pointed out to me recently. Especially if there's no reason for me to stick around."

"No reason? What about Cam?"

"Who do you think told me to go in the first place?"

"She didn't."

"Oh yes. She said it's time for us to stop pretending that I don't have to get on a plane and go back to my life. At first I thought she was putting me on, but she meant it. And she said…she said she didn't really—" No, she was not going to go there. "She said I needed to grow up and face reality."

"Cam said that?"

"Not in so many words, but I got the point. It pissed me off, of course, but the more I thought about it, the more I realized she was right. Sometimes you have to do things that"—*break your heart*—"aren't particularly pleasant. I'm going to take advantage of my opportunity and concentrate on being grateful to have a chance like this, instead of whining about what I can't have."

Nicola didn't look particularly convinced, so Alex decided to move on. "Anyway, she's the real reason I'm here. I've been looking all over for her, but she's vanished. I can't find her, and I can't get her on the phone. She's probably holed up somewhere waiting for me to leave."

"Sadly, I expect you're right. Did you try—"

"Nicola, I've tried everything I can think of, and I'm too worn out to chase after her any longer." She looked away. "I just can't bear to say good-bye in a voice mail. So can you tell her…"

"Of course. What do you want me to say?"

She met Nicola's eyes again. There was no recrimination there, only compassion, and it almost undid her. "Just tell her…tell her good-bye." She got to her feet, needing to get out of there.

"Alex, wait." Nicola put a hand on her arm. "Is there anything else I can do?"

Alex shook her head.

"When is your flight?"

"Tomorrow, from Leeds."

"So soon?"

"It was the best I could do on short notice. Everything later in the week is booked solid."

"At least let me give you a ride to the airport."

"That's kind of you, but it isn't necessary. There's not much point in you going through all the hassle of driving and parking when you'll have to say good-bye two minutes later at the security checkpoint. I'll get a cab."

"I don't mind that, silly. But if it really bothers you, I'll just drop you and drive off. What time do you need to be there?"

"The flight's at noon and they said allow about two hours, so ten o'clock, I guess."

"Right. I'll pick you up about nine thirty, so there's no rush."

On her way out, Alex paused at the library door. She looked down at her hand on the knob, realized it was trembling, and angrily shoved the door open. Time to lay at least one ghost.

She stepped into the darkened room but didn't bother with a light. She didn't need to see anything; her memories were sharp enough.

She thought of Rosamund, of how devastating the whole thing had been, how she had just collapsed as if the world had come to an end.

At the time, she had felt completely destroyed, but now the pain was only a distant echo, like an old injury that throbbed in rainy weather. It had been nothing, less than nothing, compared to what she was feeling now—or would be feeling once the chilling numbness wore off and the enormity of her loss consumed her.

By then, of course, she would be far away. Back where she belonged. The words of *Artemisia's Farewell* came to her. *O my Heart, Love will reunite us.* What utter, unadulterated crap. She turned and stalked out, slamming the door behind her.

❖

The next morning was appallingly bright and sunny. At least a cold wind was blowing down off the moor, knifing under the doors and rattling the windows. Alex made her way to the empty kitchen, glad that she had insisted on saying good-bye to Mrs. Tate the previous day and had refused the offer of one last breakfast, knowing she wouldn't have the heart to eat it. That didn't change the fact that she needed something in her stomach for the flight, so she forced down some bread and butter and half a glass of milk, unable to muster the energy even to make toast and tea.

When she had finished, she looked around the kitchen one last time. The heart of the house, indeed. This was where she and Cam had kissed, where they had touched.

A gust of wind came down the chimney, carrying the faint scent of wood smoke, and just like that she was back in Cam's arms, wanting her, needing her, the way she had that first time and every other time since. The way she did that very moment.

It hurt so much she wrapped her arms tight around her middle and staggered back a step, bumping against the table. The impact, minor as it was, seemed to jar loose something inside her. She turned and raced out of the kitchen, slamming the door behind her, as if the pain were something she could get away from if she could just go far enough, fast enough. But by the time she reached the top of the stairs she had herself more or less back under control and she paused, shivering in the icy draft that immediately enveloped her.

"Oh, Janet," she murmured, resting one hand against the rose carved into the door of the secret room. "I'm so sorry."

She went to her bedroom to grab her blazer. She had decided to wear it instead of packing it, thinking it would be easier to keep it unwrinkled that way, but as soon as she stepped into the room she saw that she needn't have bothered. Somehow, she hadn't considered the consequences when she had left it on the bed, and now Grace was curled up right on top of it, gazing at her with disdain—or perhaps that was just her guilty imagination.

"Cat hair—the gift that keeps on giving. Well, at least I'll have something to remember you by, won't I?" She lifted Grace, who mewed unhappily. As Alex picked up the jacket, the cat squirmed out of her arms and ran from the room. Apparently sentimental good-byes weren't her style.

Alex shrugged on her blazer without bothering to tidy up or straighten it, having learned from previous experience it would be pointless to try to brush away the evidence of Grace's recent occupancy.

She took a final look around, not seeing anything amiss. She had a nagging feeling she was forgetting something, but even after opening drawers and looking under the bed she didn't find anything.

She glanced at her watch. It was time.

A few minutes later, she closed the door of Dawson House behind her for the last time, stowed her laptop and bag in Nicola's car, and climbed in.

She tried to make conversation during the drive, but her heart wasn't in it, and finally she stopped, grateful that Nicola seemed willing to let the silence continue. Instead, she gazed dully out at the countryside whose beauty was just one more reminder of what she was losing. The first time she had ever seen it, Cam had been by her side.

She wondered where Cam was, how she was, what the hell she was doing, if she really was hiding or had just gone off somewhere on a job, not realizing how soon Alex would be leaving. Regardless, Alex decided it was probably for the best, since she didn't think she would have been able to stand having to see her again, to kiss her or hug her or even just clasp her hand. Touching Cam one last time and then having to walk away would have destroyed her. Maybe Cam sensed that somehow, and that's why she had taken herself off.

Finally they reached the airport. A few moments to grab her things, kiss Nicola on the cheek, and promise to keep in touch, then wave as she drove away, and just that quickly, Alex was alone.

Squaring her shoulders, she marched inside, passing by the huge lines at the airline counters, very glad she had opted not to check any bags. Of course, the line for security was even longer, but at least it was moving. Apparently someone was watching out for her, because there didn't seem to be any unnecessary delays from novice fliers setting off the metal detector after neglecting to empty their pockets, or worse, some ruggedly obtuse individualist who felt the need to argue about the regulations, as if the guards were conspiring to inconvenience them personally instead of just doing their jobs, trying to keep everyone safe.

Eventually it was Alex's turn, and as she carefully emptied the pockets of her jeans she realized that she still had her key to the Dawson House front door. Well, she would just have to mail it back. Or maybe she should keep it as a souvenir—it wasn't as if they'd miss it. It was just an ordinary key, easily replaced.

Smiling ruefully, she tossed it in the basket with her wallet before placing the container on the X-ray conveyer belt next to her laptop and carryon. Not wanting to waste anyone's time, she maneuvered past a guard whose back was turned as he assisted another passenger.

As she stepped up to the metal detector, one of the other guards started to say something to her—all she caught was the word jacket—but then the metal detector beeped. Automatically, she patted her blazer pockets and when she felt something in the right-hand one, she stuck her hand inside, encountering the familiar shape of a long, thin metal object. Not thinking, she drew it out and held it up, grasping it in her fist and staring at it in amazement.

That was when the shouting started.

CHAPTER TWENTY-NINE

Cam checked her watch as she strode down the top-floor corridor of Highgate Hall, headed for Nicola's office. It was already twenty past eleven. She'd need to get a move on if she didn't want to have to reschedule the rest of her day's appointments the way she had the morning ones.

She still wasn't sure this was a good idea, but after spending the best part of two days sitting around, then walking around, and finally driving around, going nowhere in particular and all the while trying and failing to convince herself that she was doing the right thing, she had finally given up trying to sort it out on her own. Everywhere she went, everything she did just made her think of Alex, and the heartbroken look on her face when Cam had walked out on her.

But when Cam finally reached Nicola's office, it was empty. The fellow across the hall said she was in the library, so Cam went back downstairs.

Opening the door, she stepped inside. Only a few lights were on, but she could see Nicola standing in front of the fireplace looking up at the painting above the mantel. Cam went over quietly, taking a moment to look at the painting herself before she said hello to Nicola, a bit curious but mostly trying to put off the conversation she had come there to have.

She hadn't been in this particular room in quite a while, and since the few times she'd been there had been to do a job, she hadn't paid the painting much mind. Now she studied it carefully, trying to puzzle out what was going on in the scene in front of her. Whatever it was, it looked peculiar.

"Cam."

Reluctantly, she turned to face Nicola.

"Where on earth have you been? I kept trying to ring you but you never answered, and when I asked around no one had heard from you. I was starting to get worried."

"Sorry, I had my mobile switched off. I didn't realize you'd worry." She stuck her hands in her trouser pockets. "I wasn't really anywhere, just wandering about, trying to think things through." She looked back at the painting. "What the bloody hell is that supposed to be? It's like something out of a bad horror film."

"That's *Artemisia's Farewell*. You know, when she had her deathbed vision of Lady Melissa and gave that speech about how their love would survive beyond the grave."

"Come again? Didn't Melissa throw her over, years earlier? Why would Artemisia be making speeches about their love, deathbed or no deathbed?"

"You know, you're right. That really doesn't make any sense."

"Anyway, it was Janet she was in love with, wasn't it? She wrote all those poems just for her. Stands to reason it'd be Janet she'd be thinking about at a time like that. Unless she'd gone right off her head. What was it she said, exactly?"

"*Death may have parted us, O my Heart, but Love will reunite us.*"

"Well, that doesn't sound mad, exactly, though I can't say for certain what it means."

"I think it means that they wouldn't lose each other—that somehow, their love would keep them together in spite of death. You know, it really would make a lot more sense if it had been Janet she was talking about. Perhaps she meant that Janet would have the memory of their love to comfort her."

"I'm not sure how much comfort that would be." She gestured toward the painting. "Seems to me remembering how the woman you loved died in your arms would be more likely to give you nightmares."

"Died in your arms? Hang on a moment." Nicola leaned in for a closer look. "I always thought that person with her arms around Artemisia, the one whose face you can't see, was just some servant. I've never heard anybody say any different."

"Janet *was* a servant."

Nicola's eyes were wide. "Of course it was Janet. Oh my God."

Cam looked back at the painting. "And that thing she said—with Janet holding her like that, she'd be saying it to Janet, wouldn't she?"

"You're right, Cam. That's got to be it. All these years people have been thinking Artemisia had some spooky deathbed visit from Lady Melissa's ghost, when the truth was there right in front of them." She pointed at Artemisia lying in Janet's arms. "Literally."

"Perhaps folk weren't too far wrong. Getting a deathbed visit from your ex would be spooky, I reckon."

"Will you be serious for once? Think about it. *O my Heart, Love will reunite us*—those were Artemisia's final words, and she said those words to Janet. They were together until the very moment she died. With her last breath, Artemisia was telling Janet how much she loved her."

Nicola's eyes were full of tears, and Cam's own eyes felt funny. She blinked a couple of times and looked away, clearing her throat.

Nicola's hand on her arm made her turn back. Nicola was staring at her in amazement. "Hundreds of people have looked at this painting over the years—probably hundreds of thousands have seen copies. But you're the only one who realized what it shows."

"Can't take much credit for that. Alex…" She had to clear her throat again. "Alex is the one who saw how it must have been for Janet, spending all those years and years without the woman she loved." She looked up at the painting again. "Thinking about what Alex said is what made me see what was going on." Suddenly she saw something else, something so obvious and so painful it almost choked her. "It was all about the two of them, wasn't it? Being with each other, I mean, day in, day out. Right up to the end. You can feel the joy of it, all through those poems. But what if they hadn't been brave enough?"

"Sorry?"

She turned to face Nicola, barely able to force the words out. "What if in spite of how they loved each other, they hadn't seen past what was keeping them apart?"

"I don't understand—"

"Janet was a servant, but Artemisia was a lady, for all she wore men's clothes. What if they'd let that stop them? What if they'd never found a way to be together? Artemisia would still have died and Janet would still have had to carry on afterward, but there would never have been any joy. All those years by herself, maybe it was the joy that she lived on."

She ran a hand through her hair, her thoughts racing. "What if one of them had made a huge mistake? What if one of them—Nicola, I told her to go. I *told* her to."

"That's what Alex said."

"She talked to you? When did she talk to you?"

"Yesterday. I almost didn't believe it. Cam, what were you thinking?"

"I'm thinking I've been a bloody fool. But the job—I don't know about things like that, not really. But I do know it's important. How can I ask her to choose? I can't bear to hurt her, to keep her from being who she's meant to be."

"You need to tell her that, Cam. You need to let her decide, while there's still time." Nicola turned pale. "Time. What time is it?"

"Just gone half eleven. Why?"

"She's flying out at noon. Noon today."

"What?" Cam's heart stopped.

"Leeds Airport. Go. Go now."

Cam barely heard her. She was already running, headed for her van.

Cam skidded to a halt in the parking area, not even bothering to pull into a space. She changed gear roughly, ignoring the screeching gearbox, and jammed on the hand brake in almost the same motion before leaping from the van and racing into the airport. She ran full out until she saw the enormous queue at security and stopped dead. She looked wildly about as an announcer droned, "Good morning, ladies and gentlemen. This is the final boarding call for—"

She spotted a monitor and raced over to it. Noting the time—11:54—she scanned desperately until she found Alex's flight, which showed as on time. All anyone ever did was complain of flight delays, but no, not this time.

She raced around the outside of the security queue to the spot just in front of the checkpoint and ducked under the rope, cutting right in front of the businessman about to step up to the desk. She pretended not to hear the outraged comments as she faced the guard on duty, a woman with close-cropped blond hair and flat blue eyes that got even harder as she addressed Cam.

"Kindly return to your place in the queue."

"Please," Cam said, "it's an emergency, can't I go through?"

The guard got to her feet. She was tall, taller than Cam, and solidly built. Her eyes were even stonier than before. She looked Cam up and down, no doubt noting her lack of hand luggage. "Ticketed passengers only in the queue."

"But it's an emergency—I've got to get through straight away. I won't be five minutes, I swear. It's life and death. Truly."

"Step away." When Cam didn't move, the guard pulled out her radio and started talking into it as she positioned herself between Cam and the entrance to the screening area.

Cam knew she was in trouble, but time was ticking by and she was desperate. Taking a step forward, she started to plead. "Please, just let me—"

The guard dropped the radio and reached for the Taser on her hip. "Don't move. Hands up."

A much-too-cheery voice announced, "Good afternoon, ladies and gentlemen. We are ready to begin boarding for British Airways flight—"

Afternoon. "No!" Cam whirled around, spotting a monitor nearby. The time showed 12:01. And Alex's flight was no longer listed.

The next thing Cam knew she was being tackled by what felt like an entire rugby team of very angry players. She went limp. Ordinarily her instinct would be to fight, or at least protect herself, but not now. Nothing mattered now. Alex was gone.

They dragged her to her feet and hustled her over to the nearest wall. Responding to barked instructions, she raised her hands and spread her legs as they patted her down. She knew what was coming next—handcuffs, an interrogation, probably an arrest. She tried to care but couldn't manage it.

"What are you doing to her? Leave her alone!"

Alex. It couldn't be. But even as Cam's brain protested, her body reacted.

She spun around so fast she caught security off guard, and before they could get hold of her again she had taken a step or two forward, just far enough for Alex to reach her and throw her arms around her, but only for a moment.

"You!" It was the blond guard again, but she was talking to Alex, not Cam. Her tone was exasperated but her eyes had softened to the point where she looked almost human. "I should have guessed you'd be involved somehow. Stand down, lads."

"Nice to see you again too, Officer," said Alex.

One of the other guards said, "Don't tell me this is the one that was smuggling the Holy Grail or Excalibur or whatever it was."

"I wasn't smuggling," said Alex, a little too forcefully, and the other guards took a step closer.

"Easy," Cam murmured.

"It's all right, lads," said the blonde. "I've got this." The rest of the guards dispersed, not without a few backward glances, leaving the three of them standing there.

Alex said, "Really, haven't we been over this? It was all a harmless mistake, as I've explained—many times—and as the people from the Foundation confirmed. Once you finally called them." Her tone was actually reasonable now, and surprisingly, the guard didn't seem to take offense at this bit of cheek. And was she cruising Alex?

None too pleased, Cam whispered in Alex's ear, "What have you been up to?"

In an undervoice, she muttered, "I was about to ask you the same damn question. Now shut up. Dear." To the guard, she said, "Clearly there has been another misunderstanding. This is Cam Carter, a, uh, consultant with the Foundation. Obviously, the Foundation sent her to retrieve the artifact that accidentally ended up in my possession."

"Obviously," said the guard, almost smiling. "And Ms. Carter's refusal to comply with security procedures would be down to…?"

"Devotion to duty. She really loves her job."

The woman glanced briefly at their joined hands. "So I see. Ms. Carter, may I take it that your emergency is now over?"

"Yes, absolutely. I'm sorry about all the excitement."

"May I suggest that now that you've retrieved the item that you value so highly, you take it back where it belongs?" This time, she really did smile.

Cam smiled back. "I'll see to it straight away. Come on, Alex, let's go."

Alex had thought she was utterly exhausted, thanks to the overly generous hospitality of the Leeds Airport security force that she had spent most of the morning enjoying, but now she felt amazing. She knew she must have the same goofy grin plastered on her face that Cam did, and she knew everybody was probably staring at them, but with Cam's hand still tight in hers, she didn't care a bit, and she doubted Cam did either.

Her logical mind tried to tell her that there was no reason to be so happy, just because she had missed her flight and Cam had come to the airport to find her. She told her logical mind to shut the hell up as she floated through the time it took to retrieve her things, rescue Cam's van from some very unhappy parking officials, and start the drive home, barely letting go of Cam's hand long enough to get into the van and buckle up before she grabbed it again.

Too soon, however, Cam pointed out that she really needed both hands to operate the vehicle, so Alex had to content herself with resting one hand on Cam's thigh. Unfortunately, the seats were too far apart for her to put her head on Cam's shoulder, so she turned sideways as much as the seat belt would allow and sat gazing at her, mile after mile.

Eventually of course, her hand started to go exploring. She was enjoying watching the red flush creep up Cam's neck when Cam finally grabbed her hand, growling, "Do you want us to end up in a ditch, lass? Have a heart." The lapse in concentration made them swerve, and it took a few curse-accented moments for Cam to get the vehicle back under control.

She glanced at Alex and swore again, turning abruptly off the road onto a lane that ran between high stone walls on either side. It looked barely wide enough for one vehicle. As soon as the lane broadened out a little, she pulled over onto the shoulder, turned off the engine, and unbuckled her seat belt.

At first she didn't move, but the hungry look in her eyes made Alex shiver all over. Then Cam launched herself across the space between them. As Cam scrambled over the gearshift, Alex had just enough presence of mind to unfasten her own seat belt, and then Cam was on her, kneeling over her, grabbing her head in both hands and devouring her mouth.

As the need for Alex consumed her, Cam had one tiny flash of sanity, registering just how uncomfortable it was being crammed into the position she was in and hoping she wasn't crushing Alex, but then her brain shut down completely and she gave herself up to the feel of Alex, warm and present and real, the scent of her, the taste of her, the heat of her mouth. Alex was hers, right there, right then, and nothing else mattered.

Cam couldn't stop kissing her. Never wanted to stop. It was just too good. Alex had hold of her shirt collar, tugging on it as if she wanted to pull her closer, to kiss her harder, if that was even possible. She felt Alex's hands slide down the front of her shirt, squeezing her breasts for a moment, almost too hard, then move lower, unfastening her trousers. Then Alex was touching her, insistent fingers gliding and stroking over her flesh. It was so good, so good. The pleasure built and built and then Alex was inside her and Cam was yelling against Alex's mouth as the top of her head came off.

Alex felt Cam break away from the kiss. As Cam buried her face in Alex's neck, breathing hard, Alex cradled the back of her head and ran her fingers gently through her hair as if to soothe her, even as she kept stroking with her other hand, drawing little shudders of pleasure from Cam, hoping to build her to another peak.

But apparently Cam had other ideas. She reached down and put a hand over Alex's, gently easing her away. Alex tried to protest, but Cam raised her head and grinned at her.

"My turn, love," she said and kissed Alex softly. Then she opened the door of the van and maneuvered herself over Alex and out of the vehicle with more speed than grace. Somehow she managed to extricate herself without kneeing Alex anywhere, but at the last moment something went wrong and she fell, landing with a grunt on her butt, right beside the open door.

Alex couldn't help giggling. "Oh, sweetheart, I never dreamed it could be like this with you," she simpered, but then the deflated look on Cam's face registered and she tried to assume a more sober expression. "Are you all right?"

"Well enough." She drew her knees up and wrapped her arms around them, looking up at Alex with a wry smile. "Nothing broken but the mood. It seems to be my day for ending up on the ground."

"I guess you just can't help falling for me, can you?" Alex said as she climbed out and sat on the ground beside Cam. "Sorry, I couldn't resist." She put an arm around Cam's shoulders. "Seriously, are you really all right? I almost lost my mind when I saw those guards all over you. I ran over as fast as I could."

Cam kissed her cheek. "I'm sure I've the odd bruise or two, but honestly, the moment I heard your voice, everything bad went right away. I thought I'd lost you for good, and there you were. Here you are. It's like a bloody miracle. What happened? And what was all that about smuggling?"

Instead of answering, Alex reached into her blazer pocket and pulled out the key to the secret room. "After I set off the metal detector, I found this in my pocket." She passed it to Cam.

"Oh no."

"Oh yes. At first the guards thought it was a weapon and hustled me off to the nearest clean too-well-lighted place for a little third degree. Then, once they realized what it really was, they wanted to confiscate it—and it turns out everything they confiscate gets destroyed." For some reason, Cam was frowning as she sat looking at the key, turning it over in her hand. "That blond guard just kept saying *Regulations, miss* like a goddamn parrot—she's almost as hardheaded as you, and that's hard to pull off."

When Cam didn't smile in response, Alex started speaking faster. "I swear we almost came to blows before I finally got her to contact the Foundation. And when she did get it through her head that the key was a valuable historical artifact, I had to convince her I wasn't trying to steal it."

Alex knew she was talking too much, but she couldn't seem to stop. "After all, I couldn't exactly tell her the truth—that a cat had somehow slipped it into my pocket, almost certainly at the instigation of a ghost. She'd have tossed me down the nearest oubliette and that would have been the end of me."

Finally Cam looked up, her expression grim. "So you only missed your flight by chance, then?" Her mouth twisted. "I thought you'd decided to stay." She turned her head away.

CHAPTER THIRTY

"Why do you care why I didn't get on that plane?" Alex pulled her arm away and got to her feet. "I'm here now, aren't I? A few minutes ago you seemed to think that was a pretty good thing—you used the word miracle, as I recall."

Cam stood up as well, wincing a little. "I did, didn't I? More fool me."

"Don't you dare lose your temper. It's bad enough you disappearing on me after pulling that *Dark Victory* stunt. Off somewhere hiding, I suppose—" When Cam opened her mouth to protest, Alex stepped close enough to jab a forefinger at her chest. "Don't interrupt me. And then the next time I see you, you're being mauled by a bunch of security guards. Damn it, they could have really hurt you!"

Instead of arguing, Cam put her arms around her and pulled her close. For a minute, Alex stayed stiff, resisting.

"You're right," Cam murmured in her ear, and she let her body relax into the embrace. "I've been ten different kinds of a fool." Cam kissed her neck and Alex put her arms around Cam's waist.

"Yes, you have." She felt Cam smile against her skin. "Besides, all the key did was give me time, so instead of coming to my senses somewhere over the Atlantic, too late to do anything about it, I was sitting in the airport with hours and hours to think things through." She leaned back enough to see Cam's face. "Does it really matter how we got here, as long as we're together?"

"I don't suppose it does." Cam sighed. "I know I'll regret asking, but what does *Dark Victory* have to do with anything?"

"The ending." Cam shook her head, clearly not comprehending. "You know, when Bette Davis realizes she's dying and instead of telling her husband, she pretends she's fine so he'll go off to the meeting he's supposed to be attending."

"I remember it. I just don't see what it has to do with us."

"She does it because if he stays with her, he'll miss a chance to work with other doctors trying to cure her disease." Cam still looked confused. "She sends him away because she thinks his research is more important than their relationship."

"Oh."

"Oh is right. The really bad part is that she does it because she doesn't trust the person she loves to make their own decisions. In the movie it's all gloriously tragic, but in real life it's horrible." She glared at Cam, who cringed—as well she might. "Just as well you weren't around when I figured it all out. As it is, I'm still pretty mad."

"I'm sorry, lass. Honestly, I meant it for the best."

Alex hugged her close. "You are very much an idiot. But you're my idiot. And it's not all your fault. I shouldn't have let Barbara snow me. There'll be other jobs and other chances—maybe even better ones. Regardless, job or no job, no one, but no one, is going to keep me from working on Artemisia's poems. It's not as if they can stop me."

"What do you mean?"

"It's just like you said—I need to work so I can eat. But if I have to, I can wait tables or whatever and still write about Artemisia. Maybe I'll start a blog. Or a Web TV show." She gave Cam a kiss. "You can be my camera operator."

"That might be a bit of a lark, now you mention it."

"I'd reach more people that way than through some stuffy academic journal anyway. Especially if I give my lectures wearing a bikini."

"What?"

"Just making sure you were paying attention." Alex rested her head on Cam's shoulder. "What matters is that we stay together."

"Too right."

Alex hugged Cam tighter. "Tell me something."

"Why I came to find you? Because I love you and I can't live without you."

"That's really sweet, but what I actually wanted to ask is why you got out of the van." Alex raised her head. "What exactly did you have in mind before you gave that impressive demonstration of acrobatic incompetence?"

Cam laughed and kissed her. "God"—she kissed her again—"I do love you so."

"So. What were you planning to do? You weren't running away, by any chance?" She reached up and anchored her fingers in Cam's hair, pulling her head back enough to look her dead in the eye. "Because trying to get away from me would not be a good idea."

Even as she said it, Alex stepped back against the side of the van, pulling Cam with her, and drew her head down for a long, hard kiss. Eyes closed, she felt Cam lean against her, hands braced against the van on either side of her shoulders. Alex loved the feel of Cam's body, all her weight and strength pressing against Alex's whole length, and as the kiss went on and on and the pleasure started to build in her center, she began to move her hips, needing more pressure there but getting barely any.

Just when she thought she couldn't stand it anymore, Cam shifted her legs, pushing one thigh in between Alex's. For a moment it felt so good Alex thought she was going to scream, but Cam kept pushing, pressing just hard enough to keep her from moving at all.

Confused, Alex loosened her grip on Cam's hair and pulled back from the kiss, searching Cam's eyes for some clue about what was happening.

In a teasing voice, Cam said, "No."

I'm going to kill her. "No, what?"

"No, I wasn't going to run. And I wasn't going to do this, either."

Cam moved her leg just a little, sending a jolt of pleasure through Alex that stole a groan from her throat.

Then Cam stopped moving. "So, do you really want to know what I was going to do?"

Oh, she was enjoying this, damn her. Alex managed to find her voice long enough to snarl, "Just do something, goddamn it, or I swear to God I am going to kill you."

"Not until I finish." She started kissing Alex's neck, working her way down. "Then I can die happy."

And just like that, Cam was on her knees, opening Alex's jeans, pulling them down along with her underwear. She had a moment to feel cold air on her bare skin and then Cam's mouth was on her, warm and hungry, and she was lost. Everything disappeared except the way Cam was taking her, her eager mouth seeking out all the places that made her whimper and shiver and cry out. Alex felt herself collapsing and then Cam's arm was around her, keeping her upright as she started to come, Cam's caresses never letting up, demanding every last molecule of pleasure from her until she couldn't take any more and she tugged at Cam's hair, begging her to stop.

Cam looked up at her, eyes glazed, as if she was still as lost in the pleasure as Alex had been.

Alex drew her to her feet and hugged her tenderly, whispering in her ear. "Let's go home, sweetheart."

"Oh, love, I am home."

❖

Eventually they made it back to Dawson House. As they climbed out of the van, Alex was surprised to see Ian walking along the path from the back of the house, his expression troubled. But then he caught sight of Alex and his face broke out in a huge smile.

Alex rushed over and gave him a hug. As she stepped back, Cam came over and shook his hand.

"Good to see you again, Mr. Montrose."

"Good to see both of you. Especially you, Alexandra. From the messages you left, I was afraid I would be too late."

"I'm glad to be here myself. It was a pretty close call." She took Cam's hand and smiled at her before turning back to Ian. "But what are you doing here? I mean, I'm glad to see you. I'm just surprised."

"Now, didn't I tell you that I'd be up here to view your find the instant I had the chance? I would have been here sooner if that wretched meeting of mine hadn't lasted longer than the Trojan War and Odysseus's homeward journey combined. That's the other reason I'm here. I'm afraid I've a bit of bad news and—"

"If it's bad, it'll keep. But why aren't you inside? Someone from Highgate Hall could have given you a key."

"Someone did. But it being such a lovely day, I was enjoying myself too much to go indoors. I walked about the village for a while, tut-tutting over the way things have changed in my best old-fogey fashion, and then I wandered up to Bram Tor."

"I'm glad you've been enjoying yourself, Ian, but why don't we get you in out of the wind now."

"Hold on a bit," Cam said. "I'm of a mind that bad news doesn't get better by waiting. What's going on, Mr. Montrose?"

"Well, I'm afraid I couldn't get the Board to agree to more than a token reward, in spite of your spectacular discovery. So I've only a thousand pounds for each of you." He patted the breast pocket of his jacket.

"For me?" said Cam. "What for?" Alex elbowed her and she hastily added, "That is, thank you, Mr. Montrose."

"Yes, thank you, Ian."

Ian laughed. "You are most welcome, both of you. And the what for, Cam, is that if it hadn't been for your keen observations, Artemisia's new poems would never have come to light. You are both equally responsible for the find and thus share equally in the reward. I just wish it could have been more."

As Alex unlocked the front door and they all stepped into the foyer, Cam said, "Mr. Montrose, if your notion of bad news is passing out thousand-pound checks, I'd love to know what you consider good news."

Alex closed the door and switched on the light. "I have to agree with her there."

Ian chuckled. "As a matter of fact, my dears, I do have some good news as well. To begin with, I've been up to Highgate Hall as I said, and one reason was to inform Nicola of her change in status."

"How's that, Mr. Montrose?"

"After the recent contretemps over the Prandall, it became obvious that we could do with a bit of housecleaning among the

Foundation staff in Bramfell. I was able to convince the Board to establish a permanent administrative post here instead of rotating London staff in and out."

"That sounds like a great idea, Ian."

"That it does, Mr. Montrose. Nicola's forever going on about how hard it is to always have to deal with new bosses, most of whom could care less about anything except getting back to London."

"Ian, you said Nicola's status has changed. Does that mean you've offered her the job?"

"Yes, indeed. The way she handled everything having to do with your new find left a very favorable impression. Now she'll have a great deal more responsibility and a corresponding rise in salary as well."

Cam smiled. "She was dead chuffed, I'll be bound."

"Yes, she was very pleased. But that's not the only position I was able to convince the Board to establish." He looked directly at Alex as he said this. "We're using the interest from the Prandall to establish an institute dedicated to the study of the new poems and the other materials that you found. The institute will need a director." He smiled. "We were rather hoping you'd consider it, Alexandra. Unless you have your heart set on returning to the States after the Brockenbridge ends."

As his words sank in, Cam stared at Alex, who just stood there looking stunned. After waiting a moment or two, Cam turned to Ian. "Would that be a permanent posting? And would it be Bramfell based?"

"Yes, to both questions."

"Bloody hell." She held both of Alex's hands and turned toward her, almost shaking with joy and excitement. "You heard what he said. You can stay, and you can work. What more could you ask for?"

Alex finally found her voice. "Oh, my God! I can stay. I can work. I can do my work, and I can stay with you. That is"—she turned back to Ian—"can I stay? Don't I need to get some kind of approval from the government?"

Ian said, "As to that, of course there are formalities, and it may take a while to sort out, but I'm confident that we'll be able to arrange things satisfactorily."

Cam said, "Would it be easier if she was married to a British citizen?"

Ian smiled. "I expect it would be."

She turned to Alex. "All right then. How about it?"

It took a moment before Alex reacted. But then it seemed to hit her all of a sudden, and not in the way Cam had hoped.

Alex snatched her hands from Cam's grasp, her face taut with anger. "How about it? How about it? That's your idea of a proposal—How about it?" She stalked off to the kitchen, slamming the door behind her.

Cam looked at Ian. "That went well." She wasn't sure whether to laugh or cry. She'd spoken from the heart, too caught up in the moment to think about how it sounded.

Ian raised his eyebrows. "The lady does have a point. A touch more romance might be in order."

"Any advice?"

"Grovel."

When Cam cautiously pushed open the kitchen door, Alex was pacing back and forth, wearing a path between the table and the back door. After a moment, Cam stepped inside, not daring to say anything. Alex scowled at her and started to speak, but then she looked down.

A moment later she bent down, straightening up with that ginger cat cradled in her arms. Both of them regarded her with identical glares before Alex strode over to the photo near the fireplace and began studying it as if it were the most fascinating thing she'd ever seen, all the while murmuring affectionately to Grace.

Cam could hear the beast purring all the way across the room, clearly enjoying the attention it was getting. She decided she really should be grateful instead of jealous. After all, it was the cat who was mainly responsible for Alex still being here. Which had given her yet another chance to mess things up. Only this time, she was going to put it right straight away.

She walked over to stand beside Alex and looked at the photo of Janet and the children. Now that she knew what the key and the notebook meant, the expression on Janet's face took on a new meaning.

It was Alex who finally broke the silence. "She looks so happy."

She didn't sound angry. Best to tread carefully even so. "Janet, you mean?"

"Yes. Just look at her. She looks like a woman in love."

"She must have done her share of grieving, but all I can see is joy."

"Me, too. The way she's holding the book of poems, the way the children are gathered around her. She looks so proud and so content. And from what Ian says, she didn't spend her days alone and suffering. I'd forgotten that. She might have been a widow, but her life didn't end when Artemisia's did. The people in the village really cared about her. All of those years, she had affection and laughter, hope for the future, and peace at the last."

"Not such a bad life, when you put it that way." Cam put a hand on Alex's shoulder. Apparently the cat had objections, because she started squirming until Alex let her go.

"But I bet she'd have traded all of it for one more day with Artemisia," Alex said.

"I would."

Alex turned to face her. She didn't look angry. She looked wistful. "You would what? Never mind, don't try to explain. I think I get it."

"Alex, I'm sor—"

Alex didn't want to hear the apology. She put her fingers against Cam's lips, feeling their warmth and softness. "Sh. It's all right."

Cam took her hand, gently kissing the back of it. Still clasping her hand, she got down on one knee.

Alex felt a nervous giggle rising inside but ruthlessly clamped down on it. This was impossible. The whole thing was completely insane. And completely wonderful. She hadn't ever imagined this, had never dreamed of anything like it. But now, with Cam looking up at her, her face full of tenderness, she realized that this was what she wanted, what she needed—now, this moment, and forever.

She held her breath, waiting for the words that would cast the spell over them both.

"I love you. Will you marry me?"

"Of course I will. I love you." Maybe it really was that simple. Alex felt a tiny breath of cold air across her cheek. It might have been a draft. It might have been a kiss. It felt like a blessing.

She drew Cam to her feet. She traced the tip of one finger along Cam's cheek. "We're going to drive each other crazy. You know that, right?"

Cam turned her head just enough to kiss the palm of her hand before answering. "I'm counting on it, lass."

About the Author

English teacher by day, tale spinner by night, Jo Victor is old enough to know better but still too young to care. She has been writing more or less seriously since she was in her teens and likes to think she is carrying on the family storytelling tradition that goes back to her Italian grandmother. When not fighting the good fight on behalf of black ink on white paper, she enjoys folk music, British humor, and excessive novel reading, all of which she highly recommends. She lives with her life partner in Virginia.

Jo can be contacted at: jovictor@jovictor.com

Website: www.jovictor.com

Books Available from Bold Strokes Books

Hardwired by C.P. Rowlands. Award-winning teacher Clary Stone, and Leefe Ellis, manager of the homeless shelter for small children, stand together in a part of Clary's hometown that she never knew existed. (978-1-62639-351-6)

No Good Reason by Cari Hunter. A violent kidnapping in a Peak District village pushes Detective Sanne Jensen and lifelong friend Dr. Meg Fielding closer, just as it threatens to tear everything apart. (978-1-62639-352-3)

Romance by the Book by Jo Victor. If Cam didn't keep disrupting her life, maybe Alex could uncover the secret of a century-old love story, and solve the greatest mystery of all—her own heart. (978-1-62639-353-0)

Death's Doorway by Crin Claxton. Helping the dead can be deadly: Tony may be listening to the dead, but she needs to learn to listen to the living. (978-1-62639-354-7)

Searching for Celia by Elizabeth Ridley. As American spy novelist Dayle Salvesen investigates the mysterious disappearance of her ex-lover, Celia, in London, she begins questioning how well she knew Celia—and how well she knows herself. (978-1-62639-356-1)

The 45th Parallel by Lisa Girolami. Burying her mother isn't the worst thing that can happen to Val Montague when she returns to the woodsy but peculiar town of Hemlock, Oregon. (978-1-62639-342-4)

A Royal Romance by Jenny Frame. In a country where class still divides, can love topple the last social taboo and allow Queen Georgina and Beatrice Elliot, a working class girl, their happy ever after? (978-1-62639-360-8)

Bouncing by Jaime Maddox. Basketball Coach Alex Dalton has been bouncing from woman to woman, because no one ever held her interest, until she meets her new assistant, Britain Dodge. (978-1-62639-344-8)

Same Time Next Week by Emily Smith. A chance encounter between Alex Harris and the beautiful Michelle Masters leads to a whirlwind friendship, and causes Alex to question everything she's ever known—including her own marriage. (978-1-62639-345-5)

All Things Rise by Missouri Vaun. Cole rescues a striking pilot who crash-lands near her family's farm, setting in motion a chain of events that will forever alter the course of her life. (978-1-62639-346-2)

Riding Passion by D. Jackson Leigh. Mount up for the ride through a sizzling anthology of chance encounters, buried desires, romantic surprises, and blazing passion. (978-1-62639-349-3)

Love's Bounty by Yolanda Wallace. Lobster boat captain Jake Myers stopped living the day she cheated death, but meeting greenhorn Shy Silva stirs her back to life. (978-1-62639-334-9)

Just Three Words by Melissa Brayden. Sometimes the one you want is the one you least suspect. Accountant Samantha Ennis has her ordered life disrupted when heartbreaker Hunter Blair moves into her trendy Soho loft. (978-1-62639-335-6)

Lay Down the Law by Carsen Taite. Attorney Peyton Davis returns to her Texas roots to take on big oil and the Mexican Mafia, but will her investigation thwart her chance at true love? (978-1-62639-336-3)

Playing in Shadow by Lesley Davis. Survivor's guilt threatens to keep Bryce trapped in her nightmare world unless Scarlet's love can pull her out of the darkness back into the light. (978-1-62639-337-0)

Soul Selecta by Gill McKnight. Soul mates are hell to work with. (978-1-62639-338-7)

The Revelation of Beatrice Darby by Jean Copeland. Adolescence is complicated, but Beatrice Darby is about to discover how impossible it can seem to a lesbian coming of age in conservative 1950s New England. (978-1-62639-339-4)

Twice Lucky by Mardi Alexander. For firefighter Mackenzie James and Dr. Sarah Macarthur, there's suddenly a whole lot more in life to understand, to consider, to risk…someone will need to fight for her life. (978-1-62639-325-7)

Shadow Hunt by L.L. Raand. With young to raise and her Pack under attack, Sylvan, Alpha of the wolf Weres, takes on her greatest challenge when she determines to uncover the faceless enemies known as the Shadow Lords. A Midnight Hunters novel. (978-1-62639-326-4)

Heart of the Game by Rachel Spangler. A baseball writer falls for a single mom, but can she ever love anything as much as she loves the game? (978-1-62639-327-1)

Getting Lost by Michelle Grubb. Twenty-eight days, thirteen European countries, a tour manager fighting attraction, and an accused murderer: Stella and Phoebe's journey of a lifetime begins here. (978-1-62639-328-8)

Prayer of the Handmaiden by Merry Shannon. Celibate priestess Kadrian must defend the kingdom of Ithyria from a dangerous enemy and ultimately choose between her duty to the Goddess and the love of her childhood sweetheart, Erinda. (978-1-62639-329-5)

The Witch of Stalingrad by Justine Saracen. A Soviet "night witch" pilot and American journalist meet on the Eastern Front in WW II and struggle through carnage, conflicting politics, and the deadly Russian winter. (978-1-62639-330-1)

Pedal to the Metal by Jesse J. Thoma. When unreformed thief Dubs Williams is released from prison to help Max Winters bust a car theft ring, Max learns that to catch a thief, get in bed with one. (978-1-62639-239-7)

Dragon Horse War by D. Jackson Leigh. A priestess of peace and a fiery warrior must defeat a vicious uprising that entwines their destinies and ultimately their hearts. (978-1-62639-240-3)

For the Love of Cake by Erin Dutton. When everything is on the line, and one taste can break a heart, will pastry chefs Maya and Shannon take a chance on reality? (978-1-62639-241-0)

Betting on Love by Alyssa Linn Palmer. A quiet country-girl-at-heart and a live-life-to-the-fullest biker take a risk at offering each other their hearts. (978-1-62639-242-7)

The Deadening by Yvonne Heidt. The lines between good and evil, right and wrong, have always been blurry for Shade. When Raven's actions force her to choose, which side will she come out on? (978-1-62639-243-4)

Ordinary Mayhem by Victoria A. Brownworth. Faye Blakemore has been taking photographs since she was ten, but those same photographs threaten to destroy everything she knows and everything she loves. (978-1-62639-315-8)

One Last Thing by Kim Baldwin & Xenia Alexiou. Blood is thicker than pride. The final book in the Elite Operative Series brings together foes, family, and friends to start a new order. (978-1-62639-230-4)

Songs Unfinished by Holly Stratimore. Two aspiring rock stars learn that falling in love while pursuing their dreams can be harmonious—if they can only keep their pasts from throwing them out of tune. (978-1-62639-231-1)

Beyond the Ridge by L.T. Marie. Will a contractor and a horse rancher overcome their family differences and find common ground to build a life together? (978-1-62639-232-8)

Swordfish by Andrea Bramhall. Four women battle the demons from their pasts. Will they learn to let go, or will happiness be forever beyond their grasp? (978-1-62639-233-5)

The Fiend Queen by Barbara Ann Wright. Princess Katya and her consort Starbride must turn evil against evil in order to banish Fiendish power from their kingdom, and only love will pull them back from the brink. (978-1-62639-234-2)

Up the Ante by PJ Trebelhorn. When Jordan Stryker and Ashley Noble meet again fifteen years after a short-lived affair, are either of them prepared to gamble on a chance at love? (978-1-62639-237-3)

Speakeasy by MJ Williamz. When mob leader Helen Byrne sets her sights on the girlfriend of Al Capone's right-hand man, passion and tempers flare on the streets of Chicago. (978-1-62639-238-0)

Venus in Love by Tina Michele. Morgan Blake can't afford any distractions and Ainsley Dencourt can't afford to lose control—but the beauty of life and art usually lies in the unpredictable strokes of the artist's brush. (978-1-62639-220-5)

Rules of Revenge by AJ Quinn. When a lethal operative on a collision course with her past agrees to help a CIA analyst on a critical assignment, the encounter proves explosive in ways neither woman anticipated. (978-1-62639-221-2)

The Romance Vote by Ali Vali. Chili Alexander is a sought-after campaign consultant who isn't prepared when her boss's daughter, Samantha Pellegrin, comes to work at the firm and shakes up Chili's life from the first day. (978-1-62639-222-9)

Advance: Exodus Book One by Gun Brooke. Admiral Dael Caydoc's mission to find a new homeworld for the Oconodian people is hazardous, but working with the infuriating Commander Aniwyn "Spinner" Seclan endangers her heart and soul. (978-1-62639-224-3)

UnCatholic Conduct by Stevie Mikayne. Jil Kidd goes undercover to investigate fraud at St. Marguerite's Catholic School, but life gets complicated when her student is killed—and she begins to fall for her prime target. (978-1-62639-304-2)

Season's Meetings by Amy Dunne. Catherine Birch reluctantly ventures on the festive road trip from hell with beautiful stranger Holly Daniels only to discover the road to true love has its own obstacles to maneuver. (978-1-62639-227-4)

Myth and Magic: Queer Fairy Tales edited by Radclyffe and Stacia Seaman. Myth, magic, and monsters—the stuff of childhood dreams (or nightmares) and adult fantasies. (978-1-62639-225-0)

Nine Nights on the Windy Tree by Martha Miller. Recovering drug addict, Bertha Brannon, is an attorney who is trying to stay clean when a murder sends her back to the bad end of town. (978-1-62639-179-6)

Driving Lessons by Annameekee Hesik. Dive into Abbey Brooks's sophomore year as she attempts to figure out the amazing, but sometimes complicated, life of a you-know-who girl at Gila High School. (978-1-62639-228-1)

Asher's Shot by Elizabeth Wheeler. Asher Price's candid photographs capture the truth, but when his success requires exposing an enemy, Asher discovers his only shot at happiness involves revealing secrets of his own. (978-1-62639-229-8)

Courtship by Carsen Taite. Love and justice—a lethal mix or a perfect match? (978-1-62639-210-6)

Against Doctor's Orders by Radclyffe. Corporate financier Presley Worth wants to shut down Argyle Community Hospital, but Dr. Harper Rivers will fight her every step of the way, if she can also fight their growing attraction. (978-1-62639-211-3)